Hail Judeas Caesar

Hail Judeas Caesar

Ryan Fleming

Wellspring
Books

Copyright © 2016 by Ryan Fleming

All rights reserved. No part of this book may be reproduced in any form or by any electronic or mechanical means, including information storage and retrieval systems, without permission in writing from the publisher, except by a reviewer, who may quote brief passages in a review.

Library of Congress Cataloging-in-Publication Data

Fleming, Ryan
    Hail Judeas Caesar / Ryan Fleming – 1st ed. P. cm.
    Includes bibliography, notes and references
    ISBN-13: 978-0-9715676-2-7
    ISBN-10: 0-9715676-2-X
    Library of Congress Control Number: 2017943410

Published by Wellspring Books
P.O. Box 18561
San Antonio, Texas 78218-0561
www.wellspringbooks.com

Printed in the United States of America

Table of Contents

Preface	vii
1 ~ Pontius Pilate	1
2 ~ Caesarea	6
3 ~ Barabbas	12
4 ~ Antipas	21
5 ~ High Standards	35
6 ~ Joseph of Arimathea	46
7 ~ Holy Water	57
8 ~ Two Heads Aren't Better Than One	69
9 ~ John the Baptist	74
10 ~ The Beginning	83
11 ~ Like Minds	95
12 ~ Purification	101
13 ~ Some Trips Never End	111
14 ~ The Wilderness	119
15 ~ From the Water Sprang Life	126
16 ~ Wishing for Less	135
17 ~ Misguided Blame	146
18 ~ Where Did He Go?	163

19 ~ A Day of Rest	175
20 ~ My Servant	183
21 ~ Source of Affliction	193
22 ~ The Cost of Miracles	208
23 ~ Going, Going	221
24 ~ Who's Listening?	233
25 ~ Food for Thought	236
26 ~ Word against Memory	244
27 ~ Pushing the Limit	248
28 ~ A Cornered Lion	263
29 ~ Vengeance from Within	281
30 ~ A Matter of Choice	285
31 ~ The Crucifixion	295
32 ~ From the Lair	301
Author's Note	313
Bibliography	335
Notes and References	337

Preface

This book presents a perspective of the conflict between Rome and the people of Judea during the first century CE in a different light than is commonly held in traditional Christian ideology. As a result, some readers may be sensitive to its content.

The Roman governor, Pontius Pilate, and his wife, Claudia, find a country steeped in deep religious traditions and zealot resistance. The Jewish people believe the Roman presence is a defilement to a land promised to them in a Holy Covenant with their god, fueling impassioned defiance. Pilate elicits clandestine liaisons within the Jewish community to manipulate religious forces and subvert the populace against the established religious order. He seeks to increase tax collection and recruit men for fielded armies to further Rome's power and his own political aspirations. Interwoven into this intense conflict between two vastly different cultures is the love story between Pontius and Claudia.

This is a compelling and timely book that places ancient written accounts of the origins of Christianity in an historical paradigm rather than a supernatural or theological context. It proposes a remarkable theory of Rome's direct involvement in the inadvertent formation of the early Christian movement. The story builds towards an amazing climax of one of the most important and potentially misunderstood events in the history of the world. Pilate's strategies result in a consequence of which he never dreamed—a religious offshoot of Judaism—Christianity. In one final staged miracle Jesus Christ survives a Roman crucifixion, the culmination of Pilate's actions, perpetuating a movement that otherwise would have withered, lost to history.

In the crucifixion, the book describes Jesus being tied to the cross rather than nailed. None of the early written accounts, including all four Gospels of the *New Testament*, mention anything about nails. If this method of crucifixion is not documented in written form from the first days, years, or even decades after the event, then where did this adaptation come from? The only viable answer is "word of mouth." The very concept of "word of mouth" is imbued with uncertainty, often involving exaggerations, embellishments, and sensationalism.

The *Author's Note* at the end offers more detail regarding this and many other important aspects related to the story's premise, in addition to supporting historical references.

ix

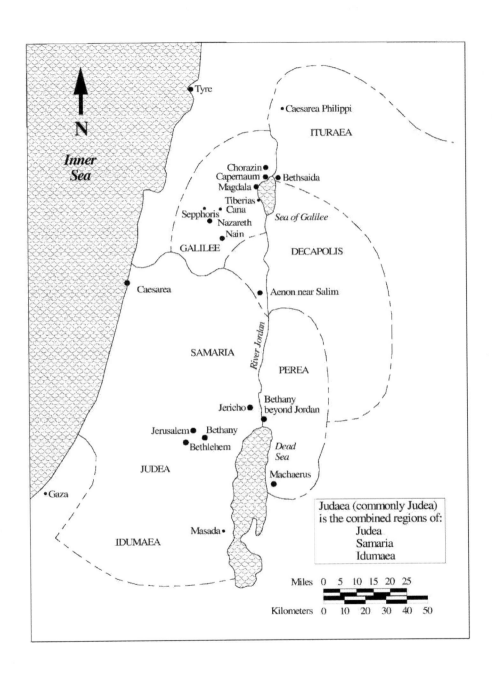

1 ~ Pontius Pilate

Pontius Pilate took the papyrus from the Senate messenger and dismissed him with a wave of his hand. He broke the seal and unrolled the scroll, recognizing it as orders for transfer of duty. Pontius clinched the bottom of the scroll, crumpling a portion in his hand.

Pontius had become accustomed to Rome; it was starting to feel like home again. Standing in the doorway of his home, he looked out at the villas on the hillside and breathed in the familiar aroma of his wife's garden. He wasn't ready to leave.

Having chosen a military life, his commission meant responding to the wishes of Caesar and the Senate. Refusal wasn't an option.

Pontius anxiously skimmed forward. *Where am I to go? Greece, Spain, Gaul, North, East—or possibly here in Italia?* His heart sank when he thought he saw the word "Judea." For a brief moment Pontius consoled himself—perhaps he had been wrong? But there it was again. The word seemed to fill the entire page, erasing all other aspects of the orders.

This can't be true, Pontius thought to himself. *After all the years I have served Rome and remained loyal to her.*

He hadn't had a brilliant career, but why Judea, why him? Pontius read on. He would be governor. Governor of what? A land of rebellious people, a land dry and dead. He had heard of their strange beliefs and profound loyalty to a single god.

How preposterous, Pontius thought. *The world is too complicated for one god. Too many things are happening at once—in the sea, in the* mountains, in the clouds, and in the lives of the citizens of Rome—for a single god to control. These Judeans do not see the complexities beyond their simple lives and barren land. Besides, a single god would experience a protracted torture of eternal loneliness, with or without the praise of his forsaken subjects. Pontius scoffed at the absurd and simplistic nature of their beliefs as he closed the door and turned to walk back inside.

His wife, Claudia, walked into the room. "Who was that?"

"A messenger from the Senate. He brought orders for my transfer."

"What does it say?" Claudia looked apprehensive, and Pontius knew why: his last assignment had been a remote military post.

Pontius hesitated. "Judea." Pontius tossed the papyrus on a table. "They've offered me the position of governor of the province." He snickered slightly. "Offered—that's the wrong term. They've ordered me to take the position. No Roman in his right mind would accept an 'offer' for such a command."

"Governor," Claudia recited with animation. "That's quite a promotion, my love. I should see a look of pride, rather than despair." She walked over to Pontius and wove her fingers through the back of his dark-brown hair. She tried to meet his eyes. "It's a position that could not better suit so great a man as my husband. The Senate thinks the title grants a sense of importance, but it is the title that will be honored by your name."

The touch of her hand calmed his spirit. Her voice erased his anxiety, and the sincerity of her words strengthened his confidence. Smiling, Pontius brought his hand up to meet hers and gently guided her delicate fingers to his lips. "I am blessed by the gods to have you as my wife and my counsel. But you do not understand. Judea is a peculiar, deviant sort of place." Pontius hesitated, finding it difficult to explain in few words. "It has long been a province of Rome, but there is no control or order. The country is full of barbaric tribes who listen to no authority. It can be very dangerous."

Claudia's confident smile turned wary. "Does this mean I will not be able to go with you?"

"No, no, my love. I have implored the gods that those days are no more, and I will have none of it. Judea is a country we will both have to endure, which only adds to my torment, realizing that you will not have the comfort and beauty of Rome to serve you."

Claudia laughed. "You speak of me as some old crone in need of luxury, rather than a woman who desires adventure. It is you I serve, not a city's cold embrace."

Pontius brought his hand up to her cheek. "But you deserve more." Then, with a new determination, Pontius added, "And I deserve more than to be sent to a barren, lifeless land crawling with ungrateful subjects."

"You speak of them as if they were serpents, Pontius, and not people! I have heard many wonderful things about the lands of the East—Egypt, Persia, and beyond. Surely, your vision of these people is distorted."

Pontius smiled. He wished the mere power of her belief would make it so. He had heard firsthand the burdensome nature of the commission and knew his perception wasn't distorted. Hoping he still had time to change the orders, Pontius left immediately for the administrative council to plead his case.

* * *

Pontius walked into the command chambers where a clerk was seated at a table too small to hold all of the scrolls and papers overflowing its edges. The clerk appeared to be unaware of Pilate's entrance, studying the papers in front of him, or possibly lost in thought. Pontius hesitantly interrupted.

"Hail Caesar!"

The clerk echoed the introduction without looking up. Finally, his eyes shifted from his work. "Pilate, what brings you here? You were recently in Spain, were you not? How were your engagements?"

Reluctant to deviate from the subject overflowing his thoughts, but feeling obligated to respond, Pilate regurgitated what had become a standard and rehearsed reply: "I counted the days with enduring pain in the absence of beautiful Rome—and my loving wife. Fortunately, there were few battles, but they seemed to last a lifetime. Hours seemed an eternity, especially when death rained in the air like hail from a vengeful black cloud. Thank the gods, they all ended in victories."

"Good, I have heard of your engagements. How long were you there?"

Pilate ignored the question, wanting to get to the point. "I received orders. Where will I be assigned?"

"Orders?" the clerk repeated. "You've received orders already? Doesn't it say?"

"Well, yes, but there's got to be some sort of mistake—Judea. The orders also mention that I am to be governor, a position of high importance which I have long dreamed of holding, and I am flattered that the Senate would consider me. If I am that important, should I not be consulted?"

"You're being consulted now, and you don't have a choice. The area is falling to the dogs. Tiberius Caesar seeks the assistance of Jewish rule, and our patience with Antipas and Philip are wearing thin."

Pilate was puzzled. Antipas was the Jewish regent of Galilee and Perea, and Philip was the regent of Iturea. "What do they have to do with me—or the province of Judea, for that matter?"

"It has everything to do with you. Rome desires a Jewish intermediary for Judea, since that position has been vacant for nearly twenty years, and these people refuse to deal directly with Roman authority. Antipas has made it known he wants control of the combined provinces, just as his father, Herod the Great, did long ago. He makes no secret of his desires, spending most of his time in Jerusalem, in the ancient palace of his father. The city has an obsessive significance to these people." The clerk scrunched his face. "Almost as if they thought of it as Rome."

Pilate laughed at the thought of comparing any city to Rome. "What about Philip? He is also a son of the ancient Herod, is he not?"

The clerk smiled. "Apparently, you already know a lot about the region. Yes, Philip is also a son. However, Tiberius Caesar favors Antipas. After all, the man built an entire city as capital of Galilee to honor the Divine Caesar. Tiberius has aspirations that Antipas should facilitate control and order of the entire region." Taking a deep breath as if to acknowledge the enormity of the task, he continued, "Caesar dreams of a province as it was during the time of Augustus Caesar with Herod the Great. However, King Herod's death over thirty years ago left the area divided, with continuous infighting amongst his heirs and a corresponding loss of control of the people."

"Well, why doesn't Caesar simply appoint Antipas as king and get beyond all of this foolishness?"

The clerk shook his head. "I said Caesar favors Antipas; I didn't say he has complete confidence in him. The man you are replacing, Valerius Gratus, does not like Antipas. Gratus felt Antipas no longer had control of anyone except the guards in his palace—and I'm not sure he has loyalty there. Jews no longer think of him as one of their own, but as a Roman puppet." The clerk paused for a moment and smiled. "Which he is; and you've got to give those worthless people some credit." The clerk shook his head as if to get back on track. "Since Valerius Gratus resigned as governor, morale among the soldiers has been low and is getting worse. Judean zealots randomly kill anything wearing a Roman uniform, even if it means their own death. They strike, and then scurry off like rodents to their pitiful lives. Executing them has no effect. Whether it's a few or many, they do not seem to care."

"I know how bad it is there. You don't have to tell me these things! But why me? What am I supposed to do?"

The clerk sat back in his chair and lowered his eyes as he looked away. "Caesar has great confidence in you. He looks to you to effect change amongst the servitude of the Judean people. We need new ideas to bring this country under control and increase collection of taxes to support the fielded armies. Caesar believes you're the right man."

Pontius thought for a moment. *New ideas from him?* Judea had been a land of experiments in Roman rule, although most had been failures. Was the Senate expressing faith in him for such a position? Pontius felt naive to believe this. However, this assignment could be his opportunity to shine in the eyes of the Senate and achieve advancement in the Roman hierarchy—maybe even the Senate itself. This could lead to permanent residence in Rome with all the privileges and wealth of a senator. But only average men were sent to Judea—and less than average men returned. Which was he to believe? Did it matter?

"Despite the misgivings of Valerius Gratus," the clerk continued, "I think your best hope lies with Antipas for regaining control—next to having their god command them to do so."

2 ~ Caesarea

It had been three weeks since they left Rome. The ship seemed to glide through the water with relative ease and it was a beautiful day. The breast of an innate gold eagle bellowed on a large square sail from a mild wind over the relatively calm Inner Sea. The water was clear and as blue as the sky. Very rarely did the ship venture far from land. Today on the last leg of the journey, the shipmaster made a straight cut for Caesarea. The gods had paid them company on this voyage, granting weather of good fortune. However, the uneventfulness of the trip only added to the boredom and sense of isolation. The desire to end the journey acted as a bond, heightening the sense of activity and movement on board.

Pontius stood near the bow, peering off to the featureless horizon, each passing wave looking just like the last. He knew Judea lay straight ahead. The fact that it could not be seen made it ghostly. It fascinated Pontius that after so many days of travel, and so many miles of endless horizons, just ahead lay a whole new people, with their own customs, daily trials, and personal struggles. He found himself anxious to meet them, despite his misgivings. The animosity that had filled his thoughts when he left Rome had softened with time and the loneliness of the trip. The loneliness turned into a sense of vulnerability, with the laws and authority of Rome so far away. It was a vulnerability he had never felt before, reminiscent, in a way, of his feelings on the battlefield. Except on the battlefield it did not have time to simmer and mature.

Pontius felt the familiar touch around his waist and only had to glance back slightly as he whispered, "Hello, my love." Her touch was all it took for his fears to subside. Pontius felt secure with his wife and he loved it—a security magnified by the humbling nature of the trip. He turned to pay her notice. "I think I've been hypnotized by the motion of the water... and the steadiness of the bow slapping wave after wave. I am so glad this ship has done most of the slapping, rather than the waves tossing us around like a toy. I have heard that the waves can be big enough to swallow a ship whole."

"Oh, Pontius, stop it. You may speak so when we are on solid, dry land and not a moment before. You're tempting the gods to make sport of us and this vessel. It's all we have between us and whatever creatures lurk below. The gods might even land one right on this deck with such talk," turning her mild scolding into a smile.

Pontius let forth a quick, unexpected laugh. Claudia always had a way of changing any mood with a strange, funny twist. "I do love you, Claudia. I would never do or say anything to cause the gods to toy with you—since I myself worship you—always by your side." Pontius smiled. "You came along at the right moment. My thoughts were turning... uncomfortable. I never realized this trip would be so long and tiresome. Perhaps a good storm would have made things a little more interesting."

"I think not! I'm perfectly happy with an uneventful trip. We have seen so many beautiful new lands—places I had never dreamed of. However, I fear where we are going, and what it will be like. In a way, Pontius, I do not want this voyage to end. What sort of people will there be? Just to think, we must live amongst them for a long while." Claudia turned to look from whence they came and added, "The voyage itself has been so wonderful. We have had so much time together, nothing else to think about, no worries about politics or acting proper amongst a gathering of your... acquaintances. Just time for us and us alone."

Pontius smiled. "But our destination serves a purpose. Tiberius Caesar told me himself that Judea is at the heart of our civilization, a central—"

Claudia interrupted, "You spoke to Tiberius? When did this happen?"

"I did not tell you?"

Claudia looked sternly into his eyes. "There are many things you do not tell me, Pontius. In Rome, you are always too busy, with so many things on your mind. Thoughts I see racing through your head, thoughts that stay locked inside, a mystery to me. Now you are more relaxed. We talk more, and I don't have to wonder what is churning in your head."

Pontius felt a little embarrassed since Claudia was close to the mark. So much was demanded of him by his position in the Roman government. Incredible demands that sometimes he felt incapable of fulfilling. The demands were taxing him as a person, and Claudia's remarks only served to confirm that it was also taxing those around him. "Tiberius explained that Judea is central to many great civilizations—some even out beyond the protection of our empire, far to the east."

"I have heard of Egypt, and Assyria, and the Arabians, and stories of people much farther beyond."

Pontius smiled and opened a pocket on his tunic, pulling out a necklace. He raised it delicately against her chest and draped it over her shoulders. "This necklace contains gems and gold from the very lands of which you speak."

Claudia gasped as she touched the brilliant opal pendant dangling from a gold chain inlaid with emeralds and pearls. "Pontius, it's beautiful!"

"It is no match for your beauty. You are my strength and my solace."

Pontius pushed back her soft flowing black hair and fastened the necklace, caressing the delicate lines of her neck. He lightly guided his fingers along her smooth olive skin to hazel-blue eyes perfectly appareled on a slender face. Suddenly they were interrupted by a loud call from above. "Land! I see land!" A crewman had climbed to a high point on the main mast and was pointing straight ahead. Pontius turned his attention beyond the bow and could see nothing.

Claudia mumbled, "What is he talking about? I see no land. All I see is water. Is this land but a ghost?"

Pontius shuddered slightly, remembering his own thoughts. It seemed uncanny that Claudia would mention the same thing. Collecting his thoughts, Pontius said, "He is not seeing things, my love. He's an experienced seaman. It is out there."

Claudia's mood dimmed as she grasped the pendant. "Oh, Pontius, I don't want it to be out there. I don't want this journey to end."

Pontius gently brought his hand up to touch her face. "This journey may end, but I will always love you."

Visions of land appeared on the horizon, followed by the faint outlines of buildings and structures. As they grew larger, the magnificence and grandeur of the architecture became apparent, seeming out of place. High on a hill stood a grand palace with a dozen massive columns that dwarfed the people who could barely be seen milling about. The marble was flawlessly white. As the ship wove through the harbor, several obelisks came into view, topped with magnificent statues commanding ever-present power and authority. Some statues were solid white, emphasizing purity and beauty, while others were lightly trimmed in gold, outlining the edges of garments or granting attention to a torch held high to the gods. Still other sculptures were completely gilded, shining in radiant brilliance.

Claudia's apprehension changed to astonishment as she broke the silence. "Have we left Rome? Has this voyage been but a dream?"

Pontius too was taken by the beauty and splendor of the coastal city. "Caesarea. I had heard it was magnificent, but I was not aware it had the beauty of Rome herself. Herod the Great built the city many years ago in tribute to Augustus Caesar and to all of Rome—a tribute that will live on to greet countless Romans. It is a wonderful sight after such a long journey."

Samaritan slaves waited at the dock to load their belongings onto a cart. The military escort who had accompanied Pontius and Claudia directed the workers as to what items to take and to whom they belonged. Three of the military escort even lent a hand, seemingly weary of doing nothing after such a long journey. Pontius turned to Claudia and whispered, "I must admit, I'm not sure where we are to go. I thought someone would be here to greet us and assist in our accommodations. I was told the governor would have a council, but they, too, seem to be ghosts."

Claudia laughed. "We arrived early, Pontius. They probably weren't expecting us until next week."

Pontius started to grow agitated. "Don't they have eyes? Surely they could see a Roman vessel as big as this approaching from the sea!"

"Pontius, we could barely see this entire land until we were almost upon it—and I'm sure they have merchant vessels that arrive every day. This one is probably no different from the rest," Claudia said with a consoling tone.

Pontius' frustration was growing. "No different from all of the rest! It only flies the banner of a Roman governor. They should have kept more careful watch. The chief council will lose a month's wages over this, I assure you."

The Roman centurion in charge of the ship escort approached Pilate. He stopped smartly at attention, and with very crisp, proud movements, struck his right fist against his chest, and then thrust it smartly forward. "Hail, Pontius Pilate, governor of Judea. With your permission, the slaves have informed me they are to take your possessions to the Palace of the Governor."

Pilate looked firmly at the centurion. "Are we to trust these slaves?"

The centurion was professional and to the point. "My Lord Pilate, as commander of your guard, I swear my allegiance to you and your protection. My soldiers are well trained, and will do whatever is necessary to protect you and your wife."

Pilate felt reassured by the sternness and confidence of his response, but still felt wary. "I doubt it would come to that. I'm just cautious of slaves who might attempt to take possession of our goods."

The centurion responded, "Your possessions are also under our sworn protection, Prefect. These slaves have pointed to the palace—there, up on the hill, overlooking the harbor. The structure with the large, marble columns: that is the Governor's Palace."

"I am impressed. I noticed this building far out to sea. I thought it to be some temple to a god." Then placing his hand on his chest in a boastful manner, Pilate added, "I suppose I must suffice as the cause of worship."

Both Pilate and the centurion smiled at the easing of spirit. Off to his right, Pilate heard the sound of footsteps running along the stone dock in their direction. By his dress the man was obviously Roman.

Approaching Pilate, and slightly out of breath, he introduced himself. "Prefect, I sincerely apologize for not having greeted you upon arrival. I wasn't expecting you this early. A runner only just informed me. I am truly sorry and hope I have not inconvenienced you or your wife in any way." Taking another breath, he continued, "Please excuse my rudeness, My Lord Pilate, I am Ascenius Tomis, the head of your advisory council."

The sincerity and friendly nature of Ascenius' demeanor quelled the slight agitation that had been brewing inside. "Yes, yes, if it were not for the magnificent architecture, I was beginning to wonder if there were any Romans within this city. Had it not been for these slaves, we would have had no welcome at all."

"I am forever in your debt, Your Nobility, and I assure you, there are a great many Romans who grace this city."

Pilate softened his attitude and realized that a simple mistake had been made—not enough to sacrifice a trust he would need to build in learning the character of this country and its people. "And pardon my rudeness; allow me to introduce my wife, Claudia."

"It is an honor to meet you, Lady Claudia. There are many who are anxious to meet you and your husband, and be of whatever service we can. I hope that your journey was pleasant."

Claudia cleared her throat and bowed slightly. "Oh, it was very pleasant—more so than I thought it would be. There were so many interesting places and people along the way, but none quite as beautiful as Caesarea. I, too, am looking forward to meeting everyone—and being of service to my husband."

3 ~ Barabbas

Several weeks passed. Pontius and Claudia had almost forgotten they were in Judea. For Pontius, there still seemed countless, insurmountable tasks that overwhelmed any awareness of where he was or how distant they were from Rome.

After a long day at the council Pontius approached the now familiar site of their new home. The aroma of fresh bread was in the air. Pontius normally helped Claudia with setting the table, but today he was tired from tasks and details for planning a trip to Jerusalem. He fell back into a chair in the front room letting out a heavy sigh. The sun's rays grew dim on the walls with the day's light beginning to fade. Claudia came into the room and lit a long, thin wick from a single, burning oil lamp. She carefully carried the flame to other lamps in the room. Pontius watched his wife in this nightly ritual, moved by her familiar, yet beautiful, comforting form. The flames provided flickering accents above the natural light. Soon, their dancing glow would be the only source to maintain the image of her radiant beauty. Pontius thought the oil lamps a true blessing from the gods to extend this treasured time. He drew near to Claudia, gently placing his left hand on hers as she lit the last lamp and guided his other arm around her waist. "How was your day, my love? I hope you are finding this country pleasing, and the people interesting and… friendly. I must admit that I myself am pleasantly surprised at the nature of Caesarea and the people here. It is not as bad as I feared."

Claudia brought the flame close to her lips as if to offer a kiss, providing a gentle force of air. Pontius felt this a true paradox. Such a gesture from such a wonderful woman should breathe life, but instead the flame disappeared, transforming into a spirit that rose to meet the gods. Claudia placed the wick sideways onto the lamp, and then turned to meet Pontius. "I am grateful that you are content, my husband. I think most of my reservations stemmed from the horrible, predisposed images we were given of this land, that truly were not justified. The sea is so beautiful, and it seems no matter where one stands in Caesarea, you can still see and hear its waves. It reminds me of when we lived in Ostia—except Ostia was so big that many times I had forgotten we were even near the sea." Claudia's voice slowed, as Pontius became entranced in her eyes. Time was irrelevant as their lips met. Her kiss brought life, providing a type of nourishment out of his trance, interrupted by discomforting thoughts of his near-term duty.

Knowing he had to tell her, Pontius frowned slightly. "In a few days I must travel to Jerusalem. I will meet with military commanders there—and Antipas. I do not wish to leave you after we have only been here for a few short weeks, but it is something I must do. I wish I could take you with me. However, it is likely to be a rough trip over strange land. I plan to stay for a couple of weeks—no more, I assure you."

Pontius was deeply affected as the light in Claudia's eyes dimmed, and her mood changed slightly as she asked, "Do you have to go? You should have them travel here to meet you. Surely they would not object to visiting this beautiful city."

"That's actually not a bad idea. But I am told that Jerusalem is the heart of this country—a place I must attend sooner or later. Politically, it is important I do it right away. It will be an important gesture to the people and to their governing council. Cooperation with these people is not to be taken lightly, and it doesn't take much to throw everything off balance."

Pontius could see the disappointment in Claudia's eyes as he continued, "I am concerned with these bands of Judean criminals who roam the countryside, attacking Roman outposts and small companies of soldiers—'zealots,' I think they call them. We will have a large escort, so there will be no trouble. Still, I do not want to place you at risk until I see the layout of the country for myself."

"Take an entire legion, Pontius," Claudia said with a developing smile on her face. "I want to make sure you come back safely to me."

Pontius laughed. "Then the legion would not be here to protect you, my dearest Claudia, and I will have none of that."

* * *

The next morning Pilate exited the front door of the palace where a contingent of soldiers had gathered. Just in front of the gate, a sergeant held Pilate's mount. The horse was adorned in red and gold trimmed cloth, and light ornamental armor around the saddle and head dressing. Most of the leatherwork was inset with gold and silver that glistened with every movement. Pilate called out for the company sergeant. "Whose idea was it to dress my mount in this manner?"

"It was mine, sir," the sergeant said with pride. "The horse is dressed with adornment recently sent from Rome, and I am afraid there is very little to add, My Lord Pilate. Perhaps you would prefer a chariot, sir?"

Pilate looked at the sergeant in disbelief. "No, I do not wish to stand all the way to Jerusalem, and no, I do not want anything added that will make me visible from every hilltop through the wilderness. I want you to take all of this off"—pointing at the horse. "Refit it with battle dress. We have a long journey ahead, and I do not want to be made a target for every zealot we might encounter!"

"Yes, sir!" The sergeant responded with a forceful fist-to-shoulder salute.

Pilate looked down the long line of horse soldiers and the greater number of foot soldiers who stood along either side of the road waiting for orders to proceed. He felt somewhat anxious realizing he had caused the entire column to wait, but quickly fought it off. He looked down at the parched, dry earth and kicked at a stone protruding from the roadway. The entire way was marked with them. His immediate thought was how a chariot ride would rattle one's bones in short order, making the experience very unpleasant and possibly painful. Pilate walked over to the centurion of the cohort and said, "We must wait a short while. I have ordered the dressing on my mount changed to something a little less conspicuous."

The centurion responded, "A good idea, sir. I had the same thoughts of your mount. There is no need to attract attention until we get to Jerusalem."

"Have you made this trip before, Centurion?"

"Yes, sir, many times. A few years ago there was no need for an escort of this size. Now the zealots are attacking small bands of Roman soldiers, hiding like cowards behind rocks and bushes in a land they know all too well. With an escort of this size and accompanying horse, I assure you we will have no problems."

"It is good to hear your confidence, Centurion. It is an impressive force of men and equipment."

It had only been a few moments when the sergeant returned with Pilate's horse. Pilate drew in a deep breath. "Yes, this is more like it. Make sure the ornamental dressing is brought along in a cart so it can be used when we near Jerusalem. It would be a shame not to show the glory and honor of Rome."

Pilate mounted his horse and sat confidently in the saddle. He rode down the length of escort, providing the customary inspection. He thought of his days in Spain when he led his own troops under more serious and life-threatening campaigns. It also reminded him of the fear that seemed to grip every ounce of his soul in preparing for battle, not knowing what arrow might meet its mark or what army might slaughter his men. Many times he had wondered whether he would see another day or Claudia again, dying without notice in a foreign land. As if he had wakened from a bad dream, Pilate realized he was nearing the end of the column and the lead centurion. He felt an incredible sense of relief that he was not on the battlefield of his previous duty, merely in a land that had long ago been conquered by many other forgotten Romans who had died in her glory. Pilate signaled to the lead centurion that it was time to proceed, turned on his horse, and rode back to the center of the column. With a few short, powerful commands, the cavalry were on their mounts, the foot soldiers were lined up in two columns, and the whole mass was on its way.

The clanking of the soldiers' equipment had a rhythm, a song of battle. Pontius remembered the times he wished his men had been as well equipped. Food, water, weapons, armor, and health—all of which were missing at one time or another—were now in plentiful supply. And they were simply traveling from one place to another.

As the sun climbed higher in the sky, the heat and dry air caused the dust to stir from pounding feet—both human and horse. It hung in the air and seemed to follow them. One of the sergeants yelled for the men to pick up their feet and not shuffle. After several hours, the dust covered everything. Pontius wasn't sure if the dryness he felt was from a coat of dust or from the heat. A quick swat at his sleeves confirmed his suspicions when a cloud filled the air. Pontius caught a glimpse of disgust from those around him as his thoughtless action had added to their misery. Pontius offered an inaudible apology.

About that time, the lead centurion motioned for the column to stop and move off to the side of the road. The snappy mood of the men had vanished as they trudged off the road, some plopping to the ground in their own cloud of dust. Pontius dismounted and walked his horse to the side. The walking felt good and he had no desire to rest his sore behind on a jagged boulder. Pontius took out the bread that only a few nights before had offered a pleasant aroma, but now was stale and hard. The morsels were nonetheless a welcome indulgence. Pontius was amazed at how the land had completely changed character immediately upon leaving Caesarea.

As the afternoon wore on, the men required more and more time for resting as the desert conditions taxed their physical abilities. The initial delay was lost in the dragging of hours of a seemingly endless march. Pontius wished he had kept in better practice at riding his horse; the soreness of his inner thighs was almost unbearable. Ignoring what the soldiers might think, Pontius dismounted and walked for a while, leading his horse. He thought it humiliating in front of his men, but he did not want to wear his backside raw so early in the trip and not be able to walk or sit when they finally reached Jerusalem. Much to his surprise, no one seemed to notice.

The road was not well traveled. The column met only the occasional traveler, who would move off to the side and wait as they passed. Some were alone, some in small groups, and some had a few animals that were either being herded or pulling carts. The travelers seemed filthy and poor. Pontius couldn't help but wonder what they were doing so far out in the middle of nowhere and how they survived. One appeared the same as the next, wearing the same dusty, worn clothing; all with dark, weathered skin beneath facial hair that was scraggly and disheveled. The only thing that distinguished one from another was the length of their beards. They offered a stark and pitiful contrast to the clean-shaven and smartly attired Roman force. It was not long before Pontius and the rest of the soldiers completely ignored the native travelers. The travelers, in turn, did not seem impressed with the Roman column, offering only the inevitable right of way. Pontius swore he caught an emotion in some of their eyes he had never seen before—not in the battlefield or in the eyes of his enemy, and not in the Senate halls of Rome. It seemed a subdued, passionate hatred, meaning to destroy the object of its rage. There were others, expressionless, where Pontius saw nothing, which chilled him to his core.

The shadows grew long and thin off to the forward left. The near-end of the day was a welcome sight, knowing there would soon be relief from the scorching heat. The lead centurion called, "Halt!" and sent a messenger back to Pilate.

"With your permission, Noble Pilate, the centurion has requested we make camp for the evening."

Pilate offered immediate approval.

The men suddenly came to life again, putting into practice their relentless hours of training and experience in setting up a secure camp in the precious light remaining. Sentries were placed at several points around the perimeter, while others put up the tents for the officers and the Roman prefect. Still others prepared fires and butchered a calf in preparation for skewering on a spit. It was not long after night fell that all of the men were fed, calling an end to a long, grueling day.

* * *

Toward the end of the third day, the column was one day's march from Jerusalem. The countryside had changed, showing more vegetation, trees, and bushes, and had also become hillier, with mountains off in the distance. It was still hot and dry, however, and the wind picked up. Pontius normally hated the wind, yet now it cleared the dust from the soldiers' feet and offered cooling from the sun's incessant rays.

Pontius' trance was suddenly interrupted by a flock of arrows flying towards the main body of soldiers, most overshooting their mark from the gusting support of the wind. A few stray arrows fell into the column, one entering a soldier's left collarbone only a few feet in front of Pontius. Two of the arrows hit horses, causing them to rear, throwing one of the unsuspecting riders and nearly throwing the second. The rearing of the horses startled the soldiers into action. Cries of warning and surprise erupted as they raised their shields over their heads. Officers barked orders, causing the soldiers to scatter to both sides of the road. On the left, the cavalry immediately turned and charged directly toward the source of the arrows' flight. No sooner had they charged than came a second wave of arrows from men jumping out from behind rocks and bushes on the hillside. The arrows fell like rain with crackling pops mostly on shields. The attackers quickly poured down the hillside, abandoning their bows in favor of clubs, axes, and swords. The screams and yells of the attacking brood grew as they approached, while the horse soldiers quickly and forcefully charged up the hill.

The attacking number was about thirty and clearly they were outnumbered by the horse soldiers alone. The foot soldiers followed behind as a second line of defense. Pontius was amazed the attackers were not hindered by the overwhelming force of the Roman counterattack, boldly charging ahead as if blinded by suicidal drive. If the outcome had been decided by the sheer intensity of their charge, they would have defeated an entire legion. Before the two forces met, members of the Roman cavalry accurately and powerfully threw their spears, silencing over half of the determined enemy. Pilate hurriedly rode down the length of the opposite-side cavalry holding their position.

None of the attackers turned and ran. They continued forward to their deaths, inevitably engaging Roman soldiers in arm-to-arm combat. Their actions were hard and enraged. As soon an attacker would become entangled and focused in a violent battle, he was impaled or struck from behind. The fighting ended almost as quickly as it began. Two of the attackers were physically subdued by several soldiers as they hopelessly continued their struggle. One attacker held tight to his sword as a soldier twisted his arm and used his fingernails to tear at his grip. The zealot gave a deafening cry and gritted his teeth as the veins in his arms were ready to burst trying to thrust his sword into anything nearby. The soldier then pulled out a dagger to pry the attacker's grip. The zealot's blood caused his hand to slip as the sword was finally pulled free.

The prisoners were forcefully taken to Pilate. The intensity of their continued struggle was matched by the fire and hatred in their eyes. A final count showed twenty-nine of the zealots had lost their lives with five Roman casualties—two dead and three wounded.

A Roman officer placed a spear to the throat of one of the prisoners and asked, "Who are you?"

The man said nothing as the officer pressed the spear harder and deeper into his throat. Pontius sensed the officer's undiminished anger from the heat of battle as the officer yelled, "Why did you attack us?! Are there any more of you in the rocks?"

The prisoners did not respond. The officer called over an interpreter who continued the line of questioning. The interrogation went on for several minutes until finally one of the prisoners started chanting in Hebrew, seemingly oblivious to what was going on around him. The officer occasionally forced the spear in deeper, breaking the skin—only temporarily interrupting the prayerful chant. "If you do not speak, you will be executed! Right here, right now! If you speak, your lives will be spared, and you will be taken prisoner."

The only reaction was a slight quickening in the prisoner's chant. The other prisoner showed no reaction as the blood from his hand dripped into a puddle on the ground.

The violent events were nothing like Pilate had ever seen. The burning fire of their attack with its hopeless outcome seemed senseless. Pilate finally found words. "It was suicide! They had to have known they had no possible hope of defeating this column."

One prisoner immediately turned his attention towards Pilate, appearing to comprehend the language of his enemy. The lead centurion responded, "I do not think it was their objective to defeat the column, my lord. I think their objective was more focused. It was no secret that you were traveling to Jerusalem."

Pilate was disgusted at the insinuation. So many lives had been severed in an attempt on his. Disturbed by the obvious stare from the one prisoner, Pilate sensed he was reacting to things being said. Pilate approached him. "Why do you throw so many lives away in an attempt on my life? You have accomplished nothing!"

Not expecting a response, Pilate turned and walked away, but was stopped in his tracks as he heard, "It is not the man—it is the position! You, as a man, mean nothing to us. It is your presence that defiles this land. We serve only the one true God and will never submit to Roman authority."

Pilate quickly turned and narrowed his attention on the zealot. Approaching, Pilate grabbed the prisoner's beard and pulled his face close. "Your friends submitted to Roman authority in their death, and you will submit in a prison for the rest of your life!" Pilate pointed to the other prisoner and said to the officer holding the spear, "Kill him."

Without hesitation, the officer thrust the spear forward, immediately silencing the chant. Pilate turned back to the zealot and said, "You, as a man, mean nothing to me."

4 ~ Antipas

In the distance, Pontius could see the walled city of Jerusalem. Signs of civilization were a welcome sight after four days in the wilderness and fighting off the band of zealots. The column halted, and Pontius ordered the dressing on his horse changed back to the original, grand decor. A messenger was sent ahead to announce their arrival to the Roman commander of the garrison at Fortress Antonia. As the column approached, the gates slowly opened, beckoning them to enter. A crowd had begun to form. They were not there to greet the Roman intruders, but drawn by curiosity. The silence seemed eerie as Pontius thought back to the savage screams of the assailants.

The lone prisoner was being pulled in chains near the rear. The two dead Roman soldiers were covered in an open cart. The bodies of the slaughtered zealots were left on the battlefield. Behind him, Pontius could hear occasional cries of "Barabbas!" He wondered what it meant and if it was something in Hebrew. *Was it a greeting, or more likely, a phrase of contempt and hatred?* Pontius leaned over to one of his officers and asked, "What do you suppose 'barabbas' means? I've heard it called out several times. I'm not sure if we should be smiling back at their greeting or throwing spears!"

"I'm not sure, my lord. I have never heard this term before." The officer called for the interpreter and asked of its meaning. The interpreter paused for a moment and then responded, "It's a name, I think—most likely of the prisoner. He must be a popular man."

Pilate's eyes lit up, realizing the simple explanation. "Of course! It is good that he is well known, for they will never see his popular face again."

The officer nodded. "We should arrest those who call out his name. If they know the prisoner, then they must know of the zealots—or even be zealots themselves."

Pilate interrupted with a touch of sarcasm in his voice, "Perhaps we should arrest the entire crowd and interrogate them all. Our first two prisoners would say nothing. I doubt we would gain much from people brave enough to call out his name. How would it look for our column to march gloriously into the city, and then disperse into the crowd, arresting people simply for calling out a name? We definitely wouldn't gain favor from a people we are tasked to rule. We must have their support, not their contempt, in order to strengthen the role of the Roman Empire in this entire region."

With this, Pilate rode back to where Barabbas was being pulled in chains. "So, you are called Barabbas. You have quite a following! Heed their calls for the last time, for I doubt you will ever hear your name called from the bowels of a dark prison cell." Pilate paused, letting the hopelessness sink in. "I will give you a new name, since I am tiring of Barabbas. We will call you... Yahweh, after your god."

Barabbas looked up. "I will not answer to Yahweh. That is the Lord, my God."

"Then you will have a silent life. If you will not speak of your zealot friends, then you have no other purpose."

The column stopped in front of Fortress Antonia, and the lead centurion dismissed the troops. Pilate dismounted and gave his horse to the sergeant. "Form a detail to transport Barabbas to a prison cell inside the fortress."

A Roman commander from the fortress approached Pilate. A flowing red robe draped from the shoulders of a polished-brass breast plate ornate with scenes of battle. An equally magnificent helmet was inlayed with gold and silver gods overseeing the scenes below. The helmet matched every movement of his head as a thick red mane quivered to keep pace. The commander slapped his fist against his breast plate in salute. "It is indeed my honor to greet you, Prefect Pontius Pilate, Governor of Judea. I am Tacitus, commander of the forces occupying this walled city. Welcome to Jerusalem and to Fortress Antonia."

The fortress was much older than the structures at Caesarea, but it was still magnificent. Pilate walked up to the main entrance and could feel his exhaustion settling in as he climbed the steps. The guards, standing on either side, snapped to attention, striking their fists against their breasts. Pilate regained his composure, acknowledging the guards' salutes. Turning to Tacitus, Pilate offered a worn smile. "Yes, Tribune, I am Pontius Pilate. Pardon me for my hesitation, but I am really feeling the burden of this trip. All I want to see is a bed and a good night's rest. As you can see, we have brought along a prisoner. His name is"—Pilate smiled before he caught himself—"Yahweh."

"Yahweh!" Tacitus exclaimed. "That is a sacred word to these people. It is the name of their god. Many will not even speak the name!"

Pilate laughed, seeing the surprise in Tacitus' eyes. "It is a name I have given him. Instruct your guards to only refer to him as Yahweh."

Tacitus smiled. "So be it, My Lord Pilate. I had heard you met with a band of zealots, and I saw the cart carrying the dead soldiers. How many men did we lose?"

"Only two. The zealots were hoping that I would be one of the dead. Had it not been for the wind, one of the arrows in their first flight may have found its mark, but the gods were with us yesterday. So much for their Yahweh—losing thirty, while our loss was only two."

Tacitus acted a little surprised. "Thirty! I did not know there were so many. Normally they travel in groups of six or eight, but rarely that many. They must have placed great importance in your capture, my lord." Tacitus thought seriously for a moment and then added, "On your way back, I will send more troops along with your escort."

"That would be greatly appreciated, but I don't think it will be necessary. My escort handled the zealots well enough. The zealots truly had their zeal, but they were no match for the training and discipline of our soldiers."

"The zealots have been around for many years—more so recently. They have grown to become a thorn in our side. These people are like none I have ever seen. I sometimes think that some day, every man, woman, and child on the streets of Jerusalem will become zealots." Tacitus smiled and then added in humor, "Eventually we will have to kill them all. Then where would our tax base be?"

Pilate's thoughts deepened, almost ignoring Tacitus' attempt at humor. "I saw hatred in the faces of many in the crowd when we rode into Jerusalem. Some were even calling out the name 'Barabbas'—err, the real name of our prisoner—as if it were a battle cry, or a challenge. My centurion was ready to arrest them all. To tell you the truth, I'm not sure that wouldn't have been the correct course. In any case, I am dead tired, and I truly must get some rest. We can speak tomorrow."

Tacitus quickly agreed. "Yes, sir, tomorrow. If it be your wish, my lord, I will take you to visit Antipas. He is a peculiar man."

* * *

The next day Pilate and Tacitus rode with an escort to the palace built by Herod the Great. Riding through the winding streets, the buildings grew smaller and older—a far cry from Caesarea. For the first time, Pilate sensed being in a foreign land with strange people. He thought of Claudia and how much he missed her even though it had only been a few days. It would be at least as many days before he would see her again.

Traveling towards the palace there was not the crowd of onlookers, just several people going about their daily lives. Pilate sensed his presence bred contempt rather than respect. Occasionally, through breaks in the buildings, massive towers of a very large structure appeared in the distance. Tacitus pointed up. "That is Antipas' palace."

Pilate shook his head. "That is not his palace. That is the palace of his late father, Herod the Great, who was our puppet king over the combined provinces many years ago. Antipas is the regent of Galilee up north. He doesn't even belong here. What brings him down from Tiberias?"

Tacitus smiled. "Antipas thinks he is the resurrected body and soul of his father. He has spent much of his time in Jerusalem, making no secret that he desires his father's kingdom. Besides, many of the people of Judea will not live in Tiberias. They feel the city is defiled. Apparently, the noble and wise Antipas built the city on the site of an old cemetery, having exhumed and moved all of the bodies. The city will never have the air and power of Jerusalem."

As they drew near, the immensity of the palace quickly became apparent, its large stone walls climbing between the massive towers, topped with parapet structures. Herod's palace was by far the most impressive structure within the city and rose in stark contrast to the smaller, less-well-kept structures that crept right up to its walls. This was definitely a fortress within a fortress, just like Fortress Antonia. Pontius could tell this city had been built over the centuries to ward off invaders, and it reeked of seclusion from the outside world. Pontius was familiar with the history of the Jews and how they had been conquered and reconquered countless times. Somehow, they always regained self-identity even after very long periods of occupation. Pontius almost felt sorry for the Jews, existing at the heart of civilization in such a barren land. The Egyptians, the Assyrians, the Philistines, the Babylonians, and now the Romans had yokes about their necks, toiling their land. Where were the landlords of the past? The Jews were still here, but the others had long since departed. Pontius wondered if the same fate lay in store for Rome, though he quickly fought off the notion, remembering Rome's might and power.

Upon entering the main hall of Herod's palace, Pilate noticed the layout was remarkably Roman. Large pillars lined either side of the large room, which was tiled with polished marble floors. At the end, a throne was elevated above the main level with a series of steps. Jewish soldiers lined each side of the hall, one to each pillar. On the throne sat the man Pilate thought to be Antipas. Pilate was all too familiar with the hierarchical layout of the room, always placing the visitors at a lower level to the king, surrounded by palace guards. In the palace of Tiberius Caesar, this seemed a natural arrangement. But here in Judea, it seemed awkward and inappropriate for a conquered king. Even so, after a guard announced their presence, Pilate, Tacitus, and four accompanying Roman soldiers walked briskly across the marble floor, quickly closing the distance to Antipas' throne. Even from afar, Pilate could tell that Antipas was uncomfortable with the situation, immediately jumping from his father's chair and exclaiming from halfway across the great hall, "Most Noble and Honorable Pontius Pilate! It is a pleasure to have you grace our fair city!" Antipas hastily proceeded down the steps to meet them. "Welcome to Judea!"

Antipas' tone seemed over-jubilant, which also seemed out of place in Pilate's eyes. His attire appeared stranger and more bizarre than the awkward situation, having a garment and robe of wildly different colors—reds, brown, yellows, and gold intermixed with odd, intricate designs. Antipas was a large man, hidden beneath layers of clothing. His headdress had four domed segments that met at a point on top accenting the oddity of his garments. Only the smartly trimmed beard on a dark-skinned face presented an air of dignity in the otherwise gaudy appearance. Pilate felt that if it were not for his well-developed sense of tact, the smile on his face would have quickly turned to laughter at the unexpected spectacle. Antipas continued, "Tribune Tacitus! It is good to see you again, honoring the halls of my palace. Have you recovered from last week's banquet? I was worried you might drown in the wine!"

Tacitus frowned at the remark in front of Pilate, but kept his composure. "Tetrarch Antipas of Galilee, this is Pontius Pilate, Roman prefect of Judea."

Pilate offered a slight nod in greeting. "Tetrarch, it is an honor to meet you. I have heard many great things of your service to Rome. I look forward to a working liaison that will prove beneficial and mutually productive. I also hope to learn about the great people of this land."

"Yes, great people," Antipas remarked with a hint of sarcasm. Antipas paused a short while and finally nodded in agreement. "A great faceted people with many different ideals, characters, and beliefs." Then Antipas quickly changed the subject. "Perhaps you would experience our great hospitality with a feast and a banquet tonight! I will have entertainment, along with great food and plenty of wine!"

Even though the gesture was contrary to the point of his visit, Pilate felt compelled to accept Antipas' offer. The performance seemed an obvious attempt to avoid political issues that needed to be discussed. "I am compelled to accept your gracious invitation—and I suppose Tacitus will not mind swimming in another pool of wine," Pilate said smiling, casually patting Tacitus on the back.

Losing his smile and assuming a more serious tone, Pilate looked at Antipas. "We have a Jewish prisoner for you. He is a murderous zealot. He should be a burden of your cells and not a Roman prison. My sergeant will bring him over with a detail later today. He is the only one left of a large group of zealots who attacked my column yesterday, killing two of my men."

Antipas' face distorted into a superficial expression of concern. "He will be punished severely. I will have him whipped in public until near death, and then... let him die. These zealots are a nuisance, but fortunately, there are few and easy to deal with."

"Nuisance!" Pilate exclaimed. "Nearly thirty of them attacked my column—well equipped with arrows and other weapons. Had it not been for the gods, we would have lost more men. When we entered Jerusalem, there were several in the crowd calling out the name of our prisoner: Barabbas."

"Barabbas!" Antipas exclaimed in recognition, but also with a pained look of disappointment. He quickly changed to a note of marked concern: "I have heard that name before. He is a criminal, a thief, and a murderer. It is good you caught this man!"

Pilate was surprised to hear Antipas' unexpected tone and knew he wasn't being forthright. He had sensed courage and honor in the few words he had exchanged with Barabbas, not the cowardice of a thief and murderer. This, however, did not seem the time or the place to question Antipas' integrity. Pilate was beginning to feel that Barabbas was the only Jew with whom he knew for certain where he stood. "You need not execute this man or have him whipped. I just want him thrown in prison, never to be released, to serve as an example to his people. He seems to be a popular man, and the execution of such a man would only create a martyr. I would rather he waste in jail, as will his memory."

"So shall it be!" Antipas exclaimed, agreeing emphatically. As their discussions continued, Antipas seemed to do or say anything to please Pilate, and Pilate perceived the facade of a mysterious man. He could not tell whether Antipas' words were truth or lies. In a sense, Pilate felt this was Antipas' only quality—the ability to disguise truth from fiction.

As they were leaving the palace, Tacitus looked over to Pilate. "He's quite a character, isn't he?" Tacitus took on a cautious grin. "He likes to entertain. I forgot to tell you. Antipas loves to throw banquets. You can tell by his size that the man has no aversion to food and drink. I think he has a banquet every night whether he has guests or not."

Pilate was surprised to detect a positive note in Tacitus' remarks. He thought Tacitus was giving Antipas far too much credit. "He is quite a character, all right, but more in the negative sense from what I observed.

I do not feel I could trust the man in anything he says or does."

"I see your point, my lord. Still, he is perfect as a figurehead without power. It is no secret he desires the kingdom of his father, and what better man for such a position. We have an administrator fulfilling the needs of the people, without any threat to Rome. Antipas will do anything and everything Rome desires. He does not have the ability to be a threat to Rome."

"If he has no power, then how can he be effective in implementing our policies? How can he have any influence over these people?"

A puzzled look came over Tacitus' face. "Listen to yourself, My Lord Pilate. Would you have a strong-willed, charismatic ruler who at a moment's notice would threaten the authority of Rome? Besides, he is not completely powerless. He's our only corridor to peacefully implement the policies of Rome—and a willing corridor."

"I suppose you're right, Tribune. I think I was reacting to the character of a man I didn't like. I just hope Antipas can help resolve some of the pressing issues Rome has directed me to deal with." Pilate shook his head as he thought of the countless problems. "Tax revenues are waning. When one thinks the cash stores could not get any lower, they vanish. The only explanation is that these people are losing their respect for Roman authority. They simply refuse to pay, hiding their assets, stocks, and stores from being counted. If it were possible, I would send every last soldier into every residence and take what is owed. But we do not have enough men. Besides, such action would instigate mass rioting and disorder. We would have to kill every last one of them, as you have said, probably at the cost of losing most of our army. It is as if every option is not an option, and I am bewildered as to a solution." Pilate paused and shook his head. "I guess I was expecting more. I was truly looking upon Antipas for assistance in this and other matters, but I don't think it's going to happen."

Tacitus took a conciliatory tone. "I think it's possible Antipas could help with increasing tax revenues. I do not see the harm in discussing ideas with him."

* * *

That night at the banquet, Pontius was surprised to see the size of the crowd gathered in the great hall. Despite the large number of people, there was no shortage of food. He had never seen so much food. The banquet rivaled even the most lavish affairs in Rome. Antipas had lost several layers of clothing, more clearly revealing the level of his obesity. He also seemed more obnoxious than earlier in the day, surrounded by people attentive to his wishes. As Pilate approached, Antipas lifted his arms. "Ahhhh, my good friend Pontius Pilate!" Looking back at his gathering of acquaintances, he exclaimed, "This is the new prefect of Judea from Rome. He has graciously accepted my invitation to come and share our festivities."

Standing next to Antipas was a beautiful, young woman who did not appear to be Jewish. Her skin was slightly darker than the other women, and her features seemed more Arabic. Pilate knew Antipas was of Idumean descent, having converted to Judaism to meet political needs. Pilate thought this must be his daughter, and he wondered how such a beautiful creature could come from such a vulgar man.

Antipas seemed to notice Pilate's temporary fixation. "Ahhhh, you have noticed my beautiful wife. Permit me to introduce Phasaelis, daughter of Aretas, king of the Perean Arabs."

Caught off guard by his mistaken perception, Pontius did not catch the full extent of the lavish introduction. Her beauty commanded any man's focus. But it also caused Pontius to think of Claudia, and how he wished she could be here to experience every little twist and turn that kept one in constant surprise. Even though he presumed Phasaelis would not understand him, Pontius directed his attention toward her and said, "It is a pleasure to meet you, my lady. Your beauty rivals that of my own wife, who I wish could be here."

Antipas placed his hand on Pilate's arm. "Maybe someday you will bring her to Jerusalem. She will enjoy the hospitality of our people, just as I am sure you will." Antipas pointed to the middle section of a long table laden with food. "Here, this is where you and Tacitus will sit, with me and my wife. From here, you will receive the best view of the entertainment. You won't want to miss anything!"

Pontius was not sure where to begin with the array of cheeses, plums, apples, dried figs, olives, broccoli, artichokes, nuts, snails, oysters, fish, and bread loaves laid out before him. Off to the side were bowls of dipping sauces including honeyed wine, cabbage in vinegar, and garum. All of the other guests took their seats, seemingly all too familiar with the proceedings. Slaves began serving skewered meats including beef, lamb, dormice, and pigeon, as well as large jars of wine, filling everyone's cup. The tables were arranged in a giant U shape with everyone sitting on the outside. The servants were hustling in every direction, responding to the many requests of those gathered. The marbled walls and floor echoed every word spoken, creating a deafening clamor of language he could not understand. Antipas' bellowing voice carried easily over the noise. "If there is anything you desire that is not here, feel free to ask, and my servants will get it for you right away!"

Pilate leaned over to Antipas, raising his own voice over the increasing din. "No thank you! There is more here than I could possibly hope to eat, and it all looks magnificent!"

Antipas smiled broadly. "I am glad it pleases you!" Antipas stood up and clapped his hands, drawing everyone's attention. The deafening noise immediately ceased. Antipas spoke in Hebrew, and Pilate was not able to understand. Whatever was said, the festive atmosphere suddenly subsided. Everyone started speaking in whispers rather than competing volume. Pilate greatly appreciated the change, which allowed him to relax somewhat, with a better chance of enjoying the meal before him.

Antipas was in his element, acting bolder and more in control than he was earlier. He slowly sat down giving a stern scan toward all of his guests. Turning towards Pilate, he continued, "Sometimes the chatter can become a little overwhelming. These walls seem to echo even the faintest whisper." His own voice was still as loud as it had been. "My guests were not considerate of your presence. I assure you, you will not need to strain your voice again tonight." Antipas took a huge bite of lamb, followed by a wash of wine. He chewed for a while until he had swallowed enough to resume speaking. "Later, you may be straining your voice in praise when you see the parade of entertainment—in your honor, of course."

Pilate laughed, pleasantly surprised at Antipas' newfound lightheartedness—likely due to the wine. Reacting to his agreeable nature, Pilate responded, "If the entertainment is as good as the food, I'm sure I won't be disappointed."

As the night wore on, Pontius was surprised to see most of the entertainment involved scantily clothed beautiful women dancing in very seductive movements. Sometimes they would dance individually, and sometimes in large groups. The music seemed foreign and bizarre. Some theatrics included muscular and agile men accompanying the women in aggressive, athletic dances. Antipas was absorbing everything as if hypnotized by the performances. The female dancers flirted with Antipas throughout the night, and Antipas played to their enticement without inhibition. Pontius felt embarrassed for Phasaelis, who sat patiently without expression. He could not understand how a man would behave so in front of his wife, and in turn, in front of so many guests.

Pontius acquired ill feelings about the evening's activities and was truly looking to its end. Everything seemed in stark contrast to the strict behavior enforced by the Jewish religion and practices he had seen in his brief time. There was far more food left on the tables than had been eaten. Pontius had tried to eat as much as he could, which ended up being very little, since his stomach was still small from the days of travel. Pontius felt a strange need to finish as much as he could, and was starting to feel pained and uncomfortable. The leftover food was such a waste and contrary to the discipline he had known as a military officer.

Tacitus was not having trouble putting the food away. He erupted in frequent bouts of laughter and applause, only becoming quiet and attentive when female dancers came close.

Finally, the entertainment ended and Pilate did not hesitate to excuse himself, offering a forced "Thank you."

Upon leaving the palace, Pilate and Tacitus immediately met up with their escort, who had waited outside the entire evening. The quiet of the night air was a welcome relief. As they walked toward their chariots accompanied by four guards, Pilate joked, "Now I know where all the tax revenues have been going."

"Tax revenues! How could you think about taxes after an evening like that?" Tacitus' words were slurred and his walk had a slight imbalance with an inconsistent rhythm in his step.

A little disgusted, Pilate replied under his breath, "If only my thoughts weighed so lightly upon my soul."

They climbed into three chariots—Pilate and Tacitus in one, the four guards in the other two. Pilate took the reins. Tacitus was semi-oblivious to what was going on around him, and was slow to grab the reins. As Pilate whipped the horses, the noise of the chariot wheels on the stone streets broke the silence of the night. Proceeding back through the dark streets softly lit by moonlight, the poverty in some areas stood in extreme contrast to the lavish display just witnessed. Pilate's first full day in Jerusalem was hardly what he had expected. Antipas would be more of a problem than a solution.

The next morning, Pontius awoke disgruntled with the previous night running through his thoughts. After a modest morning meal of cheese and bread with honeyed wine, Pontius' mood improved with the familiarity of the Roman decor and the grace of the Roman staff. Pontius thought of Claudia back in Caesarea, and spent the next three days in Fortress Antonia, never venturing into the city. It was an involuntary act rather than by design. There were several administrative tasks to be taken care of and meetings with the Roman tribunal.

Eventually, Pontius realized it was his duty to familiarize himself with the workings of Jerusalem. He had come all this way, and it only made sense to gain perspective on a city that had been the interest of so many armies and conquerors. He found himself wanting to understand what drove these people and their culture.

Venturing through the streets, the dirt and poverty again caught his eye. There were people milling about in a seemingly chaotic manner, without purpose. The marketplace was particularly crowded, with all sorts dressed in dirty, ragged clothes. Occasionally, a privileged person with fine, colorful dress could be seen walking amongst the rest. The more Pontius walked through the city, the more hopeless the prospect seemed of understanding the masses he had been sent to rule. He was an observer, an outsider, completely ignored by those scurrying around. The difficulty of a new language only added to his frustration. He would have to learn it to become effective. However, it was not a challenge he relished. In a strange way, he felt it would be more appropriate for these conquered people to learn his language and succumb to Roman ideals and culture.

Walking back into the sanctity of Fortress Antonia, Pontius saw the reassuring images of the Roman Empire adorning the halls. Proceeding into the meeting chamber, he saw a statue of Julius Caesar and a few other figures he could not name. There were a few works of art strategically placed on the barren walls. Their presence offered a sense of dignity and power. Having been forced into a peculiar land, Pontius grew to appreciate the beauty and intricacy of each work and his native culture. He spent several hours exploring the countless rooms and halls, absorbing all the details.

Pontius came across a finely detailed tapestry of a face he knew well—Tiberius Caesar. The work was of such likeness that he almost expected the lips to move and hear the familiar voice of a man he greatly respected. *If only the people of this city realized how great a man he was, they would be in awe.*

Later that afternoon, Pilate called Tacitus into his office. "Tribune! I have given thought to impressing culture on this city. An idea came to me while studying the tapestry of Tiberius Caesar in the library. Do you know the one of which I speak?"

"Yes, sir. We received it from Rome nearly four months ago."

"I want standards of his image placed outside the walls of Antonia—and throughout the city." Pilate grew more excited as the words spilled from his lips. "Smaller ones, of course, but images of Tiberius all the same. These people must know their emperor and pay homage to him."

"An exceptional idea, sir! I'll never be one to argue the merit of his divine influence."

"Yes, we need to start small and gradually introduce more of our culture, assimilating them to our way of life. We must work to the core beliefs of the people to effect any real change. This will take time. With patience, we will change their hearts. We have conquered these people militarily. Now we must conquer their minds. They must see and know the presence of Rome in order to respect her authority and understand the benefits of her presence. With time, the burden of our commission will ease, as the people become more willing to pay taxes. They will see the zealots as criminals and murderers." Pilate got up and walked around the room, visualizing the potential of his scheme.

Tacitus smiled. "We have let them live by their own laws for far too long, Noble Prefect. They have no respect for our authority—or our culture."

Pilate sat down at his desk and wrote an order. "I want twenty standards made—no, make that thirty! I want them placed on the walls outside Fortress Antonia and at other locations throughout the city. Place them under cover of night so not to bring attention. I will be returning to Caesarea next week, and I want you to see to this."

5 ~ High Standards

The journey back to Caesarea was uneventful. Tacitus had convinced Pilate to take additional soldiers, a possible ingredient for a peaceful return. Pontius was glad to be back with Claudia, although it wasn't long before he started feeling detached from the subject of his rule. Pontius recounted to Claudia the details of his trip, including the attack by the zealots. He hadn't planned on telling her, not wanting to worry her, yet he found the story too compelling to keep to himself.

With a saddened look of concern, Claudia responded, "I thought the days of worrying about your life were over, Pontius. I thought when you went from the military to politics your life would be safe." Her voice was trembling, almost pleading for reassurance.

Pontius sensed the worry in his wife's eyes. "Prefect is technically a military position, and there are some risks. But the risks are nowhere near the risks of a command in battle. We made it through those years. We can make it through these. Besides, I have started a policy that will calm the rebellious hearts of these people, not unlike the conditions here in Caesarea. Here there are many signs of Roman culture. We noticed it when we first arrived: the statues, the architecture, the monuments... even how the people dress. We can bring that to the people of Jerusalem and beyond. The culture in Jerusalem is so archaic, so simple—ripe for influence. Their lives are begging for more, and we can give it to them. All they need is to see and understand our way of life, and they will surely convert from their archaic ways."

Pontius took a deep breath and his chest swelled with pride. "I have ordered signs of Roman authority placed around Jerusalem so the people will become accustomed to our presence. I saw a truly remarkable tapestry of Tiberius Caesar in the library of Fortress Antonia that inspired me to have his image placed around the city."

Claudia turned away and shrugged her shoulders. "Do you really think placing a few standards will give these people a change of heart? I doubt you could ever place them high enough for them to revere them." Claudia smiled coyly.

"Your humor comes as a dagger, Claudia. This is very serious. I know it's a simple idea. And *no*, the standards alone, high or low, will not make a difference with these people; but we need to start somewhere. Too much, too soon will provoke them. After a few months, we will introduce more; we will expand to grander projects. In a few years, Jerusalem will appear as Caesarea and the people will be just as they are here—accustomed to our presence, our way of life, and our authority. It will happen, Claudia, I promise you. These people can be governed and become productive subjects of Rome."

* * *

In Jerusalem, Tacitus hired skilled craftsmen from the land of Persia to design and weave the standards of Tiberius. Within two weeks they had completed the first six. They were near duplicates of the tapestry from the library, matching the intricate details of Caesar's face—particularly the eyes and hair color. Tacitus immediately had one of the standards delivered to Caesarea for Pilate's approval. He hung another in his office and placed the remaining four throughout the city.

Pontius smiled as he unrolled the standard. He hung it on the wall and stood back, taking in the brilliance of the colors and the remarkable reality of the image—almost as if it were a painting and not a tapestry. His chest swelled with pride, as if he had created it himself. It *was* his creation; it *was* his idea.

As the afternoon wore on, he could not wait to show Claudia. He rolled up the standard and almost ran to the palace, his escort struggling to match his heartened pace. As Pontius neared the palace he sensed an unusual air. *Why were so many people in the streets?* They were mostly

Jewish, although Roman soldiers were running about securing the crowd. One of the soldiers ran up to Pilate. "Sir, I do not know what's going on, but you'd better come with me."

Palace guards were at the front and side entrances of the walled palace, holding back people trying to force their way in. They were chanting and yelling many things in Hebrew that Pilate could not understand. A few in the crowd recognized him and started running in his direction. Seeing the shift in the crowd's attention, Pilate and his escort ran to meet several other soldiers who had come from the main garrison. Pilate was shocked by the sudden and unexpected threat. *Are these people of Caesarea or zealots from the countryside?*

"What's going on here?!" Pilate shouted, not really knowing whom he was addressing.

Several from the mob who had run toward them stopped short of certain death from Roman swords. Quickly, Pilate turned his attention toward the palace and hastened toward the main crowd and the entrance, pushing his way through the soldiers. "Claudia!!"

Several of the soldiers immediately drew their swords and started swinging them, doing their best to stay in front of Pilate. A defenseless man who had not moved fast enough was struck in the head, then kicked back into the arms of others straining against a compressing crowd. The soldiers used their shields to plow their way forward, reaching the front gate as Pilate finally pushed his way through.

Inside, Pontius found Claudia in tears, pacing up and down the main hallway. "Pontius! I am so glad that you're all right! What's going on? Why are these people trying to get in? What are they saying?"

"I don't know! Have they threatened or harmed you in any way? When I saw the crowd out front, the first thing I thought of was you. I would never forgive myself if anything ever happened to you."

Claudia wrapped her arms around Pontius and embraced him tightly. "I'm fine, Pontius. No one has come through the soldiers. Thank the gods they're here... and you're here." Pulling back, Claudia wiped the tears from her eyes. "It all happened so fast. A couple of minutes ago things were fine, perfectly normal. And now this! What's wrong with these people? Have they lost their sanity?"

Claudia began shaking. The shouting from outside seemed to be increasing, echoing down the halls. The mob continued to grow, along with the intensity of the protest. Seeing the fear in his wife's eyes, Pontius held her in an attempt to calm her and himself down. "We are safe, Claudia. No one is getting into this palace."

At that instant, Gaius ran into the room. Gaius was an administrative assistant who knew the Hebrew language and acted as interpreter. "My Lord Pilate! What's going on, sir? I was sent to assist you."

Pilate was a little startled by Gaius' sudden entrance. "I don't know, Gaius. You're the interpreter; *you* tell me! What are they saying out there?!"

Gaius listened and tilted his head with a studied look. "They're saying something about pagan images, Prefect. Something about pagan images in the Holy City."

"Pagan images! By the gods, what are they talking about?" Pilate looked down at the standard rolled under his arm. "Pagan images? Holy City?" He shifted the tapestry, grasping it with both hands. "Surely this is not the subject of their cries!"

"Of what subject?" Claudia asked, looking at the rolled tapestry in his hands.

"This! This is the standard of Tiberius Caesar I was telling you about. I just received it today, by courier." Pilate slowly unrolled it.

"Pontius! It's beautiful! It looks just like Caesar! If it were not a cloth, I would expect his words this very minute!"

Pontius looked into Claudia's eyes, remembering his own thoughts in the library at Fortress Antonia. "The craftsmen have done a remarkable job with this standard."

Pontius laid the tapestry across a table and smoothed it with his hands. "I received a note from Tacitus, along with this standard. He said he had placed several around the city."

Claudia looked at Pontius and then the standard. "No, Pontius. I don't think this has anything to do with the mob outside. How could it? It's just a rug." Claudia paused suddenly. "I didn't mean the way it sounded. It's a beautiful standard and a wonderful idea. It's just that I can't see how this could be the subject of any complaint, much less a riot."

Pontius shook his head. "I know, it doesn't make sense, but you heard what Gaius said. Chanting about pagan images in the Holy City. What else could it be?"

"It could be any number of things, Pontius. Maybe Gaius heard wrong or misunderstood what they were saying with all of the chaos."

Gaius interrupted, "No, my lord. They keep saying it over and over again. They are also saying, 'Tear down the pagan images!'"

Pontius' face twisted in an expression of disgust. "You can't be serious! We've only placed a few! Claudia is right; this can't be the subject of their complaint. I'll find out tomorrow. By then all of this will blow over, and I'll find the true nature of their protests. Tomorrow morning, Gaius, I want you to confront the Jewish council and find out what's going on. Tonight, I want you to stay here at the palace in case I need you."

Gaius bowed respectfully. "Yes, sir! I am glad to be of assistance, My Lord Pilate."

The chanting continued well into the evening. The soldiers remained on guard. Eventually, the chanting and yells of protest diminished. Pontius and Claudia thought it would never end, but finally felt comfortable enough to get some sleep.

* * *

It was later than usual when Pontius awoke. Claudia was still asleep, so Pontius carefully climbed out of bed. He was anxious to find out what the rioting had been about the night before. His spirits were lifted: the chanting and yelling was gone. The quiet of the morning was a welcome reprieve. Pontius went to where Gaius had been sleeping, but Gaius was already gone. He walked to the front entrance and cautiously opened the door, gradually revealing a sea of people sitting motionless in the street surrounded by several Roman guards. Pilate walked up to the front gates and approached a Roman centurion. "What's wrong with them? Are they hurt? Did we injure or kill that many from the rioting last night?"

The centurion snapped to attention. "No, sir. Only one was killed, My Lord Pilate. These people seem to be in some state of shock or something. They will not speak or even move."

Pilate looked around. More people had infiltrated the quiet mass, filling almost every space. The gathering nearly surrounded the entire palace. "Centurion, I'm staying here today. I want more guards stationed around the palace. Go find Gaius and tell him to return with a representative from the Jewish council. Also, send Ascenius and my staff over. I will be working from here today until I find out the source of this madness!"

No sooner had he said this than he looked up to see Gaius escorting a man in formal Jewish attire, weaving his way through the seated crowd. Pilate felt a small sense of relief, but stood where he was, not wanting to venture out into the human sea.

As they got closer, Gaius spoke out, "My Lord Pilate, this is Josiah, head of the Jewish council."

Pilate bowed in respectful greeting while Josiah stood firm, showing little reaction to Pilate's act of courtesy. Feeling a hint of insult, Pilate shook his head slightly and turned to lead everyone back into the palace. "It is unfortunate we meet under questionable circumstances." Pilate turned to notice his guest had stopped short of the palace gates.

With little expression, Josiah addressed Pilate in slightly broken Latin: "Pontius Pilate, Prefect of Rome, I am here under extreme protest."

Pilate backtracked to the palace gates. "Protest, yes, I can see that. Perhaps we can discuss the context of your protest inside."

Josiah showed no expression. "I cannot enter into your palace," he said, seemingly oblivious to the deep insults he was slinging on a fellow man. "Could we please have our discussion here?"

Pilate remembered what he had been told about the Jews, and how they considered the Roman structures to be a defilement of their sacred lands. Sometimes, they would not even set foot in Roman buildings. He had heard it, but never experienced it. Feeling a little frustrated and losing patience, Pilate motioned his hands to the ground Josiah was standing on. "How is that ground better than this ground?"

Josiah did not show a hint of response to Pilate's inquiry. Quickly recognizing the hopeless nature of his question, and making every effort to regain his composure, Pilate continued, "Fine, we can discuss things out here. I had forgotten about your customs. I'm still learning."

Josiah seemed to ignore Pilate's attempt at reconciliation, and got straight to the point. "In our holy city of Jerusalem, we understand that by your orders tapestries bearing images of your emperor are being placed around the city. Pagan images of any type are a great insult to the one true God, desecrating all of the land from which they can be seen. This is a sacrilege of the highest level, and they must be removed."

Pilate could not believe what he was hearing. *It was the standards causing this uproar.* "Removed! We have only placed a few! Quite to the contrary, we plan to place more!" Without saying a word, Pilate rushed back into the palace and came back with the tapestry. Walking up to Josiah, Pilate unfurled it. "This is a work of art, not a pagan image." Turning his attention to those protestors seated near the gate, Pilate held the standard high for all to see. "This is your emperor, Tiberius Caesar, and this will be made known to all. He is a great man who has done many wonderful things for you and this country. He is compassionate and deserves no less than to be known by his servants!"

There was little reaction, even though he hoped that some might understand Latin. Most turned their heads in defiance, rather than gaze upon the image. Josiah pointed at the image and cried out to the people in Hebrew, "This is a desecration, an abomination to our Lord and our people! We cannot tolerate their display in Jerusalem!"

Pilate recognized words of defiance by the tone of his voice and the reaction of the crowd. "The standards will stay! You and your god will just have to become accustomed to them." Pilate motioned to Josiah that the discussion had ended, and it was time for him to leave.

Josiah's expressionless face grew pained, and the anger in his eyes could no longer be hidden. However, his voice softened as he continued to address the crowd. "Remain calm! Under no circumstance should you incite violence resulting in the death of another of our brethren." Josiah paused slightly. "Pontius Pilate, the Roman prefect, has not agreed to remove the pagan images from our Holy City!"

A slight uproar arose with a few of the protesters getting up from their seated positions.

Josiah raised his hands. "No! No! Remain seated. We will have the pagan images removed! God's justice will be served! We must maintain trust in God, and ask him for patience. If it eventually means our death, then so be it. For now, we must test our will and the will of God against the will of the Roman prefect. I vow that we will stay here in protest until the images are removed. Do not move from your places or be swayed by the threat of death!"

Josiah defiantly sat back down. Pilate didn't want to arrest Josiah. Force would likely cause more unrest. Turning toward Gaius, Pilate asked, "What was he saying?"

Hesitating, as if uncertain of his translation and with an expression of disbelief, Gaius replied, "He was telling the protestors to remain calm and stay here in protest. He said something about a test of wills between you and their god, and not to move until you have agreed to tear down the standards."

"Get a pole and place the standard higher for all to see, and place a guard at its base. We will see who wins this test of wills! These people can sit out here and swelter in the heat, while I rule from the comfort of my palace." Pilate dismissed Gaius and went inside to see if Claudia had awoken.

With each passing day, more Jews joined in the protest, with some women joining their husbands and brothers. Pontius was beginning to feel imprisoned in his own palace, but he was not willing to give in to their demands. The standards were only a first step in his grand scheme of influencing the social values of these people. He was not about to let a passive protest wither the seed that had just broken ground.

The chanting from the first day gradually gave way to a persistent deathly silence. On the third day, Pilate employed soldiers to prevent anyone from bringing the protestors food or water. Many of the protestors were becoming weak. It became difficult to tell whether those lying on the ground were conscious, sick, or even dead.

In the middle of the night Claudia awoke with a scream. Pontius extended the wick of a softly burning lamp to see Claudia shaking, drenched in beads of sweat. Crying, she brought her hands up to her face. "I saw them charging in, overpowering the guards and killing everyone!"

Pontius held her close. He could not bear to see his wife going through such torture. "The guards are well trained and will never let anyone enter this palace. I will check and make sure they remain vigilant. Tomorrow I will double their number."

"But the mob is out there, Pontius, and could slip through in the dark! If I go back to sleep, will your guards be in my dreams to settle my fears then! My dreams seem so real, Pontius, and they will come true!"

Pontius held Claudia even tighter and felt her cries tearing at his soul.

After five days, the protest seemed to gain new life. Renewed chants pierced the marble walls as if to fulfill some aspect of Claudia's dreams. Pilate ordered a full cohort of soldiers from the main garrison to surround the mass of protestors. He called upon Gaius. "I will address these people directly, and I want you to be my voice. Hopefully, I will make them understand or..." Pilate hesitated in front of Claudia.

Trembling, Claudia grasped her husband's hand. "Pontius, please don't have them killed. Please. There are women out there... and children. They are defenseless, Pontius." Claudia began crying, unable to hold back the emotion and fear that had built up over several days. "My dreams were not real. I overreacted. They mean us no harm. They can't harm us. I know I've had a difficult time over the past few days, and at times, I've even feared for our lives, but we can't do this, Pontius. Take down the standards, Pontius. It was a wonderful idea and you brought it life. I love you for it. You're a wonderful man, and you are doing everything you can, but please don't do this."

Claudia wiped the tears from her face and composed herself. "It's not our fault we don't understand the depth of their twisted faith. How can we? We've only been here a couple of months. We misunderstood a bizarre aspect of their religious beliefs. No harm was done. Let it go. It's not worth the lives of these defenseless people."

Pontius looked into Claudia's eyes. If anyone could convince him, it was she. Torn, Pontius replied, "Claudia, I can't. I can't let these people dictate the policy of Rome. Giving in to these protestors, tearing down signs of Roman authority—these actions are not good for Rome." Pontius moved away from Claudia and then led Gaius and a group of soldiers outside the palace. He couldn't bear to hear Claudia's cries and quickened his pace to his unwanted duty.

Pilate and Gaius climbed onto a wagon that had been wheeled into place. Pilate directed a soldier to stand next to Josiah, who was now lying limp on the ground. Pilate began to speak, "Subjects of Rome! Subjects of the Divine Emperor Tiberius Caesar!"

The Hebrew translation seemed to work. Those that could, slowly lifted their eyes toward Pilate. The reaction, little as it was, was startling. "I plead with you to get up and go to your homes! Go to your families! Go to your loved ones!" From a near lifeless position, Josiah slowly pushed his body into a sitting position.

"Please!—Go!—Now!" But there was no longer any reaction, no movement, not even a voice of opposition. All he heard was the faint sound of Claudia crying inside the palace. A sinking feeling pooled deep inside. He felt trapped and wished he could be anywhere but here and now. "If you do not leave, you will be executed! All you have to do is get up and leave—and your lives will be spared!" Still there was no movement.

Pilate stepped down from the wagon and walked over to Josiah. Lowering his voice, he knelt down and pleaded, "Josiah, please. Convince them to get up and leave this place. They will listen to you."

In a pained whisper, his lips barely moving, Josiah replied, "Take... down... the... images."

Each word from Josiah fueled a fire that burned inside Pilate. Josiah had barely said the last word before Pilate jumped up, screaming, "Ready your swords!" The sound of steel filled the air as the soldiers drew their blades, raising them high, ready to strike on Pilate's command. The glint of the sun on so many blades caused many to shield their eyes. Pilate could hear some protestors starting to cry—men and women alike—but he could not tell from whence the cries came, for still no one was moving. Josiah bowed his head and moved his hair over to the side, exposing his neck for a clean strike. Soon, several others did the same, showing an absurd willingness to die. Pilate realized that the next word from his mouth would mean the sudden death and slaughter of many people. The glistening of the swords would darken, stained with blood. He was almost afraid to move for fear that any motion might be misinterpreted by a soldier as an order to swing his sword through flesh and bone. Suddenly fear filled his body, realizing he did not want this, nor did he want Claudia to witness such slaughter. Making his words as clear and distinct as possible, Pilate cried out, "Stand down! Withdraw your swords! Stand down!"

Much more slowly than they had drawn them, the soldiers lowered their swords. The glare from the blades gradually diminished with several soldiers re-sheathing. Not a single life was taken. Pilate walked over to Josiah and mumbled, "I will remove the standards. I will tear them down from the streets of Jerusalem."

A near-undetectable smile came to Josiah's face as he leaned over to a couple of men and whispered. The men helped Josiah to his feet and yelled something to the crowd. The people slowly began rising and walking away, ignoring the dumbfounded soldiers they passed. Pontius could hear a distinct, faster-paced rhythm of footsteps behind him—a sound that broke through the slow shuffling of protestors. Turning, Pontius saw Claudia running toward him, wiping the tears from her eyes. Her embrace was all that kept him from sinking into despair. Her affection seemed to lift everything off his shoulders as they turned and walked back to the palace.

6 ~ Joseph of Arimathea

The next day, Pilate sent word to Jerusalem to have all of the standards removed. However, this was not an immediate cure for the heated emotions that infected the Holy City.

Claudia had gotten too close to the consequences of his actions as governor, placing her—and his command—in jeopardy. She had influenced his decision, and he was certain it hadn't been in the best interest of Rome. His plan for assimilating Roman culture into Judean society was dead before it started, never getting the chance it deserved. Without his wife present, he might have handled the protest differently. The people would now be more keenly aware of further attempts, subtle or otherwise, to introduce Roman culture.

Caesarea was too removed from the daily political affairs of the main governing bodies in Jerusalem. He had to go back to Jerusalem. Pontius didn't like the prospect of being without Claudia, but she needed to remain at a safe distance. Once things had settled he would send for her.

* * *

At Fortress Antonia, Pilate called Tacitus into his office. "Tacitus! It's good to see you again! How have you been?"

"Fine, sir. You would not believe all that has happened since you left, and the reaction of these people to the standards!"

Pilate smiled, sitting back in his chair. "Oh, yes, I would. The Jews in Caesarea put up a protest like I'd never seen."

Tacitus nodded. "Yes, sir. I heard." His tone conveyed disapproval for the way Pilate had handled the protestors. "The standards were a great idea, sir, and this city should be covered in them."

Tacitus' expression mirrored his own emotions. Trying to keep the discussion light, Pilate asked, "How many standards were made?"

"Fourteen or fifteen, my lord. One is missing. It was torn down the first night."

"Torn down!" Pilate said in surprise. "I guess we would have needed guards to protect them. I'm not so sure it was ever a good idea," Pilate muttered, trying to convince himself. "What did Antipas have to say about all of this?"

"Antipas? He has said nothing," Tacitus mumbled with disgust. "Words of protest came from the Jewish council... as well as every other Jew in this city! It's good Antipas didn't voice opposition, but he never offered a sign of support. He basically stayed out of it, staying true to his character."

"The true control over these people comes from the Jewish council and not from Antipas!" Pilate stood up and slapped the table. "By the gods! Why do we even have Antipas? What purpose does he serve, other than himself?!" Pilate paced the room, trying to understand what he was dealing with. "Perhaps we should disband the Jewish council."

"I would be all for that, sir, but if you thought we had problems with the standards, disbanding the council would pale in comparison. The Jewish council is more a religious body than a political one. It has been part of their government for many centuries. I doubt very seriously there is any hope of disbanding the council."

"I know. I was just thinking out loud, grasping for hope where none exists. What do you think we should do? Do you have any suggestions?"

Tacitus seemed pleasantly surprised. It wasn't often a politician asked a military man for advice. "Well, as a matter of fact, I do, my lord. I've been thinking of this for some time, and it could prove to be very beneficial. It won't solve all our problems, but like your standards idea, it could be a critical first step toward a larger goal."

Pilate liked what he was hearing. "You have my interest, continue."

"I don't know if you know, sir; we have spies in the field, scattered throughout the city—some more reliable than others. I think we need a spy on the Jewish council. We need to know what they're thinking, what they are planning, maybe even sway some borderline decisions to go in our favor. If the Jewish council is the true body of power, as you suggested yourself, then we need to know their inner workings."

"That's an interesting idea, Tacitus, but spies on the Jewish council? I know we have openly appointed high priests, but we do it from within their ranks, men truly devoted to Mosaic Law. Any attempts we have made otherwise have resulted in failure. The high priests who lasted any length of time had to be more dedicated to their religious doctrine than our interests. They receive so much critical attention."

"No, sir. We wouldn't need to appoint a position on the council. We would direct Antipas to make the appointment. It could be subtle enough that it would be forgotten with time. After all, we're not trying to control the Jewish council. We just need insight into their affairs. One thing I have learned in my military career is that knowledge of the enemy is valuable. Knowing what they are thinking, what they are planning, and what resources they have can allow us to strike blows where it hurts." Tacitus paused, his voice confident with Pilate's attention. "Much of the information we gain can be useless. However, every now and then you get a gem—the secret that allows us to gain a decisive advantage."

Pontius gave careful thought to Tacitus' words. "I agree. Knowledge is valuable. A spy for such a position must be cultivated, trained, and groomed—and most of all, accepted by the council."

Tacitus waved his hands, motioning to the general area outside the building. "You forget, My Lord Pilate, we have many such spies throughout the city—most of them Jewish. Some of them 'cultivated,' as you say, since they were children. We have been here for a long time, sir, and most of our spies have been here long before you or I ever heard of Judea. They're all over Judea, Galilee, and Ituraea—not just in Jerusalem. A few of them even infiltrated the zealots." Tacitus dropped his gaze to the floor. "The zealots—they've been the hardest. I must admit a couple of our spies became traitors, having other spies they knew killed. The zealots are a tough group and we have not had as much success there." Tacitus paused, exhaling. "Anyway, there is a man I know who would be perfect for this position. He is not from here, but from Arimathea, which makes it all the better, minimizing the connection with us. His name is

Joseph. He's a good man. He has influence because he has wealth—mostly through our help, of course. He has good standing with the community."

"Joseph. That's a Jewish name. Is he a Jew?"

"Oh, yes, he's Jewish; very knowledgeable of their laws and religion, but Roman at heart, my lord—Roman to the bone."

Hearing a revived tone of confidence from Tacitus, Pilate's eyes lit up. "Well, by all means, send for this man. I want to meet him. It's time we had Roman bones on the Jewish council."

* * *

At Tacitus' request, Joseph left Arimathea to visit Jerusalem. He stayed at an inn several miles from Fortress Antonia. Joseph had always been careful about concealing his affiliation with Rome; he had a lot at stake, considering his family and his wealth. In the past, he had brokered purchases of grain, wine, blankets, clothing, carts, axes, and even weapons for the garrison in Arimathea, often concealing the identity of his client in order to maintain his social standing. Joseph often provided valuable information regarding Jewish or foreign merchants, granting Rome advantage in numerous transactions, further building his status. His strict adherence to secrecy, even from his family, was a significant factor in his longevity as a Roman collaborator.

Joseph had been raised as a Jew. His mother was Jewish, and as a young boy he'd learned that his father was Greek. His mother strictly forbade him to speak of his Greek ancestry, warning him that the other children would be very cruel if they knew. She also warned that the cruelty would extend to her, since the adults of the community had their own prejudice towards outsiders. Joseph loved his mother, so he abided her wishes. Perhaps it was his lifelong practice of keeping secrets that made him a master at controlling what he wanted others to know.

The forbidden nature of his hidden half also created an intense curiosity about Greek culture, which he studied at any opportunity. He was knowledgeable in the Mosaic Law and teachings, learned through the strict regime of education required for all Jewish males. But his heart was in Greek philosophy, which broadened and enhanced his understanding of the Mosaic Law. Many times Joseph felt it was this double life in sometimes clashing philosophies that had shaped his ability to carry on the life he was now leading. He wasn't proud of his special connections with Rome, nor was he ashamed. It was just there—a life dealt him by a father he never knew.

Joseph sent word he would meet with Pilate and Tacitus in Fortress Antonia through a ruse he had carried out in the past. Jewish food merchants frequented the fortress, offering their goods to supplement the high demands of the Roman troops. Joseph saw their regular visits as a simple way of gaining access to Fortress Antonia without being detected, hidden within one of these carts.

* * *

The plan worked well. Joseph apprehensively followed Tacitus into the fortress and into Pilate's office.

Having never met with the Roman prefect, Joseph was nervous, taking a deep breath as he entered through the doorway. He bowed several times while approaching, bringing a smile to Pilate's face.

"The last time I offered a greeting to one of your people," Pilate said, "I didn't get a response. It's encouraging that someone in this land can show the common courtesy of a respectful welcome. I'm Pontius Pilate, Roman governor of Judea."

"Most Honorable Prefect, I am Joseph of Arimathea, merchant and loyal subject of Rome." Joseph felt more at ease after Pilate's friendly greeting.

"Tacitus told me you spoke Latin well, and he wasn't exaggerating. Forgive me. I have not learned your language as well. Someday I hope to do so."

"It is quite all right, Your Nobility. Hebrew is very difficult to learn, but I have no doubt you will master it."

"Actually, you're right, it's not the language I am worried about," Pilate replied confidently. "It is the nature of your religion and its laws that I'm not sure I will understand—or if I should even try."

Joseph laughed. "I'm not sure I understand it, and I've studied it since I was a boy. I think it wise that you not attempt to learn the faith of the

Hebrews—you would have no time for other duties placed upon your shoulders."

"Duties—yes, I have plenty of those in my position. In some ways, that's where I am hoping you will be of assistance. If we can learn what goes on in the minds and policies of your Jewish leadership, then maybe I can better understand what I must do to fulfill my role as governor. That's where we are counting on you, Joseph." Pilate placed his hand on Joseph's shoulder.

Pilate's casual gesture made Joseph uneasy. "Me! And a legion of angels! What you ask is no simple matter."

"A legion of what?"

"Angels. Have you never heard of angels?" Joseph asked, a little surprised. Pilate was clearly unaware of this religious intricacy.

"What are they? A group of religious teachers?" Pilate prodded.

Joseph laughed gently. "No. They are..." He paused, grasping for a way to explain the concept. "They are messengers of God."

"So they are of your priesthood?"

Joseph laughed again, and shook his head. "No. They are not men as you know them. They are not of this world, but have been with God since the beginning."

"So they are immortal?"

Fascinated by Pilate's interest in the Hebrew religion, Joseph adopted an instructive tone. "Yes, if you want to call them that."

"How do they deliver messages from your god?"

"They speak to our prophets. Daniel spoke of the angel Michael as a prince who has charge over us."

Pilate interrupted. "Your angels have names?"

"Yes, there are several named in the Scriptures: Gabriel, Ariel, Raphael, Azazel." Joseph paused. "Some have tried to assert their own will upon man. Satan tested Job and even tried to make himself as God. For this he was thrown down from heaven."

Pilate smirked and shook his head. "This Hebrew religion has all sorts of twists and turns. I thought you only had one god. Now I find you have a legion! It is not unlike our own gods who control the land, the sea—everything you see about you."

Joseph hesitated. He didn't want to offend Pilate. "Jews don't consider their angels to be gods. They are of some lesser form of the one God."

Pilate raised an eyebrow. Counting off on his fingers, he retorted, "The angels are immortal, they have their own will, they have some type of professed control over the lives of men, and they do not commonly live among us. They are gods!"

"But to the Jews, the One is higher and the creator of all things. Angels are subservient to God." Joseph paused. "Although they do, sometimes, act according to their own will."

"This is no different from our god Jupiter," Pilate shot back. "He is the supreme god with dominion and power over the rest."

Pilate had made an interesting point, Joseph realized. "Or Zeus from Greek mythology. Zeus is supreme over all immortals. That is an interesting line of reasoning, Noble Prefect, but in the faith of the Hebrews, they still do not consider angels to be gods."

Obviously annoyed, Pilate frowned. "A stone is a stone even if you wish to refer to it as a rock. These words and play of words mean nothing. The Jews believe in many immortals, and their religion is no different from many others—or the Greek mythology, as you refer to it. How is it you know of Greek theology? I would think it something not encouraged amongst your people."

"You're right; it is not. It is an interest I developed as a boy, and has been a subject of study ever since. I've always been a curious person. It's in my blood, so to speak." Joseph did not expect Pilate or Tacitus to recognize his literal meaning.

Looking somewhat disgusted, Pilate spoke of the Jewish faith as if ignoring Joseph's presence. "There is nothing special about their precious customs and scrolls, except for their insane stubbornness to blind themselves to anything that exists outside the words of their Scripture and the walls of their synagogues. We have conquered these Jews. Where was their god... gods... or should I say 'army of angels'? They refuse our rule because we are not one of their gods. We have given them roads, buildings, and irrigation for their fields. Still they refuse to accept our government. They are only making it worse for themselves by refusing to accept any form of authority other than their god."

Joseph interrupted. "Actually, at one time God lived amongst us—or so it is said in the writings. One of the ancient prophets, Moses, spoke to him in divine company, and received the commandments of obedience."

Pilate leaned forward, his curiosity awakened. "So where is he now? He lived amongst his people? Did he take wives?"

"No!" Joseph exclaimed with surprise. "He is not Zeus—or Jupiter! Zeus may have fathered Hercules through a mortal woman, but the Hebrew God did not take on such a physical existence. The mere sight of his face could blind one or strike one dead. His presence was as a spirit on a mountaintop when he spoke to Moses. The visitation of this spirit was sanctified by a sculptured ark, crafted by our Hebrew ancestors."

"So where is this ark now? Why did they not appeal for his presence to simply blind us while they were being slaughtered?" Pilate asked sarcastically.

"I do not know where the ark is," Joseph said, shaking his head. "It has somehow been lost over the centuries."

"Then their god is lost?" Pilate laughed. "How could a people lose something so precious? I thought they communicated with their god frequently, receiving divine refusal to accept our rule. Perhaps their god should have fathered a more tangible presence while he dwelt amongst them—their own 'Hercules,' you could say, to lead them into battle."

Astonished that Pilate would touch upon something so important in Jewish history, Joseph smiled. "Actually, there was such a man—King David. According to Jewish teachings, he was the son of God, and he led the Jews to throw off the bonds of the Philistine empire."

"So your god fathered a mortal human. I'm assuming he was mortal—or did this make him an angel?" Pilate inquired, grinning.

Joseph laughed, seeing the confusion in the details. These were concepts he had grown up with and accepted without question. It was easy to see how these things could appear disjointed and confusing to someone who had never heard of them before. "No, he wasn't an angel, and yes, he was mortal. He wasn't the son of God in the same sense that Hercules was of Zeus. The Scriptures say that David received special direction and guidance from God as his begotten son."

Pilate interrupted. "Ah yes! Such was the gospel of the divine birth of Augustus Caesar."

"Gospel?"

"It is a term we use in Rome to honor the birth of an heir to the throne. It means wonderful news, worthy of praise by all who serve Rome—and all who will ultimately serve her."

"The gospel of Augustus Caesar? You refer to his divine birth?"

"His mother, Litivia, was mortal, but his father was the sun god, Apollo. Litivia was impregnated one night while she slept in his temple."

Joseph paused, seeing the true paradox of their discussion. "Divine nature makes known its presence in both of our worlds—one who commands today's world, and one destined to command the world according to the Scriptures. The Hebrew nation awaits a messiah, a descendant of King David, to deliver its people out of the bonds of the Roman Empire."

"Messiah?" Pilate repeated. "I have heard the word. My predecessors executed many Jews claiming to be messiahs. Where is this family of David? Is Antipas of this house?"

"No, Antipas is not even Jewish. He is Arabic, but he practices the Jewish faith."

"Not very well... I think he is in need of more practice. If you had seen him at his banquet, you would heed my words." Pilate paused rubbing his forehead. "Actually, Antipas is indirectly related to why I've... we've"—gesturing toward Tacitus—"called you here. A few days ago Tacitus brought up a novel idea that I think is worth pursuing. I'll get straight to the point. We need eyes and ears on the Jewish council here in Jerusalem, and Tacitus thinks you're the man."

Joseph listened with concern. Was he being asked to become a spy?

"Antipas is out of touch with the people in the province of Galilee and in this land," Pilate continued. "He has lost his effectiveness as regent. However, it is still my responsibility to govern this land and its people, with or without Antipas' help. We need to understand what's going on in the hearts and minds of the Jewish people. We need to know the plans and ideas of the body that truly has their loyalty—and that body seems to be the Jewish council. Antipas can make appointments to the council, and we will request that he appoint you."

"The Jewish council!" Joseph nervously stroked his beard. "I don't know. I've never really been involved with politics. Most of my dealings have been with merchants and their supplies. The stars in heaven may not favor such a fate." Unable to hide his discomfort, Joseph averted his eyes from Pilate.

"I know you are a successful trader," said Pilate, "and we are prepared to pay you handsomely for this position. Your interactions with Rome have profited you well in the past, making you a wealthy man. With wealth comes power, and responsibility. Your wealth has also made you influential, and we believe your appointment to the council will be readily accepted. We are not asking that you control the council or redirect its policies. To the contrary, we are simply asking that you blend in with the ideals of the council members and gain their acceptance and trust, so we can know what's going on. We are not looking for an adversarial role, but a cooperative one."

Joseph nervously rubbed his hands. "Arimathea has been my home for quite some time. Jerusalem will be a difficult transition for my family."

"Tell your family you met with Antipas, and he personally requested your position on the council. You've been to Jerusalem many times, so it should come as no surprise. Tell them Antipas has developed trust in you, and truly needs your position on the council to further his political goals. Tell them he needs someone with your influence. You would be describing our goals rather than Antipas', but they are goals just the same."

Joseph realized he had little choice. He owed his livelihood to Rome, and he knew it could be easily stripped away. Besides, he liked Pilate. He'd enjoyed the brief discussion they had, and he liked the way his mind worked. Pilate's appeal seemed genuine. Joseph's real concern was not collaborating with Rome, but the combination of political and religious forces that came with such a position. He had always tried to minimize those forces, particularly the religious, in his daily work. Now he would be thrust into the middle of both, in a setting that would challenge his confidence.

"You make a convincing argument, Your Nobility. I am flattered by your faith in me. I am good at 'blending in,' as you say, and I find this the most comforting aspect of your offer. I would be truly reluctant to take an adversarial role. But, given that your offer is made in the interest of cooperation, I will do my best in service to Rome." Joseph put out his hand in the common Jewish custom for sealing a verbal agreement. With a broadening smile, Pilate reached over to grasp his hand.

The next day, Pilate and Tacitus approached Antipas about the appointment, and within the week, Joseph had a position on the Jewish council.

7 ~ Holy Water

Joseph's appointment to the council proved to be anticlimactic, as most things that follow high expectations turn out to be. None of the information they gained was earth-shattering or anything they didn't already know. There was growing mistrust for Antipas. There were general attitudes that the standards affair had been a humiliation in command and a sign of weakness that would grow with time. Pilate began seeing his handling of the standards affair as a dismal failure. But Pilate saw his new path of intelligence as more important than his temporary misjudgment in leadership. It would take time for Joseph to gain the trust of the council, if it happened at all. Only time would tell. Pontius had stretched his hands into the workings of the soul of this country, no longer a spectator in a chain of events he could not control.

A fierce battle raged in Pilate's mind: his role as governor versus his relationship with Claudia—a relationship he cherished more than life itself. He missed Claudia, but he was also becoming engrossed in a job that summoned every ounce of his being. At times, the demands caused him to forget that his wife was at least two days' travel away. Pontius detested these temporary lapses, removing him from the real bonds that truly gave him purpose in life. Ultimately, he knew Claudia had to come to Jerusalem and live there with him. *When?* That was the question. He wished it could be now, but Claudia's cries haunted his mind, and her presence had deluded his reasoning in handling a difficult decision.

Isolated in Fortress Antonia, his hopes of bringing Claudia to Jerusalem seemed within arm's reach. However, as soon as Pontius ventured into the city, his hopes would drift away. Claudia would detest Jerusalem just as he did—probably even more.

One day, on their way to Herod's palace, Pilate turned to Tacitus. "One thing I detest about this city is the dust. It's in the air, in the streets, on the buildings, in the clothes these people wear, in their hair, their beards. As a pitiful creation of the gods, it even seems to be in their skin. Is bathing forbidden in their religion?"

Tacitus laughed. "No, I don't think so, but I could be wrong. After all, I didn't think displaying the tapestry of Caesar would create such commotion."

"Please don't remind me of that," Pilate said, half-joking, echoing Tacitus' good spirits. "After visiting the streets and spending even a short period amongst these people, I feel a driving need to immerse in a Roman bath just to wash off the filth and… smell of this city."

Tacitus chuckled. "This is a desert, My Lord Pilate. Things here are naturally dry and dusty, including the people I suppose. I doubt these people ever bathe, except for the occasional trip down to the Kidron River."

"Do they not have public bathhouses?" Pilate asked, inquiring about something he had never really considered a luxury, but rather a basic need readily available in Fortress Antonia.

"I think not, my lord. Most of the water they bring up from the river is for drinking, preparing meals, or for irrigation of their fields outside the city. I have never seen a bathhouse outside of Fortress Antonia or Herod's palace."

"That's a touch of Rome that should grace this city," Pilate replied, rekindling his idea of introducing Roman culture to Jerusalem. "These people don't know what they are missing. I can't imagine anyone turning down a pool's soothing embrace. Surely filth is not worshipped, placing cleanliness at the level of a Roman tapestry."

Tacitus chuckled, then scoffed, "I doubt they would make occasional trips to the river if bathing were against their Jewish laws." Tacitus paused and changed his tone. "Where would we get the water to supply a network of public bathhouses?"

"I don't know!" Pilate exclaimed, reacting to Tacitus' defeatist attitude. "We have built numerous irrigation channels and aqueducts throughout the world and in this country! Surely we can build another."

"Yes, sir, I suppose we could. We've recently built small aqueducts to supply the needs of Fortress Antonia. I will have our engineers investigate a design, if it be your wish, my lord."

"Your foresight of my command is prophetic, Tribune. It is a task that deserves prompt and deliberate attention." Pilate felt a sense of urgency, wanting to shorten the time before introducing his wife to Jerusalem. "This could be our second chance at a first step."

A few days later, Tacitus reported to Pilate about natural springs south of the city between Bethlehem and Hebron. They were known as Solomon's Pool and could serve as a source for the aqueduct. "The springs are about twenty-three miles away, my lord, and my engineer reports they will serve as a perfect source of pure, clean water. Solomon's Pool could also serve as a source of drinking water for our soldiers. The water for Antonia has always been in short supply and a constant problem. Such an aqueduct would be a wondrous triumph for Rome, my lord."

"Wonderful news, Tribune! Excellent! Solomon's Pool?" Pilate's excitement grew, encompassing the full vision of the project. "This will also serve as a focus, a project to bring progress to Judea. A government without focus drifts aimlessly, stagnating. Quite frankly, I've had trouble focusing on anything since I've been here."

"Yes, sir. I am planning a team of engineers to visit the region. We'll do a quick, preliminary survey of the land to get an idea of how much work will be involved. You are more than welcome to come along."

"Yes, yes, by all means, Tacitus. I look forward to any excuse to get out of this city and the confines of this fortress." Taking on a more serious tone, Pilate asked, "Did the engineers have an estimate of the cost?"

"Well, not exactly, sir. I heard casual mention of fifty to one hundred thousand talents."

"Fifty to one hundred thousand talents!" Pilate retorted in disbelief.

"Yes, sir. They said they would have a better idea of the cost once they survey. We have slave labor in mass, but we will need to feed them. We will need to buy tools and materials, mainly mortar. Apparently there is plenty of rock along the way for building. We will need tools to excavate the rock and equipment to move the rock." Tacitus paused. "I would make a point, My Lord Pilate. I do not mean to be the bearer of bad news, but I feel it is my duty to bring it to light." Tacitus hesitated as Pilate's enthusiasm began to wane. "As you know, sir, there is very little money available. We have had trouble paying for necessary supplies here at Antonia and wages for the soldiers."

"Of course I am aware of the revenue problem, Tacitus! It is only a task of the highest priority!" Trying to think fast, digging for an answer, Pilate went on. "I have no intention of sacrificing the wages of the men. That will never be a consideration. If we must, we will take food from this city—by the gods, food from Herod's palace to feed the workers. We will confiscate tools and supplies if need be." Even as he spoke Pilate knew the hopelessness of his words, not expecting Tacitus to accept his ranting.

"Sir, if I may, I believe there is another way to pay for this noble venture." Tacitus' words caught Pilate's attention, since Tacitus was not prone to whimsical ideas. "As you must know from our history, my lord, the great and divine Crassus seized the treasury of the Jewish temple."

Pilate nodded in recognition of history as Tacitus continued, "The Jewish temple treasury has plenty of money to pay for our campaign. That money should be ours, my lord. The people pay to the temple what they should be paying, and don't pay, to Rome. It resides unguarded, useless, and wasting as rotted fruit."

"Of course, Tacitus! It's a brilliant idea! We are preparing a meal for the sake of their hunger and not the belly of Romans. By the gods, the ingredients should come from their bins and not ours!" Pilate clapped his hands together.

Tacitus smiled and added, "Should I form a detail of soldiers and seize the treasury right away, sir?"

"No, Tribune. The time of Crassus was completely different. Crassus conquered this land, and now I must govern it." Pilate had often thought of the great treasury that existed only a few hundred yards away, yet still felt out of reach. Its mention brought a sense of reality to what had been a forbidden fantasy. "We can persuade Antipas to authorize the use of the temple treasury, so this project will be perceived as cooperation and not one of confrontation."

Tacitus looked doubtful. "What if Antipas does not agree?"

"He will. With persuasion, he will bend easily to the desires of his one true god," Pilate said with a confident smile.

Tacitus shook his head. "What if he doesn't agree, My Lord Pilate?"

Pilate dismissed his warning, thinking it remote at best. Never suspecting he might have to make good on such a threat, Pilate looked back at Tacitus. "Then we will seize it!"

* * *

Antipas sat upon his throne hearing arguments between two merchants. He yawned, trying to remember the subject of their case as one merchant rattled off emphatic discourse filled with heated emotion. Out of the corner of his eye he noticed the other merchant slip a pouch to one of his guards, who immediately made his way up to the throne. Bowing with his arms extended, the guard dropped the pouch into Antipas' hands, which clinked with the music of coins. Antipas smiled from the weight and then stood to announce his ruling. Before he could speak he looked up towards the sound of frantic footsteps echoing from the end of the great hall. A palace guard ran towards him, eventually pushing his way through the startled assembly and hurried up the steps. Having difficulty catching his breath, the guard whispered, "Pilate is approaching!"

Antipas looked down at the gathering and shouted, "Everybody out! Guards, get these people out of here! Leave through the side entry!" Guards jumped into action pushing the bewildered merchants and their attendants toward the side access amid angry protests. Antipas slipped the pouch into a pocket in his robe and brushed away at imaginary dust to straighten his garments. Looking up he saw Pilate and Tacitus rushing in from the main entrance. Still brushing at his clothes, Antipas stumbled slightly descending the steps. "Prefect, Tribune, it is always good to welcome your presence!" Antipas felt uneasy as Pilate and Tacitus closed their distance. It had been less than a week since their previous visit, and Antipas sensed something unusual.

Tacitus was the first to break in with greeting. "Good health to you, my friend! I hope you are doing well."

Wary of such a friendly greeting, Antipas hid his concern. "Doing well. Very well, my friend." Antipas thought of the mountain of political and family turmoil that was plaguing him and was apprehensive of any further burden his guests might bring. His own infidelity was causing serious problems in his political marriage.

Pilate smiled in friendly greeting. "My apologies for our unannounced visit. Tacitus and I bring great news of a planned aqueduct from Solomon's Pool. It will bring fresh water to your palace, to Fortress Antonia, and irrigation for fields surrounding Jerusalem."

Antipas gave a suspicious smile, but with honest enthusiasm. "That is great news, Noble Prefect. Fresh water has become a serious problem, and I sincerely welcome your tidings."

Clearing his throat, Pilate replied, "Good, I was hoping for your support. Since the aqueduct will benefit the people of Jerusalem and the surrounding farmland, we will need your help to fund the project."

"My help? How am I supposed to help? There is not enough money in the palace treasury to make note of such a grand project."

Pilate responded with accusation. "Your banquets profess an air of wealth untold." Tacitus let out a quick laugh, followed by Pilate. Antipas failed to see the humor—he was too busy contemplating Pilate's true meaning. Pilate slowed his laughter and continued, "No, we wouldn't think of giving rise to your hunger, Noble Tetrarch. I am speaking of the temple treasury."

Antipas' eyes widened as he lost his superficial smile while maintaining an outward calm. "The temple treasury? You can't be serious."

Pilate reacted quickly. "I am quite serious. There is plenty of money in the temple treasury to fund this project. Most of that money is due Rome anyway in the form of unpaid taxes. And the aqueduct will benefit the people of Jerusalem."

Antipas' suspicion turned to fear. "That's impossible, Noble Prefect. That is the sacred treasure of the most Holy Temple. This treasure belongs to God, not me. I couldn't authorize its use even if I wanted to. Only Joseph Caiaphas, the high priest, can authorize its dispersal. You should be discussing this with him, not me. He was appointed by Valerius Gratus, which should wield some level of influence."

Pilate nodded his head in exaggeration. "He was appointed to appease the Jewish council and the people. We have no real power over him." Pilate became noticeably irritated. "Heed carefully my words. The treasury sits ripe for harvest in an orchard adjacent to Antonia. It's not in some nether world with your god! Your word can authorize the inevitable force of our action, as well as Caiaphas. It will much better serve our purpose—and yours—to make known your command."

"You don't understand! I can't, and I won't do this! I am a servant, not a priest of the temple over which I have no earthly authority. If I were to make a pretense of authorizing such a move, it would certainly mean my death!"

"It may mean your death if you *don't* authorize it!"

Antipas was not accustomed to threats, which sparked an unconscionable anger. He sensed Pilate's threat was a bluff as Pilate's eyes shifted from side to side, which only intensified his anger. His face turned bright red with beads of sweat surfacing on his forehead. With a rage that was ready to erupt, his thoughts somehow grasped upon a more constructive intent deep from within his soul. "Most Noble and Gracious Prefect, surely you must realize I am not of any position in Judea. I am tetrarch of Galilee. If I had the kingdom of my father, it would be a different story." Smiling, Antipas realized the perfection of his argument. The manifestation of his point calmed him considerably. "I'm not saying you can't take it. I'm just saying I'm not in a position to authorize your action. If you and your soldiers want to seize the treasury under your own authority, then do so. But I can have no part of it."

* * *

The next day, Tacitus ordered a centurion and a detail of soldiers to go into the temple. Their entry came as a complete surprise to the small contingent of Jewish soldiers standing guard. After all the anxiety and apprehension for such a move, the seizure went smoothly and without incident. The Roman soldiers counted the coins carefully, taking only a third of the temple treasury, seizing what they had been directed and nothing more. Plans were immediately put in motion for building the aqueduct.

As expected, Joseph Caiaphas and the Jewish council issued impassioned protests, demanding the return of the sacred treasure. The demands became more heated, quickly backed with threats to incite insurrection amongst the people.

Pilate called Joseph of Arimathea to Fortress Antonia. "Do you think the council will carry through with their threat to incite the masses?"

Joseph nodded emphatically. "Yes! They are enraged." Pointing in the direction of the council chambers, Joseph continued, "I no longer consider their mood as council, but as an angry mob. Some have even threatened your life if given the chance." Joseph walked over to the window and gazed off in the distance. "However, others are afraid of taking their case to the masses. They fear the announcement may not have the effect on the public they would hope. The temple treasury is not as visible as the standards, and they are concerned this may not be enough to instigate a large and sustained resistance."

"Interesting—a very interesting point, Joseph. And they're right. Nothing will come of their threat."

Joseph took a deep breath and slowly exhaled. "Antipas has been openly speaking of plans to build an aqueduct to provide additional irrigation for the farmers. The idea is proving to be very popular with the people. So popular, the council is concerned it may hurt their chances to incite resistance against Rome."

"This is good news," Tacitus interjected, giving Pilate a knowing look.

Joseph nervously stroked his beard, shaking his head. "But I do think the council will carry through with the threat of calling for mass protests. I have also heard talk of pursuing legal appeals to the Roman tribunal."

Pontius let out a short laugh, quickly followed by Tacitus.

Joseph continued, "I sensed desperation, since the idea of popular resistance is seeming less and less plausible."

Turning to Tacitus, Pilate gave a nod of understanding. "We will keep the treasury."

* * *

The Jewish council made good on their threat, instigating sporadic protests, and eventually scheduling an appeal to the Roman tribunal.

The day before the appeal, Pilate met with Tacitus in his office. Anxiously tapping his fingers on the desk, Pilate muttered, "We can't let their protest continue to build unchecked. We have to test the limits of their resolve."

Pilate was consumed in thought as Tacitus asked, "Are you concerned about the protests or the tribunal?"

Pilate's eyes widened. "The tribunal?! By the gods, no! I am just uncertain how large and how long the protests will grow. They seem to be gaining strength every day, and I wonder if this will continue or if they will break and fade. If I understand what Joseph has been telling us, it will eventually peak and fade. However, there is a danger in letting discontent build without consequences."

"I sense you have something in mind, my lord. What are you suggesting?"

Pilate's tone became aggressive. "We must respond to their protest with force and demonstrate a cost for disobedience. My course of action in Caesarea was flawed. Having the soldiers with their swords drawn, surrounding helpless men, women, and children, led to a situation where we were cursed no matter what we did."

Tacitus shook his head and sighed deeply. Pilate sensed disappointment. "Don't misinterpret my resolve and my intentions, Tacitus. I am committed to this project, and I won't let it die. We will confront these people. I just don't want it to be so obvious and prepared. I want the blow to come as a complete surprise—not giving them time to demonstrate a willingness to die for their stupid cause."

Tacitus lifted his head with renewed attention as Pilate continued. "Tomorrow, I'm sure there will be a crowd of protestors gathered in front of the tribunal when we arrive, along with the Jewish council. I want you to assign fifteen to twenty men and have them dress as common people of Jerusalem. Obviously, you must pick soldiers who bear resemblance. I want all of them to carry weapons concealed under their clothing."

"Have the soldiers dressed as civilians? Will you have them attack the protestors? If they are carrying swords, won't everyone know they are Roman, my lord?"

Pilate shook his head. "No, no! They will not attack the crowd. I want them to intermix with the crowd—blend in while they are gathering. The Jewish protests usually teeter on the brink of violence. Our soldiers will simply push the chaotic mess over the edge. They will pay with the violence they themselves seed." Pilate paused slightly, trying to work the details of the plan as he went. "You're right. They should not carry swords. That would be too obvious." Pilate mulled over the options racing through his mind. "Many times there are those in their midst who carry sticks or clubs." Pilate paused and let out a quick laugh. "Thinking they pose some semblance of threat." Pilate shook his head. "Our soldiers will carry clubs, only this time it will be a threat we will make real. It doesn't matter if they conceal them or not, only that they are willing to use them."

"In front of the Roman tribunal? With the Jewish council present? The crowd will be under strict orders from their own council to appear peaceful, giving their appeal a chance."

Pilate raised his shoulders in a confident jester. "Our soldiers will carry clubs making the crowd appear unruly and reckless—prone to violence!" Pilate paused, thinking on the details. "It doesn't matter if they conceal their clubs or not! When I give the order, I want them to start beating the crowd! I want them to beat them until there are none present. I will give the order through a signal."

"A signal? What kind of signal?"

Pilate raised his arms over his head, crossing them back and forth. "When I do this," he demonstrated. "I will address them first, making a few short appeals for them to disperse, and then I'll do this." Pilate waved his arms again. "I'll make it appear I'm trying to get their attention. That is when I want your soldiers to start beating them. Surprise will work in our favor."

Tacitus nodded. "A powerful idea, my lord! The shock will drive the life out of their resistance—that is, unless we beat it out of them! They'll never know from whence the blows come."

* * *

The next day, Pilate visited the tribunal to face the appeal by the Jewish council. A crowd was forming as expected. Pilate went into the building and talked to the tribunal members, who emphatically regarded the appeal as a waste of their time. Pilate informed the tribunal of his plans to disperse the crowd by force.

About that time, members of the Jewish council started arriving outside with cheers and cries of support from the crowd. Pilate smiled and bowed, excusing himself from the company of the tribunal. "Well, it looks like I'm needed outside." Looking back over his shoulder, he jokingly added, "They're calling for me! By the gods, it feels good to be so popular!"

As Pilate continued toward the exit, he encountered a lone councilman nervously juggling an armful of scrolls, nearly dropping one as he passed. Pilate walked out onto a balcony. The crowd had grown in size and disorder. Two council members were speaking to the crowd, further instigating heated emotions. The crowd was more animated and active than the protestors in Caesarea. A brief rush of fear raced through Pilate. *Are the soldiers out there? Will there be enough?* He scanned the crowd. At first, he could not distinguish Jew from Roman, but finally caught glimpses of familiar faces. Down the street a large number of fully dressed soldiers were gathered in case they were needed for control. A large contingent was also inside the building. Pilate slowly raised one hand, crying out, trying to get the crowd's attention. Careful not to give the signal too soon, his arms felt like lead weights as one lay limp along his side. "People! People of Jerusalem!" Pilate felt awkward restricting his arm movement. Still, Pilate wanted to appear as if he were appealing to their conscience. "People of Jerusalem! You must leave!"

The light roar and turmoil of the crowd gradually increased. "You are not doing any good here!" Pilate cried out again. He paused, scanning the sea of faces. "The aqueduct will bring water to your fields! Life to your crops!" With this, the noise subsided somewhat; evidently a few of the people understood his words. For an instant, Pilate felt the urge to continue his appeal given the slight reaction of the crowd. The noise quickly regained in strength, however, and he realized such an appeal was hopeless. Slowly, Pilate raised both arms over his head and began crossing them back and forth.

Screams erupted from the crowd, and several people started running. The soldiers had pulled out their clubs and began striking anyone who stood nearby—men and women alike. Earlier, Tacitus had put twice as many men in the crowd, seeing how large it had grown during the day. As people began running, Pilate could see the clubs swinging through the air, coming to abrupt, thudding halts as they met their targets again and again. There were sharp, gruesome cracks as the clubs fell upon heads or broke bones. The screams came from every direction, some cut short as clubs contacted faces. The soldiers would strike at one person and then another, oblivious to the pain and death they were inflicting. Several of the protestors were beaten so badly they died after only a few blows. Others died later after being taken away. Most of those who littered the street were unconscious or too injured to move. Pleas for mercy were usually met with incessant blows from soldiers who had lost control—men who'd cultivated hate and anger for a people they held with disdain.

In the following days, Pontius unequivocally attained the morbid fruition of his plan. The protests ceased and construction on the aqueduct soon began, bringing water paid in full by the sacred treasury of the temple and by the blood of several innocent people. One day, while visiting Solomon's Pool, Pilate took one of the coins from the treasury and threw it into its depths. "Here is your sacred offering, oh waters of Solomon! With this, make your waters holy so it pleases the gods!"

8 ~ Two Heads Aren't Better Than One

Pilate summoned Joseph of Arimathea to Fortress Antonia. Joseph's visits to Antonia became quite frequent—at least weekly—and Joseph had resorted to less cumbersome means to affect his visits. The cart arrangement took too long and resulted in too many missed meetings. Joseph eventually entered the fortress wearing bulky clothing and hooded garments to mask his identity. As Joseph entered Pilate's office, Pilate greeted him with a warm smile. "Good day, my friend! How is your family? Doing well, I hope."

Joseph smiled, but appeared uneasy. "They're fine, Your Nobility. It's the council you should worry about. There is persistent discontent, and it is growing instead of passing." Joseph shook his head while looking down away from Pilate. "Any issues pertaining to Roman authority is met with dissension and resistance. Where once there were arguments discussing different points of view, now there is unity—unity against anything benefiting Rome. There is a lot of mistrust on the council. I sometimes find it difficult to hold my tongue for fear of revealing my position."

"You are wise to do so, Joseph. It is more important that I have an ear on the true matters of the council, rather than a single voice viewed with suspicion. Rome is blessed with your service, Joseph." Pilate placed his hand on Joseph's shoulder. "It takes a very intelligent, level-headed man to have their trust, and you have more than fulfilled that role. By the gods, you even have my trust." With cunning and deception Pilate added with sincerity in his eyes, "I have grown to think of you as a friend, not just someone I work with."

"I am honored, Noble Prefect. It is good to hear your words. It is, perhaps, a situation that fate has placed upon us, having to depend upon each other in our work."

Pilate nodded. "You're right; it is a unique situation. I'd like to think we would have developed a friendship no matter what the circumstances might have been." Pilate maintained a subtle smile, hoping he wasn't overacting his part.

Joseph nodded without expression. "I would like to think so, too, Noble Prefect."

"I don't expect such formal address when we are alone," Pilate said with a confident smile. "On the other hand, it is good to maintain the habit for public occasion. I just want you to know I don't expect it. I even feel a little uncomfortable hearing it from you. It somehow belittles the trust that has developed between us."

"No offense, Your Nobility, but that will take some getting used to. After all, you are the Roman prefect, and I have become accustomed to referring to you as such." Joseph managed a brief smile. "But I will work on it."

At this, Pilate laughed and slapped Joseph on the shoulder. "I'm sure you will, Joseph. I'm sure you will." Pilate paused. "I feel we have won a battle, and it is a good feeling. But it is not enough. I truly want to win the hearts of these people, even if I have to force it down their throats."

Joseph acted a little surprised. "How can you win their hearts by forcing it down their throats?"

"It is like a bitter herb—medicine to cure an illness. It might seem unpleasant, but in the end it is for the good and health of the body." Pilate prided himself on his ability to pick a simple human experience to illustrate more complicated political concepts.

Joseph shrugged his shoulders. "I do not question that the aqueduct is for the betterment of this city and its people, but I do not think beating them to death will win their hearts."

Pilate gave Joseph a stern glance. "I did not think it would go that far. Tacitus put more men in the crowd than we had planned—and they got carried away. It's unfortunate, but what has happened, has happened. I can't go back and change that." Pilate softened his tone. "But you have to understand, submission is the first step to gaining hearts. That is the way it must be with a conquered people. I saw it many times in Spain. It did not matter how badly we slaughtered their armies, or even their villages, they would eventually come around to offer their servitude. Through fear perhaps, but servitude all the same."

"But Judea was conquered many decades ago, Noble Prefect, and fear cannot go on forever—especially with Jews. They have a strange immunity to fear, and they submit only to their God. It is only through their God that you can gain submission. Forcing it down their throats only builds defiance."

Pontius showed concern, recognizing the truth of Joseph's words. Even though the construction of the aqueduct was going well, the atmosphere in Jerusalem was still very tense. Whether he was dealing with a member of the Jewish council or a vendor on the street, Pontius could see the hate in their eyes.

Joseph took on a bolder instructive tone. "A heavy hand will continue to build dissent and rebellion amongst the people. The activities of the zealots have been on the rise recently, as you well know, costing the lives of several good soldiers. Any attempt to interfere is met with unparalleled resistance, which in turn fuels the zealots. It's like a childish, parasitic relationship, each one building and growing off the other, and I don't know how far it will go."

Pilate thought on Joseph's words, then shook his head in disagreement. "I wouldn't say there isn't anything that would interfere with devotion to their god. In the short time I have been here, I have sentenced a man to death for insurrection against Rome. His movement had strong religious overtones supporting outright defiance to Roman authority. He developed a large following, living in caves in the mountains east of here. With his death, the insurrection stopped, as if by a spell. I had never seen anything like it. One minute there were several followers showing intense support, with rebellion in their veins—and then the next, they scattered like sheep. Prior to my term, Valerius Gratus executed countless leaders. The people seem willing to throw their blind support toward someone proclaiming to be a messiah—most of them promising to rid this land of the gracious presence of Rome." Pilate walked over to the window that looked down upon the large courtyard in the center of Fortress Antonia. "Of course, we have dealt with them severely and immediately, before sedition might develop." Pilate paused, realizing his diction had turned dark. "However, there have been others, here and there, who have cultivated moderate followings without such a rebellious nature, and we have left them alone."

Joseph appeared puzzled. Breaking a short pause, he changed the subject. "I suppose with time they will come around. When the farmers see the benefit of the irrigation for their fields, they will perhaps forget how it was paid for."

Pilate sensed Joseph's disapproval. This angered Pilate, although he felt partially deserving of such a reaction for deceiving Joseph about the field irrigation. Pilate had had no intention of directing the project toward this end, but he never informed Joseph. He wasn't sure how and when he would tell Joseph—or if he ever would. Pilate hoped for a turn of events that would take attention away from the project. In any case, the conflict of anger and betrayal churned in Pilate's thoughts.

Joseph continued, "When you slap at smoke, it scatters, but it still gets in your eyes with stinging blindness as you walk into the flame."

Feeling the effect of another rebuke, Pilate's face flushed with hidden anger as he spoke more aggressively. "I was sent here nearly eight months ago to do a job. I have constantly felt my hands bound. Everything I try is met with opposition. These are not forgiving people. I have been very surprised at how they react to even minor aspects of policy. When I force a heavy hand, you're right, it does feel like I have stepped into the fire to rid the smoke. But what am I to do, Joseph? The people and the council do not respect me. I can see it in their eyes. They think of me as some type of defiled humanity, just because I do not believe in their god."

"It is not you personally, Prefect. It is just a deeply ingrained bias of our religion not to accept outside influence. This is a country based on religion and undivided devotion to God. They consider themselves a priestly race to serve as a light to the world in their covenant with God—not to be led by pagan authority. They will never pledge allegiance to one who is not their own."

"What am I supposed to do?" Pilate asked with a true sense of concern. "Convert to Judaism in order to become an effective leader? Pledge allegiance to their god? Not only would it be political suicide for me back in Rome, but no one here would ever believe it. I could not put on an air and make it believable." Pilate threw up his hands and then pointed in the general direction of Herod's palace. "Look at Antipas. He is a professed Jew, but he has no real power or ability to control the people!"

"Antipas is seen as a puppet of Rome. He is seen as an extravagant fool, the worst type of hypocrite to profess the Jewish faith. Only the authority given him by Rome keeps him in power."

Pilate nodded his head in strong agreement. "I know. Antipas maintains favor with Tiberius. He does and says all to please Caesar. He has built many magnificent monuments and buildings in Tiberias to please the gods. His devotion to Rome is unwavering and consistent, but he is removed from his people. In that sense, Antipas is smart. He knows where he has to place his allegiance to maintain his own wealth and position. But it does not solve my problem of how to make these people good subjects of Rome. It is like a body with two heads, paralyzed from the neck down."

9 ~ John the Baptist

In Nain of Galilee lived an only son, John, of an elderly couple, Zechariah and Elizabeth. As a child, John's parents were considered old. Growing into manhood, Zechariah would often tell John, "Your mother and I thought we would never be blessed with a child. But as it is written in the Scriptures, so it was with your mother and me. Abraham and Sarah bore Isaac late in life, while Manoah and his barren wife bore Samson. Just as with Isaac and Samson, I feel that God has great plans for you, my son. You must follow in the priesthood to lead and teach his people."

Now in the prime of his life, John's parents were fragile. He was twenty-nine and frequently helped them in their daily lives. They were not helpless, but many of their daily chores and tasks were becoming difficult. Zechariah was the rural priest for Nain of the order Abijah, and it was expected for sons to follow in the priesthood. However, John had chosen a different path, a move which his father did not approve and frequently reminded him. The family line was of Aaronic descent—a priestly lineage. Zechariah viewed John's choices as a failure of sacred duty and a break in a destined lineage.

John was a good man, who under any other circumstances would have made any father proud. John knew he had not lived up to his father's expectations, which always left a slight emptiness. John was pleasant in appearance. He was slightly taller than average, with a stature that portrayed strength and confidence. He had pronounced facial features: a carved chin and a strong jaw accompanied by an unexpected impression of humility.

John had grown up with the daily workings of the synagogue. He had been saturated with the Jewish teachings, rituals, and routine. John took the teachings to heart and lived according to the Mosaic Law, but did not want to follow in the priesthood. He had a basic drive to please people, pulling him in many directions, cultivating self-inflicted pressure. Many of his friends would tell him he tried too hard to be everything to everybody. John considered this a curse on his life, but it seemed beyond his nature to let it go. Most of all, he wanted to please his father, but he could never voice the true extent of his feelings.

The rituals of the temple and incessant sacrifices seemed meaningless to John, and in a sense, wasteful. However, these were practices that had strong meaning to his father; more than just meaning, they *were* his life. John respected his father's devotion and had no desire to argue points that would belittle his father's work. There were times when John would find himself wanting to confide in his mother, but he would always cut himself short, knowing his mother and father were truly one. John felt his parents were incapable of keeping secrets from each other—a wonderful strength in their relationship. John believed in God and loved God. However, he could not see himself practicing the rituals day in and day out.

One day, in one of many such conversations, John told his father, "I perform service to God and his people by bringing the goods in from the land and distributing them within the marketplace. The service I provide helps others, just as you do in priestly service."

"It also does you a great service by placing money in your pocket," Zechariah said with disgust in his voice.

"Yes, Father, but it is a living. It serves a definite, worthwhile purpose. I provide the farmer the means to trade his crop for money—bountiful crops that otherwise would rot in their bins."

Zechariah interrupted, "You say that as if my duties do not serve a purpose."

"No, I didn't say that. I was merely saying what I do *also* serves a purpose. Many benefit from the fruits of my labor, Father, just as they do from yours. Although, I must admit, my work does not have the direct nurturing to their spiritual needs, but it is what I have chosen to do."

John had a talent in dealing with people and he was never known to cheat or swindle, which seemed common practice among merchants. This was part of what made John so successful. He was well liked and trusted by just about everyone who met him. Trust went a long way toward developing long-term, solid relationships, as well as building his market. John wasn't the richest and most powerful of the merchants, yet his confidence and basic presence made him influential. He despised those who would put forth a front of strong devotion to Mosaic Law and rituals, but in turn think nothing of cheating a poor man out of his goods and money. The poor usually had little recourse, or voice, to pursue vindication, and most of the time, it would simply go unnoticed.

Zechariah used his age to bring John closer and more deeply into priestly duties. Each year, during his allotted time, Zechariah would take pilgrimage to the Temple of Jerusalem to present sacrifices—a great honor for a rural priest. The whole trip usually took about two weeks, and a group of about five to ten people would accompany him. When John was younger, there had been times he went along.

The time for the fall pilgrimage was approaching, and Zechariah confided in John, "My son, I could use your help on the journey to Jerusalem this year. I was wondering if you could join me." Zechariah paused as if to sense an initial reaction. "As you know, I am growing old. I doubt I have many years left to visit the Temple. This may even be my last. It has been many years since you have gone with me to Jerusalem. I want you to come with me this time."

"I would love to go with you," John said, giving him a reassuring smile. "It has been a great while since you asked. I must admit, sometimes I would get so busy in my trade that the time would just come and go, and then you were off."

With an expression of surprise, Zechariah responded, "I did not ask because you always seemed so busy. If I had known you were expecting me to ask after you had grown, I would have every time."

"I am honored and pleased to go with you, Father. However—and please don't take this the wrong way—it is not something I would do every year. It is not my profession or my calling. I am concerned that you cannot make this trip alone anymore. Someday, perhaps, you should consider letting someone else lead this pilgrimage. You have provided so much service and honor to the people of Nain. They, in turn, owe you a great debt."

"I will make the trip to Jerusalem for as long as I am able to walk or crawl on my hands and knees."

In John's heart, he knew his father meant every word. It saddened him to think the day would come when his father would be put to the test. Even if the mind is willing, the body might not be capable, and this would be an emotional death for his father.

* * *

John, Zechariah, and six others from the village walked down the street to the inn just inside the gates of Jerusalem. It brought back memories from years past, and it was a welcome sight after the four long days of travel. The trip had been fairly slow, driving the cumbersome ox-drawn cart carrying the goats, sheep, and chickens the villagers had ceded for sacrificial offerings. John saw the pain in his father's eyes, wrenching his face with each step, validating his constant complaining about his sore knees and hips. The pain did not present a dilemma of whether or not to assume his father's duties, only in how to persuade his father to relinquish his duties to younger men.

John and Zechariah walked into the inn, searching for the keeper. An elderly, heavy-set man strolled in from a side door. "Zechariah, it is wonderful to see you! It does not seem a year has come and gone since you were here last. Who is this handsome young man here with you? No, wait, is this John? I can't believe this is your son!"

"Yes, this is John. I'm surprised you remembered, for it has been… let's see, over ten years."

The innkeeper laughed confidently. "I cannot forget such a handsome, noble face. Besides, you speak of him every year. He seems to have filled out, though—stouter and stronger. He's not the boy I remember!"

John felt embarrassed by the outdated attention he was receiving. It had been a long time since anyone had referred to him as a "boy." It seemed a strange greeting in front of his father. "Yes, I am John. I've come to help my father. I'm sorry, I don't remember your name, sir. I remember you, but it's been a very long time."

"Nathaniel, my name is Nathaniel. Now I hope I don't have to repeat that in ten years when you come again!" John remembered Nathaniel's pleasant nature and how he always had a smile upon greeting them. Placing his hand on John's shoulder, Nathaniel continued, "Your father has always spoken proudly of you. That means a lot coming from such a man."

Zechariah managed a forced smile through obvious discomfort. "I'm sorry, Nathaniel. I am very tired, and I must get off these worn old bones. There are eight of us, and we will need to keep our animals in the manger out back."

"Oh, of course you're tired. It's probably been a very long day for you. We can talk more tomorrow after you have had time to rest."

* * *

The next morning, bright beams of sunlight streamed in thin layers through the wooden window slats. John inevitably felt the soft tugs drawing him away from his sleep, until an annoying glare caught his eye. John squinted as he tried to open his eyes, feebly using his hand to block the rays. For a moment he wondered what day it was, his mind playing tricks as it listed the merchants he would meet in the town center. Looking around, the room had no familiarity. A slight confusion set in, until he noticed his father lying on a mat across the room. Remembering he was in Jerusalem brought quick relief—reason enough to turn over away from the light.

Feeling a hand on his shoulder, John recognized his father's voice as he woke a second time. "John, John, everyone is starting to get up. Can you smell the fresh bread in the air? Nathaniel must have made some for his guests. He usually does this to welcome us. Come, let's prepare to meet the day before all of Jerusalem gets a whiff and there is none left for us."

John pulled out a clean garment from his bag and slipped on his sandals. His other clothes were dirty and dusty from the long trip. He threw them into the corner, thinking he would take care of them later. One of the travelers, Joshua, brought in a large bowl of water for cleaning and shaving. Some had already left for breakfast.

As John and Zechariah walked into the room, there were warm

greetings from fellow members of the group, as well as from Nathaniel and his wife, Sarah. Zechariah smiled. "Peace be with you, Sarah. May blessings from God rain heavily upon you. I am sure you are the one responsible for this most pleasant aroma that fills the air. Truly, this very room must be the envy of all of Jerusalem. Your talent in cooking can only be matched by your warm smile."

"Zechariah! Your words are kind and full of grace. Nathaniel told me you had arrived last night. This must be your son John. Nathaniel told me what a handsome man he had become. This, I think, is an understatement."

John dropped his eyes away from Sarah's focused gaze as she continued, "You must have a beautiful wife back in Nain."

John was caught off guard by the sudden personal attention. He had never married, and the subject made him uneasy. John was not certain why he had not taken a wife; it was not center in his mind. Attempting a well-rehearsed explanation, John said, "No, I'm not married. My work keeps me very busy. I also spend much of my time caring for my mother, Elizabeth, and my father. I am their only son, and they were fairly advanced in age when I was born."

Zechariah politely interrupted, going into his own story of Abraham and Sarah, and Manoah and Samson. John appreciated the interruption, as it diverted attention from an uncomfortable subject. He had seen many of his friends grow up and go through many different types of relationships. Some were simple and predestined, while others were more complicated and intense. He did not have strong desires for a woman. Instead, he felt more comfortable with other men and attractions he would never discuss with anyone, especially his parents. John found it easy to dismiss these inconsistencies, and seldom let them occupy his thoughts. The care of his parents and his work left him little time for anything else.

After a fair amount of discussion in which John had lost interest, Nathaniel added, "So the Lord must have great plans for this young man. God must have willed it for you and Elizabeth to have a son, after such a long period without children—a design of most holy and divine ambition."

Zechariah smiled with a confident note. "Yes! Maybe you can help my son recognize the divine covenant of his priestly calling!" The mood instantly turned quiet and serious. John started feeling uncomfortable, with an uneasiness building in the room. This was a discussion amongst mostly strangers—a discussion he hadn't expected.

Nathaniel quickly interjected to change the subject, "Maybe John can think of a way to force our Roman governor back to Caesarea. Have you heard, Zechariah? Pontius Pilate, the Roman prefect, has moved to Jerusalem to better rule his 'subjects.' He is a fool! All Romans are fools! Do they not know we are subjects to no one but God?"

Every turn in the conversation made John feel out of place. He had met several Romans in his merchant dealings in Nain, many of them from Caesarea. He thought highly of most of them, even more so than some of the Jewish merchants. He had never met or even seen Pontius Pilate, and the thought that the governor was here in Jerusalem intrigued him.

* * *

Fortress Antonia was adjacent to the temple and was almost as big and magnificent. Zechariah's group passed in front on their way to the temple. John noticed Roman soldiers ordained in shiny, silver armor standing guard at the main entrance. Crafted golden eagle sculptures were perched atop tapestry standards on long poles standing straight on either side of the entrance, projecting Roman power and authority. The Roman guards were proud in stature—perfectly still with their feet shoulder-width apart holding spears canted forward. The soldiers ignored anything and everyone who passed by on the street or through the entryway. Such a display seemed a world away from the everyday life of Nain. One could not help but be impressed by the discipline and strength of the presentation.

The group went quiet as they passed in front of the magnificent fortress. Soon someone started mumbling, and then all joined in a low tone. John did not hear any of it, for he was still hypnotized by the majesty and opulence of a world with which he had only brief encounters.

John's attention was interrupted by his father. "John, John! It's quite impressive, isn't it? Only rarely do I see the presence of Roman authority, and it never ceases to amaze me how they need such pageant in a worthless attempt to demand respect and fear. The outpost of soldiers in Nain is one thing, but this is another. They defile this ground with their presence. The Lord will surely make them pay for being so close to the temple." Zechariah paused as if in thought, and then continued, "It wasn't like this in the past when the Roman prefect remained in Caesarea. It is only a matter of time before the Lord will strike him dead for defiling this Holy City!"

John sensed the anger in his father's voice. He was a little surprised at the intensity of his father's words. John didn't feel the same hatred and anger.

The teenage boy, Joshua, broke in, asking, "Why would Pontius Pilate choose to live next to the temple, knowing it would offend us?"

Zechariah immediately bellowed, "That is probably his very intention, to wave his Roman authority in our faces, just as he did with the standards of Tiberius."

John doubted this was the sole reason for choosing Fortress Antonia. "Or perhaps it is the most secure structure for them to stay—outside of Herod's palace." Several in the procession stopped short, giving disapproving looks for John's hint of defense. John immediately recognized the uneasiness and made light of it. "Or *maybe* he was trying to get as far away from Antipas and still be within the walls of the city!"

Everyone laughed and it seemed to ease the tension. If there was anyone hated as much or more than the Romans, it was Antipas. Since he was a practicing Jew, his cooperation with Roman authority was looked upon by many as betrayal or even treason.

The main door of the fortress suddenly opened and out stepped a man dressed in a purple robe with gold trim. He was talking with two Roman centurions, whose brass-plated armor with gold inlays was even more magnificent and lustrous than the guards'. The guards, without hesitation, immediately snapped to attention, bringing their spears directly upright, tightly to their sides with a spontaneous clank of armor. The sudden movement startled the group and brought their attention to the three men leaving the fortress. Both of the centurions had their attention keenly focused upon the words and actions of the man grandly attired. He stood and walked proudly. He was of medium height, with dark hair, and was clean shaven—obviously a Roman. John slowed his steps, almost forcing the others to slow their procession. He stared at the three. *Could one of them be Pontius Pilate? It had to be.* He had never seen centurions dressed so, and he had never seen them treat another person with such submissiveness and humility.

Pontius met John's stare. John, in his mere appearance, stood out from other men and was easily noticed. Pilate interrupted one of his centurions, asking, "Who is that man—there with the group of people and animals, the one looking this way?"

The centurions looked at the group, whose pace again quickened—except for John's. One of the centurions answered, "They are a group proceeding to the temple with their sacrifices. The one dressed in the long gray vestures and the red cap is a priest, probably from an outlying city."

John noticed the three had shifted their attention toward them and uncomfortably looked away. Realizing he had fallen behind, John hastily caught up, trying to mix unnoticed.

Pilate shook his head. "No, I'm not talking about the priest. I'm talking about the man who was looking this way—the tall, clean-shaven one leading the lamb."

"Oh, that one, sir. I do not know who any of them might be. Aside from the priest, they are probably common peasants, accompanying the priest from some distant city. They are of no concern, Your Nobility, and do not pose any form of threat. These type pass by every day, on their way to the temple."

Pontius smiled. "No, I am not worried of threat, Centurion. It will just take time for me to become accustomed to the processions of people and animals outside my home."

10 ~ The Beginning

The evening air was quiet and still. The sun had just dropped below the horizon as John, Zechariah, and the rest were walking back toward the inn. The glare of the sun was gone, taking the strain from their eyes. The air was neither warm nor cool, providing no sense of presence. The quietness heightened the beauty of everything around them: the pattern of the buildings that lined the streets, the bushes and the flowers in the courtyard across the way, the people walking along the hillside in the distance, and the birds racing to beat the coming darkness. John wanted to stop and fall behind the others, hoping to be free of even the sound of their footsteps. Zechariah broke the silence. "John, I am so thankful you came along with me to Jerusalem. Not only for the help to an old man, but for the time we have spent together. Back home, sometimes we get so busy with life that I fail to appreciate you... and your mother. I forget how lucky I am to have you as a son."

John related keenly with every word from his father's lips. "I know, Father. I feel the same. This has been a wonderful time with you also. We really should do this more often. Let us hope we don't have to travel all the way to Jerusalem to do so. It would be nice to take more time like this, and include Mother. I really miss her and wish she could be here with us."

Zechariah nodded. "Yes, I've been thinking of Elizabeth, too. Maybe something closer to home would be better, because I know she would have a very difficult time with such a long trip."

As they walked on, Zechariah suddenly raised his hand. "Oh, that reminds me. Tomorrow, I will be meeting with the council to present an appeal from Nain."

"What appeal?" John interrupted, curious. "You are meeting with the Jewish council? What business would you have with the Jewish council? They are not associated with the temple."

"Yes, the Jewish council. What other council would I be dealing with?" Zechariah said in a rhetorical tone. "You know of Shadrach, the head of the town council?"

"Yes, of course. I deal with him every once in a while. I know he is not well liked by the rest of the council. That goes for the rest of the people of Nain, for that matter."

"I have been asked to voice a complaint to the Jerusalem council regarding Shadrach. He seems to have taken on a personal vendetta against most of the others. They want him replaced. We're hoping the Jerusalem council will hear our pleas and appoint a new leader. I have a letter signed by every member of the council and several other prominent people of Nain, including myself."

John placed his hand on his father's shoulder. "Well, they picked a fine man to present their appeal." John smiled, adding, "With your charm and appeal, they'll probably appoint *you* head of the council!"

Zechariah laughed. "I think not! It would surely send me to an early grave, serving on that council."

Zechariah suddenly slowed his pace and paused to catch his breath. "I was wondering if you would go along to support your charismatic father."

John did not relish the idea of visiting the Jewish council, but he felt he could not deny his father's request. Feigning enthusiasm, John responded, "Of course I'll go with you. I'm not sure what good I'll do, being overshadowed by the power of your domineering presence," John added in a humorous attempt to build up his father's esteem.

Zechariah scoffed and shrugged his shoulders. The light in the evening sky was quickly fading as they picked up their pace. Between breaths, Zechariah added, "We are scheduled to meet with them tomorrow afternoon. It will just be us and our little letter."

* * *

The next day, Zechariah and John neared the building in a part of the city they had rarely seen. A few blocks away, Herod's palace loomed high towards the heavens. It offered a fatherly presence to the spawn of buildings in its shadow. Zechariah pointed towards a large building that hugged the skirt of Herod's palace. "There, on the right. From the description and directions I was given, that is the council building."

John and Zechariah walked up the steps to the entry. Polished marble floors reflected objects and people down the hall. Zechariah approached a finely clothed gentleman. "We are looking for the council chambers. Do you know where it might be?"

The man pointed down the hall. "Yes, take the hallway to the right and you will find it there."

Obediently, Zechariah proceeded in the given direction, John following close behind. A number of people were gathered outside the chamber door, some leaving and some entering. Two Jewish soldiers stood on either side of the doorway, seemingly oblivious to all the surrounding activity. Across from the doorway, a custodian sat at a desk talking to another gentleman bent on keeping his attention. Zechariah walked over next to the desk and waited patiently for the other man to finish his case. However, the custodian soon interrupted the other gentleman in mid-sentence, seeming to welcome the chance to break from the prodding. "Yes, sir. May I help you?"

Zechariah cleared his throat, appearing startled by the sudden attention. "Well, yes. I am Zechariah, rural priest of Nain." Motioning his arm toward John, he added, "This is my son John. We are scheduled to meet with the council this afternoon."

The custodian ran his finger down the ledger looking through the day's appointments. He stopped on Zechariah's name. He looked up, smiling. "Yes. You are welcome to go into the council chambers and take a seat. They will call your name when it is your time."

In the council chambers, only about a quarter of the seats were filled and there was no problem finding a place to sit. Ten council members were seated behind a long table at the front of the room. A single man was standing before the council, presenting a case with dedicated and impassioned emotion. Several of the council members were talking amongst themselves, seemingly unconcerned with what the man was saying, while a couple gave their undivided attention, occasionally nodding their heads and offering appropriate facial expressions.

Three additional cases were heard, taking most of an hour. Occasionally, members of the council would ask questions or respond to statements made by the presenters. Sometimes a few members argued amongst themselves, but it would quickly subside. Zechariah leaned over and whispered to John, "I recognize the head council member. He has been to Nain a few times."

John nodded and leaned toward his father. "Yes, I have seen him before, too." John scanned the other faces. The council member to the far right also looked familiar, though he couldn't place the name or recall where he had met him. The feeling was more annoying than important.

After the fourth presenter finished his case, the head councilman called a recess to the proceedings. Most of them rose, leaving the room through the side door, including the council member that caught John's interest. Eventually the councilman returned, taking his place at the far end of the table. With John's curiosity getting the best of him, he stood up and walked over to the man, introducing himself. The councilman glanced up, not really offering his attention, but addressed him all the same. "You must wait to present your case when your name is called. Please, go take your seat."

John was taken aback by the brush-off, as he continued politely. "I'm sorry, sir, you look familiar to me. I can't quite place how I would have known you. I have come a long way, and I didn't expect to see a familiar face. Have you ever been to Nain, sir?"

The councilman paused, giving John more attention, saying, "No, I am from Arimathea. My name is Joseph."

John pondered the name. It sounded familiar. Finally, he placed it. "Joseph of Arimathea. That's how I have known you. I think I remember seeing you here in Jerusalem several years ago. My name is John from the house of Zechariah in Nain. You and I, sir, are of a similar trade." John smiled, motioning his hands toward his chest. "However, I am not on the Jewish council!"

An unavoidable smile appeared on Joseph's face, reacting to John's pleasant nature. Joseph rolled John's name off his lips, "John of Nain. I have heard of you, too, sir. However, I don't remember meeting you. You employ a profitable marketing trade in Galilee, do you not, sir?"

"I am flattered you have heard of me. Your name is well known in the marketing circles throughout all of Israel. We met only briefly here in Jerusalem. It must have been five or six years ago. I never forget a face."

By this time, all of the council members had returned. The head councilman called the room to order. John felt their conversation cut short as Joseph added, "We will have to talk more! With hope, after today's sessions."

John bowed his head slightly. "I look forward to it, sir." Turning, John went back to sit next to his father.

Zechariah and John were called next. The presentation of their case went well, especially with the newfound support from Joseph. Zechariah appeared pleased at the positive and immediate response he had obtained from the council. Leaving the council chambers, John pulled lightly at his father's garment, motioning him to stop. "I will remain here for the rest of the afternoon. The council member who was giving us support is Joseph of Arimathea, a very successful merchant, similar to my line of work."

Zechariah's demeanor turned from satisfaction to puzzled concern. "Joseph of Arimathea? Should I know this man?"

John shook his head. "No. He is well known in marketing circles. In fact, I met him briefly here in Jerusalem several years ago. I am going to stay for a while and talk to him when the session has ended." John hesitated, thinking of the long walk his father would make back to the inn, adding, "Unless it is your wish I walk back with you."

"No! No! I'll be fine walking back to the inn. It's the middle of the afternoon, and I'm not that helpless!"

John smiled. Taking the opportunity to take a friendly jab at his father, he responded, "I'm not so sure. The way you've been talking lately, there are times I think I will have to carry you."

Zechariah laughed with an air of someone acknowledging his guilt. "I suppose I have carried on at times. I have really appreciated your assistance and your company on this trip. I have to admit your presence here today certainly made our case much easier. If you hadn't been here, I doubt things would have gone quite so well. You never cease to amaze me, John. We travel over seventy miles from home, and you have connections on the Jerusalem council!"

John shrugged his shoulders. "Connections, maybe. He is simply someone I met very briefly. He is a good one to know in my work, and a 'connection' is precisely what I wish to make of him." John paused in order to emphasize his point. "Connections are very important in my line of work."

"And mine!" Zechariah replied, appearing somewhat annoyed by John's presumptuous remark. With that, Zechariah bid him farewell and headed off for the inn.

John strolled around the area, pleasantly taking in the sights and sounds of Jerusalem before returning to the council chambers.

The afternoon session continued for another hour, and John found several cases very interesting. The whole process was fascinating, hearing the many different problems and how most of them were quickly decided. He got the sense of things being accomplished—important things, things that affected many people's lives.

* * *

After the session ended, Joseph saw John sitting on one of the benches. He stood up and walked over. "Peace to you, sir. I am pleased you managed to stay through the sometimes torturous wanderings of these proceedings. We have these sessions twice a week, and sometimes they can get a little drawn out and boring."

John shook his head. "Oh, no! I find them very interesting. The power and control you have over solving important problems is fascinating!"

"I must admit, I find this more interesting than I thought it would be. I've only been here for about three months, and I really didn't know what to expect," Joseph confessed.

"Only three months! Your bearing on the council seems far more experienced. How was it you came to be on the council?"

Joseph hesitated, apprehensive with his answer. "I was appointed by Antipas."

The smile on John's face lost its luster and Joseph could detect the slight change in John's expression. Trying to downplay a connection with an unpopular man that didn't exist anyway, Joseph added, "I didn't really know Antipas. He just knew of me through my work—much like yourself—and he wanted a merchant on the council." Joseph felt a little uneasy, unsure if John would accept such a simple explanation.

John reacted favorably. Joseph sensed the positive change in John's expression, but still felt it was time to change the subject. "How is it that you came to Jerusalem? Surely you did not come all this way to present a fifteen-minute case on—who was it? Oh, Shadrach."

"Oh, no. I didn't even know we—my father and I—were presenting to the council until yesterday. The true purpose of my trip is to assist my father in his annual visit to the temple. He is the rural priest of our synagogue in Nain. We are here for a few days to present offerings and sacrifices to the temple."

Joseph's attitude dimmed, for he did not favor making a connection with the religious aspect of Jewish society, no matter how personable the man presented himself. "I thought your father was a priest by the manner of his dress. Are you training to be a priest to follow in your father's path?"

John shook his head. "No. I never had any desire to go into the priesthood. I am simply assisting my father because he is getting too old for his duties. He needs to step down and let someone else take over. He always thought and hoped I would fulfill that role. I am not one for the religious ceremonies and rituals of the practiced faith." John paused with a sheepish expression, as if he had said too much. Clearing his throat, he continued, "I enjoy my work too much to give it up, much to my father's disapproval."

Noticing John's uneasiness, Joseph reacted on a positive note. "I don't blame you. I would find priestly servitude too mundane and repetitious." Joseph turned and started walking toward his office, motioning for John to follow. The subject matter did not faze Joseph, but he was sensitive to the possibility that someone might overhear their conversation. On their way to his office, Joseph continued, "Many times I fail to see the significance of killing a goat in sacrifice and how such an act is pleasing to God."

With a pleasant note of surprise, John reacted, "Many times I have felt the same way."

As they walked into Joseph's office, Joseph partially closed the door behind them. Continuing, John added, "To me, such sacrifices are a loss of valuable necessities—meat and milk that could go to feed desperate families. Sometimes these sacrifices come from families who have little else. It bothers me to stand by and see such waste."

Joseph nodded in agreement. Their thoughts and values intermeshed as finely woven cloth. Their discussion went on for several hours, talking of their work experiences, families, and hometowns. They agreed they should get together in some future trading venture, but Joseph admitted his new job was taking most of his time. "I miss my work, yet also enjoy this new facet of my life. I like Jerusalem—and my family likes it, too. It's only been a few months, but I find my previous work a lifetime away."

John smiled and seemed to relax. "I envy you. I enjoy dealing with people in my work, but most of the time, money is the single motivating factor. In your case, justice and reason seem to be the basis of your interactions." Pausing in thought, John continued, "Does your work ever interfere or clash with the Roman presence?"

Joseph's eyes widened, feeling the question hit uncomfortably close to the mark. Before Joseph could respond, John went on, "How do you decide what issues you deal with versus what the Roman government deals with?"

Joseph responded in a matter-of-fact tone, "We deal with every issue brought to us. The Roman government has nothing to do with our proceedings, and they leave us alone. Most of the time, it is us making appeals to the Roman government, rather than the other way around."

"Such as the aqueduct affair, I presume?" John inquired.

Joseph cleared his throat. "Well, yes—although our appeals went unheeded."

John continued with his line of discussion as Joseph nervously fidgeted in his chair. "I find it amazing the contrast between how the Roman prefect handled this compared to the standards affair last year. It is as if he were two different men. I believe I saw him a couple of days ago in front of Fortress Antonia."

Joseph cleared his throat again and gave a minimal reaction. "Is that so?"

John continued, "I must admit I found myself thinking I would like to meet the man—find out who he really is. I always find people of different cultures and different lands very interesting, good or bad. In your position on the council, have you ever met Pontius Pilate?"

Joseph's heart quickened. He was even more surprised at hearing John's expressed desire to meet anyone like Pilate. "Yes, I have met the man on occasion. He's not a tyrant, as the aqueduct affair would portray him to be. I think the reaction at the protest got out of hand, the fault of soldiers who lost control, beyond Pilate's direction. He really seems to have good intentions at providing improvements for this country and its people."

John canted his head and raised an eyebrow in skeptical surprise. "So you have met him?" John softened his expression as he continued. "What type of man is he, or have you met with him enough to even know?"

Joseph thought back over his discussion with Pilate about their "friendship" and how he really did consider Pilate to be a friend, despite some disagreements. However, Joseph didn't want to reveal the extent of his relationship to someone he had just met, someone whom he had already told more than he should have. "I really don't know the man. I've only met him a couple of times."

While they were talking, an idea came to Joseph. *His position had been successful. Could it work again?* In a moment of inspiration, Joseph wondered if his position, or something similar to it, could be applied to other cities throughout Judea. Joseph thought Pilate might be pleased at the idea of extending a liaison that had proven to be beneficial, for him as well as Rome. Realizing he should first mention the idea to Pilate, Joseph asked, "How long are you here in Jerusalem?"

"For about another week. Why?"

"Another week, huh?" Joseph repeated, rubbing his chin. "Well, maybe you could get the chance to meet Pontius Pilate. Let me know where you and your father are staying. I will get back to you if I can make arrangements."

John looked away and nervously tapped his fingers against his folded arms. After an uncomfortable pause, John finally responded, "We are staying at Nathaniel's inn on the north side of the city." Bowing in a departing gesture, John continued, "It's been enjoyable talking to you, sir. I look forward to hearing from you."

With that, the two parted company. Joseph was intrigued by the nature of the man he had just met. In a society so dominated by religious forces and law, it was rare to have such discussions. The thoughts and attitudes were not rare, but such discussions were.

Joseph was excited about presenting his idea to Pilate. Pilate had been desperately seeking suggestions toward permeating the tight knit fiber of the Judean people. Each time, Joseph felt helpless to provide any real solutions. Now he had a solid idea that would enable Pilate to get a feel for the thoughts and character of the masses throughout Judea, not just in Jerusalem.

* * *

The next day Joseph met with Pilate. Joseph said, "Remember how we discussed ways of trying to get the people to be more accepting of Roman authority?"

Pontius raised his eyebrows slightly. "Yes, of course. You are asking me? I am usually the one asking you for advice on such matters!"

Joseph laughed slightly. "No, I am not asking your advice, sir... not that I don't value it. I am offering an idea."

"I am always willing to listen to ideas, especially good ones."

Joseph continued, "Yesterday I met a man—a man from Nain in Galilee. His name is John. He is here assisting his father, a rural priest from Nain, on his annual trip to the temple. He is a merchant, much like myself—a remarkable man to talk to. His ideas and thoughts on Mosaic Law are very open and progressive. He also expressed a desire to meet you of all things!"

Pilate expressed surprise at such an unexpected notion. In a sense of bewildered flattery, Pilate exclaimed, "To meet me! What is he? A zealot in disguise who would sacrifice his own life to sink a dagger into my chest?"

Joseph shook his head. "No, no. Lest I be a very poor judge of character, his thoughts were genuine, Your Nobility. I have heard of him in my work, and according to him, we met briefly several years ago." Joseph scratched his head, adding, "Although I do not remember such a meeting." Joseph felt slightly uncomfortable with the degree of uncertainty he had surfaced.

"How will this one man help the cause of Roman authority in this region?" Pilate asked with a note of rhetorical skepticism.

Joseph was quick to respond, now even more anxious to present his idea. "It will not just be one man. It could be several. He would only be the beginning." Joseph paused, remembering his own role. "Or I guess I was the beginning. If we had several council positions in different cities throughout Judea, the interaction could prove to be very valuable. You could have foreknowledge of issues and problems important to the people throughout the land. With knowledge, you will be able to predict how people will react to your actions and decisions."

"You steer a convincing argument, Joseph. I must admit, I'm not sure I would have proceeded with the aqueduct project if I hadn't had your insights into the true feelings of the people."

Pilate thought for a moment and then asked, "How are we supposed to secretly recruit several people to occupy important positions throughout all of Judea? Your chance meeting with John sounds exceptional and may be difficult to reproduce time and time again."

Joseph placed his hand on his chest, saying, "You and Tacitus found me, didn't you? Are there not others available?"

"Of course! We have many spies throughout Judea, but none with your reputation and position." Pontius stopped as if catching himself in an inappropriate admission. "'Spy' is perhaps the wrong term. I did not mean it in that manner. I think of you more as a Roman official on the Jewish council. A position that should exist, anyway."

In a strange sense, Joseph felt complimented by Pilate's statement and his willingness to make such a distinction. Subconsciously, almost in reflex, Joseph's chest swelled with a feeling of pride. "It will come with time. In my trade, I know many people and have many connections throughout Judea, Galilee, and Iturea. It will not be difficult to find people to fill such positions."

Pontius responded with a cautious smile. "An important key to the success of our relationship is secrecy. Having numerous people in such high positions across the country will be very difficult to keep hidden. If one position is revealed, the whole network could quickly unravel, revealing even your position on the Jewish council."

Joseph lowered his eyes and brought his hand up to rub the back of his head.

As quickly as Pontius had delved into the negative argument, he reversed himself. "I have no objections to meeting John. In fact, I look forward to meeting him, if he is as impressive as you say."

11 ~ Like Minds

Joseph escorted John through the halls of Fortress Antonia. The display of Roman paraphernalia on the outside was nothing compared to the decor and statues inside. Each hall—indeed, every room—had several pieces of magnificent artwork gracing its walls or laying watch as if by the artists' design. John had been uncomfortable with the painstaking secrecy Joseph prescribed for the visit. Joseph had insisted that John not even tell his father about the meeting. With every step in the marbled halls, John became more uneasy, wondering what was in store. He had never been nervous about meeting any man, but for some reason this occasion was different. What would he say? After all, meeting the Roman prefect was merely an expressed idea that seemed interesting at the time. But now, it would become a reality. Joseph seemed a good man, but why was he so helpful at facilitating the meeting? How was it he had the connections to arrange it so quickly? All of these questions raced through John's mind as they went further and further into the maze of halls. John sensed Joseph's mind was occupied also, for neither of them said much as they made their way.

* * *

Pilate stood as the two entered the room. He extended a cordial greeting. "Joseph! It is good to see you!" Turning toward John, Pontius immediately recognized him as the man he had seen in the small procession. Pontius hesitated, meeting John's stare in a mutual sense of admiration. The quiet communiqué lasted for only a few seconds. Joseph broke the silence. "Prefect Pilate, this is John of Nain, from the house of Zechariah. The man who I was telling you had expressed a desire to meet you, sir."

"Yes, we've met," Pontius responded without missing a beat. Seeing Joseph's surprise, Pontius continued, "Well, we didn't exactly meet. We saw each other outside the fortress as he was proceeding with a group of friends and fowl." Pontius paused as if trying to recall a picture. "...and goats, and pigs, and..."

John laughed. With a serious expression, Joseph interjected, "For a minute, I thought you were making reference to foul friends and not the fowl of feather, Your Nobility."

Pontius turned his eyes toward Joseph, slowly raising his eyebrows in comic disbelief. He had a sarcastic smile that quickly changed to laughter. All three were laughing after having only just met and with just a few words exchanged. The air amongst the three was very easy and carefree, and it seemed a natural mixing of personalities. Finally, John broke his unintended silence, addressing Pilate in his language: "Peace and good fortune to you, Prefect. This is truly an unexpected honor. I have always admired your culture and writings."

Pilate presented an even greater expression of pleasant surprise, responding, "You speak Latin very well, sir. I am impressed!"

"Thank you, sir. I have met several Roman merchants in my time. It has become a necessity for me, as I am sure it has been for Joseph."

Joseph nodded. "That is one of the things I liked very much about the market—meeting different people from all over the world. From Romans to Egyptians, to Greeks to Assyrians, I find them all fascinating with a wealth of experiences. Unfortunately, my recent line of work has narrowed my interactions to this corner of the world."

John acted surprised as he turned to Joseph and said, "With the diversity of issues and problems I heard in one afternoon, surely you must find the council very exciting and interesting! I know I did. The problems seemed very important and relevant, having strong effects on many people's lives."

Joseph shook his head. "Don't get me wrong. I truly enjoy my work on the council and feel it is very important. It's just that when one gets used to a line of work, you tend to miss it when it's gone."

Pilate jumped in. "Don't miss it too much. There's a lot of work ahead of us." Pilate stopped, realizing what he had just said in front of John. The conversation had become so casual, it slipped out. Maintaining his composure and noting the anxious look on Joseph's face, Pilate added, "Your work on the council is very important toward keeping this city working. It saves *us*"—pointing to himself—"a lot of work on *our* side."

Pilate tried to change the subject. "There are some peoples of the world whom I'd wished I'd never met. Perhaps your experiences have been mostly pleasant ones, and most of mine have been as well. But there are some that are ruthless and blood-thirsty. Like the barbarians of northern Europe in Gaul. They are dirty creatures, barely human, living in disorganized tribes throughout the land. The winters are very long and cold. Sometimes I wonder how any of them survive."

"You have seen these people?" John said with a heightened sense of curiosity.

Seeing the opportunity to speak of his life experiences, Pilate's pride was ignited. "Yes, I have. In my younger years, I commanded cohorts in northern Europe, and most recently even a legion in Spain. Spain was far more preferable to the barbarians of northern Europe. The barbarians dressed in crude, animal-skinned garments, with the fur still intact—to keep them warm, I suppose. They were hairy people, never clean shaven. Sometimes you couldn't tell where their hair stopped and the garments began."

Joseph interrupted. "That sounds like the dress of our prophets. One of our most famous, Elijah, wore a garment of camel hair and a leather girdle. He must have looked something like the barbarians you speak of."

John added in, "Yes, in the book of Zechariah from the Scriptures, it speaks of the hairy mantle as the mark of a Jewish prophet."

Pontius looked surprised. "The book of Zechariah? Your father has written a book for the Jewish Scriptures?"

John laughed, shaking his head. "No! Of course, no," and then looked surprised. "You have heard of my father?"

Pontius nodded. "Joseph has told me all about you and the purpose of your visit to Jerusalem."

John nodded his understanding. "The book of Zechariah was written many centuries ago. Perhaps my father was named after *it*. In any case, being the book with my father's name, I know it well."

Pontius smiled. "I have had previous discussions on the Jewish religion with Joseph, and I have found them both confusing and fascinating. I have learned of angels—who are immortals, but not gods. I have learned of the son of your god, David—who was not immortal, but a king. And I have learned of a messiah, meant to be a leader of your people, a descendent of this King David. And now I hear you speak of prophets. Were they immortal?"

John became noticeably surprised at the turn in the exchange. "No, they were not immortal. They were just men who had been given special gifts from God to foretell the future. They were revered amongst the ancient Jews, who looked to them for guidance and direction in times of trouble. They were not kings, but they had the power of kings."

Pontius nodded, jabbing his finger in the air to emphasize a point. "That's what I need! A prophet, to offer *me* direction in how to rule this land."

John smiled and shook his head. "No offense, Your Nobility, I do not think a Jewish prophet would be caught dead giving advice to a Roman governor."

Joseph laughed. "He wouldn't be a prophet for long. Prophets strictly offer their guidance to Jews."

Pilate's face turned puzzled. "Well, how do your people know when someone is a prophet, one to seek guidance from?"

John took on a proud, instructive tone. "Well, like I said before, the hairy mantle is the known mark of a prophet, but many times the people would not accept a man as a prophet until his prophecies were fulfilled." John paused. "Although, that wasn't always the case. Zechariah, the prophet from the book I spoke of, along with another prophet, Haggai, prophesized that one of our kings, King Zerubbabel, was the true messiah. They predicted the imminent overthrow of the Persian Empire, the worldwide manifestation of God, and glorification of Zerubbabel. The population even built and completed a new temple here in Jerusalem based on their prophecy. But the prophecies were never realized; Israel remained under the bondage of the Persian Empire; and Zerubbabel sort of disappeared from history. But Zechariah and Haggai were considered prophets even before their prophecies were realized."

Hearing this, a marvelous idea began to form in Pilate's mind. The thought was more inspiration than solid plans. Even though he didn't know the details, it excited him greatly. Pontius was starting to believe he could use the hidden aspects of this religion to work for him, rather than against him, in effecting his control over the Jews. The idea excited him so much that he paid little attention to the rest of their conversation. His anxiety reached such a level, in fact, that he wished the conversation would end so that he could think on it more on his own. He wanted to work out details that were only starting to form. Eventually, Pontius' thoughts returned to the conversation. Looking at John, he inquired, "So, how much longer did you say you will be staying in Jerusalem?"

"Only a few more days, Noble Prefect, and then we will be heading back to Nain."

Pontius thought for a moment and then added, "Is there any way you could extend your engagements in Jerusalem? I find our conversation truly fascinating and I wish to continue more of this, but at a later date."

"I really must go back with my father. He is old and needs my help. That was the entire purpose of my trip—to assist my father. Although he is not entirely as helpless as he leads others to believe, I cannot let him go back alone."

Pilate turned noticeably disappointed, but not angered, saying, "This is unfortunate, but I understand. This is indeed sudden. I, too, was not expecting such an enlightened meeting." Being careful with his words, yet hoping to further cultivate a beneficial relationship, Pilate added, "It is rare that I engage in such interesting and enjoyable conversation, even amongst Romans. Quite frankly, I have developed a close friendship with Joseph in such discussions. I cherish friendships as much, or even more, than my role as governor."

John bowed. "I understand your position, Noble Prefect. I, too, cherish friendships to a high degree, but I have my family obligations that dictate that I must return with my father."

Pontius smiled, detecting the positive note in John's response. "Then you must come back to Jerusalem. I've enjoyed our meeting, and I look forward to more in the future. I oversee numerous arrangements with local and regional merchants, and I hope someday you will become involved."

John nodded. "I look forward to any way that I could be of assistance, Your Nobility."

*　*　*

The three exchanged farewells and left the meeting in goodwill. John felt a sense of confidence building inside. This was the "connection" he had hoped for, although with a different man—certainly not expecting the Roman prefect. This was more than he had dreamed possible. Not necessarily because of the money, but because of the variety of opportunities it would open and the people with whom he would interact. John was amazed at how emotionally profitable this trip had been and how comfortable he had become with a man who most in Judea despised—an unjust hatred, he felt.

On their way out, Joseph turned to John and whispered, "You must keep your interactions with Pontius Pilate secret for your role to remain effective. In my own trading experience, interactions with the Romans are looked down upon and better left untold."

12 ~ Purification

Over the course of three months, Pilate and Joseph coordinated merchant deals for John. The arrangements were very lucrative. Even more important to John were the new areas of trade with Egyptian, Ethiopian, Greek, Roman, Persian, and Eastern merchants, and the whole new class of people he was meeting. John made frequent trips to Jerusalem, stopping in to visit Pilate and Joseph. He exercised care to maintain secrecy, although not to the level Joseph had taken. Joseph constantly reminded John of the need for secrecy, but John did not see the intense need. Joseph brought this up to Pilate, who finally agreed to conduct their meetings at a farmhouse outside of Jerusalem. Pilate was reluctant at first, but as their meetings became more frequent, he realized the need for a less conspicuous location.

John was more freewheeling than Joseph, less serious on a wide range of issues and ways of approaching different problems. But Joseph's level-headedness and past experience proved invaluable, not only in merchant arrangements that kept John's interest, but by providing a balance on discussions pertinent to their trade—ranging from wheat, to weapon supplies, to religion.

On several occasions, Tacitus accompanied Pilate to the farmhouse. Tacitus, too, grew to like John. Pilate's and Tacitus' image of the Jewish people naturally improved as a result of the meetings. John and Joseph served, in a way, as representatives of their own people. Their impressions and familiarity grew fonder with each meeting.

One day, in private with Pilate, Joseph inquired, "Begging your pardon, sir, but when do you plan on asking John about serving on the Nain council? I feel the time has been right for a good while now. John is a man we can trust and depend on."

"I couldn't agree with you more, Joseph. But the reason I haven't asked him yet is because I have grander plans for John. Plans I have contemplated for some time—actually since the first day we met." Pontius paused, wondering if the time was right for such a scheme and how Joseph would accept it. Pontius recognized his self-haste, always impatient for grand results. But he had thought this through and was certain it could work.

Joseph resumed the discussion. "I'm not sure if it's the same thing, but I've had bigger thoughts regarding John's role, too. John is a remarkable man. With his intelligence and natural ability to work with people, I think his role on the Nain council would expand very quickly. I think he can do a lot of good, and I also think he has very strong potential to become head of the council in short order. In such a position, he would have great influence."

Pontius poured two glasses of wine, handing one to Joseph. "You are reading my mind, Joseph. But I am planning on skipping the part regarding the Nain council and have John go directly to being a leader... or a teacher. I want to be careful not to rival Antipas." Pontius paused, seeing Joseph's heightened interest. "We have garrisons in Nain and the other cities you speak of. I do not want to complicate the relationships of the governing councils with local Roman authority. Our main problem is in the countryside where zealots roam freely. I want to facilitate a movement of your own people to counter the spread of the zealots... or even absorb them." Pontius looked up at Joseph and continued, "Do you remember when we discussed the role of the prophet?"

"Prophet!" Joseph exclaimed. "You're getting into something that you do not understand."

Pontius showed little concern at toying with a religion or Joseph's expressed anxiety. Quickly reacting to counter his charge, Pontius replied, "I have had scholars research your prophets of old and you were right. They were men who were revered and looked upon for guidance and direction. For most of them, it took time before they were accepted as prophets, acting mostly on their own. Just think how much more strongly and quickly we can develop the role with support from Rome."

"They were prophets due to help from God. They were not of their own accord!"

"But the people won't know that! How will they know whether he is getting assistance from us or your god?!"

Joseph shook his head. "You're asking us to betray our people!"

"I am not asking you or John, for that matter, to turn away from your god or betray anyone. I am just asking for a leader who Jews will trust and listen to. By the gods, my predecessor, Valerius Gratus, appointed the high priest of your temple, Joseph Caiaphas, and he still holds that position today. Your people may have felt a betrayal at first, but now he is well established and accepted in the highest position of your practiced faith. Rome, however, in all its wisdom, has directed that I can no longer fire or appoint a high priest." Pontius paused, almost angry Rome had curtailed such power. "I personally think Valerius Gratus got carried away, appointing and firing a succession of five high priests. I don't think it did any good, anyway. Now I'm the one suffering the consequences. I feel my hands are tied."

Joseph finished his glass of wine and Pontius poured him another. He sensed Joseph uneasiness, but continued, "I will need your help in order for John to teach and lead according to your laws—laws that pacify rather than incite violence. Surely there are laws that deal with treating others with dignity... respect... fairness. I know we, as Romans, are not considered as deserving of such courtesy, instead being looked upon as enemies. Perhaps we can change that view. Get them to understand we are here to help—improve their infrastructure, provide security, order, and protect them from invasion. There are many forces to the east that would have overrun this area and slaughtered your people if it were not for our presence. *Our* armies have dealt with these forces, requiring all the strength and power of Rome to keep them at bay. And quite frankly, it hasn't been easy. There have been battles won, and battles lost. It is imperative we maintain the support of the people to serve in our armies and pay their taxes, not only to preserve their own existence, but to honor the gracious presence of their protector." Pausing to make a point, Pontius concluded, "Instead, our armies expend resources to maintain order with the very people we are burdened to protect—a people for whom rebellion seems to permeate every aspect of your culture."

Pontius sat down in his chair and looked up at the ceiling. "John is the seed that will harvest a new resolve amongst your people. This resolve cannot be chiseled or hammered by a Roman. It can, however, be kneaded and shaped from within."

Listening to Pilate, Joseph almost finished his second glass of wine. Speaking in a hesitant, low tone, he finally replied, "You're asking a lot, Noble Prefect. How can you be so sure they will not see the hand of Rome in the work of a Jewish baker? Almost the entire Jewish population abhors the mere presence of Roman occupation. They would consider any outside influence as an enemy of the Jewish State. It's as if you are asking them to love their enemies as one of their own, and I'm not sure that will ever happen."

"Love thine enemy," Pilate repeated aloud. "That is a good start, Joseph. Good fortune rides upon your thoughts." Pilate smiled and nodded with approval. "Let us hope with time, they won't consider us their enemy. I am familiar with your history, and I know this area has been overrun many times by countless armies. This area lies at the heart of the world, between East and West. With our presence, the past hundred years has been the longest period of peace and prosperity that your people have ever known. I truly believe our presence has been much kinder to your people than any previous conqueror. Previous conquerors have slaughtered your people, scattered them to the four corners of the earth, or enslaved them. We have done none of that. Instead, we build roads, buildings, entire cities, aqueducts, provide protection, and at the same time we have allowed autonomous rule."

The intense concern slowly began to subside from Joseph's face. "You make a strong argument, Prefect, and I agree with you. But to declare John a prophet, it could very well be a disastrous move—for John in particular. Blasphemy, especially on this scale, could mean death."

"Hear me. I am not saying we should declare him a prophet, or that he declares himself a prophet. I'm just saying he could become a leader amongst your people—someone they will place their trust in. With our help, we can pave the way for him. Then it is up to the people to make of him what they will. I do not care whether they call him a prophet, or a teacher, or a messiah. All that matters is that we have someone under the control and influence of Rome to instill new attitudes amongst the population. I will need your help, Joseph. I need someone who is well versed in the Jewish laws, so that I know what we can and cannot do or say."

Joseph rubbed his eyes and took in a deep breath. "There are many aspects of Mosaic Law that are good in their own right, and some that are not so good. I like the idea of emphasizing aspects of Mosaic Law that will improve our society and even the relationship with Roman authority." Joseph stroked his beard in careful thought. "I suppose, if we do not declare him a prophet, but simply permit him to present teachings to the people, there could be no harm in that."

"Exactly! However, there are things we could do to help *promote* the idea of him being a prophet."

Joseph quickly interrupted. "Most Noble Prefect, your reference to the position of prophet is much too carefree. You're touching on very sensitive ground. This is a very sacred concept in the faith and beliefs of every Jew."

Pontius' tone became slightly annoyed. "*Everything* is sacred to your people! Is there nothing I can touch upon that will not insult even the ground I stand on?" Seeing Joseph shake his head, Pontius continued, "Nonetheless, I am interested in learning more about these prophets. Tell me more about Elijah. What did he talk about? Where did he teach?"

"Well, as you may remember from our discussion a few months ago, Elijah wore a garment of camel hair and a leather girdle. He led a very austere lifestyle. Elijah spent most of his time in the wilderness, preaching from there. In fact, it is said he was taken up into heaven in an area north of here, along the Jordan River, southeast of Jericho. Elijah spoke mostly of preparing one's self for the imminent judgment of the Lord."

"In the wilderness?" Pontius smiled, seeing a connection with his thoughts. "Was Elijah effective in his teachings?"

Joseph nodded. "He attracted people from many different cities, rather than just one. The people tend to identify heavily with aspects and events of their own city and ignore others. The countryside is a neutral area—less threatening to allegiance."

"Interesting point, Joseph," Pontius responded. "It would also be safer for concealing our association here in Jerusalem. John would be far enough from Galilee so that he would not draw attention from Antipas' government in Tiberias, giving us time to build a basis." Pontius paused, relishing a dream of truly effecting rule over the thoughts and attitudes of the Jews. Continuing, Pilate added, "Eventually spreading throughout all of Judea, and maybe into Galilee, deposing Antipas of the kingdom he desires."

"Aren't we getting a little ahead of ourselves? We haven't even asked John if he wants to do this. When we present the idea, we should describe the role as a leader or teacher, and nothing more. The stories of Elijah can be our guide, but that's as far as I would go with it. We must be careful about using the word 'prophet,' since I don't think it would sit well with John. He would probably react the way I did, only stronger."

Pontius seemed a little perturbed with Joseph's modification to his plans. But the basics remained the same. He liked the idea of building a new leader, and John seemed perfect for that role. "Yes, yes, I suppose you're right. That is the reason I have you, to help me with these details."

* * *

The next day, Pilate and Joseph met with John in the farmhouse they had come to know well. Pilate explained how he wanted John to be his "leader of the people," someone who would help define and guide the direction of Judea. Pilate again presented a convincing argument of Rome's role in effecting peace and progress in the area for the past hundred years. Pilate concluded, "Your role could eventually expand to your home in Galilee, serving as the Jewish representative of the region—possibly ousting Antipas."

John felt cautious but excited. The idea of serving as a representative of his people to the Roman government sounded appealing. He didn't like Antipas as the leader of his region—a feeling he shared with many others, and now, it seemed, with Pontius Pilate. Here was an opportunity to effect real change in a country he loved, and with the power of Rome behind him. He had been envious of Joseph's position on the Jewish council, and now he was being offered a similar role. Serving as liaison between his people and the Roman government would certainly be a job of purpose and importance that could be rivaled by little else. He enjoyed working with Joseph and Pilate, and such a position would ensure their interaction for many months to come. He was hesitant, though. It was definitely an important role that deserved serious thought before giving acceptance.

Pilate walked over to John and placed his hand on his shoulder. "My basic goal is to improve the relationship between Rome and the Judean people. I want to learn more about them, through you. And I want them to learn more about us—again, through you. You will be the focal point in this whole affair. You will have the full support of Rome for whatever you need to perform your role, and of course, you will be paid handsomely for your services." Glancing over towards Joseph, Pilate added, "I have learned so much about your people and your customs through Joseph. Of course—as with Joseph—you must keep your connections with me secret in order to gain support from your people."

Warming to the idea, John asked Pilate, "Where would I begin in such a role? Would I gain a position on the Jewish council?"

Joseph interjected, "No. We want you to deal more closely with the common people. We want you to start off slow at first, possibly in a role as teacher, intermixing directly with the common people. You have the character and strength to become a great leader, John. You interact and present yourself very well. You have a strong and confident stature."

Pontius smiled and placed his hand on John's shoulder. "We understand it will be slow-going at first, and if it doesn't work, we have lost nothing. We must start somewhere to lay the seeds of cooperation between Rome and the Judean people, rather than having us at each other's throats."

John felt the words forming in his mouth, even though warnings were sounding in his mind. He really enjoyed the air of friendliness and sense of goodwill he felt inside. Here he was, in the unlikely company of the highest Roman official in Judea and a member of the Jewish council, and everyone was getting along wonderfully. In fact, they had become good friends over the past several months and he wished others could do the same. Finally, John broke his silence. "I'm not sure what all this entails, but I am willing to give it a try. I sincerely appreciate the confidence you express in me, and I hope I can live up to your expectations."

Pontius shook his head. "I wouldn't think of it in terms of expectations. Now, we have nothing. We can only build from here. We will lay the foundation for changing the attitudes of the people toward Roman authority." Pontius paused, turning his gaze towards the floor. "And it will also change our attitude toward you."

Joseph gave a reassuring nod as his chest swelled slightly, his shoulders squared. Joseph turned to John. "In order to attract as many people from different cities as possible, not just Jerusalem, we were thinking you should be based outside of Jerusalem. It will also serve to conceal your relation with the Roman government." Joseph paused as if in thought. "In order to attract the most attention, it would probably be best if we based your work in the area southeast of Jericho near the Jordan River. There is a small community there, Bethany beyond Jordan. It is easily accessible from Jerusalem and many other cities. It's also a little closer to your home."

John's smile turned to a sneer, dismayed with the idea of spending time away from the main cities. "Bethany beyond Jordan!" John exclaimed. "Jerusalem is the seat of power."

Joseph quickly interrupted. "Jerusalem is too close to Antipas. We can't risk interfering with him here or his government in Tiberias. It is important that he not get word of this too quickly, for he might see it as a threat to his own role as tetrarch."

John raised his eyebrows and nodded. "Of course, you're right, Joseph. The way you were talking, I was naturally thinking of Jerusalem, here with you—and working more closely with you." John paused, feeling an odd sense of relief that the role would be less stressful away from Jerusalem. "Bethany is in beautiful country. I have always liked the river and the countryside it feeds. The trees and wildlife have their appeal, compared to the endless lines of stone and brick in the city." John wasn't sure if he meant what he was saying. Maybe he was trying to convince himself. John had spent most of his life in Nain. Even though he had spent time traveling between cities and was no stranger to the wilderness, he was not sure if he was ready to make it his home.

Pilate took a deep breath. "There may be a few hardships at first, but we will ensure your good care."

John smiled, looking back at Pilate. "How about a palace on the river?

Now that has appeal I can live with."

Pilate laughed. "I wouldn't mind a palace on the river myself, but I'm afraid that might give us away, don't you think?"

John quickly turned serious again, wanting to discuss the realities of such an arrangement. "At least I won't need to worry about water. I couldn't imagine trying to survive in areas away from the river. For that matter, it would be very important for people visiting the area, if any do come."

Pontius smiled, adding with a humorous note, "If they do come, maybe you could get them to bathe in the river. I've noticed many of the people in the streets look like they've never seen water. Isn't cleansing and washing important amongst your people?" Before John or Joseph could answer, Pontius turned more serious. "That's one aspect I would like put into practice more often. In fact, when the aqueduct is completed, we are planning to build bathhouses around the city. Bathing is a common Roman custom worthy of attention from your people. In Rome, before performing ceremonial sacrifices to the gods, one performs an act of purification by bathing in the living stream of the Tiber River."

At first John thought Pilate was joking about bathing. But as Pilate went on, he realized Pilate was obsessed with introducing Roman customs.

Before John could respond, Joseph replied, "Washing is a common ritual in Mosaic Law. Mostly, it involves washing the hands in preparation for meals, or washing the feet before entering a place of worship, like the temple. But washing the whole body is not as common. Fresh water is a precious commodity, and one must be careful of its use."

Pontius went on. "At the river there is no shortage of water. Bathing in a river is not only an act of purification, it could be as appealing as it is useful. You'll need something to counter the hot, dry desert."

John raised his finger, as if to make a point. "It was a common theme of prophets of old to prepare one's self for the imminent judgment of God." Pilate and Joseph looked at each other, and then John continued, "Repentance is a type of cleansing of the soul in preparation for presenting sacrifices to the temple. However, many times I have seen people entering the temple with complete disregard for their appearance; some are even filthy. Out of respect to God, people should make themselves more presentable before entering His House. Cleansing the body, as well as the soul, is an appropriate act, showing piety toward God."

Pontius nodded. "Your words complement my thoughts. You will deal mostly through Joseph, as will I. Joseph will be our messenger; more than a messenger—central to the success of our campaign. He will pass messages or themes that I want you to present over time." Pontius paused, appearing anxious to get across some of his ideas. "One of the first things I want to change is the deep irreverence towards taxes. We must instill an understanding of how necessary they are to provide stability for your people. And the image of the tax collector—the tax collectors we employ serve a critical role in collecting the revenues we need to support our presence. Among your people, they are looked down upon, even seen as traitors in some circles."

John took a deep breath, raising his eyebrows. "A simple desire, Your Nobility, but very difficult to instill. Tax collectors are seen as having direct connection to Roman authority and that, in itself, makes them evil in many eyes."

The three went on, discussing the details of John's role and the manner of his presentation. The next day, Joseph went with John to Bethany to search for a place to live.

13 ~ Some Trips Never End

Pontius read the note from Claudia. He could picture her face from the words on the page. It was times like these that he realized how much he missed her. So much had happened during his stay in Jerusalem that he had almost forgotten the amount of time that had lapsed. His days in Caesarea seemed a lifetime away—and so did Claudia. He felt uncomfortable with such thoughts and realized he needed to bring her to Jerusalem. Pontius felt he had accomplished a great deal, laying the groundwork for many plans, but still he had nothing to show for it—yet. To Claudia, Jerusalem would be a backward, old city. How could he explain to her that beneath the surface, it was changing—change that would take time, possibly years to fully realize? It would be impossible for him to wait that long to bring her here. Looking back, Pontius realized how foolish he had been, expecting change would happen faster.

Pontius called Tacitus to his office. "Do you have a date for completion of the aqueduct?" Pontius had taken several trips to inspect the progress, and to him it seemed painstakingly slow.

Tacitus shook his head. "It is still a few months away, Your Nobility. I am going there in a few days and should know more then. You are welcome to attend."

Pontius shook his head. "I will not be accompanying you this time. I have my own trip that I cannot bear to delay any longer."

Tacitus smiled. "To Caesarea?"

"You know me too well," Pontius said, a little surprised that Tacitus picked up on his intentions so quickly.

"I was wondering when you might be sending for her. You speak of her often, and when you do you always get this"—Tacitus paused—"*softer* tone in your voice." Then he smiled and added, "...and hopelessly glazed look in your eyes."

Pontius laughed. "What? Me speak softly! How can I as governor of these people? Sometimes I must think as their god to understand them."

"Oh, so now you're a god! When did you get promoted? Next thing you'll be telling me is you're going back to Rome as emperor!"

Pontius burst out laughing, appreciating Tacitus' casual nature. He also appreciated that Tacitus was not insisting upon his company to the aqueduct. Tacitus caught his breath and added, "You speak fondly of her, and I can tell you miss her. I know I'm glad to have my family here. I was wondering when I would finally meet Claudia. She must be a fine woman."

Pontius smiled and nodded. The more they talked about her, the more Pontius felt an urgent desire to see her again. He felt foolish realizing that perhaps he had underestimated her ability to adapt to Jerusalem. "Please assign a contingent of soldiers to accompany me to Caesarea tomorrow morning."

"That's very noble of you to go all the way to Caesarea to personally escort Claudia. Any other man would simply send for his wife," Tacitus said with an admiring smile.

As Pilate walked away, he stopped and turned back toward Tacitus. "Could you check that Barabbas is still in prison? I wouldn't want him leading our welcoming committee when we return."

* * *

Pontius sent a messenger to inform Claudia he was on his way. Again, the trip took several days, but this time he was more familiar with the land. Being late fall, the air was cooler and the winds were calm. Finally drawing near to Caesarea, the familiar shape of the buildings, the Roman architecture, and the cleanliness of the paved streets were a welcome sight. *Someday, Jerusalem will look like this—with or without Judean help.*

Riding up to his palace, Pontius dismounted, hoping Claudia was waiting inside. He could not bear the thought she might be away. As he walked through the gate, the front door flew open revealing her familiar silhouette. His pace quickened. Claudia ran from the door straight into Pontius' arms. As they embraced, Claudia felt so soft and delicate, he swore he would never part from her again. Pontius was overwhelmed by a feeling that permeated every ounce of his being. He was holding the body, soul, and life that could know no equal in his love. He squeezed her tighter and felt Claudia respond. Neither wanted the embrace to end, as each wished they could truly become part of the other. Finally, Claudia interrupted her tears, saying, "Oh, Pontius, I have missed you so. I never want to be away from you like this again."

Feeling her tears as he brushed against her cheek, Pontius backed off just enough to gaze into Claudia's eyes. Unable to find the words that could possibly express what he was feeling, Pontius kissed her, forgetting the entire world that loomed over him. He gently touched her face, wiping away the tears, enchanted by the soft texture of her skin. Pontius whispered, "I love you, Claudia." Caressing her shoulders, Pontius confided, "A friend told me that when I spoke of you, it was as if I were a different man. Even worlds apart, my love for you transcends distance and time—neither of which I ever want to grow so distant."

Claudia fell back softly into Pontius' arms and said, "I must go back with you to Jerusalem, Pontius. I could not bear to stay here without you any longer."

Pontius smiled, not expecting the subject of his trip to come up so soon. "My thoughts also, Claudia. Such is the purpose of my trip: to convince you to come back with me. I have waited this long only because I was concerned for your safety. I only hope you will like it there. It is not Caesarea, but I think its charms will grow on you. We will be living in Fortress Antonia. It is beautiful, with wonderful paintings and sculptures. The city itself has tremendous marketplaces where items from all over the world can be found."

With a reassuring expression, Claudia responded, "I don't care if it's the deserts of Egypt, I want to go with you, Pontius. I have not liked being apart from you this long. I thought those days were over."

"Those days *are* over. It was just a silly concern about your safety, Claudia. I would never forgive myself if anything happened to you."

Pontius held her close and gently caressed her shoulders. Barely letting her go, they turned and walked back into the palace. "I have made great progress in Jerusalem. I feel very comfortable bringing you there now. There is still a lot to be done to bring it up to the level of Caesarea, but the groundwork has been laid. Even now, my engineers are building a great aqueduct to the city in order to provide bathhouses for the people."

Pontius hesitated to tell Claudia about Joseph and John; he felt this would delve too deep into political work. He was wary of how the standards affair had affected her disposition, and not sure she would understand the brutality against the protesters of the aqueduct. He had to exercise discipline to keep her at arm's length regarding his political decisions. Diverting his thoughts, he went on to describe the city. "You will be fascinated by a palace built long ago by Herod the Great in honor of Rome. It is truly the most magnificent structure in all of Judea. One of Herod's sons has claimed the palace as his own. He is a vulgar man, surrounding himself with extravagance. He loves to throw dinner banquets. I am sure you will get to know the palace well." Pontius paused, seeing the gleam in Claudia's eyes at the mention of dinner parties and magnificent palaces. "Next to Fortress Antonia is a huge temple to the Jewish god. It is very old, hundreds of years, and it truly amazes me that they could have built such a massive and majestic structure so long ago." Cautious not to build things up too much, Pontius added, "But I have to warn you, most of the city is old and simple—almost dirty in a sense, certainly compared to Caesarea. The people will take some getting used to. Very few of them live up to the standards of even our servants."

Shaking her head, Claudia said, "It sounds like a strange mixture of wealth and poverty, luxury and bare minimums, religion and vulgarity. How do these people live with such contrasts all around them?"

* * *

For the trip back to Jerusalem, Pontius enlisted a wagon to carry Claudia and himself, as well as several other wagons to carry the bulk of their possessions. A few extra soldiers were taken to ensure greater security. Much to Pontius' relief, the entire trip went without incident.

On elevated terrain overlooking Jerusalem, Pontius pointed out the many features that were now familiar to him. Drawing Claudia's attention and pointing toward the city, Pontius proclaimed, "Jerusalem! You can see almost the entire city from here." Then, pointing a little towards the left to give her a reference point for Fortress Antonia, Pontius added, "Do you see the large structure, over on the left? That is the Jewish temple."

Claudia strained to pick out the building Pontius was referring to amongst the tangled mass of rock walls and structures. Instead, Claudia pointed towards higher ground, walled off from the rest of the city. "What is that area, with the large walls and towers?"

"Oh, that's Herod's palace," Pontius responded, somewhat disappointed.

"Herod's palace!" Claudia exclaimed. "I was hoping that was Fortress Antonia."

"No. Fortress Antonia is down to the left, next to the Jewish temple." Eventually, Pontius pointed out several areas of interest, providing a long-distance tour. He figured this tour was much more pleasant than the one up close.

Nearing the city, a crowd of spiritless onlookers gathered similar to the one that had welcomed him almost a year before. This time they were not crying out the name "Barabbas." They were more subdued with expressions of curiosity rather than animated voices of veiled defiance. Very little was said as they rode through the streets to Fortress Antonia. Pontius thought this highly inappropriate, for he felt the crowd should be cheering with open arms for such a wonderful woman gracing their city. Instead, it felt like a funeral march with all the peering eyes wishing to see a Roman wrapped in burial garb. Pontius shrugged off the insolent behavior, thinking that someday the people would change their ways, showing respect and admiration for Romans.

Helping Claudia down off the wagon, Pontius smiled and offered her his hand. "Welcome to your new home!"

All of the soldiers were dismissed, and the wagons carrying their possessions were taken in through a utility gate. Pontius and Claudia walked in through the front door, with a greeting from Marcellus: "Hail, Pontius Pilate! Welcome back, my lord. I presume this is your lovely wife Claudia."

Pontius noticed a subdued tone in his voice and realized the mood in

Fortress Antonia wasn't much better than the crowd of townspeople. Even though he was disappointed by Marcellus' somber attitude, Pontius returned his greeting. "Greetings, Marcellus. Yes, this is my wife." Pontius was starting to turn angry and agitated at the lack of fanfare for welcoming his wife. Trying to hide his disappointment in front of Claudia, Pontius whispered to Marcellus, "Why the somber mood and long faces amongst those milling about?"

Pilate recognized the emptiness of Marcellus' smile as Marcellus dropped his eyes away. "Sir, if I may, a word in private, my lord."

Marcellus' burdened eyes finally lifted to meet Pilate's. Pontius sensed something was desperately wrong. Without hesitation, he turned back toward Claudia. "A moment, Claudia. I need a brief word with Marcellus."

Marcellus pulled Pilate into the nearest room, being careful to whisper so Claudia wouldn't hear. In private, the smile on his face turned to pain. Afraid to hear Marcellus' words, Pontius finally grabbed him by the shoulders. "What is it? What news has you so bound that you cannot speak?"

Marcellus took full control of his senses and forced the words: "It's Tribune Tacitus, My Lord Pilate. He's dead."

Pilate's expression went blank and his body felt limp. He couldn't believe what he was hearing; in his mind it didn't make sense. His lungs seemed numb having difficulty pushing out the air to speak. Finally, with a forced breath, Pilate pleaded, "What?"

Tears finally dropped from Marcellus' flooded eyes. "Tacitus, my lord. He was killed two days ago, on his way back from inspecting the aqueduct."

Pilate let out a cry that could be heard for several rooms. He had grown to love Tacitus, and he could not believe that somehow he might actually be gone. Pilate fell back into a chair and placed his head in his hands, still not believing what he had heard. "He can't be dead! What happened? How did he die?"

Marcellus pulled himself together. "He was about fifteen miles out, my lord, and his group was attacked by zealots... a large group. They outnumbered his soldiers. Tacitus took a stray arrow and died instantly, my lord."

Pilate's face came out of his hands looking up at Marcellus. Marcellus' emotions faded in and out as he recounted the details. "One other soldier died, and the rest gave chase after the band. The zealots scattered into the hills, but the soldiers were able to kill three of them and capture another four."

With his disbelief turning to anger, Pilate shouted, "By the gods, how could this happen? Tacitus was a good man. These people don't realize what they've done! With an ignorant, stupid action, they have snuffed out the life of a man far greater than they will ever know!" Pilate's anger tumbled back into sadness. "And his family. How is Phaedra handling this? And his children?"

Marcellus shook his head slowly. "She is taking it pretty hard, my lord. She and her children have spent most of the time locked in their rooms. Several of the wives have visited them, but they do not wish to talk to anyone."

"Perhaps Claudia could go talk to her." But then Pontius paused, wondering if it would be appropriate. "Phaedra doesn't know Claudia; still it would be good for her. We cannot let her drift into isolation."

Pontius' compassion quickly returned to anger. "What of the prisoners?"

"They are in the prison cells here in Fortress Antonia, My Lord Pilate. We held them, waiting for your return."

Without hesitation and with strong meaning in his voice, Pilate grumbled, "I want them crucified. But first, I want them whipped and beaten in public so that they go to the cross in pain." Pilate stood up, adding, "I want it done now."

Marcellus hesitated. "Sir, at this moment?"

Pilate nodded. "Yes, now. The impudent gathering outside these walls will witness the swift judgment passed upon zealots, providing retribution for their rude welcome."

With that, Marcellus took leave to administer the execution of Pilate's order. Pilate went back into the hall, deciding not to mention the upcoming crucifixions to Claudia. He did not want to make things worse for Claudia's first moments in Jerusalem.

Claudia approached Pontius with sadness and tears in her eyes. "What has happened, my husband? It pains me to see you so." She paused and began sobbing lightly. "Before we entered this city, you were happy and eagerly describing the features we could see in the distance. Now, it is as if a beast had swallowed you as I heard you cry out."

The depth of her concern and sincerity compelled Pontius to confide in her. In a way, he had to tell her, for she was the only one who could begin to ease the pain crippling his soul. After relating the great injustice dealt upon the world that day, Pontius went on to tell her stories of a man he knew far too briefly.

14 ~ The Wilderness

John and Joseph entered an abandoned cabin, only a few hundred yards from the Jordan River. The area was fairly remote, about four miles north of Bethany. Joseph had the place stocked with food and enough furniture to provide a comfortable living. The area was very beautiful—green, full of trees and scattered underbrush. Less than a mile away, the land reverted back to the dry, rocky ground. The banks of the Jordan River were an oasis of life-giving water that ran through an otherwise harsh and unforgiving land. From the cabin, Joseph could just hear the pleasant sound of the river.

Joseph looked around, suggesting to John, "I think you'll find this place comfortable."

John took a deep breath, seeming to enjoy the fresh air. "Yes, I find it pleasant enough—more than I was expecting."

"I think I would rather have your job, John. All you have to do is sit out here and wait. You might be able to scrounge up time to relax every now and then," Joseph added, smiling.

John smiled back. "With the supply of bread, at least I won't need to scrounge for food. You have given me a role as teacher. At first, there will be few to listen, if it ever grows to more than that. Here we do not have a synagogue. It will take time to prepare what to say and how. I must find some way to address Pilate's concern of tax collectors. This will involve a few sleepless nights."

"I'll help you with that, John. Periodically I'll continue to meet with Pilate. I have no doubt he will have plenty of his own ideas. Until such time, we must concentrate on a basic subject, something that will draw people's attention."

"I know, let's talk about throwing off the bonds of the Roman Empire."

Joseph laughed. "Pilate will probably have something to say about that. Besides, that would make you no different than countless others scattered throughout this land." Joseph smiled and added, "We need to think of something a little more conservative."

John nodded, joining in Joseph's laughter. "I know, I know. But there could not be a better theme to draw hordes of those we must change." As their laughter subsided, John turned serious again. "Actually, I have thought of a message. We must start with a theme that is simple and basic in order to form an initial gathering. A common theme from prophets in the Scriptures is repentance of sins, preparing one's self for the judgment of the Lord. It is a recurrent theme that should work well for us. I know I have heard my father speak of it many times. It has an emotional, healing nature that tugs on the soul."

"Great, John. Actually, I was thinking along the same lines. While I'm here, I'll go over some of my ideas with you. When I get back to Jerusalem, I'll start spreading the news that you are teaching in the land of Elijah. Curiosity should develop to draw crowds. Then it will be up to you to keep their interest." Joseph looked firmly in John's eyes and said, "I have confidence in you, John. I have personally been fascinated by your thoughts and discussions. I think you will have the same effect on the people."

"I hope this to be true. For if not, this will be a short-lived experiment." Shrugging his shoulders, John continued, "I don't think it is contrary to the Jewish faith to live in mutual cooperation with Roman authority, especially since they let us fully practice our own Jewish customs and laws. There is no law that states we should hate and kill Romans."

Joseph nodded his head slowly.

For the rest of the morning, Joseph showed John the locations of the different supplies provided by Rome. There were even weapons for protection against any type of creature—human or otherwise. Rome had even provided animal traps to assist in food variety. Joseph reassured John that he would be resupplied periodically to keep his stores plentiful.

If he needed anything immediate, it was a short trip to Bethany.

As the day turned to early afternoon, Joseph said, "I need to leave soon so that I can reach Bethany before dark. If I may suggest, John, since you will be teaching out in the wilderness, you ought to dress the part. Plus, it will be turning cool soon, and we have provided you with this clothing." Joseph walked over and opened a chest near the bed. He pulled out a fur garment and held it up for John to see.

John walked over and touched the garment, asking, "Isn't this camel hair?" John shook his head with disapproval. "This will incite reproach among those who come. They know camel hair to be the garment of a prophet—a presumptuous display."

"No, no. I just think you must fit the part of living in the wilderness. It will make your presence here all the more convincing. I think as long as you're not claiming to be a prophet, then the people can think what they will. There will be nothing dishonest or misleading on your part."

Joseph noticed the disapproval building in John's demeanor. "Look, you don't have to wear the animal skins. It was just a suggestion. However, if you wear your normal clothing out here, that too will appear odd."

Joseph wasn't sure if he was getting through to John, or if John was detecting his true intentions. Starting to wonder if they were doing the right thing, Joseph added, "I only ask that you give it careful thought. I will leave them in your care. As for now, I must be getting back while there is daylight."

For the first time, fear tugged upon Joseph. There was so much riding on John's ability to play a convincing role. If the true nature of John's charge was revealed, it could uncover his own role. Trying his best to shrug off the thought, Joseph smiled and grasped John's arm in an affectionate gesture of farewell. "Take care of yourself, John. I am fortunate to have met you, and I've enjoyed spending these past few days with you. I will visit quite frequently to monitor progress and communicate Pilate's desires. Of course, you can always make your way back to Jerusalem if you need anything."

John offered a reassuring smile as the two embraced in a strong, emotional farewell.

* * *

Over the next few weeks, John became very familiar with the area around his new home. He also spent a great deal of time preparing messages he would share with the people—if they came. He grew a beard to better effect his upcoming role as teacher.

Joseph visited every couple of weeks just as he'd promised. Very little progress was reported over time. Finally, though, people started coming to find the man of whom word was spreading. As Pilate and Joseph had hoped and expected, John was a fine speaker, pleasing most who heard him. The crowds were sporadic at first, barely enough to report as progress to Pilate.

As John became familiar with his role and his surroundings, he became more comfortable wearing the clothes Joseph had provided. Some of his own clothes had started to wear thin due to the harsh treatment of living away from the city and repeated, frequent washings. As the weather cooled, the warm comfort of the insulated animal skins became a welcomed advantage.

One day, while speaking to a small group of people along the banks of the Jordan River, John noticed another crowd gathering on the opposite side. Seeing their predicament, he called out to them, "If you go upstream a ways, there is a place you can cross!" John motioned his arms up to the north, directing the people where they might go. He excused himself from his immediate company and proceeded up the banks to show them where to cross. A few of his company followed along. John yelled across again as they neared the point. "It is not much farther ahead! It only gets a little more than waist deep there, and it is not difficult to cross!"

As they reached the area, John motioned for them to cross. Some were reluctant to wade out into the river and John had to call out again, "There is nothing to fear! It is not very deep here! The water is not cold and the air is warm today! You shouldn't have any problems!" Noticing there were a few women in the group, and a few others who were still reluctant to enter, John waded out to offer assistance. "Come! I will help you!" As John reached the deepest part, some were already passing him by. John offered a warm greeting and welcoming smile to each person. He was flattered that these people would come this far to see him. John had a warm, positive sense about these people, although he knew Joseph and Pilate had been disappointed with the light numbers. John was beginning to sense that Joseph and Pilate were losing interest in the project, and he wasn't sure how much longer it would last. Joseph had been the main architect of his teachings, but John had interjected many of his own values and thoughts. His message deviated from the strict guidelines of Mosaic Law, which seemed to have a fresh appeal to the few who came. He appreciated the uniqueness of his position—a forum to impress his thoughts and desires on people willing to listen. He recognized that most who came had some type of need to be filled. John was beginning to appreciate the role his father played to the people of Nain with a strength he had never felt before.

Some who came were there out of curiosity, and John could immediately detect their motivation. They would not stay long as their superficial interest faded.

Looking up, John noticed one of the women who had entered the water. John smiled as she grew near. She responded with a quivering smile fighting a fearful anxiety as she inched her way through the soft current. As John offered his hand, the woman reached for his—and then suddenly slipped and went straight into the water. She let out a brief scream before she vanished. John immediately reached under the water, feeling frantically for her, eventually grabbing an arm. As he pulled her out of the water, the woman gasped for air—more out of surprise than for lack of oxygen. She clung tightly to John as he led her to the bank. Several onlookers gathered as they came out of the river. Water was still dripping from her nose and face as John asked, "Are you all right?"

The woman looked up through wet strands that snaked across her face. A shaking expression of shock relaxed to a broadening, beautiful smile. Soon they were both laughing at the unexpected turn of events. The woman wiped the hair away from her face and muttered, "I was in need of a bath anyway." Her lightheartedness brought everyone to laughter. The newcomers exchanged greetings with those already present. With her words, John remembered Pilate's odd biddings. Taking advantage of the opportunity, John said, "Now that your body is clean, we must also provide the same care for the soul."

Seeing that his statement attracted everyone's attention, John continued, "In the same way that a body can be cleansed by dipping into the water, so is it with the spirit! In the same simple way that one can wash off the dirt and soil from the body, so can the sins of the spirit be washed away—cleansed by repentance!"

The laughter slowly subsided, and everyone's attention was on John. Seeing the effect of his words, John spoke with renewed feeling: "In the same way a man must take action to wash away the dirt, so must a man take action to wash away the sins of the spirit. If a man chooses not to cleanse himself, then he will stay dirty. If a man chooses not to repent, then his spirit will remain gripped by sin—forever turned away from the grace of God!"

A silence fell upon the crowd, waiting for his next words. John was greatly moved by the accidental illustration of a message he had been trying to convey. He waded back into the water, motioning for all to follow. Some started splashing water on themselves, cleansing away the symbolic sins that spoiled their souls. Some even started crying, overcome with emotion. One cried out to John, "What does it mean to repent? What must I do to cleanse my soul?"

John felt strong compassion for the man. "I can help you cleanse your soul from sin! I can teach you what it means to repent." Grabbing the man by the hand and leading him out into deeper water, John said, "In the same way that I can help you cleanse your body..."—John started taking handfuls of water, pouring it over the man's head and shoulders—"I can help cleanse your spirit of sin."

The man immersed himself completely under the water. Somewhat surprised by the intensity of his action, John reached under and brought the man back up. Even with the water drenching his hair and face, John saw the tears streaming from his eyes. John placed his arms around the man and said, "Even with this action, I can see you have repented. I know the Lord is filled with compassion and has forgiven you of your sins."

Tears still streaming from his eyes, the man looked up at John. "Thank you, Master. I can't express what I'm feeling inside. Is this what it means to be cleansed in spirit?" The man embraced John and soon, all of the others were walking out into the water to be cleansed. One by one, John started pouring water over the people. Just as the first had done, they immersed themselves, and John would pull them up, giving them each consoling words on God's willingness to accept even the worst of sinners through the simple act of repentance.

15 ~ From the Water Sprang Life

Word spread quickly throughout all of Judea and Perea of John's cleansing ritual. He quickly became known as John the Baptist, coming from the word *baptize*, which means to dip or cleanse in water. Great throngs traveled from near and far to hear John speak and to be cleansed by him in the Jordan River. To John's surprise, he soon had to deal with an influx of tithes insisted upon by the countless visitors day to day. The members of his flock had no way of knowing of his worldly support. With time, John found it easier to accept the tithes rather than continually deny their persistent offering. This also meant Joseph had something to take back to Jerusalem, which Pilate perceived as justified, but a mere pittance compared to that owed Rome.

In his teachings John emphasized righteousness, rather than strict adherence to Mosaic Law, as an approach that would ease the population's attitudes towards Roman authority.

* * *

John's increased popularity and the large crowds sparked renewed attention from Pilate. One day John was surprised to see Pilate accompanying Joseph as they entered through his doorway. John immediately stood and practically knocked the chair out from under him. "Noble Prefect! I wasn't expecting you! It's truly good to see you again!"

Pilate walked over and offered a cordial greeting. "I hope you are in good health, John."

"Yes, Noble Prefect, I am in good health. Peace to you, sir." In a near state of shock, John continued, "I'm not sure if I'm more surprised to see you or your common attire!" Even with Pilate's warm greeting, John sensed something was missing—a spark that had always been in his eyes and in his voice. John suspected it was the death of Tacitus. "I'm sorry to have heard about Tribune Tacitus, Your Nobility. May the Lord comfort you for the horrible loss of a good man and friend."

Pontius shrugged off John's condolences, heightening a peculiar sense that hung in the air. Expressionless, Pontius nodded. "It was a deplorable act." Pontius paused, with John and Joseph waiting for him to continue. Instead, Pontius changed the subject. "I have heard great things about you, John. It sounds like you are drawing tremendous crowds. I can honestly say I've seen a tendency toward a..."—Pontius paused again—"calming of the spirit in the people of Jerusalem." Pontius smiled and added, "Or maybe it's just because they are all coming out here to see you."

John and Joseph's laughter was short-lived as Pilate lost his smile and continued with business. "I heard about your cleansing ritual. That was brilliant, John. It really seems to have attracted attention."

John smiled and nodded his head slightly at Pilate's compliment. Pilate's serious expression softened. "I just didn't expect you to take me so literally about bathing in the Jordan River."

John chuckled under his breath. "Actually, it all happened quite by accident." John explained the incident in the river and how the woman had slipped. "Now, it's become quite overwhelming. Every week, there are dozens of new people coming out, growing into the hundreds, and all of them want to be cleansed in the river. I have resorted to cleansing only once, unless they really press for it again. The task is quickly becoming too much for one man. I am going to need help." John paused, seeing their quizzical expressions. "There are a couple of people I have met already who have expressed a strong desire to offer their service in God's work."

"Help?" Joseph interrupted. "How well do you know these men?"

"I have only just met them, but they seem like good men with good intentions. Their names are Andrew and James, both from Bethsaida on the Sea of Galilee."

Joseph gave a cautious, questioning look towards Pilate. Pilate gave a reassuring nod, and Joseph turned back to John. "Your idea may have merit, John. Just don't tell them very much."

John shook his head. "Oh, I wouldn't think of it. They have no need to know about support from Rome. They are just involved with the ministry, helping with the cleansing..." John paused before it came out, the word *ritual* grinding in his thoughts. What had started out as being a very strong, emotional experience to illustrate a point *was* becoming a ritual. He had repeated the act thousands of times, and to him, it had become an action losing most of its meaning. He could not recapture the deep emotion those few had experienced on the first day. Still they kept coming. John justified it, in his own mind, as an act that helped illustrate a point—a point that many people still wanted to learn.

Before John could continue with his argument for additional help, Pilate inserted a question. "Have you talked about tax collectors, as I originally asked?"

John felt a little embarrassed by Pilate's pointed question. "Well, no, Noble Prefect. I haven't found a way to work tax collectors into my sermons."

John felt somewhat insulted that Pilate, despite his remarkable success, had quickly highlighted a shortcoming. Interceding, Joseph suggested, "I have thought of a way to support tax obedience into your teaching, John." Both John and Pilate turned their attention toward Joseph. "We could have tax collectors visit John. Many would witness John cleansing them in the river, offering a type of acceptance to their profession."

Pilate immediately shook his head. "No, Joseph. Acceptance? It will do just the opposite! It will make their work appear sinful, as if they were in need of cleansing."

Joseph quickly replied, "John has told me, some have asked what they must do to better themselves in the eyes of God. When the tax collector approaches, simply tell him, 'Collect no more than is appointed.' This will be an indirect license for the commissioned amount, while commanding discipline in their course. Given the size of your growing audience, such sanction will reach many ears."

A near-imperceptible smile appeared on Pilate's hardened face, and he finally offered a slight nod. "I will talk to officials back in Jerusalem and have them make arrangements."

John let out a concerned sigh. He felt wary of expressing a thought that might appear contrary to his teachings. "A main theme of my teachings has been repentance of sin, promising not to continue in such a life once one has been cleansed. The people will expect me to tell them to turn away from their profession and collect no more taxes."

Seeing a slight look of disgust appear on Pilate's face, Joseph quickly interrupted again. "You forget, John. We are not trying to imply the tax collector's work is wrong or sinful, as you put it. We are offering public notice to their work, making their profession appear more acceptable."

John felt hesitant, realizing the practice would not fare well. John shook his head in an apparent sense of refusal. Taking a firmer tone, Joseph continued, "Look, John, you agreed in the beginning that taxes played an important, proper role in supporting the Roman government. You understood that first we must gain their hearts and confidence before introducing concepts that at first may seem contrary to traditional ways— reversing destructive forces building in this country. Would you prefer a heavier hand from the Roman Empire if anarchical forces grow unchecked?"

John understood the reality of such a threat and how vulnerable their people would be to the legions of Rome. Softening his tone, Joseph continued, "Now that we have the confidence of the masses, now that we have their attention... we cannot shy away from the purpose we agreed upon in the beginning."

John was caught off guard. Over the months he had grown accustomed to his non-confrontational role as teacher and he had grown confident with the multitudes that looked to him for guidance. John felt justifiably cornered in his changing attitude. Nervous, John responded, "No, I'm not changing my mind. I suppose you're right. I have developed a strong following. If they hear such a statement, it will go far toward justifying the role of tax collection."

Joseph looked up at the ceiling, letting out a sigh of relief.

Undaunted, Pilate pressed on. "The same should go for Jewish soldiers. We need more of your people volunteering to serve in the military, to assist in our campaigns against the Persians. When these soldiers approach, I want you to offer public acceptance so that all may hear." Pontius paused in thought and added, "Warn them not to take the spoils of war."

Every word from Pilate's mouth seemed crazier than the last. John smirked under his breath and exclaimed in disbelief, "The spoils of war!"

"Yes! The spoils are meant for Roman soldiers. We need the spoils to supplement the taxes we aren't receiving from your people! There are regiments of Jewish soldiers who have started seizing spoils for themselves, and it has to stop!" Pilate's voice became angrier. "And tell them to be satisfied with the wages they receive."

Pilate said it with such forcefulness that neither John nor Joseph offered words of disagreement. John wanted to argue about going too far, too fast, but held his tongue.

As Pilate had directed, so it happened. Tax collectors and Jewish soldiers visited John, being cleansed by him in the river. When John openly proclaimed the legitimacy of their professions, many in the crowd would leave in protest.

Andrew and James' assistance proved to be invaluable as the crowds grew steadily in number. Even though John, Andrew, and James had resorted to only baptizing people once, their task took the better part of an hour every day to cleanse newcomers. The cleansing cultivated a passion, offering the people a distinct identity with a greater whole while bringing the whole closer to God. It overshadowed the ironic attention given to two scorned professions.

John suddenly found himself facing growing opposition. The swelling crowds caught the attention of the court of the high priest, raising suspicion of the power behind John's teachings. One day, while getting ready to preach to a large crowd, a man approached John. He was a Sadducee, strongly devoted to strict observance of Mosaic Law. The Sadducee yelled out so that others could hear, "How is it that you can survive here in the wilderness? Even with the shelter of your cabin, there is not enough food for a man to survive!" The Sadducee's face twisted into a sneer. "Do you live by eating the weeds and the locusts?!" With that, several in the crowd began snickering.

Taken aback by such an abrupt and unexpected attack, John was speechless for a moment, knowing he could not give the true answer. He had anticipated such an inquiry with a carefully planned answer, but the man's abruptness caught him off guard. Before John could answer, the Sadducee turned to the crowd. "Everyone knows that the wilderness is filled with demons. It is the land of wild beasts who serve the demons to destroy man. This is not holy land, like the temple in Jerusalem. And this man," pointing at John, "is a servant of demons!"

Feeling he needed to say something, John thought of food he had found on the land. "I do not serve the demons of the wilderness! I serve God! The demons of the wilderness do not provide hospice for my stay! There is food on this land. I have consumed honey, and yes, some locusts, of which there are plenty for a man to survive!"

John was not completely lying, for he had eaten honey during the early days exploring the area and scrounging for food on days when his supplies ran low. However, he felt deceitful not telling the full truth of his sustenance.

Seeming to ignore John's response, the Sadducee continued his attack, turning his attention back to John. "By what authority do you invoke this new cleansing ritual on the people?" As if to answer his own question, the Sadducee continued, "By the authority of the demons you serve! The Scriptures already list the rituals required by Mosaic Law! Rituals commanded by God for his chosen people. How is it that *you* command this new ritual upon the people?"

John took offense to the man's attack. "No! It is not a ritual, sir! It is a simple act demonstrating a parallel with cleansing the soul through repentance! It shows reverence toward God, preparing one's self to serve Him."

The man immediately responded, "It has the very appearance of a ritual! A ritual one must perform to enter your fold!"

At this point, the crowd began heckling the man, openly annoyed with his continuous attacks. John shot back, "No, the people do not need to be cleansed in the river to gain remission of their sins. Only repentance and a commitment to sin no more can serve that purpose! They do not need to be cleansed in the river to join my fold. I have no fold! I am simply a teacher, teaching repentance in preparation for the final judgment of the Lord. The people partake of being cleansed in the river of their own free will! It is a service I do for them to demonstrate how easy it is to cleanse your own spirit by the simple act of repentance—an act that I am willing to help you understand, as your servant."

The Sadducee was clearly not convinced by John's words, and did not waiver. Before he could get out another word from a pulpit he seemed unwilling to relinquish, a group of men forced him away.

After his sermon, even though he had clearly won in the confrontation with the Sadducee, John was troubled that the attack was from a religious man ordained by Mosaic Law. He was also troubled that he had hidden the truth regarding his survival in the wilderness. The man had made an accurate observation, and humiliated for it. In a way, John felt compassion for him, but it was impossible for John to rectify his position.

This incident only added to the other points that had started to rankle him, like the constant reference to the cleansing as a ritual, and his frequent and repeated staging of tax collectors and Jewish soldiers. John was beginning to identify more with the crowds who came to listen than with Pilate and Joseph. He started feeling like he was betraying the people through his hidden relationship with Roman authority. The conflict raged in his mind, becoming unbearable at times. John resorted to frequent fasting to punish himself for the role he had grown to resent.

The hardship of fasting offered John contrition that helped him deal with the unending dissonance. All of this served to make him appear more righteous, which in turn served to increase the number of people who perceived John as a blessed teacher, ordained by God. Some even saw him as a prophet, or Elijah himself, come down from heaven—a rumor that took on a life of its own, despite John's disapproval.

John, however, did not let his growing role swell his self-image. He always felt he was doing good for the people, helping them be more at peace with a situation that had been forced upon them long ago. He did not like the killing and rebellious nature of the zealots, for he felt it served no purpose in the day-to-day lives of the common people.

The clerical attacks became more frequent and intense. John understood their attacks, but strongly disagreed. However, John perceived the ill effect it was having on his followers. Sometimes their stares seemed to show discontent or even anger—replacing the interest and wonderment from months before. John had not anticipated the opposition and attacks from the Jewish religious order, which only added to the discord growing inside. The conflict brewed his own distrust for many who would gather, beyond the priests and Sadducees. John began to question whether each and every person was another tax collector or soldier sent by Joseph, or perhaps a spy from the Jewish council to build a case for blasphemy.

On one occasion, after having spoken to a very large group, a priest who had been sent from Jerusalem came up to John and asked, "Who are you?"

John stared at the man with a puzzled look. "I am John, John of Nain. Why do you ask?"

The priest's demeanor turned impatient. "I know your name is John and you are of Nain, but who are you, really?"

John's puzzled look grew more intense. "What do you mean, 'Who am I, really?'?"

The priest pointed an accusing finger at John's clothing. "You wear the garments of Elijah, in the land where Elijah was taken up into heaven." With arrogant sarcasm he asked, "Are you Elijah come down from heaven? Are you a prophet?"

John sensed the rhetorical tone and the man's attempt to provoke anger from the crowd. Quickly trying to avert misunderstanding, John replied, "No! I am not a prophet! I am not Elijah!" John was disgusted by the open and abrupt provocation. Turning back toward the crowd, he called out, "Hear my words! I have heard rumors about who people say that I am! I am not a prophet! I am not Elijah! I am not the Messiah! I am just a man, teaching how to walk a straighter path with God!"

Seeing the look of disappointment appearing on many faces, John sensed the misconception, and who they expected him to be. John's brewed, defensive anger spilled over onto the crowd—an anger that none could have known was fueled from many angles. "You are a race of spiteful people! Do not presume self-importance or worthiness for simply being descendants of Abraham. Such attitudes are hideous sins in the eyes of God from which you must repent! I tell you, God can raise up people more worthy than yourselves from these very stones! If you do not repent, you will be cut down and thrown into the fire!" John could see the shock on everyone's faces, matching the sudden intensity of rage that was welling inside. Shaken over what he had said, but more concerned for what might still transpire, John turned and walked away, leaving everyone in deathly silence.

* * *

The word of John's actions reached Jerusalem. Pontius called for Joseph to meet at Fortress Antonia. Pontius sensed that Joseph was also dumbfounded as he walked into the governor's chamber. "What is John doing?" Pontius asked with an angry tone.

Joseph shrugged his shoulders. "I have been noticing discontent in John's behavior."

"But he has accomplished so much, and the fact that some consider him a prophet is remarkable. His role is starting to mature just as we had hoped."

"Yes, but after a long, slow start. With his recent popularity has come focused attention from the council, and scrutiny from the religious order. They question the basis of his authority."

Pontius shook his head. "I am not worried about your priestly order. Many of your people look at priests with suspicion, and we want to build on that. The masses love John. He is a great man, and a great leader. The more your priests and scribes openly criticize him, the more 'discontent and disillusion'—as you put it—grows for their authority, not John's."

"You're right, sir. John is a good man, charismatic, and loved by all who hear him. But he has a weakness of character. Sometimes I think he is too honest, and too caring—at odds with his ability to lead."

"Too caring!" Pilate exclaimed. "A leader cares about his men."

Joseph nodded. "But he cares too much about how they, everyone, perceives him."

Pilate's face twisted in disgust. "Insulting those gathered is hardly caring about what they think of him! I think his newfound power is going to his head. The masses adore him, and *they* are looking to him as a prophet. His open denial is beyond reprieve! How can we hope to depose Antipas if he misses opportunities like this? John needs to be reminded from whence his power comes." Pontius paced back and forth, quickening his steps with growing anger. "Send for him at once!"

16 ~ Wishing for Less

Marcellus helped Claudia into an ornate, veiled carriage that delicately bowed to her gentle weight on the step. Claudia felt a sense of excitement as the front gates of Fortress Antonia opened as if to release her from the confines of a walled prison. The cushioned ride through the gates turned to awkward rocking as the carriage and accompanying escort proceeded into the narrow streets of the city. As the wheels met rocks and potholes, Claudia grabbed a rail to steady herself. She pulled back the curtains to reveal buildings more ancient than she had imagined, with many of the walls crumbling in disrepair. She wondered if people were inside or if they'd been abandoned long ago. Ahead she could see people milling about in the streets, but as she passed they seemed to disappear, except for a few children that were following along at a cautious distance. The scene was quite different from Caesarea, and she became disheartened as she began to doubt she could like Jerusalem, or even tolerate it.

The number of children following the procession kept growing, with an occasional parent rushing in to pull a child out of the mix. The children were laughing and cheerfully chanting in playful song. Claudia called for the driver to stop as she opened the small door and stepped out. Their playful nature abruptly ended as several of the children screamed and ran. Several others remained, but backed off in fearful silence in bonds of curiosity. Claudia waved to the children and called out with a welcoming smile, "Don't be afraid!" But the children backed off further, preparing to run.

Claudia reached into the carriage and pulled out fine fabric with intricate, colorful designs. "Here, this is for you." Claudia motioned for the soldiers to move and make a path for the children.

Several of the children's eyes lit up as smiles returned to their faces. With continued coaxing, the children approached and reached out to touch the fabric. Claudia's kind, nurturing smile had its effect on the children as they became more at ease. The fabric seemed to tickle their fingers as they giggled, daring others to reach in.

A young boy climbed onto the step of the carriage as a soldier grabbed him by the shoulder, pulling him down. Claudia turned and cried out, "No! It's all right." She motioned for the soldier to move back as she helped the boy back onto the step. Claudia pulled back the curtain for him to peer inside. Soon all of the children were tightly gathering around Claudia, jumping with excitement, pleading for their turn.

Claudia flinched as she heard a woman screaming for her child and saw her running towards them. One of the guards jumped in front of the woman, while another grabbed her, holding her back. Her cries became frantic as she motioned towards one of the children and began beating her breast. The horses reared, causing the carriage to surge back, with the front wheel rolling over another child. The child cried out in pain as he tried to roll free. The wheel lurched forward as the horses came back down, running over him again. A soldier grabbed the horses, steadying them. Claudia reached down to help the boy to his feet, his face wrenched in pain.

The mother broke her grip from the shocked soldiers as she ran up to another child and scolded him, slapping at him to leave. Then she ran over and helped Claudia pull the injured boy from underneath the carriage. She called out to several children, directing them to lift the boy and carry him off. With the boy's screams fading down the narrow streets, Claudia began crying as she climbed back into the carriage. She used the delicate cloth to wipe away her tears, wishing she had never presented it to attract the children. Claudia sighed as she folded it neatly and placed it on the seat beside her. The sound of the boy's screams was gone, as well as the children's laughter. Claudia put her hand on her chest and suddenly realized her pendant was gone! Claudia gasped and then looked out into the empty streets. Her eyes raced back and forth from inside to outside. She frantically patted around the seats hopelessly searching for the necklace, finally realizing it was gone. She fell back and started crying again. Wiping away her tears, she called out to the driver, "Take me back."

Claudia clinched the tear-soaked cloth pressing it against her chest. *How was she going to tell Pontius?* She realized she could never tell Pontius. He was different since Tacitus' death and she did not want to add to his anguish. *What good would it do? He probably doesn't even remember the necklace.* Claudia pulled back the curtain and threw the cloth out into the empty street.

* * *

Entering Jerusalem, John attempted to conceal his identity. He knew if he had announced his visit, there would be throngs cheering him as he walked through the streets. Instead there was no notice—a state he was beginning to prefer over the entangled mess of his role as John the Baptist.

It had been several months since he had made the same entrance with his father. Things seemed so much simpler then, and John yearned for those days. With each building he passed, the urge became stronger to return to his former life. John had come to Jerusalem with the intention of telling Pilate and Joseph he did not want to continue in his role, and he hoped they would understand. His life could never be the same, but he hoped the frenzy over his role would fade with time.

John first went to Joseph's home to let him know he had arrived. Upon entering the house, John was met by Joseph's wife, Matheshia, whom he had met several times before on his previous stays. Matheshia greeted John with an enthusiastic smile. "You have become very famous, John. It honors me that I knew you before all of this. I have asked Joseph many times if we could go to the Jordan River, and his reply is always the same: 'Some day.'"

"Yes, yes, some day. But for now, John is with us seeking quiet, private time, away from his ministries. It is important we tell no one, to allow him his rest."

With a caring smile Matheshia replied, "Of course." As she looked back towards John her expression saddened. "Forgive me. I did not notice the weariness in your eyes. Please place your things in the room to the left." As John walked away, Matheshia leaned over to Joseph and whispered, "His eyes are more than weary—I see despair. I have never seen him like this."

During dinner, after John had rested for several hours, Matheshia brought up the latest gossip—too irresistible to ignore in conversation. "Antipas divorced Phasaelis out of lust for another woman. He is a disgusting, foolish man! He nurtured an adulterous desire for his niece, Herodias. Not only is she his kin, but she is also his half-brother's wife!" Matheshia shook her head in disbelief, sharing a feeling held by most throughout Judea. "Since Philip is still alive, isn't it a sin?"

Joseph nodded. "Yes, according to our law, he is living in sin. To make matters worse, his ex-wife's father is a very powerful man, Aretas, king of the Perean Arabs. There is news he has waged war against Antipas." Joseph leaned over to John and whispered, "This makes your role even more important. Pilate gloats at every word of Antipas' demise."

John looked away from Joseph's inquisitive eyes. He wondered if he should tell his friend. But John understood Joseph's point, and this did not seem the right time to reveal his desire to end those dreams. It would have to wait until they were with Pilate.

Every mention of Antipas' name brought a noticeable look of disgust on John's face. It was common for people to dislike Antipas, particularly those involved in priestly duties. Finally, John mumbled to himself, "Antipas is an idiot."

Matheshia paused, noticeably surprised. John's words were true, but he had never been so abrasive in front of her. Joseph motioned for Matheshia to leave the room. After she had left, Joseph looked at John with a sense of urgency and said, "John, you have to be careful about what you say. It's without risk for my wife to make such comments, but in your position, you have to be careful."

John acknowledged Joseph's warning, but inside gave it little meaning, knowing his plans.

* * *

The next day, John and Joseph met with Pilate. Pilate grumbled as they walked in. The timing of their meeting was not good: Pilate was disgruntled with news that Aretas was massing a large army in the east.

The greeting from Pilate was less than cordial, which heightened the apprehension among the three. Pilate started off, not as a friend, but as a commander looking for an explanation for insubordination. "I called you here to find out what is going on. First, I hear you give a less-than-enthusiastic response to the taxmen and soldiers we have sent. Then you deny an opportunity to advance your position, your influence, and your power over these people. They're the ones who have given you this privilege. They're the ones who think of you as a prophet. The rumors have spread throughout all of Judea, John. It was right there." Pilate reached out as if to grab the metaphorical fruit. "All you had to do was reach out and take it!"

Showing deep concern, John responded, "That's the problem, Noble Prefect. People think of me as more than I am. I feel that I am living a lie, and I am finding it difficult to continue with such deception." John paused, turning his gaze to the ground in despair. "Several days ago a man brought his sick wife. She was very ill and in great pain. I don't think she even knew where she was. I wanted to help her, but there was nothing I could do. I didn't even know what was wrong with her. The husband and another man, possibly their son, had carried her a great distance. They had such strong faith believing I could help her." A tear came to John's eye as he gave a slight tremble. "I prayed over her. I found myself believing, with a strength of will I had never known before, that through God's mercy she could be spared her pain and suffering. I held her hand and talked to her. I don't even know if she heard me." John placed his hands over his face. "I don't know if I am haunted more by her pain and suffering, or by the looks on their faces when I finally told them there was nothing I could do. It was the saddest, deepest disappointment I have ever experienced."

Pontius couldn't help but be moved by John's emotions. However, he thought John was taking it too hard. He didn't see John as having been the source of the woman's pain, and he felt John was holding guilt over something for which he had no control. Finding it difficult to relate completely with John's ordeal, and not expecting this type of behavior, Pontius realized the discussion was not going as he had planned. Joseph was speechless. Pontius tried to offer some consolation, but felt he was fighting a losing battle with someone for whom he had strong hopes. "Comfort your thoughts, John. It's not your fault that people suffer. I'm not asking you to take on the burden of the world. If they think of you as a prophet, then that's their fault. You should be flattered by their high regard and not worry about things you cannot control."

John looked up to meet Pilate's consolation, then turned to Joseph. He brought his hands up, forcing them through his hair as he let out a heavy sigh. "I no longer wish to serve in this manner. I ask to be released of my duties to you, and to Rome."

Whatever compassion had been on Pilate's face quickly disappeared as he looked straight at John. John's eyes shifted off to one side. Pilate then looked over at Joseph, as his expression changed to disappointed shock. Immediately turning back, Pilate shouted, "You can't simply forfeit such responsibility!"

Pilate quickly eased his tone, taking on a more conciliatory note. "You've made such important progress. You have a great many people who depend on you, John. You made a commitment to carry through with plans that cannot and will not be taken lightly."

John shook his head. "I honestly didn't expect it would go this far. I certainly didn't expect that I would deceive people, like I feel I am. I had a simple, good life before all of this started, and I want it back."

Pilate shifted his feet irritably. His plans were starting to crumble before him, after it seemed they were well on their way to creating real change in Judea. "You can't have your old life back! Everywhere you go, people will know who you are, and wonder why you gave up." Pilate's impatience grew into anger. "What are you going to tell them?! What will you tell the thousands who travel to see you? *Forget everything I have taught you! Go back to living the way you were! I am!* You are not thinking clearly, John! You are not weighing the consequences of your actions."

As the meeting was getting out of control, Joseph quickly interjected, "Surely someone else could carry on with John's work."

John gave Joseph a thankful nod, adding, "Yes, I can think of a few people who would love to be in my position."

Joseph nervously asked, "Are you speaking of Andrew and James?"

John shook his head. "No, they are excellent help, and they are very committed to the ministries, but they know nothing of the cooperation with Rome. I'm afraid if they did know, it would not sit well with their convictions. They have a distaste toward Roman authority, although milder than others."

Pontius turned his astonished attention from John back to Joseph. "Do you presume my acceptance? I haven't agreed with finding someone else to carry on with this work. I don't know where you are getting your ideas, Joseph. I don't think it will be that simple. John has worked long and hard for a rapport with the people that can't just be assumed by someone else!"

John's expression became stern. "Well, maybe *you* don't have a choice."

Joseph's eyes widened, fixed on Pilate with a fearful stare. Pontius took John's statement as an insult that burned inside, but held back his anger. He realized if he lost his temper, he might lose what little was left of his plans. Somehow, Pontius calmed his outward appearance, hiding the anger building inside. He changed his tone, addressing John: "You could be right. If you feel you can't handle it, then it's time to leave." Sarcastically, Pontius added, "How do you suppose to pick another to rule in your stead? If you were a king and you had children, then one would stand to inherit your throne. However, you are neither a king nor do you have children. So what do you propose we do?"

John's expression tightened in response to Pilate's belittling tone. "I have a cousin in Nazareth, who like myself, has always had a favorable attitude toward Romans. I have known him since we were children. We are nearly the same age. He's a good man, and I think he is more than willing to take on this role."

Pontius gave John a suspicious look. "How can you be so sure? What if he dislikes what he hears, and decides to expose the whole thing?"

John fidgeted slightly in his chair and nervously cleared his throat. "I've already discussed it with him and he's expressed a willingness to help."

Joseph brought his hand up to his forehead and mumbled, "May God have mercy."

Pilate's anger had built to a threshold that was ready to spill over, drowning anyone in its wake. If this had been one of his soldiers, he would have killed him right there for insubordination and revealing military secrets. It was treason under Roman law to be so free with one's tongue when ordered to keep a secret. Holding back the best he could, yet with a tone that bordered on disgust, Pilate responded, "You were right about not having a choice." Pilate paused, trying to think what needed to be done next. Finally, Pilate continued, "Tell your cousin I want to meet him. What's his name?"

"His name is Jesus," John replied.

"Well, then tell Jesus I want to see him," Pilate retorted.

After John had left the room, Joseph looked at Pilate and said, "For an instant I thought you were going to strike him or worse."

Pontius shook his head unconvincingly, turning away. "No." Then, turning back Pontius added, "If I had, it would have been better he turn the other cheek. Better to be struck again, than serve an unforgiving blade."

Noticeably shocked, Joseph reacted, "You speak of him as some type of slave, and not a servant of Rome. Only a slave would show such submission."

Pontius mustered a perverted smile. "Something I think your people could stand to learn."

Fear oozed from Joseph's expression as he backed away towards the door, anxiously bowing to dismiss himself.

Pontius could not simply let John abandon his commission. Insubordination could not go unpunished. He also feared that John's lack of discipline and loose talk would eventually reveal his involvement with Joseph's position on the Jewish council.

* * *

Joseph planned for Jesus to come to Jerusalem to meet with Pilate. However, rumors were quickly spreading that John was in the city. The rumors drew more attention than if he had appeared publicly. The hearsay fell in line with his mysterious absence from the Jordan River. In order to avoid further attention, Pilate decided to have the meeting with Jesus take place up north.

As John headed for the gates of Jerusalem, some people recognized him and followed for a short distance. John noticed he was being shadowed by several people, but he wasn't in the mood for hosting a gathering. The streets of Jerusalem seemed strange to him compared to his forum on the banks of the river. Eventually someone called out, "It's John the Baptist! I know it is. I've seen him on the Jordan River!" His words were like a spark that drew everyone's attention as they rushed over to John. One man grew near, looking closely at John's face, asking in a quavering voice, "Are you John the Baptist?"

John reluctantly removed his hood and said, "Yes, I am John. And who might you be, sir?"

The man looked down. "I am Absalom. I have a farm just outside the city, Master."

John shook his head. "Do not refer to me as such. I am just a man. I promise you, there is one to come after me who is much greater than I, one whose sandals I am not fit to tie. I am not the deliverer who people seek; I am only a man commissioned by God to speak of things to come." Catching himself, for he did not want the people to think of him as a prophet, John recalled a verse from the Scriptures: "I am but a voice, crying in the wilderness, preparing the way for one to come who is greater than I."

With a look of surprise, the man said, "I heard you speak near the Jordan River, and you are truly blessed by God—more than just a man."

John smiled. "Blessed? Maybe. But a man? Definitely. I have spoken the simple truth of righteousness, the need for man to repent in order to turn away from the sins of the world, and to take up a more intimate walk with God. If you prepare yourself through repentance, it pleases God, and he will make straight your path to heaven."

The gathering crowd turned deathly silent, waiting for the expected, impassioned sermon. However, John was hesitant to speak further, knowing the long journey ahead. Trying to excuse himself, he pleaded, "I have a long way to go today, and I must be on my way." John bowed and proceeded toward the gates. Another man pressed further, "Why have you come to Jerusalem?"

John stopped and turned to face the crowd. "I have come to visit friends." John felt relieved he was able to give an explanation as a common man. "I have been to Jerusalem many times, and I am sure I will be back many times to come."

Another man cried out, "Have you heard of Antipas' marriage to Herodias? Have you not come to Jerusalem to chastise Antipas? There are many of us who are sickened by his actions, but there is nothing we can do about it. Someone should tell him what he is doing is wrong—someone like you. Surely he is not immune to the judgment of the Lord!" Many of those present started talking amongst themselves, nodding their heads in agreement.

John had no desire to get into a public discussion about what he thought of Antipas. Besides, he remembered Joseph's warning. Keeping his answer simple, John stated, "Antipas' marriage to his half-brother's wife is clearly unlawful. My message has always been to those who will listen, those who want to learn how to cleanse their spirit from the bonds of sin. It is not my position to teach those who will not listen or to give guidance to those who think they need no help." Many people in the crowd appeared puzzled. They waited, as if expecting a much bolder statement. John pulled his hood over his head and continued on his way.

As the news of his judgment spread, many of John's words were exaggerated to fit the purposes of those relaying witness. Rumors spread quickly throughout Jerusalem, including to Pilate and Antipas.

* * *

Back at the Jordan River over the next few days, John began to prepare his followers for a change, telling them that someone else would soon be assuming his ministries. He promised a truly wonderful and caring man, but he would not reveal his name. He wanted Pilate and Joseph to first meet with Jesus, respecting their wishes.

Joseph came to the cabin several days later to make arrangements for Pilate and Jesus to meet. "Have you calmed your spirit after Pilate's reaction the other day?"

John nodded. "I stopped thinking of it the moment I left Jerusalem."

Joseph took a deep breath. "I don't know how your soul can be so assured. You really should have spoken to us before mentioning your intentions to anyone else. What if Pilate does not approve of this man?

You have placed us all at serious risk."

In a slight fit of frustration, John shook his head. "This has primarily been my ministry, built upon mostly my ideas. I think I can be the judge of who can carry on."

"I know, John. I cast no doubts. You still should have consulted us first."

"My main concern was that before I could propose leaving my ministry, I needed to offer an alternative. I needed to bring hope of continuity to our work, rather than end those hopes—not just for you and Pilate, but for all of the people. I have known Jesus for a long time. He is a good man for this position, perhaps even better than I."

After pausing for a tense moment, Joseph brought up another point. "I heard what you said of Antipas."

John let out a sigh. "I really didn't say much. I was forced into speaking from the crowd's persistent questions. I remembered what you had said and actually held my tongue."

"Well, what's been said has been said. Let's hope Antipas does not take offense to it. He is a man who has jailed others for less."

John laughed. "I doubt he would do that. I'm sure he has much more to worry about than what I have to say."

Joseph and John went on to discuss arrangements for Pilate's meeting with Jesus. They agreed a place further north would be safer than the immediate area, in order to avoid the crowds that gathered daily.

17 ~ Misguided Blame

Lying in bed that night, Pontius was more agitated than usual. Claudia reached over and placed her arm over Pontius' chest, which calmed him a little. Taking a breath, she asked, "Your mind seems troubled, my husband. What are you thinking?"

A flood of events and issues filled Pontius' thoughts—so much so that he barely heard Claudia's plea. He turned away, trying to make sense of the conflicts raging in his mind. Claudia pulled back her arm.

Through the night Pontius worried about John's change of heart. If it went too far, John might accidentally let things slip, which could jeopardize Joseph's position on the Jewish council. Pilate was wary of the people and how they might react if they discovered he had been manipulating them through the guise of Jewish law. He was also thinking of Rome. Rome didn't look kindly on leadership experiments they hadn't been fully informed of—especially when they failed.

The next morning, Pilate sensed the distance growing in Claudia's eyes. He could not bear her silence and missed her caring smile. "I'm sorry, my love. I wish I could be more open about my work, and my dealings with the tangled factions in this province. Most of it would bore you anyway." Seeing he was getting no reaction, Pontius continued, "I heard about your incident in the city. I hope the boy will be alright."

Claudia sighed. "Yes, me too. I have no idea what became of him."

Pontius breathed out relief, at least getting some reaction.

Claudia pulled a bowl out of the water and began drying it. "The soldiers were far too wary of the children, and of a mother who had approached for fear of her child."

Pontius nodded. "Yes, I know. But you remember what happened in Caesarea? You were grateful for their protection then."

"But these were young children. And they were just playing."

Pontius walked over and placed his hands on Claudia's shoulders. "They are just doing their jobs. It is their duty to protect you—and my duty."

Claudia closed her eyes. "I have heard that several months ago, our soldiers beat several protestors to death, including women and children."

Pilate's grip tightened as he clenched his teeth. "The protesters came with clubs and knives. Their protest became violent and our soldiers had to contain the violence."

"I have heard our soldiers were disguised and carrying clubs... not the protesters. And they started beating innocent people without provocation!"

Pilate released his grip and backed away. "How I govern these people is not your concern. I have difficult choices to make every day, and I cannot seek your approval for every decision!"

Claudia's eyes widened. "You knew that was going to happen! Of course you knew! You probably ordered it!"

"You do not understand the pressure I am under from Rome! I could not let them trample us like they did in Caesarea!"

Her look of shock turned to horror as the bowl slipped from her hands, shattering on the floor. Lowering her eyes, she placed her hand against the counter steadying herself. "Women and children cannot trample the armies of Rome."

Pilate shook his head. "There's far more than you know about this province, including ruthless armies to the east that would march against Rome herself. And these people will not lift an axe to help us defend against them. Instead, they look upon us as some sort of plague on their sacred land. They would kill every last one of us if they could, or call upon their god to do so."

Seeing he was getting no reaction from Claudia, Pilate turned to leave. "I have to go see Antipas."

* * *

Antipas sat in the throne room, the ever-present guards and aides at his side. The courtroom door flew open as a frantic guard ran up. Before he could recite his purpose, Pilate walked in. Antipas stood and offered a customary exchange of greetings.

Pilate ignored the formalities and asked, "Have you heard of the man who is causing insurrection up around the city of Bethany beyond the Jordan River?"

Antipas thought for a moment. "Are you referring to John the Baptist?"

Pilate nodded. "Yes, the one involved in sedition against you and your court."

Antipas was dumbfounded. "Are we talking about the same man? I would hardly think that John the Baptist was inciting insurrection."

"He is gathering large masses in the north and teaching his own law. Have you not heard what he has said about you?"

"John the Baptist?! Well, no. What are you talking about?"

"Apparently he was in Jerusalem last week, and he made comments about your marriage to Herodias."

Antipas had been expecting much worse. "Oh, that! Yes, I have heard of his comments." Then he shifted uneasily on his throne. Antipas had been bombarded from many sides regarding his marriage to Herodias, and he felt slightly embarrassed that Pilate, too, would bring it up in front of his subjects. "I have received criticism from many people—and now him? It certainly hasn't helped matters, but I would hardly think of his statement as sedition."

Pilate approached Antipas and spoke softly, "Could I have a word with you? In private?"

Puzzled by Pilate's change in tone, Antipas agreed and they went off to a side room.

Closing the door behind him, Pilate said, "I want you to arrest this man. I am concerned his influence is growing too powerful, and he is starting to say things against the state."

Antipas grew anxious. He had heard of John's teaching and knew him to be a righteous man. "If I arrest John, then *this* will cause insurrection. Why don't you arrest him and throw him in a Roman prison, if you are so concerned?"

Pilate's face flushed with anger. "Because he is not rebelling against the Roman state. He is acting against your court, accusing you of unlawful behavior. That is a direct attack against your authority, and he should be arrested."

When it came down to the direct threat of Pilate's anger versus a Jewish peasant, there was no question. John's popularity could be short-lived, and Pilate was here to stay. Still baffled by the reason for Pilate's concern, Antipas agreed to Pilate's demand.

"I want no word that Rome was behind his arrest," Pilate said. Then he added, "And I want him put away so he can speak to no one."

* * *

A few days later after having traveled back from the north, Joseph came into Pilate's office. "Good afternoon, Your Nobility. If it pleases you, John and I have made arrangements for you to meet Jesus in three days."

Pilate did not expect the meeting to take place due to John's imminent arrest, but reacted superficially, "Yes, that's fine."

Joseph added, "There are rumors Antipas is going to arrest John."

Pontius paraded a show of concern. "Yes, I have heard."

Then Joseph added, "Maybe you should talk to Antipas, convince him to change his mind."

Pontius shook his head. "I don't think so. I don't want to risk revealing that I—and you—are involved in this. Besides, this is between Antipas and John. We warned John about making such statements."

Joseph blinked with an expression of surprise and disappointment. "I know John has a habit of saying whatever is on his mind, but I don't think his intentions were to threaten Antipas. Maybe if you tried to persuade Antipas, he would listen."

With a look of compassion, Pilate put his arm on Joseph's shoulder. "All right, Joseph, I'll see what I can do." Pilate concluded with a reassuring smile, having no intention of carrying through with his words.

Joseph gave a thankful nod. "We found a location about twelve miles north of his old place. John is in Aenon near Salim right now, waiting for Jesus to arrive from Nazareth. They'll travel, together, to the meeting place tomorrow or the next day. They'll stay there until we arrive."

Suddenly realizing Antipas' soldiers wouldn't know where to find John, Pilate's voice took on a nervous tone. "In three days?" Pilate's first thought was to tell Antipas where John would be, but then realized it would point obvious blame his way. Hoping to argue his way out of the meeting, Pilate pointed out, "Is it a good idea to plan the meeting while Antipas' soldiers are looking for him?"

Pilate realized his timid display was out of character, unconvincing, and possibly hurting his position, as Joseph looked at him with an expression of surprised anger. With slight disgust, Joseph responded, "It's not a question of whether it's a good idea or not. I think we owe it to John. He's made an honest effort to help us find someone who will carry on with our work. Sure, he's made a few mistakes. But we can't abandon him on the mere threat of trouble! Besides, Antipas' soldiers don't know where he is. They'll never find him. There are rumors John left the area to avoid capture."

Feeling he had little choice, Pilate tentatively agreed to the meeting. Joseph was right. There was little chance Antipas' soldiers would find them in such a short time, unless John had talked to others—which crossed Pilate's mind, but he thought was unlikely. Maybe there was some merit in meeting Jesus before it was too late. For the first time, Pontius began toying with the idea that maybe Jesus could carry on with their work.

* * *

Three days later, Joseph led Pilate to John's temporary refuge. They were on horseback and stayed well away from John's previous area so as not to attract attention. Hundreds continued visiting the area, waiting for John's return. Andrew and James still performed baptisms, while Antipas' soldiers lurked around, searching for clues about where John might have gone.

Riding up to the abandoned farmhouse, the place appeared quiet and deserted. As they were dismounting, John opened the front door and walked out to greet them. Breathing a sigh of relief, Joseph said, "Peace to you, John! It is good to witness your presence. I was beginning to wonder if you were here."

John let out a carefree laugh. "Well, of course I'm here. I said I'd be." Turning and motioning to the man who had come to the doorway, John added, "This is Jesus, the man I was telling you about."

Jesus smiled with John's introduction and said, "Peace be to those who come. John has told me a great deal about the two of you."

Pilate felt brief apprehension as Jesus walked toward him, but then Jesus stopped short, bowing in a sincere show of respect. "You must be the Roman prefect, Pontius Pilate. It is an honor to meet you, sir."

Pontius had learned much of the Hebrew language in his interactions with Joseph and John, and clearly understood Jesus' greeting. Pontius' immediate feelings were mixed. On the one hand, Jesus' gentle nature made him feel at ease. On the other hand, this man lacked John's stature. He was plain looking, shorter than average, and slightly overweight. It was difficult to conclude that he and John were even related. The disappointment showed as Pilate returned Jesus' greeting in Latin, with Joseph serving as interpreter. "Yes, I am Pontius Pilate. I guess these clothes do a poor job of hiding my identity."

Jesus smiled, pointing toward Joseph. "No, Joseph has the traditional beard, so it was a simple matter of elimination."

Upon hearing Joseph's interpretation Pontius started laughing, quickly followed by John, as they all turned to walk into the house. Joseph broke a smile—barely perceptible through the worry on his face. Upon entering the house, Pontius turned his eyes upon Jesus and said, "I have learned some of the Hebrew language, however I am not well-versed. I was hoping you would know Latin."

In his own broken Latin, Jesus replied, "I know some Latin, as do many people around Nazareth. I grew up near Sepphoris and was exposed to outside cultures, mainly Roman."

Pontius nodded in pleasant recognition. Sincerely wanting to learn more of Jesus, Pontius inquired, "So John tells me you're cousins?"

Jesus nodded. "Yes, through our mothers. Our mothers are aunt and niece. In fact, John and I spent a lot of time together when we were little, until his family moved away to Nain. We still stay in touch, though, mainly through John's travels in his work. I've always envied my cousin on his travels, wishing I could see the world as he does."

John shook his head. "Like I've always told you, one place is much like another. Traveling only serves to increase your appreciation for home."

Jesus wrinkled his eyebrows in disagreement. "We've had this discussion many times before."

Joseph broke in on the questioning. "So what is it you do?"

"I am a carpenter, as was my father, and my father's father." Looking toward Pilate, Jesus explained, "It is common for sons to follow in their father's line of work." Jesus paused, wrinkling his eyebrows again, adding, "Whether they like it or not"—showing strong disapproval for the custom. Pausing again and looking at John, Jesus added with admiration, "Now John is the exception. His work is of his own desire and liking, breaking away from the tradition of his father. Of course, John has the unique skills and qualities to do as he wishes."

Smiling at Jesus' compliment, John responded, "A job that I am honestly looking forward to getting back to. I truly miss my work. I knew I would miss it, I just didn't know how much." John grew noticeably nervous with his continuing confessions.

Joseph sighed with a look of deep concern. "So, John. Do you think Jesus is a good candidate to carry on with your... our ministry?"

John smiled. "Yes, I think he's the right man."

Pontius immediately interrupted, addressing his question toward Jesus. "Do you know what we are doing here?"

Jesus nodded. "Yes, I believe so. John has told me it is a forum for improving the relations between the population and Roman authority."

Pontius was impressed by such a simple grasp of the arrangement. He was also impressed that John had revealed the genuine nature of his role, rather than some self-indulgent explanation. Nodding his approval, Pontius added, "Yes, that's basically correct. We are trying to implement an avenue of dialogue between the two of us, both ways, without instigating hostility." All three made slight nodding motions. "In fact, that is an important quality of a true leader: communication. The ability to get one's ideas across and have people accept and follow your command."

Jesus nodded. "I think the day-to-day lives of the common people are relatively unaffected by the Roman presence. That's good as far as I'm concerned. Being God's chosen people, many are focused on themselves and are blind to the qualities of other nations. If they are not careful, God will take away His Covenant and give it to those more deserving of his mercy."

Joseph cleared his throat, shaking off an expression of surprise. "We are not taking an adversarial role. We are attempting to gain favor."

Jesus nodded and smiled, acknowledging Joseph's position. Jesus got up and poured the contents of an open jar into a large cup. "May I offer anyone some wine?"

Pilate gave a pleasant nod, while Joseph and John refrained. Pouring a second cup, Jesus continued, "It is not the fault of the common Jew. It is the hypocritical nature of those who study and teach the Law. The scribes, the chief priests, the Pharisees, the Sadducees, and those who study and keep the Law are hypocrites. I abhor the religious clergy who claim to teach the word of God, but instead incite religious fervor in the hearts of zealots."

Joseph shook his head and leaned over to John, whispering, "His views are rather extreme. Does he have any loyalties?" Before John could answer, Joseph looked at Jesus and responded, "You criticize practically everyone who studies and teaches the Scriptures."

Jesus lowered the cup from his lips as he swallowed and cleared his throat. "As well I should. They are responsible for the lives of an entire nation, and they squander their power! They instruct a view of the Mosaic Law that is too literal in its meaning. Some of the laws are old and outdated." Jesus paused in thought, then continued, "The Pharisees wash their hands before every meal simply because it is written in the Mosaic Law. It is a ridiculous ritual and a complete waste of time."

John nodded cautiously. "But Jesus, I believe some of the laws have a purpose." He held up his hand to emphasize his point. "Take pork, being from an animal that does not chew its cud. It is said that long ago several who ate pork became possessed by demons, ravaging their bodies. They convulsed, vomited, developed fevers, and several even died."

Jesus laughed, dismissing John's statement. "Those are just myths, John—old stories. Pork is forbidden because the animal is filthy and repulsive." Jesus cringed in disgust. "You see, John, I have lived my thirty years rarely washing my hands before meals, and I have never been possessed. Do you not see that whatever goes into the mouth passes into the stomach, and so passes on? So what is the purpose of such a useless law?"

John shrugged his shoulders in blithe uncertainty. Pontius sat dumbfounded, wondering the point of the conversation, but he liked the objections Jesus was raising toward traditional Jewish authority and practices.

Pilate directed an inquisitive look towards Jesus, which prompted him to continue. "The chief priests speak strongly of tithing, but that is all that is important to these hypocrites. They seize the money and squander it on their robes and temples, and for the betterment of their own lives." Seeming to correct himself, Jesus added, "Please understand, the collection of monies is justified through its intention. The taxes collected by Rome serve a purpose by providing the people of Judea stability and protection."

Pontius smiled from ear to ear. Continuing along Jesus' line of thought, Pilate said, "You hit the nail on the head, Jesus. You must be a skilled carpenter."

They all burst into laughter as Pilate continued, "Our main problem is collecting taxes rightfully owed to Rome. We mint thousands upon thousands of coins, but once they leave the mint, they disappear. This country absorbs them like a great sponge. With as many coins as we've minted, the streets should be littered with them like pebbles. Don't the people know they're dealing with minted currency, property of Rome, and not trading stones? These coins have the head of Caesar, not images of Herod."

Joseph nodded and muttered under his breath, "Give unto Caesar that which is Caesar's."

With a pleasant look of surprise, Pontius glanced at Joseph and asked, "What words do you speak?"

Joseph looked back, almost as if being wakened from a dream. "What words?"

"The words of Caesar."

Joseph shrugged his shoulders, humbly gratified by Pilate's sudden interest. "Oh, that. I was just thinking out loud—give unto Caesar that which is Caesar's."

Pontius slapped Joseph on the arm. "Well put, Joseph! I couldn't have said it better!"

John rolled his eyes. "Clever words, but it is the only currency Rome allows." Then with a note of sarcasm, John added, "Would you have me give all of my income to Caesar?"

Jesus let out a quick laugh, while Pilate was not amused. John seemed to realize his rashness as he attempted to get back on subject. "Given the power and strength of the Roman Empire, it is remarkable they offer minimal interference in our daily lives. There have been numerous adversaries in our history who have destroyed our temple, tried to force their own gods and their own customs, essentially attempting to destroy our identity."

Jesus nodded. "Rome has been sensitive to the customs and religious practices of our people. Sometimes I wonder if the people realize their blessings. Sometimes complacency can lead to misery over the slightest complaint."

Again, Pilate smiled, liking what he was hearing. His smile was contagious, spreading quickly to John and Joseph.

Pilate felt a sense of reassurance, thinking Jesus' viewpoint had to be common among a large segment of the Jewish population. *Most,* Pilate thought, *are simply too afraid to express these ideas.* Pilate was almost speechless at hearing Jesus' words. There was nothing more that needed to be said. He had been prepared to go through the entire appeal he had made before Joseph and John, but no longer felt it necessary. Instead, Pilate responded with a note of thanks: "It's nice to hear a word of appreciation—and put so well."

Jesus shrugged his shoulders. "People must live in peace with forces beyond their control. I abhor the violent nature of the zealots, blindly convinced of their cause, no matter the cost or the means to obtain their ends. Both John and I have seen many a good man die needlessly for perverted, fanatical causes. It is a horrible waste, not only of their lives, but of the lives they destroy."

Their discussion went on for some time, and Pontius grew to like Jesus and his words. It wasn't long before Pontius became very comfortable with the idea that Jesus would take over John's position, regardless of what happened to John. Showing confidence in accepting Jesus' role, Pontius inquired, "So, how do we transfer the ministry to Jesus?"

John was the first to respond. "I think the change should be gradual, having Jesus take on a role similar to Andrew and James'. Eventually, Jesus would assume the full role of interacting between Joseph and the people, and their interest in me would slowly fade. I have been telling them over the past several weeks to expect someone else, so it won't be a surprise."

Pontius cringed over the idea that John had taken it upon himself to initiate the transfer. John continued, "It would be as if nothing ever happened. No break in the original goals of our plan."

Joseph shifted in his chair. His expression turned to one of despair. "John, I guess you haven't heard."

John looked back at Joseph, seemingly surprised at his solemn tone. "Heard of what?"

Joseph dropped his eyes and gave an emotional sigh. "Antipas is sending soldiers to have you arrested."

John's eyes widened in bewildered concern. "For what? What could I possibly have done to be arrested? Antipas hasn't been involved in any of this. What concern could this be of his?" Looking at Pilate, then back at Joseph, he asked, "Do you think it is what I said in Jerusalem?!"

Jesus looked at his cousin, inquiring, "What did you say?"

"Some people had stopped me while I was in Jerusalem. They were asking questions, wanting me to speak. Finally, one of them asked what I thought of Antipas' marriage to Herodias. I just said his marriage to his brother's wife was unlawful and nothing more."

Joseph interrupted, "Look, John. It was a simple statement, relatively harmless. I can't imagine Antipas will hold you for any length of time. I imagine he is just trying to frighten you. You'll be in his court for a couple of days, and then you'll be free."

Joseph's words seemed to calm John considerably. Joseph pointed toward Pilate and continued, "Besides, His Nobility has agreed to put some pressure on Antipas to have you released, if you are arrested."

Caught off guard, Pontius responded, "Yes, I will do what I can. This is really Antipas' affair and, like Joseph, I can't imagine Antipas will carry it too far." Pontius was beginning to doubt if having John arrested was the right course of action. Up until this moment, he had never seriously considered that John's handpicked successor could actually carry on their work.

Joseph finally spoke. "I know this is going to sound difficult, but I do not think it is wise to avoid arrest by Antipas' soldiers. The more you run—err—elude capture by staying hidden, the more complicated things will become. You must go back to the Jordan as soon as possible, and let yourself be taken."

John nodded in reluctant agreement. Pontius quickly returned to an immediate point of his renewed interest. "We should also set things in motion to bring about Jesus' succession."

John looked over at Jesus. "Are you sure you want to do this, after hearing what I will have to go through?"

Jesus thought on John's words for a moment. "You know how I feel about this, John. I have always envied you. Look at the position you have attained"—nodding towards Pilate—"and with generous compensation from Rome. I am a lowly carpenter, soon to be thirty years old." Jesus paused, shaking his head. "I have worked hard all of my life, with little or nothing to show for it." With strong conviction, Jesus continued, "Yes, I do want to serve as an emissary to my people. Do you think I would pass up this opportunity to offer an alternative to the perverted power of the chief priests and scribes?" Jesus then looked at John with consoling eyes. "Besides, you'll be all right. What can Antipas do? You haven't done anything but state what is already known."

Joseph looked at John. "He's right, John. There's nothing to worry about. You should go back to the Jordan River tomorrow, and start back on your ministry. Antipas' soldiers should be there to arrest you before long." Joseph paused a moment. "Perhaps Jesus should go with you. You should baptize Jesus and begin suggesting he is the one to follow in your ministry. You must inform James and Andrew. They will be valuable assistance to Jesus in this transition."

John nodded. "Oh, it won't be difficult to convince them. I've been telling them not to expect my servitude much longer. The hardest thing will be convincing them it is someone else, besides themselves, who will lead the ministry. I'm not sure, but I think Andrew has aspirations to follow in my stead. Both of them have expressed devotion as if called by God. I have provided for them from the generous shares of Roman supplies and even from the tithing of our fold."

Pontius lightly slapped his hand on the table. "Very well then. We have a sound plan worthy of preparation. The two of you can work out the details. I agree with Joseph we should get started immediately."

With a tone of optimism, Joseph added, "Maybe Antipas has forgotten about all this, calling back his soldiers. It only makes sense he'd realize it's not worth the effort."

Pontius looked at Jesus and said, "If John does happen to be arrested, I want you to come straight back here and wait for a few days—allow things to settle down. I will have provisions sent up as soon as I get back to Jerusalem tomorrow. Either Joseph, or myself, or both of us, will be back to talk to you further."

Then Joseph interrupted, "And if he isn't arrested?"

Pontius looked at Joseph as if a little bothered by his question. "If John isn't arrested, then we will just continue along the same arrangement, having the three of you meet periodically, letting the transition occur gradually."

They all agreed to the plans and slept over that night. The next morning, John and Jesus headed south on foot to the Jordan River, while Pilate and Joseph headed back—a roundabout way to Jerusalem.

* * *

As John and Jesus neared the area, John thought it best if they did not walk in together. He didn't want to have Jesus connected with him in case he was arrested right away. John also felt it would be best to introduce Jesus to a large crowd at one of his sermons. He thought baptizing Jesus was the perfect opportunity for such an introduction.

They separated, and John walked into the clearing first. A large number of people were there, and they crowded around John as he approached. Several expressed relief to see him, inundating him with concern for his well-being. Finally, one of those gathered asked if he knew that Antipas' soldiers were seeking his arrest. John acknowledged their worries, but assured them that he wasn't concerned.

A great multitude had gathered along the banks of the river—more than he had ever seen. Perhaps it was due to the publicity over his pending arrest, or maybe they had accumulated over time waiting to hear him speak.

Later that day, standing on the banks of the Jordan River, John looked out upon the sea of faces. Most were strangers, with only a few he recognized. Still, he felt a responsibility toward them. A strong sense of sadness settled into his spirit realizing his efforts to return to his former life would soon become a reality. Seeing their expressions, how much they looked up to him for guidance, and possibly even purpose, made John wonder if he was doing the right thing. Finding it difficult to gaze into their hungry eyes with conflicting emotions filling his soul, John closed his eyes and raised his hands toward the heavens. A deathly silence fell over the crowd. Not a voice could be heard. All John could hear was the chirping of the birds in the distance. Everyone was waiting for John to speak, some even holding their breaths. It was so quiet that for a moment, John imagined he was alone, quieting his soul. As he opened his eyes, a silent reaction drifted through the crowd as if by a current of air.

Putting forth all the strength he could, John spoke: "To the spirit in each of us it is a simple covenant! There are only *ten* commandments from God that we *must* follow! They were not suggestions from God. He was not asking us. He *commanded* what we must do. There are only ten!" Pausing, trying to look into each and every eye that was locked his way, he continued, "Then why do we all fail?" John could see a wide range of reactions on their faces—from looks of bewilderment to looks of concern, to hidden smiles, to imperceptible nods of agreement. Sweeping his hands through the air, motioning to the entire crowd and to himself, John continued, "Yes! The flesh of the body is weak, even though the spirit is willing. We fall short of the glory of God. Do we fail because we are destined to? Or is it because the flesh convinces us there are commandments less than the others?" Again looking out at the great multitude, motioning his arms to all, John asked, "Who can tell me which of God's commandments are more important than the others?" Looking out over the crowd waiting for an answer, no one spoke. Making his point, John continued, "None of his commandments are more or less than the others! God did not give us a ranking of his commandments. God did not give consent to break one, to follow another!" With a powerful emotion he had never felt, John slowly cried out each commandment, pausing between each one, emphasizing the depth of his conviction. "He *commanded* us not to have any other gods before him! He *commanded* us not to make false idols! He *commanded* us not to use his name lightly or in vain! He *commanded* us to keep the Sabbath holy! He *commanded* us to honor our mothers and our fathers! He *commanded* us not to kill! He *commanded* us not to commit adultery! He *commanded* us not to steal! He *commanded* us not to lie! He *commanded* us not to covet anything our neighbors possess, or his wife!" Feeling emotionally exhausted, John lowered his arms, then lowered his eyes to the ground. It was as if the world was motionless, waiting for a power to push it along its way.

Slowly John raised his eyes. "They are *all* important. And when we fail, we should all be ashamed that we have disobeyed a commandment of the Lord." His voice desperate, almost pleading, John continued, "We are filled with desires that cause us to turn our eyes from God and break his commandments." Then suddenly, calling up a force that could be felt as well as heard, John added, "We must recognize our failure, recognize our sin, and plead for God's mercy in his forgiveness!" Stretching forth his hand and slowly pointing to everyone in the crowd, John said, "If you do not recognize that you have sinned!... If you are content with your failure!... Then you should not be here! You will never walk in peace with the Lord!" Suddenly, John's voice took on a tranquil solace: "You must be ashamed of your sins and constantly strive to make straight your path with the Lord. As easy as it is to wash clean your body by being baptized in the river, so it is to wash clean your soul by acts of repentance to God." Smiling to all those present, John proceeded to walk down to the river and wade into its softly flowing current. Motioning to the people, he waited as they followed him to be baptized.

Jesus stood amongst the crowd and was openly moved by John's words. He stood on the bank and watched for several hours as John baptized the hundreds who gathered in a snaking line. Eventually, John recognized Jesus standing near the river's edge. Remembering his duty to introduce Jesus to the people, and also feeling a sense of urgency, John raised his voice to all of those still present, saying, "I have told you there is one to come who will continue my ministry! One who is better than I! One who will not only baptize you with water, but will baptize you with the fire of his message!" Pointing to Jesus, John directed everyone's attention his way and said, "This is the man of whom I spoke!"

Everyone looked toward Jesus, who was visibly stricken by the sudden attention. John could say no wrong. His command was a gentle breeze that drifted from John to Jesus. Jesus' look of surprise turned to determination as he walked into the water. Growing near, Jesus said, "I want you to baptize me."

John lowered Jesus into the water and then pulled him up, saying, "Just as your body is cleansed by the water, so is your soul cleansed of its sins through your repentance." Gripping Jesus by the shoulder, John turned to the crowd and said, "God is well pleased with this man. He is indeed a man worthy to carry on the message of God's word!"

Standing nearby, a man called out, "How was this man chosen?"

Taken aback, John responded, "He was standing on the shore, and I was moved by his presence. I'm sure God is speaking to me, telling me this is the one who is to carry on with this ministry." John was starting to feel uncomfortable, feeling the frailties of his flesh gripping his spirit, forcing him to possibly break one of the very commandments he had been preaching. In a way, he wasn't lying. He was compelled to have Jesus take over his ministry and return to the life he had known. After all, it was just a ministry. He had already told the people he was not a prophet or the messiah.

But the man persisted. "Did you know this man?"

John felt nervous realizing the truth might not be taken well. He felt saying yes could expose and unravel all of the hard work and careful planning he had gone through to transfer his work to Jesus. John could see Jesus looking back at him, slightly shaking his head no. Feeling the now all-too-familiar sense of deception, John shook his head and said, "No, I did not know this man."

John immediately fell silent and turned to walk out of the river. He felt he had betrayed himself through his cowering answer—one he should have prepared for, but there hadn't been time. John was greatly troubled by his denial to avoid uncomfortable explanations. He walked off a great distance and sat by himself for several hours, sinking into depression until the day's light began to fade.

Realizing it would soon be dark, John stood up and started walking back to his cabin. He caught a glimpse of soldiers approaching from the direction of the river. One of the soldiers called out, "Are you John the

Baptist?"

"Yes, I am John the Baptist." As the soldiers grew closer, John almost welcomed the arrest, still feeling torn by his transgression. He was immediately taken to Jerusalem.

18 ~ Where Did He Go?

Antipas sat high on his throne as John was escorted in shackles and thrown to the floor. Several soldiers encircled him, but they were not needed for he offered no resistance. His body slumped sadly, as he made no effort to push himself up. Antipas was fascinated by John, the righteous man from the wilderness—a man who had attracted incredible multitudes just by his words. Antipas was expecting a bombardment of such words, but there was only silence. He was expecting a man shouting incantations, chastising him for any number of things he had done as tetrarch. He was expecting pleas for mercy or explanations of defense for what he had said. Instead, there was silence.

Typically, Antipas would use his own silence to intimidate people into spilling forth information. Instead, he felt intimidated by the silence of a man who had great power and popularity amongst the people. Finally, Antipas was the first to speak: "I thought you were a man of many words. Instead, I find a man who cannot speak. Are you the one they call 'John the Baptist'?"

John lifted his head, acknowledging Antipas' presence for the first time. "Yes, I am John. I preach of righteousness and repentance of sins, not of baptism."

Antipas nodded. "Yes, I know of what you teach. It is well known over all the land. In fact, I expected you to come in here preaching to me."

Finally, with the defiance Antipas had expected, John responded, "I only preach to those who will listen."

Antipas immediately felt the focus of John's insolence, but felt it was treatment he deserved from the degrading nature of his own comment. Antipas dismissed the insult with only a slight hint of anger. "Then why is it you choose to preach *about* me to others?"

"I did not choose to say anything about you. I was asked, and I spoke what I knew to be the truth according to the law."

Antipas hesitated to ask the next question, but had to in order to effect John's arrest. "What truth do you speak of?"

John closed his eyes briefly, then, taking a deep breath said, "It is clear under Mosaic Law that it is illegal for a man to marry his brother's wife when she has borne children. Your marriage to Herodias is such. The marriage is unlawful."

Antipas had no need of further comment. He was reluctant to arrest John, but such a blatant statement in his own court gave him no choice. Showing no enthusiasm for his order and almost with sadness, Antipas muttered, "Take him away."

The soldiers pulled John to his feet and yanked his shackles as they led him to a prison wagon waiting outside. One soldier carefully helped John up through the small, barred door, while another slammed it shut, barely missing the first soldier's hands pushing the chains inside. A few of his followers reached in to touch John as the wagon made its way down the streets. As it neared the front gates of the city, John rose to his knees and pressed his face against the bars. He cried out to the driver with sudden fear, "Where are we going?! The prison is back in the city—near Herod's palace!"

A guard riding alongside swung a club, impacting John's hands and causing him to reel back, crying in pain. John fell back to the hard floor. The driver yelled at the guard, "Careful with my wagon! You'll crack the bars and have some explaining to do!"

The guard let out a quick laugh and hit the walls a couple more times, provoking him. The driver redirected his frustration by whipping the horses, causing the wagon to lurch forward, throwing John against the back wall. The driver turned his head back towards the guard and yelled, "It's going to be a long day to Machaerus if you keep this up!"

John pushed himself back up and cautiously approached the bars, keeping a watchful eye for the club. With heightening desperation laced with fear, John called out again, "Did you say 'Machaerus'? That's a day's ride, far to the south, on the other side of the Dead Sea!" The driver paid no attention, apparently hardened to the countless pleas of mercy from countless forsaken cargo.

* * *

Joseph walked into the abandoned farmhouse, searching briefly only to find Jesus was not there. He walked out to his horse and pack mule. Reluctantly, he started unloading supplies to relieve the weight from his weary companion. Joseph was tired of the constant travel over the past few days. His length of absence from the council was starting to concern him. However, he was under strict orders from Pilate to carry through with the plans set in motion by John's arrest.

In a way, Joseph had hoped Jesus would not be there, so he could just head back to Jerusalem the next day. Considering the possibility, Joseph hesitated a moment before hauling the supplies inside. His mind growing wearier, Joseph heard his name called from behind the trees next to the house. Turning, he saw that it was Jesus. Returning his call, Joseph replied, "Peace to you."

Jesus walked up. "And to you, peace. I was out for a walk, getting to know the area a little. I've been here for four days and I was beginning to wonder if you would show up."

Grief-stricken over John's arrest, Joseph shook his head. "As soon as I heard of John's arrest, I gathered the supplies and was on my way. I guess I knew it would happen soon, but it still comes as a shock. I pray his trial before Antipas goes well, but I could not stay to find out. Pilate will be coming out soon, and we can get news from him."

Jesus nodded in sorrowful agreement. "Yes, he was arrested the very day we arrived at the Jordan River. Apparently, it was just a few hours after he had delivered a sermon to many who had gathered there. I heard him speak. He is truly a remarkable man. I was moved by his message—and the way he delivered it. His ritual of baptism was as moving as his words. Hundreds had gathered for the rite. Two others were assisting him, and they baptized each and every person."

"I have seen him speak, too. The power he has over the people can only be seen to be believed. There are many times I wished Pilate could have heard him speak. I think he would have appreciated John more if he had." Joseph shook his head in frustration. "But I suppose it would be far too risky for Pilate to stand amongst the crowd. Just the other day, you singled out Pilate when you first met him."

Jesus laughed. "Even in rags, I could tell he was Roman."

They both started picking up bags of supplies from the mule and carried them inside. Helping Joseph with one of the larger sacks, Jesus asked, "So where do we go from here?"

Letting out a grunt, Joseph replied, "Pilate told me he wanted to go over several things with you before we started your ministry. In fact, he should be here in a couple of days to discuss it with us personally." Setting the package down on the table, Joseph caught his breath and continued, "I think he was disappointed we did not spend much time in the beginning with John. I don't think Pilate was happy with the flavor behind some of John's messages."

"Like what messages?"

"Like many of the topics we discussed when we were all here last—too many things to go over right now. We will have plenty of time to talk about them over the next few days." Several thoughts raced through Joseph's mind. "There are also other issues we will need to discuss, including how we are to make your introduction, how we are to carry on once John is released, and where you should start your ministry. Should it be in John's area where the crowds have gathered, or somewhere else?"

Jesus interrupted, "I suppose I should tell you. John has already introduced me, pointing me out to those gathered that day. He also baptized me, saying I was the one who would carry on his ministry. There were many who saw me, and a few who asked my name."

Joseph shook his head in disapproval. "Oh, this is not good. John shouldn't have been so hasty. What will everyone think now that you have disappeared so quickly? I was hoping the transition would be much more gradual and controlled, and take place when John is released."

Jesus nodded. "I was wondering about that myself. I was feeling a little uncomfortable with disappearing so fast. But I knew I needed to follow through with Pilate's instructions."

"Yes, I suppose that's the best we can do until John is released." Turning his thoughts to what Jesus had told him, Joseph asked, "What exactly did he say when he introduced you?"

Jesus tilted his head, trying to remember the details. "He pointed me out, saying I was the one he had been speaking of—the one better than he, who would carry on with his ministry." After pausing in recollection, Jesus went on, "Things got very quiet as attention turned my way. I slowly waded out into the river toward John. Anyway, I told you he baptized me. He then told those standing around that I would continue to baptize them with the message of my ministry, and that my ministry would spread like a fire throughout all of Israel." Jesus shook his head. "He was very confident—more commanding than I had ever seen him. And that's the last I saw him." Jesus picked up one of the skins of wine Joseph had brought and poured it into two cups. Offering one to Joseph, Jesus continued, "Someone asked how I had been chosen and if John had known me. I could tell John was upset when he said no. I don't know if others noticed it, but I did. John left the river and walked into the trees. I stayed around for a little while, telling several who I was and where I was from. I learned a short time later that John had been arrested even before reaching his cabin."

The next morning, the aroma of apple cider filled the air as Joseph heated it over the fire. His activity finally woke Jesus. Seeing Jesus rubbing his face, Joseph offered a greeting: "Good morning, Jesus. I hope you slept as well as I did last night. The weariness of my travel commanded a hard sleep."

Jesus took a deep breath, smiling from the pleasant aroma. "I don't think it was just your weariness. This place seems to have a hypnotic effect. I don't know if it's just being away from people, or if it's just the natural beauty of the area, but this place has definitely calmed my spirit."

Joseph nodded. "I feel the same way. This seems the perfect place to escape the demands of the council, yet we fulfill the commands of Pilate." Joseph walked over and pulled a pan of bread off the fire to let it cool. Then, pouring a cup, Joseph looked at Jesus and asked, "Will you have some cider?"

Jesus pulled a cup from the cupboard and presented it to Joseph. Joseph smiled as he poured. "How familiar are you with what John has taught?"

Jesus took a light sip. "We have had brief discussions, and I listened intently to his sermon last week."

Joseph's face took on a look of satisfaction. "Good. That makes our work a little easier. We must continue with the same basic theme. When he gets back, John will spend more time with you to make sure there is a consistent transfer." Joseph took another careful sip. "The basic theme of his teachings was to repent, for the kingdom of heaven is at hand."

Jesus raised his eyebrows and said jokingly, "Now where have I heard that before?"

Joseph shook his head. "I know. It's a common theme from prophets of old. That's why we chose it. It offers a type of legitimacy to his ministry, creating a stronger platform for the other messages we want to convey."

Jesus nodded. "I see."

Realizing he had Jesus' understanding, Joseph continued, "We can't just come out and say, 'Pay your taxes to Rome because there is so much they do for you.' Or, 'Be kind to Roman authority, so we can live in peace with what they have to offer.' It has to be more subtle than that."

Joseph and Jesus sat down at the table with their breakfast. Joseph took a bite of bread and washed it down with the cooling cider. Then he reached into his purse and pulled out a piece of paper. "One of the first things Pilate wants us to emphasize is submissive behavior." Unfolding the paper so he could read it, Joseph went on, "A couple of days ago I jotted down some words." Clearing his throat, Joseph started reading. "Blessed are the poor in spirit, for theirs is the kingdom of heaven. Blessed are they who mourn, for they shall be comforted. Blessed are the meek, for they shall inherit the earth. Blessed are those who hunger and thirst for righteousness, for they shall be satisfied. Blessed are the merciful, for they shall see mercy. Blessed are the pure in heart, for they shall see God. Blessed are the peacemakers, for they shall be called sons of God." Joseph put the paper down and looked up at Jesus, adding, "That's all I've written so far. We'll have to work on it while I'm here."

Astonished, Jesus said, "You speak of a humble spirit that is contrary to the bold and priestly heritage of our people. It may not go over well, but the life you give these words has touched my heart. Maybe it will touch theirs." Jesus walked over and looked at the paper, running his finger across the last line. "But 'sons of God'? You are equating peacemakers to King David? David was a great leader and defender of our nation. I would hardly consider him a peacemaker. He brought war upon those who sought to enslave and persecute us."

Joseph shook his head. "I know, but he also brought peace to our people, once he had broken the bondage of the Philistines. I think it is the virtue of denouncing conflict that makes us children of God, rather than the conquering of nations. We, as a people, must serve as an example to other nations in our priesthood and in our peaceful existence with Rome."

Jesus leaned back with a quizzical look. "That goes against the long-held tradition and teachings of our people."

"That's the whole purpose of your ministry."

His tone skeptical, Jesus replied, "I understand what you are saying, Joseph, but I have doubts the people will be so understanding. Prophets of old have warned against straying from our traditional ways."

Trying to calm Jesus' concerns, Joseph said, "We are not here to abolish the law and the prophets, we are simply trying to put a different light on them. There is a story I remember from Greek writings." After pausing to recall it, Joseph continued, "A master had several servants whom he loved and cared for dearly. When he began to prosper—for himself, his family, and servants alike—he gave one of his trusted servants a large portion of his savings with which to go into town and buy several tools to make easier their labor. Another servant saw this and immediately thought the one servant would run off with the money and never return, for he had no trust or reason in his heart. This servant schemed to intercept the first along the way and kill him, and took the money for himself. Many suffered as a result of his mistrust: the master, his family, and the other servants who could have used the tools. But no one suffered more than the servant who would not trust, because he had an innocent man's blood on his hands and the hatred of many others tormenting his heart."

Jesus nodded as his eyes lowered in sadness. Joseph went on, "I envision Israel as the servant who could not trust good when seen, bringing harm upon her own people. We must put the vision of trust into their eyes."

Jesus asked, "Where did you hear this story? It relates very well to your message."

Joseph smiled. "It's a parable—a story illustrating a moral lesson. They're very common in Greek literature. I've also written a few of my own."

Joseph told Jesus more parables. He had told John many of the same, but John was never receptive to using them.

Over the next several days, Joseph and Jesus worked on the sermon, expanding on the idea of subservience and humility, while building on mistrust of traditional Jewish authority and the priestly lineage.

"Pilate has asked us to promote kindness and love towards those you consider enemies, particularly the Romans—promote attitudes of peace, rather than rebellion; promote submissive behavior towards oppression, rather than pride and violence. He also wants us to promote obedience towards paying taxes, and improve the image and standing of tax collectors."

Jesus let out a sigh.

* * *

After a couple of days, Pilate arrived at the farmhouse. Upon entering the house, Joseph and Pilate exchanged hearty greetings. Joseph informed Pilate of their progress. "Jesus and I have gone over a great deal of information. We've been writing a sermon, and I've been teaching him the art of storytelling."

Pilate nodded and smiled with approval.

Joseph quickly changed the subject. "Have you spoken to John?"

"No."

Joseph looked down, sighing with concern. Offering a point of excuse, Pontius hesitantly added, "Antipas sent him to Machaerus."

"Machaerus! As a prisoner?" Joseph asked in shock.

Pilate bowed his head slowly. "Yes, as a prisoner."

Joseph threw his hands in the air. "Antipas is crazy! Why would he send him all the way to Machaerus?"

Pilate shook his head. "It's hard to understand what goes on in the mind of a madman. I tried talking to him, but he was completely enraged by John's comments, particularly in his own court. He has taken them as personal attacks and acts of insurrection." Pontius looked over toward

Jesus, who was nursing a cup of wine. "That is why it is so important for you to avoid any type of political comments, and say only what you have been instructed. If you do so, I guarantee the power of Rome in protecting your safety."

Jesus shook his head. "I'm not sure how I can keep political issues out of everything Joseph and I have discussed."

"By political, I mean Antipas. Antipas will squander his position through his own doing. He will not require any assistance in his ruin."

The two men nodded, Jesus answering, "I understand, Your Nobility. I see no need to speak of Antipas. Sedition will grow against him, with or without his mention."

* * *

The next day, the three of them hiked up a peak overlooking the Jordan River valley. The ascent took nearly five hours at an easy pace. Upon reaching the summit, there were few clouds to restrict the view in all directions. Pilate could see the Jordan River running all the way from its source in the north, the Sea of Galilee, to its final destination, the Dead Sea. Joseph drank from his water bag and sat down to eat bread he pulled from his pouch. Pilate pointed in a great circular motion toward the distant horizon. "This is the land I have been tasked to rule by Rome. It is not just a land, it is people. A people with customs so foreign to me, it seems the longer I'm here the less I know of it." Placing his hand on Jesus' shoulder, Pontius added, "I need your help, Jesus. If this works, your influence will spread to every person in the land you see before you." Inspiration filled Pontius' soul as he looked out over the magnificent scene. Imagining his vision taking root in the barren land, Pontius scanned the distant horizon. "Maybe even further." Turning back to Jesus, he noticed Jesus was intently focused on his words. "I'm not sure if this is important to you, but I assure you, you will be rewarded handsomely and looked upon with great favor from Rome."

Jesus shook his head. "That's not important to me. I want peace and security for the people of this land. Something everyone deserves, Jew or Gentile."

With a curious look, Pontius turned. "Gentile? What do you mean,

'Gentile'?"

Jesus looked back, motioning toward him. "You are a Gentile. The people out beyond the horizon you speak of are Gentile. It is a term we use for those not Jewish. There are many trees in the forest and we, the chosen people of God, are the fruit trees. In the past, the prophets have preached of God wielding an ax against the roots of the trees of the forest for transgressions they have dealt upon us. Now God is wielding an ax against the roots of the fruit trees, evidenced by the violence and divisions that have ripped our people. I believe there is no longer a distinction between the trees of the forest and the fruit trees, between you and me. I believe we are all equal in the eyes of God, all worthy of his love and mercy."

Pilate nodded, seeing Jesus' attitudes meshing with his own vision. With a hint of sarcasm Joseph interrupted. "Perhaps we should first concentrate on the fruit trees."

* * *

As time went on, Pilate and Joseph traveled back and forth to Jerusalem several times, leaving Jesus to spend many days on his own. The periodic visits went on for a few weeks as they put in more preparation with Jesus. They worked hard to ensure that the turn of events that befell John would not happen again. They had attained so much success with John and could have gone much further, had it not been for John's indiscretions.

Soon, rumors spread throughout the land about what had happened to the man chosen by John to continue his ministry. The brief introduction at the river acted as perfect publicity. The mystery of Jesus' sudden disappearance worked to their advantage in spreading the news and fervor.

During one of Pilate's visits, Joseph addressed Jesus: "It's amazing, but your name is already becoming known. In my travels back and forth to Jerusalem, I have heard your name mentioned several times. It seems word of your disappearance and persisting absence is spreading as fire in parched woods. With John's absence, the people are in a void that you must fill."

Pontius smiled and nodded with confident assurance. "Excellent news. That's the kind of promotion we need to get things going again. It's funny how the mystery of the unknown can gain so much more than a thousand mouths." Then turning toward Joseph, Pontius asked, "So, what have they been saying?"

Joseph raised his arms in astonishment, his view less optimistic. "I have heard everything and anything. It amazes me what can spread by word of mouth. I have heard Jesus was taken up into heaven by a whirlwind, like Elijah of long ago."

Pilate smiled with confidence as Joseph nervously continued, "But mostly I've heard that he was taken away by the demons of the wilderness. In fact, the old, dying view that John was supported by demons is gaining new life. It seems to be growing in popularity now that John is away."

Jesus turned towards Pilate. "Do you know how long John will be in prison? Is he in good health?"

"He's fine. But I do not know how long Antipas intends to keep him."

Jesus continued, "If John isn't released soon, we may lose the momentum that is building throughout the land."

Pilate emphatically shook his head. "We cannot wait until Antipas releases John. You're right, Jesus. The fervor is high with news of transition. We must take advantage of the passion of your mystery before it withers—forgotten."

A deep concern overtook Jesus' face. "With all this attention, how will we handle my return without John's presence? Where will I say I've been?"

Pontius shrugged his shoulders. "I don't know. Maybe we won't need to say anything."

Joseph shook his head, strongly disagreeing. "Rumors have been widespread and persistent. We cannot ignore them."

Pilate sensed the depth of concern in Joseph's voice. "Maybe we should build upon the idea that he was taken into heaven."

Joseph's eyes widened in shock. Jesus was the first to react. "If you would have me stoned the first day, then you would have me address them so. The mere mention of having been taken into heaven would be blasphemy!"

Pontius threw his hands in the air. "These are not my words! These are words created from the mouths of the people who must believe them. I'm just saying we could cultivate the seeds already sown."

Joseph reiterated Jesus' point. "We could never propose that, or suggest Jesus may have looked upon God. There are many who would rather tear their ears from their head than hear those words. Truly I plead, Noble Prefect, we must be careful what we have Jesus say."

Pontius gazed at Joseph, searching for an answer. "Well, you are the ones telling me we must say something. All I'm proposing is that we play upon the rumors."

Joseph nodded. "Your argument has merit, but I feel we should turn our attention upon others. Maybe we should play upon the rumor that he was taken away by the demons of the wilderness and tempted for their support."

Pilate raised his eyes in bewilderment. Jesus' expression was little changed from when the first idea was broached. Looking over at Jesus, Joseph continued, "Your return could be looked upon as a victory over their power, and how they could not bind you." Joseph paused as if searching for support. "Do you not see? We could turn a superstition into our favor. If we say Jesus was attacked and besieged by demons of the wilderness, but did not submit, then we can claim victory over popular folklore rather than meddle with a sacred concept of scripture."

19 ~ A Day of Rest

It was the Jewish Sabbath. Jesus and Joseph were seated at a table in the farmhouse, finishing their bread and wine, when Pilate walked in accompanied by two men Jesus did not recognize. They appeared to be Jewish, which surprised Jesus. Pilate used the table to steady himself as he sat down next to Joseph. With a weary arm motion, Pilate made the introduction: "Joseph, Jesus, this is Glaucus. And this is Decius." From the names it was immediately clear they were not Jews. Pilate continued, "They are soldiers of the Roman garrison from Caesarea. They look Jewish, don't they?"

Joseph nodded. "Well, yes, and with the clothes, you could have fooled me."

The two men introduced themselves using perfect Hebrew. Joseph looked over at Pilate and said, "Are you sure they're Roman?"

Pilate replied with a confident smile and a slight nod of his head. Pointing to the clothes Pilate was wearing, Joseph continued, "You, too, have grown to a convincing role. You seem to have taken well to Jewish attire."

Pontius lost some of his smile looking down at his clothes, wiping at the dust. "Yes, sometimes I think a little too convincing. When we left Jericho early this morning, you wouldn't believe some of the stares we were getting from people. Some even cursed at us! Glaucus told me they were rebuking us for traveling on the Jewish Sabbath!"

Jesus and Joseph looked at each other and smiled. Joseph's smile turned to a quick laugh as he said, "You are experiencing, firsthand, judgment according to our law, Noble Prefect."

Clearly not amused, Pontius continued, "We couldn't even get feed for our horses or extra food for ourselves along the way! I think it is ridiculous how your people refuse to do anything on Saturdays! The world can't come to a complete stop just because you decide to sanctify it!"

With an instructional tone Jesus interjected, "It all goes back to the creation of the earth and how, after six days of labor, God rested on the seventh. Jews live by his example and rest on the seventh day. All forms of work and travel are forbidden on the Sabbath."

Feeling his stomach, Pontius got up and walked over to the cupboard and pulled out some bread. Stuffing some in his mouth, Pontius said in a muffled voice, "Is it forbidden to eat on the Sabbath?"

Jesus and Joseph laughed at Pilate's obvious disdain. After washing down the bread with wine, Pontius added, "I think there are some things you can carry too far. This Jewish law is one of them." Looking over at Joseph, Pontius added, "That's one of the things I want to work on."

Joseph raised his eyebrows and scratched his head. He slowly nodded, as if agreeing to Pilate's request. Then he glanced at the two soldiers and said, "These men aren't the usual contingent that accompanies you. I still can't believe they're Roman. You've done well to choose a convincing escort."

Pontius studied Glaucus and Decius. "Well, I hope they're convincing. I want them to serve with Jesus in his ministries throughout Judea. I know the work became too great for John. I believe it is a good idea to provide Jesus with assistance from the very start."

Jesus turned his attention towards the two soldiers, trying to hide a sudden sense of fear. Pilate continued, "John recruited disciples during his short ministry. It only makes sense that Jesus will do the same."

Joseph shook his head and let out an audible sigh. Pilate rolled his eyes. "Don't worry. They're under strict orders to do anything and everything directed by Jesus. They will follow his command."

Jesus felt somewhat reassured, but Joseph countered, "That's all well and good, but I'm more concerned about their common, everyday interactions with the pe—"

Pilate interrupted, "You, yourself, found them very convincing. And you heard them speak."

"Yes, but that was only a few words. How convincing will they be portraying Jews day in and day out? Besides, some of John's disciples may be willing to transfer over to Jesus' ministries. After all, they were there when John handed his ministry to Jesus. Surely they are willing to carry on with their work."

Pilate nodded. "I have no objections to having them help Jesus with his duties. I'm just saying these men will supplement them, not be the exclusive disciples of Jesus. They will also provide me with a more direct link as to what is going on. There were many times I lost touch with John's work."

Jesus did not like the idea of being under the constant watchful eye of Roman soldiers. However, he liked the idea of the security and protection they might bring, especially since they would be under his direction. With slight reluctance, Jesus agreed to their service. "We obviously can't refer to them as Glaucus and Decius. They'll need Jewish names."

Glaucus immediately responded, "This is not the first time we have worked in the Jewish community. We already have names. I am Thaddaeus of Tyre and this is Simon the Cananaean." Decius smiled and bowed slightly at the mention of his alias. Decius had a rougher look compared to Glaucus, with darker skin and dense, unkempt facial hair. Putting his hand on Decius' shoulder, Glaucus continued, "Decius—or should I say Simon—has spent a fair amount of time with zealot bands. He is well accepted amongst their ranks. So you see, we have already spent a great deal of time amongst your people. We will have no difficulty continuing with this role."

Jesus walked over to greet them. "Thaddaeus of Tyre and Simon the Cananaean. I look forward to working with you gentlemen."

* * *

Pilate stayed for two days before heading back to Jerusalem. Glaucus and Decius escorted him back, and then immediately returned to begin their duties with Jesus.

Joseph unfolded the letter from Pontius and skimmed through the words. He then closed his eyes, and with a nervous exhale looked up at

Jesus. "He wants us to return to the Jordan River." He shook his head handing the letter to Jesus. "I asked him to wait until John is released, but he doesn't want to wait."

Jesus skimmed the letter, then looked back at Joseph. "It's been over a month, Joseph. If we wait any longer, there won't be anyone to return to."

Joseph pulled a bag from underneath his bunk. "I suppose we'll find out soon enough."

The next morning, the four of them traveled to John's old cabin. Thaddaeus was the first to enter. He eventually came back to the front door and waved them in. The place was in order and well kept. Jesus found his way to a chair as Joseph stood silently in the center of the room.

After a short rest, Jesus and Joseph walked down to the river. Joseph obviously knew his way, as they soon came across people milling about. Jesus saw a large crowd as they neared the river. Jesus recognized Andrew and James at the head of twisting lines working against the river's current. Joseph said, "Obviously, you will have to do this on your own. I believe that's James and Andrew out there—two of John's disciples."

Jesus nodded. "Yes, I met them very briefly before. I hope they'll remember me."

Joseph placed his hand on Jesus' shoulder. "How could they not? Were they not there when John introduced and baptized you?"

"Yes, but will they heed his call and follow me?" Jesus asked, his face uncertain.

Joseph gave a reassuring nod. "As for me, I'm going to visit John at Machaerus."

"Machaerus? Just be careful traveling through that area. It is said that Aretas is waging war on Antipas' armies for the dishonor he brought to his daughter."

Joseph nodded. "Yes, I know, but I think the battles are more to the northeast, away from Machaerus. I will be careful all the same." Joseph looked over his left shoulder towards the south and let out a heavy sigh. "I feel I need to go and see how he is doing."

"Does Pilate know you are going?"

"No. I pray he is as concerned as I am and will want to know about

John. But sometimes I wonder." Joseph closed his eyes and turned his face to the heavens, taking in a few deep breaths. "Sometimes we have yokes to bear: I, having to travel through war-torn country; you, taking up the mission of a new ministry; and John, suffering Antipas' wrath." Joseph opened his eyes and looked at Jesus. "I don't think you should spend much time around here. You should move your ministry farther north, maybe closer to your home of Nazareth. I think you need to get away from Jerusalem, and Antipas, until things settle down a little. Besides, you would probably be more comfortable up there."

Jesus nodded. "But will they follow?"—pointing to the crowds and John's disciples.

Joseph turned in the direction of John's cabin, while Jesus waded out into the river to meet with Andrew and James. Drawing near, some of those gathered recognized him from the weeks before. A hush fell over the crowd. Gradually, attention was turned towards Jesus as he pushed his way through the water. James called out, "Andrew! Look there!" pointing to shore. "It's Jesus!"

Both of them excused themselves from the line of congregants and started making their way toward Jesus. James was the first to reach Jesus, hugging him with surprising intensity. Releasing his embrace, James stood back and said, "I can't believe it! You've come back! I was beginning to wonder if you would ever return!"

By this time, Andrew had reached Jesus, offering his hand in a more subdued yet friendly greeting. James stood back slightly asking, "What happened to you anyway? Where have you been?"

Jesus took a deep breath and shrugged his shoulders. "It's a long story. I will tell you about it in time. For now, John has given me an understanding of my responsibilities, and I think I'll need your help."

Andrew and James nodded, with Andrew replying, "We have stayed here carrying on John's work, and we have no plans to leave. We have collected large sums in tithing and stored the money in John's cabin, except for the amount John would have given us." Andrew's tone then grew more concerned, looking Jesus squarely in the eye. "Have you heard anything from John?"

Jesus shook his head. "Unfortunately, I haven't heard anything since he went to Machaerus. However, I am confident he will be fine. There are forces at work to see to his release. I am sure God is looking after him."

Jesus sensed Andrew cared for John greatly. Seeing how much his words settled Andrew's soul, Jesus went on, "I have a friend who is on his way to Machaerus right now to pay witness to his welfare." Then turning towards James, Jesus added, "I suppose you know that even after he is released from prison, John will not be coming back to his ministries. He has commissioned me, and I hope you will continue to help me as you would have with John."

Both Andrew and James gave nods of devoted and reassuring approval.

By this time, a large portion of the crowd was making its way toward the three of them. Turning around and pointing at the growing number of people, James said, "As you can see, we've been busy in the time you've been away. Andrew has given most of the sermons from what we can remember about John's teachings. Unfortunately, I'm not a good speaker, so I haven't been much help there."

Jesus smiled at James' humility and said, "It's not so much how you say it, but what you have to say that is important."

Andrew raised his eyebrows a little and said, "That's part of the problem. We've run out of ideas for sermons. We've resorted back to more traditional teachings of the Scriptures—not so different from what one would hear in the synagogues. The people have come out here not only to be baptized, but to be consoled. We must give them something." Andrew lowered his eyes and shook his head. "Even though it appears there are a lot of people here today, there were many more at one time. It's been steadily tapering off since a couple of weeks ago."

James interrupted, "After John was arrested, there were a great many people who came out, probably more curious than anything to see what was going on. We were really overwhelmed at first. We called upon our brothers in Bethsaida to help, but by the time they arrived, the crowds were already starting to thin. They were eager to help and stayed for a few days. But when it became obvious they were no longer needed, they left."

Worried, Jesus asked, "Why did they leave so quickly?"

James placed his hand on his chest and said, "I'm a fisherman by trade. Both of my brothers are fishermen. We helped my father on the Sea of Galilee since we were boys. When there was no need for their services, Aaron and John went back to Bethsaida to help my father."

Andrew nodded. "The same is true for my brother, Simon." Placing his hand on James' shoulder, Andrew added, "That's how James and I knew each other. Our families have fished the Sea of Galilee for as long as I can remember."

James gave a quick, sarcastic laugh. "I am a lot better at pulling fish out of the sea than I am at pulling people out of the river."

Jesus and Andrew laughed abruptly. Then Andrew hit James across the shoulder. "You don't have to be so disrespectful! You've been doing this too long!"

James gave Andrew a friendly shove, nearly pushing him back into the water. "You didn't have to laugh either!" With this, their laughter grew louder, almost reckless. Even though Jesus thought they were carrying this too far, he quickly got caught up in the contagious nature of their laughter. For an instant he thought of them as fishers of men, but held his tongue.

Jesus turned his attention to those gathering around. He raised his hands and said, "I am Jesus, the one John told you would come after him! I was commissioned by John to carry on his work. I am your humble and willing servant to spread good news—the gospel of the Lord—to his people!"

Jesus had heard Joseph use the Roman term "gospel" several times in their discussions. The word presented an air of power and glory he hoped to convey in his first introduction. He scanned the crowd, not sensing disapproval, but rather looks of people breathlessly awaiting his next word. "John is doing fine! He has been arrested by Antipas, but he is doing fine! By God's will, and with all of your prayers, he will be released soon. John has lived as an example we must follow. He is a righteous and good man, and so must we live our lives. Repent from any evil ways that may be controlling your lives, for the kingdom of heaven is at hand. God's powerful hand will come down in judgment, lifting those up who live according to his will and smashing those who forsake his divine guidance." Jesus went on with a lesson he and Joseph had worked on, his confidence slowly building.

With a look of astonishment, James leaned over to Andrew and whispered, "His words are fascinating. He speaks with such ease and meaning. We have struggled for weeks and could not affect the power of his words."

After concluding his sermon, Jesus, Andrew, and James walked back to John's cabin. Jesus told them about the two other disciples waiting for them. Then remembering what Joseph had suggested, Jesus added, "I have been thinking of moving the ministry up north, closer to the Sea of Galilee. I, too, am from the region—Nazareth in Galilee."

At first Andrew smiled, but then a look of obvious disappointment infected his expression. He leaned over to his brother and whispered, "That's too bad. He is a Nazarene. I was hoping he was from the house of David—maybe even the Christ, the Messiah. Now I know this cannot be. The prophets have said the Christ would come from the City of David, Bethlehem." Pausing, he took a deep breath. "Can anything good come from Nazareth?"

Jesus interrupted their private exchange, "If the ministry moves up north, do you think your brothers will join us?"

Jesus had hoped they would react favorably to a move closer to their home, and was puzzled at Andrew's sudden change in mood. However, they both nodded as James replied with some uncertainty, "I believe they will."

20 ~ My Servant

Jesus, Andrew, James, Thaddaeus, and Simon proceeded north to Bethsaida along the eastern shores of the Sea of Galilee, passing through several small towns and villages. Coming upon Andrew's hometown, Jesus could see several small fishing boats offshore. He could barely make out the figures of men throwing their nets into the sea and hauling back their catch. As they reached the point on shore nearest to the fleet of fishing boats, Andrew strained his eyes. "I think my father's boat is out there, but I can't be sure."

Andrew located the nearest boat on the beach and waved for the others to get in. James and Jesus jumped into the boat to give Andrew a hand at setting sail. Simon and Thaddaeus elected to stay on shore.

Once they'd hoisted the sail, the boat grudgingly cut through the waves that were pushing them back to shore. Soon the breaking waves turned into mild swells that no longer impeded their gradually increasing speed.

After they had gone halfway, many of the boats were raising their nets and setting their sails, giving up their work and heading for shore. James pointed to the distant horizon. "There's a storm brewing, beyond the fleet of boats. They're pulling in their nets."

Soon, all of the boats were headed back. James went up to the bow to get a clearer view. "We'd better turn back, Andrew! They're all coming in."

Andrew held steady on the rudder and shook his head. "Most of the boats are still twenty to thirty minutes out. Some of them might get caught in high seas!"

James stumbled back to Andrew, holding onto the low railing as the sea started to turn rough. Placing his hand on Andrew's shoulder, James confided, "Our fathers have spent countless years at sea. Their skill and experience will serve them well. However, it has been a while since we have commanded a boat."

Andrew reluctantly ordered the boat around, but continued looking back as the fleet closed its distance. As they neared the shore, a few boats were coming within earshot. Going to the rear of the boat, Andrew stood and called out, "Have you seen Azor!" As they waited for a distant response, a voice called from behind. Turning and looking toward shore, a man was waving his arms with others standing nearby. Andrew called out, "Simon!"

James leaned over to Jesus, pointing. "That's Andrew's brother, Simon, and his father."

Urgently, Andrew pulled on the rope to add more tension to the sails. Still the boat plodded at its own pace, which seemed to slow as they neared shore. The instant the boat touched bottom, Andrew was in the water running toward his father.

"Father, I have missed you! It's been far too long!" The two embraced.

"Andrew, my son, I didn't think you would ever come home," his father replied with a joyful tear.

Andrew shook his head, saying, "You know I couldn't stay away from the people and the life I love. If it were not for God's calling, I would have been home long ago, but there has been so much work to do."

Andrew's brother Simon broke in on the elated greetings, giving Andrew a sturdy embrace with strong pats on the back. Watching the boat, Simon raised his arm and waved a greeting at James. "Good life and peace to you, James!"

By this time James and Jesus were out of the boat, trying, with Glaucus and Decius' assistance, to pull it up onto the sand. Simon walked over, giving them a hand and shouted jovially, "It was nice of you to go out and do our work today!" Then turning and noting that the boat was empty, he added with a large grin, "But I see you have returned, as usual, with no fish."

James clutched Simon's arm in confident friendship and returned his smile. "If it had been fish we were looking for, this boat wouldn't have been big enough even for a single throw of my net!"

Simon offered a hearty laugh, and then looked over at Jesus. "It looks like you have found new fishing partners."

James turned, appearing apologetic. "Oh! This is the man Andrew and I were telling you about when you were down at the Jordan. This is Jesus, the one prophesized by John. And this is Thaddaeus of Tyre and Simon the Cananaean."

Jesus was the first to respond. "Peace to you, Simon."

In awe, Simon answered, "And peace to you, Master."

Feeling emboldened by Simon's blind respect, Jesus continued, "Your brother told me how much you helped with John's ministry."

Simon nodded. "Yes, for a short time they needed our help." He pointed at James. "His brothers helped too." Clearing his throat and shifting his eyes slightly, Simon added, "After a while, I had to return to help my father."

Jesus turned to face the strong breeze. In the distance, deep clouds were building over the choppy water. He studied the line of boats clinging to the soft sand along a narrow beach that quickly transitioned to sporadic groves of trees and thick vegetation unique to the sea. "It's a beautiful country. It's easy to understand why you would long to be here." Looking at James and Andrew, Jesus went on, "We have decided to move our ministry up to this area. Both of them have told me you were invaluable help, and I was hoping you would consider working with us."

Simon's chest swelled at Jesus' show of confidence, but he hesitated in answering. Pointing at the numerous boats starting to come on shore, Jesus continued, "There are a great many fishermen to gather fish from the sea. Follow me and I will make you fishers of men."

Simon cringed slightly and leaned over to James. "What an odd thing to say. We pull hundreds of fish from the sea each day. They all die and get fed to the masses."

Jesus heard Simon and shook his head in disbelief.

James let out a quick laugh. "No, Simon! He's referring to the baptism ritual. Andrew and I were joking about it last week—pulling people out of the river like fish."

Jesus wasn't amused as Andrew joined in the laughter. Simon's expression lightened somewhat, but still gave a quick shudder of disapproval. Turning serious, he asked, "What about my family and our livelihood? I have a wife, although I don't have children. Andrew and I have worked with our father since we were young, and he has grown to depend on us."

Undeterred, Jesus replied, "Surely your father has others who can help with the daily tasks. You have been called by God to spread his gospel to all of his people." Glancing at Simon's father, Jesus continued, "I assure you, your family will be provided for. They will continue to have food to eat." Then looking back at Simon, Jesus said, "God will provide for us also, giving us food to eat and places to lay our heads." Jesus remembered something his father used to tell him as a boy. Looking up into the sky and pointing toward some birds, Jesus said, "Look at these birds. They do not concern themselves about what they will eat next. God provides for them and cares for them. How much more important are we to God than they?"

Simon smiled at Jesus' reassurances. Glaucus smirked and whispered to Decius, "Has he ever been away from Nazareth? A few years back I saw death from starvation and famine, including children—in villages not far from here."

Decius nodded, but gave Glaucus a stern look. "Careful of your words, Thaddaeus. We are here to support Jesus, not offer words of dissension."

Simon still would not give an answer gathering up his equipment to return with Azor. Following behind their father, Simon turned to Andrew. "Thaddaeus and Simon seem of good character and fortitude. How is it Jesus came upon their service?"

Andrew shook his head with an uncertain look. "I don't know. But they offer unwavering support. They are good men and are very dedicated." Andrew offered a confident smile, and added, "They offer a fine example, Simon—one that should help in your decision to return to John's ministries."

Simon paused and let the heavy coil of rope fall from his shoulder and hit the ground with a loud *thump*. He rubbed his lower back, his face grimacing. "How is John? Have you heard from him?"

Andrew shook his head. "No. But Jesus says he will be released soon. It will be good to see him again."

"Yes, it will be good to see him again." Simon paused with a studied expression. "Father is planning on giving up on fishing, and I'm not sure I want to continue on my own." Simon massaged the small of his back again as he reached over to pick up the rope.

The next day, one of James' brothers, John, also agreed to join them.

Jesus' disciples now numbered six as they started going about the country presenting most of the material Jesus, Joseph, and Pilate had worked on during their forty days of seclusion.

* * *

In Jerusalem, the Roman centurion from Capernaum walked into Pilate's office, smartly hitting his fist against his shoulder. Pilate looked up from his desk, returning the gesture. The centurion dutifully announced his name and position. "Sir, Centurion Bartimius of the garrison at Capernaum, reporting as ordered."

With this, Pilate stood from behind his desk and walked over to personally greet him. "Ah, Bartimius! We meet again." Offering a friendly slap on the back, Pilate continued, "Relax, Bartimius. You may stand at ease." Pilate walked over, shut the door, and pointed toward a chair. "In fact, you may sit." Pilate walked back and took his own seat.

The centurion dutifully walked to the chair and sat down, his trembling fingers grasping the arms. Seeing that Bartimius was tense, Pilate tried to relieve the stress. "I appreciate your coming so far on such short notice. I know it's not an easy journey. Was your trip without incident?"

Bartimius nodded. "Yes, sir. It was fine. I've made the trip many times, and I know it well, my lord."

Pilate smiled. "Good, good." Then getting straight to the point, realizing it would be merciful to a man who seemed to be dreadfully anticipating every word, he began, "There's a man, a Jew, who is moving up into your area to preach—how should I say it—a variation of the Jewish faith. He is actually under Roman support and direction, and it's important it stay that way. The people don't know of our support and that's also crucial. Anyway, I want you to let him have clear reign over the area. I don't want you, or any of your men, to give him any trouble."

A load seemed to be lifted from Bartimius as he nodded in complete agreement. "Consider it done, my lord. If I may ask, sir, who is this man?"

"His name is Jesus, and he will have a following of five to ten disciples. It's possible there will be even more who follow him from place to place as he gives his message."

"Jesus, huh?" Bartimius repeated. "I've never heard of him. The way you were talking, I thought you were speaking of John the Baptist." Pausing only a second, Bartimius continued, "But he's in prison, isn't he?"

"Yes, he is. At Machaerus. But you're right, he's a lot like John the Baptist." In nervous agitation, Pilate pushed himself out of his chair and walked over to the window. Bartimius immediately jumped out of his chair, but Pilate quickly motioned to him. "Oh no, Bartimius, please remain seated."

In a respectful tone Bartimius responded, "Thank you, sir, but I'd feel more comfortable standing."

Pilate lifted an eyebrow. "So be it, as you please." He then looked out the window and observed a small group of soldiers lined up for inspection in the courtyard below. Turning back to Bartimius, Pilate said, "One of the reasons we are supporting Jesus is that he is trying to improve the image of the Roman soldier with Jews."

Bartimius jerked back his head letting out an audible sneer.

Pilate walked closer to him. "That's where you come in—again."

Bartimius raised his eyebrows. Continuing, Pilate explained, "I want you to meet with Jesus—in secret, of course. Make arrangements for him to perform some type of miracle on you or your family." Pausing in thought, Pilate asked, "Are you married? Do you have children?"

Bartimius nodded. "Yes, I have a wife and five children." Growing noticeably uneasy, and in a skeptical tone, Bartimius asked, "What kind of miracle?"

Pilate slightly shook his head. "Oh, it doesn't matter. We've been having him heal the sick and cure physical disabilities. Even last week, I had one of my soldiers dress up in leper's clothing, covered from head to toe, and we had Jesus 'cure him.' Throwing off his coverings, the crowd was truly amazed at what they perceived to be a true miracle from their god." Chuckling to himself, Pilate added, "We didn't even need to alter his physical appearance. All we had to do was put a hood over his head, and their imagination did the rest. These people are so gullible, as they thirst for wondrous acts. These miracles have become an incredible tool with which to manipulate their loyalties. I only wish I had thought of it long ago."

Bartimius scratched his head. "I remember hearing a vague rumor before I left. Something about a Jew performing magic acts of healing. I didn't know that's who you were referring to."

Pilate nodded. "Yes, that's him. These miracles have made him very popular. Now is the perfect time for us to get involved."

Bartimius shook his head with knowing concern. "I don't want to get my family involved in this."

Pilate's voice grew stern and more direct. "Heed my words. A lot of the people who have acted out afflictions have been Roman. The only thing is, no one knows they're Roman. This time I want a miracle involving a Roman citizen, so these people will see we don't have to be excluded from their society."

"Well, I'm not going to act like I have leprosy—or paralyzed. I'm known too well there. Besides, I think it would appear strange for me to all of a sudden come down with some serious 'affliction,' as you put it, just in time to be healed by this... who did you say it was?"

"Jesus! His name is Jesus. I'm not asking you to come down with some affliction. I don't think it would look good to your men. That's why I was asking about your family," Pilate said, feeling like he had made his point.

Bartimius shook his head again. "I don't want my family to be part of this, sir. I keep them shielded from my work. I don't want to get them involved in something so... conspicuous."

Pontius' enthusiasm waned. Bartimius grew noticeably uneasy. His anxious expression relaxed, however, as he added, "But I do have servants in my house."

Pilate's eyes narrowed. "Are they Roman?"

"No! They're not Roman, sir." Looking up at the ceiling as if to recall them one by one, Bartimius continued, "One is Ethiopian, and the other two are Greek, I believe. We had a Jewish servant at one time—Samaritan, I think. She didn't last very long, due to the pressure she was receiving from her family about entering a Roman household."

"That's what I'm talking about! The disdain these people have towards anything Roman!" Pilate raised his hands with his fingers splayed, resigned to some level of cooperation. "May the gods be merciful—that will have to do! I want you to meet with Jesus when you return to Capernaum. You will need to work out the details with him."

Returning to attention, Bartimius responded, "Yes, my lord." He gave another salute, bowed, and left.

Immediately after dismissing Bartimius, while still looking down at the soldiers in the courtyard, another scheme took root in Pilate's mind. He recognized a soldier below who was known to have discipline problems—obnoxious and unruly. The soldier was particularly large, intimidating, and overbearing, sometimes on the verge of disobedience to garrison commanders. Pilate had avoided the commander's requests for arrest, but now had an idea for a mission that would suit the soldier's attributes.

Calling the soldier to his office, Pilate kept him at attention. "Your name is Dracus, is it not?"

"Yes, sir," he replied, with beads of sweat building on his forehead.

Seeing that he was intimidating the large man, Pilate capitalized by getting closer. "I have a special mission for you, Dracus." Then circling around, accentuating the soldier's motionless captivity, Pilate continued, "It will just involve you and your special talents."

Dracus nervously moved his eyes toward Pilate, then quickly forward. Pilate finally broke a span of silence. "Are you capable of using these talents in the service of Rome?"

Dracus immediately responded, "Yes, sir!"

Walking in front of Dracus, Pilate continued, "You will go up to the village of Gadara on the east bank of the Sea of Galilee. You will go there disguised as a Jewish commoner and not as a Roman soldier. All I want you to do is what you do here so well: terrorize the people for a few weeks."

With a quizzical look, Dracus responded, "You want me to go up there as a Jew, sir?"

Pilate turned and walked away, and in a matter-of-fact voice, replied, "Yes. We frequently send soldiers into the field secretly, to gather information."

Dracus' expression turned to concern. "Sir, I do not know Hebrew very well. I know a little, but I do not think I could interact with them on a day-to-day basis to gather information."

With growing emphasis, Pilate nearly shouted, "I'm not asking you to gather information. I'm ordering you to terrorize the people of the village for a few weeks. I want you to act as if you were possessed by one of their demons and speak gibberish for all I care." Pilate rubbed his chin and sat down at his desk. "Just don't try to say anything in Hebrew and don't let them know you're Roman." Taking on a very stern tone, Pilate looked directly at him. "You act as a crazed man in the midst of your fellow soldiers. Now it is time you offer your antics where they will serve a purpose."

Clearly apprehensive, Dracus pleaded, "Sir, I swear I will settle my actions and cease my threats. Sometimes I don't know why I do the things I do, but I will discipline my thoughts and control my actions."

Pilate nodded. "That's good, Dracus. When you return, I'll hold you to that."

"But sir, what if I'm arrested?"

"See to it that you're not arrested. I'm not telling you to kill anybody. I just want you to harass the villagers. If you act crazy enough, they won't arrest you, they'll just think you're possessed and leave you alone." Pilate actually wasn't sure of this, but felt it did some good in settling the soldier's fears.

"You will only need to do this for a few weeks—long enough to really become a persistent thorn in their sides. Then I am going to send a Jewish man called Jesus, who will drive out your demons. You can then return to Jerusalem and your normal duties." Pilate prided in thought on how an entire village would witness Jesus' miracle.

Dracus gave an incredulous blink, then asked, "Could I please take a couple of men with me, sir? Men who can speak Hebrew. I don't know how I would have a chance, otherwise."

Pilate agreed. "And by the gods, man, be convincing!"

* * *

In Capernaum, Bartimius met with Jesus and laid out the details of their planned performance. The next day, as Jesus entered Capernaum with his disciples, Bartimius ran up to him and pleaded, "Lord, my servant is lying paralyzed at home in terrible distress."

Most of the people stood back as the centurion approached. Everyone appeared stunned to hear the centurion call Jesus "Lord." A strange silence filled the air, as they waited to see how Jesus would react.

Jesus smiled and turned towards Bartimius. "I will come and heal him."

Several in the crowd began voicing shock and disapproval as a low murmur turned into a roar. One man called out, "Last week, Ephram called upon you to heal his wife, only to have you rebuke him, as you cursed a generation that demanded so many signs, with so little faith. Now, you are bowing to the wishes of a Roman who does not even practice our faith!"

The crowd became silent again. Jesus turned away and started walking with Bartimius toward his home. As if by some unknown force, many turned and followed. After they had walked a short distance, Bartimius raised his voice so that all could hear. "Lord, I am not worthy to have you come into my home, but only say the word and my servant will be healed. For I am a man of authority with soldiers under me. And I say to one, 'Go,' and he goes, and to another, 'Come,' and he comes, and to my slave, 'Do this,' and he does it."

Turning to the rest of the crowd, Jesus addressed them, saying, "Truly I say to you, not even in Israel have I found such faith."

Many in the crowd started yelling at Jesus and openly threatened the centurion. Several in the crowd picked up stones, but none wanted to be the first. Jesus waved his hands in the air and started yelling, "I tell you, many who are not Jewish will come from afar to sit at the table with Abraham, Isaac, and Jacob in the kingdom of heaven, while Jews will be thrown into the outer darkness. There, men will weep and gnash their teeth."

Turning back to Bartimius, Jesus said, "Go, your servant is healed as you have believed."

21 ~ Source of Affliction

Having the same name, one of the Simons, Andrew's brother, soon acquired a nickname. He was average height and solid in stature, with a stern and quiet demeanor. Many of the disciples called him Peter, meaning "the rock." Peter was dumfounded as he watched the centurion walk away. He had seen him on rare occasions, but never like this. He was still in a state of shock when he felt Jesus tap him on the shoulder. "We will need a place to stay tonight. Don't your in-laws live in Capernaum?"

Peter nodded, knowing what Jesus was asking. "Yes, I can go over and ask if they have room."

Jesus nodded. Still trying to make sense of what he had just seen, Peter turned to make his way, welcoming the chance to clear his head. Approaching his in-law's home, he saw someone walking toward him out of the corner of his eye. From his dress, he recognized the man to be a tax collector. Quickening his pace, he heard the man call out, "Aren't you one of the teacher's disciples?"

Peter turned and gave an imperceptible nod. "Yes." Seeing the man was still approaching, Peter knew he could not simply turn and be on his way. "And who might you be, sir?"

Almost out of breath, the man answered, "I am Salazar, collector of the half-shekel tax. Does your teacher pay the tax?"

Peter recalled how Jesus always spoke favorably of tax collectors, and without hesitation replied, "Yes."

Salazar smiled and asked, "Then will you give one shekel to pay for yourself and your Master?"

Peter felt somewhat offended that he was asked to pay for both of them. He was also in a hurry to reach his in-laws and did not want to be bothered further. "Sorry, I do not have any money with me. When I see my Master, I will collect for both of us and pay you later."

Arriving at his in-laws, Peter soon learned that his mother-in-law was not feeling well. Before he could gather his things to warn the others, he heard a knock at the door and Jesus' familiar call. Peter's father-in-law, Jorim, answered the door, inviting them to come in. Visibly surprised to see such a large group, Jorim turned to Peter and asked, "What fills your days, Simon, and who are your friends?" Peter quickly explained their ministry and how they had gained sudden popularity.

Jorim nodded, but with a strong look of disapproval asked, "So how is Tiersa?"

Peter shifted in his chair, taking a defensive posture. "Tiersa is doing fine, and she is staying with my parents while I am away. I get back there every couple of weeks or so." Peter sensed Jorim was still disappointed. Hoping to change the subject, Peter asked, "So Mathesia is not feeling well? Where is she?"

Jorim wearily shook his head. "She is in her room. She has been very sick for the past couple of days."

"What's wrong with her?"

"Oh," Jorim said with a bearish tone, "a couple of days ago she became ill. She has been very sick, unable to eat. She developed a fever, and I've kept her in bed." Jorim was obviously distressed over the pain his wife was going through, adding, "Last night she got the chills, and I covered her with several blankets trying to keep her warm." Shaking his head, Jorim continued, "Poor thing. She complains of chills, while her sweat has soaked her clothes and bedding."

Andrew nervously interrupted, "Can her affliction spread to others?" Hearing this several of the other disciples sat up in their chairs, as if preparing to leave.

Jorim shrugged his shoulders and grumbled, "I don't know."

Peter looked at Jesus, and began wondering if he could heal her as he had done with so many others over the past several weeks. Trying to catch Jesus' gaze, Peter asked, "Jesus, could you go up and look at Mathesia to see if there's anything you can do?"

Jesus nervously tapped his finger on a table next to his chair, seeming to take longer than usual to respond. Eventually he met each of their stares and finally responded, "Well, sure, I suppose I could go—"

Jesus was suddenly interrupted—everyone's attention was directed towards the stairs as Mathesia slowly made her way down. She was pale and in a weakened state. She had a smile on her face, however, as she precariously steadied herself against the wall. "I thought I heard commotion down here. Simon! It's so good to see you!"

Jorim immediately stood, going over to assist his wife. "Wife! You shouldn't be up. There is no need for you to be down here." Then, trying to turn her back, Jorim pleaded, "Here, let me help you back up to your room."

Mathesia held on to her husband's arm, but resisted his motions. "No, husband! I'm feeling much better now, and I'd like something to eat."

Giving in, Jorim helped her to an adjacent room to get food and water. Slowly, all of the disciples' eyes turned upon Jesus. Jesus quickly got up and walked into the adjoining room. Jesus addressed Mathesia. "As much as we would appreciate your hospitality, it is clear you need your rest. I am so glad to see you are feeling better." Pointing at the two of them, Jesus went on, "Both of you need your rest. We should not burden you any further."

Visibly relieved, Jorim offered token rebuttal. "No, it is all right for you to stay. Any friends of Simon are always welcome in our house."

Peter had entered the room as Jesus bowed towards Jorim. "For now, the important thing is for both of you to get some rest."

Jorim placed his hand on his wife's forehead. The loving concern on his face became a smile. "Your fever is gone, my wife." Standing up, Jorim patted Jesus on the arm and said, "Thank you, Jesus. I'm sorry we could not be better hosts. In the future, I hope we get the chance to extend our hospitality."

Peter was greatly relieved to see the smile on Jorim's face. It also gave him a sense of pride to see how Jorim had suddenly taken to Jesus and his friends. Walking back into the front room, Jesus addressed the rest of the disciples. "Mathesia is doing well. We must be on our way to give them rest."

No one offered objections, as some had already gathered up their things and were ready to leave.

As they left the house, Peter told Jesus of his encounter with the tax collector.

Jesus stopped and looked at Peter. "You did not pay him?"

Feeling slighted Peter replied, "You have provided for us in our ministries, and you have shared in the tithes collected. But I do not receive the income of my trade as a fisherman. Should the tithes of a ministry be taxed as if it were a trade?"

Jesus thought for a moment and then replied, "Are the coins pulled from the sea any different from the coins earned from our ministries?"

Peter shook his head. "No."

Jesus pulled a shekel from his purse, and gave it to him. "Go, give this to him for me and for yourself, being careful not to show further offense."

* * *

A few weeks later when Jesus met with Joseph, Jesus made a plea for a home somewhere in Galilee, where he and his disciples could have a place to stay and lay their heads. Going from day to day without knowing where they would stay, and constantly having to impose themselves on friends, family, and strangers, was starting to wear on their morale. Jesus explained that there wouldn't be enough room for them at his own home in Nazareth, for he had several brothers and sisters who lived with his mother in a modest home. He explained that since his absence, bad feelings had ensued among his siblings. Some in his family viewed him as forsaking his responsibilities.

Joseph agreed to Jesus' request, and they soon found a large home in Capernaum. Joseph had little difficulty convincing Pilate to provide the necessary support. Jesus' ministry was drawing large crowds and interest throughout all of Israel.

* * *

Dracus had been in Gadara for several days. He and his two companions, Tomis and Catullus, camped in a cave near the tombs, where privacy was assured. Each day, Dracus harassed the people of the town.

On one occasion, he slapped a mule's rump, causing it to run and spill its cargo. The owner ran after it, frantically picking up spilled goods. Sometimes Dracus would simply walk through the middle of town, screaming gibberish at everyone who passed. At night, Dracus would go back to the tombs to camp with his companions. He spent the evenings telling his stories of the day's events, sending the three of them into horrendous bouts of laughter.

After a couple of weeks, the humor of his duty wore thin as Dracus grew weary of the reactions of the townspeople. At first their stares were of surprise and fear, but soon they turned to hatred and disgust. Many simply ignored him. The negative feelings Dracus generated soon affected his own spirits, making him dread each day. The evenings turned from nights filled with drinking and laughter to quiet, drunken nights of cursing the day's events. Soon, Dracus found himself drinking in the morning to work up the courage and will to proceed with his annoying existence. When their supply of wine ran low, Dracus would simply steal from the town stores. Tomis and Catullus also grew weary and bored of their commission, frequently threatening to abandon their posts and return to Jerusalem.

With each passing day, Dracus grew increasingly anxious and impatient for Jesus' arrival. Their evenings were soon occupied by no other subject.

One day, Dracus rested in front of a bakery absorbing the pleasant aroma of fresh bread baking in the ovens. It was the only pleasure he could afford himself in this scornful community. Barely opening his eyes, Dracus noticed a man dressed in religious garb. A ray of hope shot through him, thinking this could be Jesus. Standing, Dracus perceived fear in the man's eyes as he stopped in his tracks several feet away. Dracus quickly asked, "Are you Jesus?"—reciting in Hebrew what Tomis had instructed.

The man seemed to ignore him, orchestrating strange motions with his arms, reciting his own garble of words. Every now and then, Dracus could make out the Hebrew word for "demon," but he was uncertain how he was supposed to react. *Was this Jesus?* After a short while, Dracus walked toward the rabbi, who quickly became silent backing away with each approaching step. Frustrated, Dracus yelled out, "Are you Jesus?"

Instead of showing recognition of Jesus' name, the rabbi continued to back away, resuming his religious incantations. Seeing he was getting no reaction, Dracus quickly and angrily turned away from the rabbi and started pushing his way through a crowd that had formed. Several people started running as he approached, but three men grabbed Dracus in hopes of subduing him. Dracus quickly pulled his right arm from the clutches of one man, then started beating at a couple of others who had grabbed him around the waist and left arm. Being large and strong, the force of his punches crumpled one and sent another falling to the ground. Another man grabbed him from behind. As if by instinct, and recalling the training he had received in close-order combat, Dracus thrust his right elbow back around, hitting the man squarely in the head, sending him to the ground with a cry of pain. Having freed himself, Dracus started running, trying to get away from an ever-growing contingent that had gathered to assist their fellow townsmen. Dracus had run several yards, gaining all the speed he could muster, before someone grabbed at his feet causing him to trip, sending his hands and face into the ground. Dazed, Dracus slowly pushed himself to his hands and knees, trying rise. Someone kicked him in his side causing him to fall over onto his back as he cried out in excruciating pain. Realizing he had to get up faster, Dracus continued rolling away from the man, gaining enough momentum to jump back to his feet. But he was hopelessly surrounded. He instinctively reached at his side where his sword would have been, patting for his last hope of escape. Unwilling to relinquish his freedom, Dracus continued to flail, landing several hard punches before finally being subdued by too many men and exhaustion.

Having no jail, the men took Dracus to a sturdy post and bound him with fetters and chains, planning to take him to Capernaum the next day.

It was getting dark. Periodically, Dracus yanked hard at the chains, grimacing as the fetters cut into his wrists. A few people remained, gawking and exchanging bouts of laughter. Each tug was met with solid resistance, making his efforts seem useless. Dracus had trouble breathing and wanted to bring his hand down to massage the pain from a broken rib. He was exhausted and wished he could lose consciousness.

Dracus awoke after an unknown span of time, hearing a familiar voice. He lifted his head and opened his eyes seeing Tomis trying to get his attention. The sight of his friend calmed him considerably. Dracus fell back against the post doing his best to remain conscious.

Catullus slapped his face, whispering, "Dracus, Dracus, it's me, Catullus. Tomis and I have come to get you out of here."

Dracus moaned from the aches from every ounce of his body. He tried to move his arm to wipe away the blood and dirt from his face—only to be painfully reminded his arms were bound overhead. Finally, seeing the familiar look of his friends in the soft torchlight, Dracus cleared his throat with a couple of coughs. "I knew you would come get me out of this." He looked around at a quiet, dark town. "Where did everybody go?"

Catullus quickly whispered, "Keep it down! It's the middle of the night and everyone's gone. We waited a good while to make sure no one was coming back." Catullus waved his torch over towards Tomis. "Tomis told me you were chained, so we brought axes."

Dracus looked at the metal ring on the post where his chain was securely bound. "This will need to be quick."

Catullus placed a large spike through one of the links on Dracus' feet. Tomis took aim at the chain on Dracus' hands as it lay against the post. Giving each other a look of "ready," both Tomis and Catullus let fly their axes, creating a loud *crack*, splitting the night air. The spike instantly cut the link at Dracus' feet, but the post only rattled as the ax found its mark. Getting to his feet, Dracus tugged at the upper chains to no avail. Tomis desperately took aim for a second hit, directing Dracus to lay the chain against the post. The impact only served to send another alarming announcement of their unwelcome presence. Catullus quickly pulled his spike from the ground and forced it through one of the links, near where Tomis had been hitting. With one final blow, the spike shattered the link into several pieces as Dracus pulled the chain through the confines of the ring. Tomis and Catullus quickly drowned their torches in the dirt as the three of them ran off into the darkness. Not sure if anyone had seen them, they kept running, each of them pulling at the chains to help Dracus along.

By the time the first of the townspeople awoke and ran to their doors, there was nothing to be seen. The sound of clanking chains could be heard, fading towards the tombs. A few made their way to the post only to find a few broken links—and their prisoner gone.

From that time on, Dracus stayed in the area of the tombs, never going back into town. The people of Gadara thought Dracus had broken his chains with the help of demonic forces, and feared him greatly. Very rarely did anyone venture to the tombs. If they did, Dracus would taunt them and throw stones when they approached. Occasionally Dracus would run nude through the tombs, emphasizing his bizarre behavior and hoping it would discourage further visits. Rumors spread of seeing more than one man roaming the tombs.

As the days dragged on, Dracus, Tomis, and Catullus started making their own elaborate plans for the welcome day when Jesus would come to call, putting an end to their strange duties. Each morning, the three of them would see a large herd of swine grazing precariously atop a large, grassy plateau next to a steep slope that fell down to the sea. Having far more time than duty, they devised an elaborate extension of the planned exorcism.

The three finally received a welcome visit from Glaucus—the one named Thaddaeus amongst the disciples. Glaucus explained that Jesus would arrive across the sea from Capernaum during the next couple of days. With a profound sense of relief, Dracus threw his hand up to the heavens. "Thank the gods! Why has it taken so long?!"

Showing little response to Dracus' sudden emotion, Glaucus replied, "We only learned of Gadara last week."

Dracus' euphoria ended as he grimaced. "Last week! We have been here for almost three!"

Catullus walked over to Glaucus and grasped his arm in a firm, friendly grip. "Well, never mind that. At least it will be over in a couple of days!" Then pointing back towards Tomis and Dracus, Catullus smiled. "We're more than ready for his arrival. Tell Jesus he must come here, to the tombs, for the exorcism. And it has to be between the third and fifth hour after sunrise."

Glaucus nodded as Tomis offered him dried bacon. For the first time, a smile came to Glaucus' face as he brought the bacon up to his nose. "My favorite meal. It's been a while since I've had the pleasure." Glaucus sat down on a rock and took in a deep, satisfying breath savoring the familiar taste. Dracus presented goblets of their fine wine to share, as the four conversed in a celebratory mood. After finishing his meal, Glaucus excused himself for his trip back to the disciples.

* * *

Jesus arrived by boat with the disciples, who by this time numbered eight. As Jesus walked into Gadara, he was met by a large, enthusiastic crowd who had also anticipated his arrival. Jesus nodded as several told him of the crazed, possessed man living amongst the tombs. Calling out, Jesus said, "I will go out to the tombs tomorrow morning, to see this man you speak of!"

The next morning, Jesus went out to the tombs, followed by his disciples and many of the townspeople. As the group approached, Dracus jumped out from behind a rock and screamed in near-perfect, well-rehearsed Hebrew, "What have you to do with me, Jesus, Son of the Most High God?"

Several of the townspeople were visibly surprised as one of them whispered, "The demon calls him by name, and blasphemes!" Several stooped to pick up a stone, as Jesus motioned them to stop. Jesus remembered his discussions with Pilate regarding King David, and immediately thought Dracus' reference to him as a "begotten one" was instruction from Pilate. Jesus grew nearer as Dracus continued to recite his memorized lines: "I adjure you by God, do not torment me!"

When he was nearly upon Dracus, Jesus finally opened his mouth and commanded, "Come out of the man, you unclean spirit!"

But Dracus continued to recite the words he and Tomis had planned over the past several days. Jesus rolled his eyes and shook his head in dismay.

Dracus continued, "My name is Legion, for we are many."

Standing nearby, Glaucus leaned over to Decius and whispered, "He is not responding to Jesus' command."

Decius gave a disgusted, disapproving look as he leaned back over to Glaucus. "Did he really just say 'legion'? Everyone will know he's a Roman."

Glaucus scoffed. "Or maybe they'll think his demon is Roman." Glaucus laughed and shrugged his shoulders. "They said they had something special planned."

Dracus continued with his performance. "Please do not send us into the abyss. Send us into the herd of swine over on the hill."

Looking up, Jesus could see the herd of swine on the distant hill. With uncertainty and concern beginning to show, Jesus again commanded with an even louder, if not angrier, voice, "Come out of the man, Legion of unclean spirits!"

With this, Dracus let out a deafening scream that sent shivers down everyone's spine. He threw himself to the ground as his cries echoed through the hollows of final rest. Even the herdsmen on the distant hill turned their attention from their herd towards the death-defying scream.

Tomis and Catullus were in hiding behind bushes on the plateau. On cue, they jumped out and started running toward the pigs, screaming, "Come back! Come back!"

All attention was on the distant hill as the pigs started running and pouring over the steep incline, falling to the sea. Everyone stared in helpless disbelief, even Jesus. Several climbed on top of rocks to get a better view. The herdsmen ran down the slopes trying to save their herd. Many of the women let out fearful cries, and several men rushed from the group to help the herdsmen. Soon others followed. In just a matter of minutes, nearly everyone except for Jesus and four of his disciples was down in the water, trying to push the pigs back to shore and gather as much of the herd as they could. They saved several from drowning, but a few ran up the banks on the other side and off into the wilderness. The entire incident took all of the attention away from Dracus, as he slowly stood to his feet. Jesus walked over to him and asked, "How did you do that?"

Dracus smiled with pride, replying, "Did you hear the screaming from the hill? That was Tomis and Catullus. They drove the pigs over the cliff."

"Whose idea was this?!"

With a look of surprise, Dracus answered, "We all thought of it. And it went quite well!"

With disbelief Jesus retorted, "Demons don't possess pigs! They're just stupid animals, with no sense of will or choice! Where did you get the idea that a demon could possess an animal?!"

Dracus turned and approached Jesus, putting his face up close. "Who are you to address me so! You need to watch your place, Jew!"

Glaucus lunged at Dracus and grabbed his shoulder, pulling him away from Jesus. "We're under orders! Watch your words, Dracus!"

Dracus pushed off Glaucus, but quickly composed himself. Turning back towards Jesus, Dracus replied, "Watch *yourself.*" Then with a didactic tone, Dracus continued, "It is common knowledge that the gods control animals."

"Not in our faith!" Jesus exclaimed. "This isn't Rome! Did you consult Joseph?"

"Who's Joseph?" Dracus replied.

Jesus shook his head in disapproval. "Oh never mind! It will blow over—hopefully."

Later that day, a group of townspeople went back to the tombs to find Dracus with Jesus, properly dressed and of sound mind. Dracus appeared uneasy as the group he had terrorized for so long approached. Jesus stood to greet the crowd, half expecting them to thank him for expelling the demons. Instead, everyone had expressions of dismay and even anger. There were no smiles or friendly greetings. Keeping his distance, the leader had a firm, serious look. "What happened here was not from God! We have never seen such a strange and frightening spectacle! Several of our herdsmen have lost everything they have worked for!" Several in the crowd began nodding and voicing threats, as the leader continued, "How is it that a demon knew your name?"

Jesus ignored him as he began motioning towards his disciples that it was time to leave. The townspeople were adamant and unyielding in their pleas for them all to leave their town.

Jesus and his disciples immediately left Gadara and returned across the Sea of Galilee to Capernaum. There, Jesus met with Joseph and quickly explained the vain attempt at winning the hearts of the people of Gadara. Shrugging off the failure as the fault of Dracus and his companions, Joseph immediately informed Jesus of the next scheduled healing of a paralytic.

* * *

Four men carried a fifth, who pretended to be paralyzed, to Jesus' home. They did so on a day when Jesus was planning to teach from there. Jesus had gained such fame and attention that these forums usually attracted large crowds, and this day was no different. As the five neared the front of the house, several people overflowed from the front entrance. The crowd included many people with true afflictions—some with obvious physical abnormalities, and others who were covered, hiding their disfigurements.

The four men started pushing their way through, making little headway with such large cargo. Finally, one of the four, Nidal, struggled to keep his grip on the pallet. "We're too late. We can't push our way through this crowd. We'll have to do this some other time."

One of the others, Eliud, let out a disapproving grunt. "I'm not sleeping in the hills another night. I need to get back to Damascus."

Eliud let go of his grip, nearly causing the pallet to fall, as the other three set Ahaz on the ground. Eliud ran over to a wall on the side of the house and jumped up on a storage bin. He looked over the wall and then turned back towards the other four, shaking his head. "There's a large crowd out back, too."

Ahaz shook his head in disgust and got up from the pallet, then carried it over to Eliud. The other three followed in resignation. Nidal climbed up next to Eliud to check for himself. Preparing to climb down, Eliud looked towards the house and then nudged Nidal. "Look. There's a loose panel on the roof." As the others turned their gaze, Eliud continued, "It looks big enough. We can get in that way."

Eliud climbed on top of the wall, then pulled himself up on the roof. Pointing at Ahaz, Eliud ordered, "Give me the pallet."

Ahaz picked up the pallet and stretched to hand it to Eliud. Pulling it up, Eliud then turned to Nidal and gave him a hand up onto the roof. Then calling out to Ahaz again, Eliud said, "We'll need some rope."

Ahaz shook his head. "I'm not saying I'm agreeing to this!"

Eliud laughed. "It's not that high. We'll lower you down on the pallet, and you'll be fine."

Achim nodded. "I saw some rope a few houses back."

Eliud clasped his hands together. "Go get it!"

After they had all climbed onto the roof, Ahaz checked the knots on the pallet. Squinting up at Eliud, Ahaz warned, "If you drop me, you'll pay for this!" Then, under his breath, he added, "And then I really will be paralyzed."

Eliud laughed. "We won't drop you!" Looking around at the people still trying to get into the house, Eliud continued, "Besides, if we did, you'd have a soft landing." Eliud gave a twisted smile. "There's plenty of people to break your fall."

Nidal's face wrenched in disapproval. "Maybe we should consult Joseph about this. It might not look good, imposing ourselves in front of all of these other people. Don't you think it will make us appear self-serving? Such a display is clearly contrary to the purpose of our task. People will think we're better than all of those who have been waiting for God knows how long. I doubt that is the impression Joseph wants."

Eliud raised his hands and started looking around in a sarcastic manner. "I don't see Joseph anywhere." Then more seriously, he continued, "We've come this far and we're almost finished. No one's going to care if we've pushed ourselves to the front." Eliud laughed, then shook his head in disgust. "When did you develop a conscience? No one in there is going to get healed! The only difference is that Ahaz will. I think Joseph will be very disappointed if he hears of a crowd of this size and no healing taking place."

Eliud then motioned to Achim. "Help me with this."

Achim stooped down and began prying at the loose panel. Nidal lifted one corner and soon they were raising it off to one side.

Many of those outside backed away for a better view of the source of the clamor. With the noise interrupting his preaching, Jesus looked up with surprise and annoyance at the hole that was forming. He had seen his fair share of tactics to get close to him, but this was the most brazen and intrusive. Pushing his way through the crowd, Jesus looked up toward the ceiling and cried out, "Hey! Who's up there?! What are you doing? This is—" Then Jesus saw Eliud's face peering down through the hole, making him hold his tongue.

The four started lowering Ahaz, who lay on the pallet. Jesus had been wondering when they would show up, but he certainly didn't expect this. At first he was upset, but he slowly became impressed by their ingenuity. Not only had they avoided the crowds, but their antics were drawing more attention. Everyone had grown quiet, and all eyes were turned upon the pallet being lowered from the ceiling. Jesus pushed his way through the crowd and cleared a space for Ahaz to be lowered to the floor.

Jesus looked down at Ahaz and asked, "What is wrong with you, my son?"

Ahaz looked up at Jesus with convincing sadness and desperation. "I am paralyzed, my lord. I have been paralyzed for several years, and I wish to walk again. I know you can heal me."

Jesus looked with pity upon Ahaz, then turned to the crowd, saying, "It is man's imperfect relation with God that causes imperfection in our physical being." Jesus was using the popular notion that physical ailments were due to disfavor with God through sin or some other transgression. His statement reaffirmed the myth, causing several of those with physical infirmities to cringe uneasily.

One woman who had been blind since birth appeared greatly confused. She leaned over to her escort and whispered, "What have I done to warrant such punishment? I did not ask to be born. I do not even understand my failed sense, except that I am a burden and must rely on others to prepare even the food I eat." She sobbed and quivered with a vulnerable note of guilt.

Her escort placed her hand on the woman's face to still her quivers and wipe away the tears falling from her empty lids. "You have done nothing wrong, Eliana. He speaks in generalities and does not know you. You are *not* a burden. You are a wonderful person, with a deep, strong faith—a loving example we all admire."

Eliana smiled at her sister's words, although the tears continued to stream down her face. Her sister squeezed her hands and continued, "Jesus will heal your blindness—you will see, through your faith in God. You are not guilty of a sin against God. You were only a baby." With this she resumed a fruitless effort to push through the crowd that had tightened around Jesus with the spectacle.

Jesus looked down at Ahaz and said, "My son, your sins are forgiven."

Judas Iscariot, one of Jesus' disciples standing amongst the crowd, had a puzzled look on his face as he leaned over to James and asked, "How does Jesus presume to forgive the man's sins? Would not his sacrificial offerings cleanse his soul? Is this not what is taught in the Scriptures?"

Shaking his head, James looked back at Judas with the same

expression. "I don't know. Maybe Jesus knows the man's sacrificial offerings had not been in true faith, or that he has not offered them at all. I have always suspected that people suffer from their disobedience and sins against God. He is paralyzed for the very transgressions he has not repented for." James became noticeably uncomfortable as he looked around the room.

Amongst the crowd was a scribe, who called out, "Why does this man speak so? It is blasphemy! Who can forgive sins but God alone? There are no verses in the Scriptures that say one man can forgive the sins of another!"

Ahaz, who continued to lie on the pallet, appeared confused by Jesus' statement. Jesus noticed this, and could also see that several people were upset by his words. Attempting to explain himself but not willing to relinquish his train of thought, Jesus continued, "Why do you question thus in your hearts? Which is easier to say to the paralytic, 'Your sins are forgiven,' or to say, 'Rise, take up your pallet, and walk'?" Still seeing the questioning look on their faces, Jesus continued, "But that you may know that the Son of Man has authority on earth to forgive sins." He then turned to Ahaz and said, "I say to you, rise, take up your pallet, and go home."

With this, Ahaz immediately stood up, took his pallet, and went out before all of them. The entire house turned silent as the people cleared a path.

Judas and Andrew remained expressionless as Ahaz walked out the door. Judas turned to Andrew and whispered, "If there is no difference between the forgiveness of sins and the healing of an affliction, then why did the man not get up and walk upon Jesus' first command, when he forgave his sins?"

"Maybe the paralytic did not understand he had been healed."

Judas shook his head. "It was several minutes between the time Jesus forgave his sins, and then reacted to the questioning—finally spelling out the meaning of his command." Judas' voice turned skeptical. "Was the man's understanding necessary if such a command was to heal him anyway?"

22 ~ The Cost of Miracles

Claudia covered her head with veils, a headband over her forehead, and bands under her chin to secure a hairnet. She lifted a hood of coarse fabric that caught the hairnet as she fluffed it to make it hang evenly. "How do the Hebrew women wear these things? My head is squeezed from all sides and I can barely move it under this hood!"

Marcellus laughed as he helped her into a wooden cart that seemed unsteady despite its heavy build and weight. "You must look the part, my lady, before proceeding back into Jerusalem."

Claudia offered a reassuring smile. "Thank you for finding the mother of the boy that was injured."

Marcellus bowed. "It was my honor, my lady. It was not difficult to find the home of the injured boy. All of Jerusalem is talking about it."

"Have you heard how the boy is doing?"

"No, my lady."

Claudia shook her head in disappointment. "I hope he is well. I cannot bear to think he might have been killed due to my actions."

"It was not your fault, my lady. The Jewish woman caused the horses to rear."

"Yes, yes, I know. But I cannot forget the child's screams as they carried him away." Claudia bowed her head under the strain of the hood. "And they were so happy and playful."

Marcellus pointed towards the Roman soldiers dressed as Jewish farmers. "Antorus and Sevius know the way to the woman's home. They will protect you with their lives."

Claudia shook her head. "I doubt it will come to that."

* * *

Esther backed away from the door as the soldiers forced their way in. Claudia entered and bowed to the woman. One of the soldiers translated for her. "Please forgive my intrusion. I am Claudia, wife of the Roman prefect Pontius Pilate."

The woman shook with fear as she backed up against the wall. "I know who you are."

"Please do not be afraid. I mean you no harm. I am here to help your son."

Esther slowly dropped her quivering hands from her face, as the mere sound of Claudia's compassionate voice seemed to calm her fears. Esther looked at the interpreter as she replied, "We do not need your help."

With deep concern in her eyes, Claudia asked, "Is your son doing well? He seemed to be in such pain when he was carried off."

Esther shifted her eyes between Claudia and the interpreter. "He is fine. We do not need your help."

Claudia smiled as she pulled her hood off and started to loosen the veils. "Oh, thank the gods!" Claudia found a chair and sat down, seeming to release bundles of worry that had built over time. She wiped away a joyful tear. "The children were so happy, and I have had many sleepless nights hearing his screams in my dreams."

The woman approached Claudia and knelt beside her as awareness of the soldiers seemed to fade. "It was not your fault. I heard what happened. I heard how you helped pull my son from underneath the wagon."

Claudia offered a compassionate smile as she touched the woman's hand.

Esther bowed her head and started crying.

Claudia placed her hand on the woman's head and pleaded, "What's the matter? We mean you no harm. We will leave right away." Claudia looked up at the interpreter, motioning for him to repeat her assurances.

Esther continued crying and pulled herself into another chair. "My son is not doing well. His right leg is bent at the knee. He cannot straighten or bend it, and is still in a lot of pain."

Claudia's smile turned to despair. Esther continued, "I fear he will be crippled for the rest of his life."

Claudia stood, walked over to the woman, and knelt beside her. "I am so sorry." Claudia looked over at Sevius. "I have brought a physician. Maybe he could look at your son."

Sevius shrugged. "I'm not sure I can do anything for him here, but we could take him back to Antonia and treat him there."

Claudia nodded, and with pleading eyes looked back at Esther. As the woman heard the interpretation, she sat up in fear. Esther slowly shook her head and with a quivering voice said, "No. He cannot go to Fortress Antonia."

Claudia nodded. "I understand. Then our physicians will visit here."

Sevius shook his head. "Begging your pardon, my lady, but our physicians have duties at Antonia—more than you know. We had agreed that the boy would come with us."

Esther looked at Claudia and said, "I cannot have Roman physicians visiting my home."

A deep sense of despair filled Claudia's soul as her tearing eyes shifted between Esther and Sevius.

Esther reacted to Claudia's comforting touch, and emotionally the two seemed to meld woman-to-woman. Suddenly, Esther straightened up and her face grew stern, calling to one of her sons in the next room. "Jacob! Jacob! Come in here!"

A door slowly opened as a boy appeared in the doorway. "Run over to Nadim's house and tell him to bring the necklace. Tell him Roman soldiers will be there if he does not bring it right away!"

Claudia sat up, her eyes widening as Jacob ran out of the house. Esther wiped away her tears with a more controlled expression. "One of the older boys took your necklace in the commotion. He is a good boy, but he is very poor—as I am."

Claudia was speechless. She didn't know how to respond as Esther continued, "Your offer to help is very gracious. It was an accident. He shouldn't have been climbing on your carriage."

Esther wiped away another tear. "I am going to take my son to see a man named Jesus. He is a man of God. He is teaching in the wilderness and he has been healing those who cannot walk, or cannot see. He will heal my son."

Claudia turned to the interpreter, not sure she was hearing him correctly. "Jesus! A religious man?! Are you sure? Her son needs a physician!"

The interpreter nodded, but Claudia quickly interrupted, "No, don't tell her that!" Looking back at Esther, Claudia pleaded, "Are you sure? My husband is Pontius Pilate, and I can persuade him to have physicians visit here in complete discretion. No one would ever know."

Esther shook her head. "No. I have heard of many wonderful works this man has performed and he will heal my son."

An older boy, who Claudia recognized, suddenly appeared in the doorway holding a beautiful necklace that was awkwardly out of place in the poor surroundings. He slowly walked over to Esther and placed it in her hands, and she quickly gave it to Claudia.

* * *

After several weeks Pilate called Joseph to his office. "I have heard news of Gadara, and it is not good."

Joseph bowed in concession. "Yes, but fascination with his miracles has spread—even to Jerusalem. The general opinion is positive, sir, far outweighing the news from Gadara. And even with Gadara, I have heard heightened curiosity of the spectacle rather than news of the reactions of the townspeople."

Pilate nodded, relieved that an act of his design was not a total failure. "Good, I am pleased to hear that." Pilate paused in thought, confident in the progression of their plans. "I want Jesus to take on a tax collector as one of his disciples."

Joseph raised his eyebrows looking away from Pilate. "I think it's too early, Your Nobility. You do not understand how poorly tax collectors are looked upon by the common people—the very ones whose hearts we are trying to win. Tax collectors are viewed with disdain and mistrust, bordering on sin."

"I know, Joseph. That's what we are trying to change."

"But we should introduce these changes more gradually—give the people more time to adjust. They already have the religious obligation of tithing. Taxes only add to their burden." Joseph walked over to pull back the curtain. "Burden or not, most simply despise Rome for being the recipient of the collected revenues."

Pilate became noticeably annoyed with Joseph's counterarguments. "I am not asking you to take on a tax collector, I am ordering you."

Joseph turned quiet, his face expressionless. Calming himself with a forced smile, Pilate continued, "We discussed this long ago, even with John. We must improve the acceptance of tax collectors amongst your people, and what better place than with Jesus' disciples."

Joseph gave a slight nod. "I know many tax collectors from my trade and connections on the council. Jesus' popularity has grown tenfold over the past several weeks. I'm sure I can find someone who is willing."

* * *

Joseph met with several tax collectors in Capernaum. One man, Matthew, stood out from the rest. He knew Matthew to be of good character and work ethic.

"Matthew, I have asked you here for a reason. Have you heard of Jesus?"

Matthew responded with a broadening smile and compassionate tone. "Yes. I have heard many great things about Jesus. He speaks well of our profession, which has improved my day-to-day toil."

Joseph noticed a disgruntled tone when Matthew mumbled the words "day-to-day toil," which surprised him to some degree. But before he could inquire, Matthew continued, "I get a few nods of approval these days, and even cordial greetings, rather than the constant bickering, arguing, and excuses."

Joseph smiled and placed his hand on Matthew's shoulder. "I know Jesus and interact with him frequently." Joseph sensed he had sparked Matthew's interest. "He is looking for a man like you to help in his ministries. What better way to improve the standing of your profession than to have a tax collector work as one of his disciples?"

Matthew showed a hint of excitement but shook his head. "I am the chief tax collector here in Capernaum and have obligations to the local

Roman garrison. They will not simply relieve me of my duties and the taxes I collect. Besides, how will I support my family?"

"I have connections on the Jewish council, and can make arrangements with the Roman garrison. As for your family, do you not know that Jesus receives tithes from those who follow him—far more than your wages as a tax collector?"

Matthew smiled with boyish excitement. "Yes, I have wanted to meet Jesus. But he would take on a great risk since I am well-known. How do I know he would be willing?"

Joseph smiled. "Don't worry. I know."

* * *

The news of adding a tax collector to his following disheartened Jesus in light of other complications he had been encountering. Pockets of disfavor were starting to build amongst the people, especially with his attempts at relaxing Sabbath restrictions. Jesus had performed miracles on the Sabbath, only to be met with severe and immediate reproach. Embracing a tax collector as a close disciple was sure to increase negative sentiment. Joseph set up a meeting between Jesus and Matthew. They were to meet at Matthew's home for dinner. Several other tax collectors would attend as well.

That evening, food and wine flowed in abundance. Several of Jesus' disciples also attended the feast. Knowledge of the affair quickly spread, upsetting many in the community. Chief priests and scribes of different religious councils seized the news as more evidence to discredit Jesus.

Even though there were pockets of disfavor, Jesus' popularity was still growing due to the rumors and fascination with his miracles. Scribes angrily denounced his teachings for straying from Mosaic Law. His growing popularity only served to fuel their fear and outrage. For the most part, the anger was not out of jealousy or envy, but from devotion and love for teachings they had held sacred for countless centuries.

The next day, several people, including one who had been a disciple of John the Baptist, approached Jesus to inquire about the feast and drinking with the tax collectors. Some perceived Jesus' actions as frivolous and indulgent. The one who had been John's disciple asked,

"Why is it you do not fast? It is said that fasting is a sign of religious discipline and obedience to God. We, as John's disciples, fasted, as do the Pharisees and the Essenes. Why do you and your disciples not fast?"

Jesus had always been sensitive to his weakness for food and drink. He rarely practiced the ritual of fasting, and it had never been an issue until now. Feeling flustered and uncertain as to how to answer such a pointed question, Jesus responded with another question: "Can the wedding guests fast while the bridegroom is with them? As long as they have the bridegroom with them, they cannot fast."

Seeing confusion and skepticism in their reaction, Jesus continued, "Doesn't anyone in this country appreciate my presence? Do you not see? I am the bridegroom. Since I am here, it is a time for celebration, not a time for fasting!"

Several people in the crowd, including his own disciples, became increasingly agitated, as did Jesus. "Someday, when I am gone, you will appreciate who I was and what I am doing. When the bridegroom leaves with his bride, then you can make of the feast what you will, and return to your fasting."

Jesus immediately saw the value of disjointed parables to distract attention from uncomfortable or pointed attacks. Continuing, Jesus looked directly at John's disciple and said, "No one sews a piece of unshrunk cloth on an old garment. If he does, the patch tears away, the new from the old, and a worse tear is made."

To Jesus' surprise, everyone started nodding. Quickly trying to remember other parables, Jesus continued, almost without thinking, "No one puts new wine into old wineskins. If he does, the wine will burst the skins and the wine is lost, and so are the skins. New wine is for fresh skins."

His comments were having the desired effect as some in the group continued nodding. Others seemed to drift off in thought, contemplating the meaning of his words. One person asked, "How would fresh wine burst used wine skins? Are you of such wealth that you can use fresh wine skins for every serving of wine?"

Many in the crowd started laughing, and Jesus sensed that his strategy had suddenly turned. He was about to slip away when one of the Pharisees called out angrily, "Are you referring to the teachings and laws of God as old, worn-out clothing? Are you referring to the sacred Scripture as old wineskins?!"

With everyone's attention turned towards the Pharisee, Jesus noticed the anger building in the Pharisee's eyes. Jesus tried to slip away, but his path was blocked by others gathering tightly around him. The Pharisee pointed at Jesus, focusing the crowd's unwelcome attention. "Is he referring to himself as the new wine, and his teachings as a patch on worn-out clothing?!" The Pharisee began pushing his way through the crowd towards Jesus. "Behold, a glutton and a drunkard, a friend of tax collectors and sinners!"

Jesus knew he had to regain his composure and gather his thoughts. Turning back towards the crowd, Jesus called out, "For John the Baptist has come eating no bread and drinking no wine, and you say, 'He has a demon.' The Son of Man has come eating and drinking, and you say I am guilty of gluttony and drunkenness. You offer ill judgment for either extreme, but lack the wisdom for its basis!" Turning away, Jesus forced his way through the crowd, retreating to his home in Capernaum and spending the rest of the day in seclusion.

* * *

In another staged miracle, Jesus and his disciples came upon a crowd that had gathered to hear him speak. A man came up to him and kneeled. "Lord, have mercy on my son, for he is an epileptic and he suffers terribly. Whenever the demon seizes him, it dashes him down, and he foams and grinds his teeth and becomes rigid. Can you heal him?"

Jesus was growing weary of the countless staged miracles. Their pageant was starting to mix and confuse with the greater number of legitimate requests he had to turn away. Even though the miracles were attracting a lot of attention, Jesus was growing sensitive to the pockets of criticism. He turned to the crowd. "You are a faithless and perverse generation, in need of miracles to prove my authority. I cannot do this forever." With a tone of sarcasm, he continued, "How are you going to manage when I am gone?"

Turning back toward the father of the epileptic child, Jesus said, "Bring him here to me."

As the man approached, the crowd cleared a wide path. Jesus looked around and recognized the fear in everyone's eyes as they backed away from the child. He remembered his own intense fear several years ago when he witnessed a real epileptic seizure. The man had been perfectly normal, explaining the details of carpentry work to be performed. Then suddenly in mid-sentence, he stopped talking and appeared disoriented. He then fell to the ground and hit his head and started shaking. The disgusting image of saliva spilling from the man's mouth and frequent, uncontrolled grunts filled Jesus' mind. The man's arms and legs curled into twisted knots. He remembered the presence of a powerful demon possessing a man only a few feet away, still sending shivers down his spine. He thought for sure the man was going to die, and he and his coworkers backed away in hopeless fear. But a few minutes later, the convulsions stopped, followed by intermittent, jerking breaths. The man appeared to regain control from the demon and started making attempts to rise. Jesus remembered how he and his friends turned and ran, fearing the demon might jump into one of them.

Jesus paused, wondering if they should be toying with powerful demonic forces he knew to be real.

As the man neared Jesus, the boy fell to the ground and started convulsing on cue. He began rolling around violently, churning bubbles of saliva pushed to his lips. Jesus rolled his eyes, realizing the boy was supposed to go rigid as his father had explained. Jesus quickly looked at the father and asked, "How long has he had this?"

"From childhood. The demon often casts him into the fire, or into the water, trying to destroy him. If you can do anything, have pity on us and help us."

"If you can!" Jesus exclaimed, almost feeling insulted at the man's choice of words. Even though they had gone over the general plan, Jesus had become lax in discussing things in detail, and it was beginning to show. Trying to salvage what was turning into yet another debacle, Jesus gave the father a stern look and said, "All things are possible to him who believes."

The father immediately cried out, "I believe. Help my unbelief!"

Jesus held up his hand and rebuked the demon that possessed the child. "You dumb and deaf spirit, I command you, come out of this boy, and never enter him again!"

On cue, the boy gave a violent scream, signaling the exit of the unclean spirit, and then became entirely motionless. Jesus paused, expecting the boy to get up. Rolling his eyes again, he bent over and nudged the boy, telling him to get up. As the boy slowly rose, exaggerating every motion, he eagerly took in the attention focused his way. Finally on his feet, he brushed the dirt from his clothes and turned to his father with teary eyes. The father gave him a strong, emotional embrace as the crowd slowly moved in, seeming to lose their fear. The sincere and awe-inspired reaction of the crowd calmed Jesus. This was the type of reaction he liked to see.

Jesus repeated this scenario many times, driving out demons that were the source of dumbness, deafness, and other physical infirmities. In many instances, the performances required minimal staging to present the desired illusion. On one occasion, a woman portrayed a physical deformity by simply hunching over and dragging a lifeless left leg. She bunched up her clothing under her shawl to present the appearance of a deformed shoulder. Jesus freed her from the bonds of demonic spirits, and she immediately straightened herself into a normal posture, pulling her garment to release it from the weight of her shawl.

There were several people in the towns of the area who became skeptical of the works and miracles Jesus was performing. His inconsistent approach of chastising many for their pleas of mercy while praising others bred contempt. Works performed on the Sabbath also fueled disillusion.

One Sabbath, Jesus and his disciples were going through a grain field. As they made their way, they began to pluck ears of grain. Pharisees heard what they had done and approached Jesus. "Why are your disciples doing what is not lawful on the Sabbath?"

"Have you not read how David, when he was hungry, entered the house of God and ate the holy bread that was only meant to be eaten by the priests?"

The Pharisee looked back at Jesus and said, "Yes, that is well known. He and his men were very hungry from having been at battle for many days. You, however, do not appear to be wanting of food. Besides, he was violating a rule of the priests, not a commandment of God."

Jesus responded, "The Sabbath was made for man, not man for the Sabbath."

The Pharisee lunged at Jesus, raising his hand as if to strike him, but instead grabbed Jesus by the garment on his shoulder. Immediately, Jesus brought his arm up, breaking the Pharisee's grip. He could feel the spit from the Pharisee's breath as he yelled inches from his face, "The Sabbath is a holy day of God's design, not yours!"

The Pharisee pushed Jesus away violently and turned towards the crowd. In a calmer voice, he continued, "It was a day that God rested. It was a day made by God through his own actions and not the actions of man. It is the fourth commandment of God, directed to his people, to keep the Sabbath holy. The Sabbath is a holy day of God, not a holy day of man!"

Suddenly, Jesus felt he had lost the argument, but he maintained his position, remembering Pilate's directive. Jesus knew he could not back down. "How can you judge what is meant to keep the Sabbath holy? Maybe we have carried the intent of God's commandment too far."

* * *

Jesus continued to perform acts of healing on the Sabbath. On one occasion, he drove out a demon from a dumb man, and the dumb man immediately spoke. Instead of getting the reaction he had come to expect, one man called out, "He casts out demons by Be-el'zebul, the prince of demons." Soon others in the crowd started nodding.

Hearing this for the first time, Jesus was shocked and insulted by the accusation. Angered by the attack, Jesus called out, "Truly, I say to you, all sins will be forgiven the sons of men, and whatever blasphemies they utter." Then with vindictive fire in his voice, Jesus motioned with his hands to everyone standing there. "But you are guilty of an eternal sin that can never be forgiven! Whoever blasphemes against the Holy Spirit never has forgiveness. You have called the Holy Spirit that resides in me the prince of demons, and for this, you will never be forgiven!"

The anger in his voice was so powerful that the crowd became silent and the nods of support quickly ceased, seemingly gripped by fear. The man who had called out leaned over and whispered to his friend, "He has taken on the divine authority to forgive sins, and now he is denying forgiveness to those who question *his* authority." The man's face was twisted with disgust.

His friend replied in a trembling voice, "I have seen his great works. We are but normal men. Has your doubt condemned us to eternal separation from God?"

The man smirked and looked around at everyone gathered. Then, turning his attention back towards his friend, he replied, "Are we condemning ourselves by listening to this man and ignoring the Mosaic Law that has been handed down through generations? Are we condemning ourselves by ignoring the warnings from our rabbis?" The man turned and walked away, shaking his head.

As time went on, many people questioned the source of Jesus' wisdom and took offense. There were several in Capernaum who still could not forget Jesus' interaction with the Roman centurion. His radical attitude toward the Sabbath, and his blatant disrespect for prominent religious leaders, started taking its toll on much of the support he had gained.

Jesus became increasingly agitated with a community to which he became too familiar. One day, while having to turn away still more people who had traveled from afar, Jesus turned his frustration on the crowd, pointing an accusing finger. "This generation is an evil generation. It seeks a sign, but no sign shall be given to it except the sign of Jonah." Feeling a strong sense of failure and rejection, he became burdened with defeatism and disappointment. It seemed he had reached his limit of compassion with the people he had been commissioned to change.

One man called out, "How is our generation any different from any other—other than having you to condemn us?!"

Jesus' emotions boiled over, as sorrow and sadness quickly turned to anger. Looking out over the sea of hapless faces, Jesus began screaming, "Woe to you, Chorazin! Woe to you, Bethsaida! For if the mighty works done in you had been done in Tyre and Sidon, they would have repented long ago. But I tell you, it shall be more tolerable on the day of judgment for Tyre and Sidon than for you." With his anger continuing to build, Jesus cursed at them. "And you, Capernaum, will you be exalted to heaven? You shall be brought down to Hades. For if the mighty works done in you had been done in Sodom, it would have remained until this day. But I tell you that it shall be more tolerable on the day of judgment for the land of Sodom than for you!"

The crowd became deathly still. Expressionless, Peter leaned over to Andrew. "What is Jesus talking about? Why is he so angry?" Keeping his voice low Peter continued, "Why has he condemned entire cities for the action of a few? My wife's family lives in Capernaum, and they accepted him into their home."

Andrew shrugged his shoulders. "I don't know. And why does he refer to Hades—a Greek god? Is Jesus implying Hades has dominion over Sheol?"

Peter shook his head. "No, there is no other God but Yahweh. We simply misunderstand the true meaning of his words." Peter paused in deep thought. "We have seen the power of his miraculous works that no other can do—not even the Pharisees. He calls upon the one true God when performing miracles, and there can be no other power behind the wonder and goodness of his works."

Andrew nodded. He looked around at the people, who were slowly starting to leave. "I do not understand why Jesus tires in the performance of these amazing works, but it is clear he does. These people demand too much of Jesus."

23 ~ Going, Going

Even with several prisoners sharing his cell, John felt alone and isolated. It had been five months since he had been imprisoned, and John was beginning to lose hope. He had some visitors, but Machaerus was so far removed from his homeland they tended to be few. His parents had visited once, about a month into his stay. Their age had made it difficult for them to travel the distance. His father made a trip to Jerusalem to make an appeal to the Jewish council and to Antipas, but to no avail.

John received sympathy and outrage from just about everyone who visited, but these emotions did little to break the massive wooden planks of his cell door.

John could feel his body deteriorating with each passing day. Yet this paled to the weakening of his spirit. Prisoners were never allowed from their cells to exercise or even bathe. His hair was growing long and matted, blending with his animal-skin clothing. If slaves waited too long to service their cells, his stool pot often leaked and many times overflowed. Some days, John would go without food or water. The guards had other duties that took their attention from the prisoners, counting on death and disease to dwindle their numbers.

The proud, confident stature that once graced a wonderful man quickly changed into a frail, weak body of skin, bones, hair, and filth. Most who visited John did not recognize him, and questioned whether this was truly he—until they heard him speak. Enough of John's character still came through to prove he was still amongst the living.

* * *

The quiet nights weighed on Claudia's soul. She felt Pontius drifting away, drowning in a turbulent sea. Claudia lit the final lamp and tried to break the silence: "I have heard of a Jewish religious man who performs acts of healing in the wilderness."

Pontius looked surprise. "Where have you heard this?"

"I go out into the city sometimes, to the markets and local gardens—with escort, of course."

Pontius nodded. "But who told you of this man?"

"Everyone talks of this man. He is even mentioned within the walls of Antonia."

Pontius smiled. "What have you heard of him?"

Claudia was a little surprised at Pontius' interest. "I have heard many great things about him. The people are fascinated with him. Some even speak of him as if he were a god." Claudia paused, seeing Pontius' eyes widen. "I think he is called Jesus. Have you heard of him?"

Pontius let out a quick laugh. "Yes, I have heard of him."

"What's so funny? The people of Jerusalem seem to be very serious about this man."

Pontius did not respond as Claudia continued, "Have you heard of the boy who was injured from my carriage?"

Pontius nodded.

"His mother tried to take him to Jesus, but could not get near him. She saw many others healed, but the crowds were too thick for her to make her way with her son."

Seeing she still had Pontius' interest, Claudia poured a cup of wine. "She tried several times, but it was always the same. She said there were always so many people who needed his help that she finally gave up trying."

"You spoke with her?"

"Yes. I have visited her several times. At first, that was the only way she felt comfortable having our physicians visit her son."

Pontius offered an approving nod. "You are a remarkable woman, Claudia. It does not surprise me you would see to the boy's care."

"Thank you, Pontius." Claudia walked over into the caress of her husband's arms. "The boy is fine now. He is walking normally."

Pontius held Claudia tight and whispered into her ear, "I can see how much this has affected you. The boy's family is lucky you were there to help them."

Claudia smiled and pulled back a little. "It's odd, though, but the mother is still fascinated with this Jesus. Even though it was our physicians who straightened her son's leg and enabled him to walk again, she still speaks of Jesus with adoration and reverence. Sometimes I feel she credits his recovery with her visits to Jesus rather than the efforts of our physicians."

Pontius laughed. "We know that's not true."

"Well tell that to Esther. It became very discomforting towards the end, hearing her speak of Jesus, and not offering thanks for our help."

* * *

Joseph wanted to visit John, but his duties with Jesus over the first month prevented him from taking the time. After that, Pilate implored Joseph not to visit John so as to keep his position on the council concealed. Despite Pilate's appeals, Joseph occasionally visited his friend, making the long, arduous trip through the harsh lands on the east side of the Dead Sea. On one occasion Joseph brought John a change of clothes in order to rid the animal skins that were now tattered, filthy rags. Feeling the soft, clean cloth in his hands, John began crying, covering his face with the aroma of the outside world. Joseph wanted so much to hold and comfort his friend. He could tell John was falling into an abyss of dark insanity from his isolation.

On each visit, John asked if Pilate had been able to work an appeal for his release through Antipas. Each time, Joseph had to give the same frustrating, negative response. Joseph was as confused as John as to why Pilate could not wield enough power to free him. Or maybe he was just unwilling to. Joseph was starting to feel the latter was the case. Joseph suspected Pilate was simply not willing to risk his position and the growing popularity of Jesus to free John. On the other hand, maybe Pilate had been making appeals, as he promised, and Antipas was simply too stubborn.

On Joseph's fourth visit after five months in prison, John had stopped pleading for appeals. Instead, he assumed a more aggressive tone. Before Joseph left, John reached out and pulled on his garment. "Joseph, I want you to do something for me."

Joseph could hear the determination in John's voice—a vexed tone that was easy to recognize. Hesitant to respond but feeling the tug of loyalty, Joseph answered, "Of course, John, anything. What is it you want?"

John looked squarely at Joseph and took a deep breath. "I want you to tell Pilate something for me. I want you to tell him that if he doesn't do something to get me out of here, I am going to start talking about the details of our plan."

Joseph's eyes widened listening to John's threat. It was the last thing he had expected from John, and in a way, he felt partially the target of his words. "If you say anything, it will reveal my position on the Jewish council, John. You can't do that!"

John shook his head. "Oh, it is common to have Roman ties on the many different groups of our government. Even the high priest was appointed by a Roman prefect, and he is still alive and well today, if not the most powerful man in this country. Your life will not be threatened."

Joseph listened incredulously to each word from John's mouth. He knew John's reasoning was being affected by his stay in prison, but he never thought John would resort to this. Shocked, Joseph responded, "What about my family and friends? I could not adjust to their hatred and ridicule!"

John's voice quickly turned to outright anger: "What?! Do you expect me to adjust to this filth and these prison walls?" John backed away and calmed his voice. "Comfort your thoughts, Joseph. I would not say anything about you. I would leave you completely out of it. I would just speak of my role with Pilate."

Joseph knew his own role could not be hidden despite John's assurances. Deep inside, he could not blame John for trying to free himself from this rat-infested existence. On the surface, though, he was still frightened by the possibility of having his own position revealed. However, maybe John's threat would spur Pilate to action.

"All right, John. I'll tell Pilate. I hope this works. Otherwise, we could be in a lot of trouble." Feeling discouraged and shaken, Joseph turned and walked away. Nearing a torch on the wall on his way to the exit, he heard faint sobs echoing from behind.

* * *

Pontius sensed something was troubling Joseph when he walked into his office. Joseph's face had little expression, and his shoulders drooped as if bearing a ghostly weight. Pontius was pleased with the phenomenal success Jesus was having in such a short time. Trying to read the look on Joseph's face, he suddenly feared news that could sway their course, as happened so often. His first thought was that something had happened to Jesus or one of his disciples, or that his position had been discovered. Pontius finally greeted Joseph, not certain he wanted to hear what he had to say. "Joseph! I haven't seen you for a while. Have you seen Jesus?"

The expression on Joseph's face did not alter. "No, I was not in that area."

Pontius was expecting Joseph to go on, but was relieved the news did not involve Jesus. The determination on Joseph's face faded as his eyes dropped away. After a short silence, Pontius' expression turned more demanding. "Well, what is it, man? Where have you been? What weighs on you?"

Joseph looked up, a hint of guilt and deep sadness in his eyes. "I went to Machaerus to visit John."

Pilate hid his reaction to Joseph's admission, forcing a smile. "So how is he doing?"

The question seemed to release Joseph's restraint as his emotions gushed forth. "He is not doing well at all, Honorable Prefect. He's not the same man he used to be. The conditions are horrid. Physically and emotionally, I would say he's as close to being dead as a man could be, while maintaining a presence in this world. I don't understand how Antipas could put anyone through this, especially someone who has done nothing wrong."

Pontius felt Joseph's hurt and pain, and for a brief instant, the tug of guilt. He would do nothing, though, except offer deceitful consolation. "I will speak to Antipas about conditions at the prison. Surely he will understand that men shouldn't be treated so."

Pilate's words were meaningless. Prison conditions had always been appalling, and they would continue to be that way no matter what he said or did. Little interest or concern had ever been paid to those taken away from society, probably never to be seen again.

Joseph walked over to a chair and slowly sat down. His fingers massaged his forehead as he stared at the floor. "Like I said, John isn't himself. No man could be in that place." Joseph paused and cleared his throat. "John said some things I'm not sure he meant—"

Pontius impatiently interrupted, "He said some things? What did he say?"

Joseph shifted uncomfortably. His hands trembled as he dropped them away from his face and looked at Pilate. "He threatened he would reveal everything, unless you effect his release."

The expression on Pilate's face did not change. Inside, however, his thoughts were exploding. He felt an anger he had never experienced before. He wanted to take his hand and strike Joseph for even conveying the words. But something held him. Anger filled his body until it seemed his very bones would break from the pressure. Pontius was not sure if he had ever been threatened by anyone, especially a Jew. Somehow he took control of his emotions realizing he still needed Joseph for his position on the council and interactions with Jesus. In fact, Joseph had become invaluable to him. Finally, Pontius found the words he hoped would satisfy Joseph and send him away; he was wary of continuing a conversation that could send him over the edge at any instant. Carefully picking his words, Pontius asked, "Doesn't John know this is out of my jurisdiction? There is very little I can do. Go tell John I will do everything I can. Tell him I will speak to Antipas—and not to do anything foolish."

A smile flickered across Joseph's face. With a sense of urgency Joseph bowed until he was nearly prostrate. "Thank you, Your Nobility. I know John will be very pleased to hear this. Thank you so very much." He continued bowing as he backed away from Pilate, eventually turning and almost running out of his office.

Joseph quickly prepared for another long trip. Even before he had left the room, Pontius was making his own plans for a much shorter trip to Herod's palace.

* * *

That afternoon, Pilate met privately with Antipas. "I will get right to the point. I have received seditious reports that a great number of followers of John the Baptist are planning to infiltrate Machaerus and make an attempt to free him. By the gods, they might already be there!"

Antipas expressed mild surprise. Acting almost embarrassed, he said, "I have not heard of such reports. How did you come upon this information?"

"Do you not have spies in the field? Something must be wrong with your intelligence."

Antipas nodded with superficial concern. "I will have it looked into immediately."

Pilate continued, "In the meantime, we must deal with this imminent threat. I want John the Baptist executed immediately, without delay!"

Antipas raised his eyebrows in surprise. "Upon your authority?"

"No! As I told you, I don't want Rome involved in this in any way!"

"I cannot execute this man! Even though he has been in prison for six months, his memory has not faded. He is righteous, and there are many who seem disposed to do everything he would say. I have received criticism and hatred for having him arrested. I'm sure the same will continue, tenfold, if I have him executed! You cannot place this upon me."

Calming himself, Pontius continued, "You don't have to take the blame. You can place it upon someone else. Your wife, Herodias, was also affected by his accusations."

"Herodias! What does she have to do with this? I doubt she has even heard of the man, much less cares what he might have said about our marriage. For that matter, John stands amongst a multitude who have criticized me for having taken Herodias as my wife. What would you have me do? Execute half the population of Jerusalem?"

Pontius took offense at Antipas' display of anger and resistance. Losing his temper, Pontius gave him a death-threatening glance. "Hear what I say! You know and I know your armies in the east have suffered defeat against Aretas—all because lust decided your foreign policy! Your poor judgment has cost the lives of many men. Executing John is the least of your worries!"

Antipas sat down slowly and fell back into his chair. Phasaelis had escaped to Perea long ago when she received word that Antipas would take Herodias as his wife. Some of Antipas' armies had been destroyed by the Arabs.

Continuing with his threat, Pilate added, "If you desire assistance from Rome, then you will do as I say and order John's execution immediately! It makes no difference to me to have Aretas rule in your stead." Pilate was not true in his threat; he knew Rome would never approve of such a move, but his voice never wavered.

Antipas narrowed his eyes in anger and gave a hesitant, reluctant nod.

Pilate returned Antipas' loathing stare as he placed his hand on the hilt of his sheathed sword and gritted his teeth. "Once John is dead, I will send three cohorts to save your armies, but not a moment sooner."

* * *

After Pilate left, Antipas began scheming of ways to distance himself from the planned execution. Pilate had certainly touched upon his weaknesses, of which there were many. John's execution could be the fatal blow that would lead to his imminent downfall. With his devastating losses to Aretas, he was critically dependent on Rome's mercy for his survival, and Pilate's threat stuck within his ribs.

Antipas thought over Pilate's suggestion to shift the blame to his wife, misdirecting the focus of the execution. She would demand John's execution and not him. Such a demand from his wife would need to be made publicly in order to make it believable. A private request would simply lead to accusations of transferring the blame, bringing obvious attention to the true nature of his contrivance.

Later that evening Antipas consulted his wife. Uncertain as to how to bring up the subject, and feeling a bit awkward, Antipas asked, "Do you know of the man John the Baptist, whom I had arrested several months ago?"

Herodias nodded. "Yes, I remember him. He was the teacher from the east, near the Jordan River, I believe."

"Yes, that's the one. He made comments about our marriage." Seeing she was showing little reaction, Antipas continued, "He made a public statement in my court that our marriage was unlawful."

"He did? In your court, directly to your face? I had heard about the statements he made. Isn't that the reason you had him arrested?"

"Yes, it was. But there are now rumors his followers are planning to break him out of prison."

Sounding more surprised than alarmed, Herodias responded, "Isn't he in Machaerus? I doubt that is possible. How would his followers hope to succeed?"

Antipas shook his head. "I don't know! In any case, I plan to have him executed."

Herodias reacted with casual surprise. "Why are you telling me this?"

Antipas took her hand and said, "Because I am going to need your help."

"My help? What can I do? Why do you want him dead anyway? If he's in prison, what harm can be done there?" Herodias' indifference turned into concern as she looked at Antipas. "No one's going to free him from Machaerus! Is he really that much of a threat?"

"It's not me who wants him dead. It's Pontius Pilate. But he wants his hands washed of this man's blood, so he has asked me to order his execution."

Herodias fixed Antipas with a questioning look. She raised her hands, perplexed. "And?"

"I have received enough grief over having him arrested. The man is very popular amongst the people, and he is a good man." Still seeing she was confused, Antipas turned more serious and direct. "Heed my words, woman. He insulted our marriage, and you're involved in this, too!"

Raising her voice, Herodias asked, "Is he talking about us from his cell?"

"Well, no."

"Is he making it his life mission to speak out against our marriage?"

"No!"

"Well, I would think you would be more concerned about the criticism we are getting from Agrippa. He *has* made it his life mission to criticize our marriage."

Antipas was aware of the animosity building between Herodias and her brother Agrippa. But in his own mind, he felt Herodias' fears were unfounded and meaningless.

Herodias looked sternly at Antipas and continued, "He's the one you should fear and not some worthless Jew!"

Antipas laughed at the threat posed by his wife. "Why should I fear Agrippa? I have him in a position of menial importance in Tiberias where he'll never amount to anything."

"I have heard he plans to leave Galilee and travel to Rome—"

"Rome! He will never go to Rome! He has amassed so much debt and so many enemies there, he can't set foot in Italia! Besides, such a trip would be a blessing from God—I'd lose his interference with my affairs."

Herodias shook her head in frustration. "I think it is his intention to gain favor with Tiberius and gain the kingdom of our grandfather—a kingdom that should be yours, my husband. You should act now, before it's too late. He's the one who should be executed!"

"You would have me execute your brother?"

Herodias lashed out, "And why not? Your father had my father killed! He had several of your brothers killed." Herodias started crying as she fell into Antipas' arms.

Antipas felt a sudden compassion for his wife at the release of her deepest emotions. He remembered the horrid and paranoid antics of his father toward the end of his life. There were times he had feared for his own life, wondering if his father would let any of his sons live. The memories brought shudders as he did his best to block them away. Wondering how they had strayed from his original subject, Antipas responded, "I am not going to have Agrippa killed. How did we get off in a discussion about Agrippa?"

As Herodias continued to cry, Antipas held her more tightly and rocked her in his arms, which seemed to calm her. After a short while, Antipas continued, "Listen. I didn't mean to yell at you. I know this is a lot for you to bear all at once. We have been through so much together, and we won't solve all of our problems overnight. We must be strong, together, and we'll pull through whatever Rome, or our own families, bestow upon us." Antipas slowly let her go, and then held her at arm's length. Wanting to continue with his original purpose, Antipas asked, "Do you know how I sometimes joke at some of our dinner parties that I would give half my kingdom to see Salome dance?"

Salome was Herodias' daughter through Philip and was a beautiful young girl. Herodias' demeanor turned cautious as she gave a stern look. "Yes, I have seen you look at her many times. If she was not so young—and my daughter—it would be a cause for jealousy."

Antipas nodded, ignoring her accusation. "Well, next Friday evening, at the dinner party we have planned, I am going to get drunk on wine—"

Herodias interrupted, "You mean, drunker than usual."

Antipas rolled his eyes. "Yes, drunker than usual. Only this time, I will not just speak of it. I will openly promise Salome anything she wants if she dances for me."

Antipas could see rebellion returning to his wife's eyes as he continued, "She will dance, and then she will ask for the head of John the Baptist."

Pushing Antipas away in disgust, Herodias screamed, "Antipas! I don't know what you're talking about! What does *he* have to do with any of this and why should I care?"

Antipas felt his anger and frustration turn to rage. He had gone through every extreme in emotion today, and it taxed his sanity. There were so many aspects in his world in which he had lost control. With strong conviction, Antipas replied, "You should care because I am ordering it. I am your king, not just your husband!"

"That's ridiculous, Antipas! How will you expect anyone to believe that? Why would she ask for the head of John the Baptist, when she could ask for anything else?"

"I'm not expecting them to believe it! I'm expecting them to see it with their own eyes and hear it with their own ears; then they won't have to believe it. Their witness will be proof!" Antipas' towering voice filled the room. Herodias backed away, trembling as she took a long, deep breath. In her silence, Antipas continued, "If she asks for anything else, and not the head of John the Baptist, it will be *her* head I will have on a platter!"

Herodias fell against the wall, barely able to breathe. It took time before she could even motion a slight nod, agreeing to his demands. With that, Antipas pointed toward the door and ordered, "Now go! Get out of my sight!"

Herodias slid against the wall as if escaping to get away. As she closed the door, Antipas sat down on the bed and placed his head in his hands.

He began moaning, wondering how he had gotten himself into this.

* * *

So it happened just as Antipas had directed. Even with careful planning, the young Salome paused when asked of her desire, hesitating to give her incredulous line in a scripted play. The low roar of the dinner party turned into uncomfortable silence as Salome walked over to Herodias for whispered reassurance. Herodias almost bit into her ear as she whispered with forced calm, "You know your answer: the head of John the Baptist!" Herodias pushed Salome's head towards Antipas, as if forcing the words from her mouth.

Salome walked back to the middle of the room, taking her place on an odd stage with increased attention from a curious audience. "I want the head of John the Baptist."

24 ~ Who's Listening?

John sat motionless against the wall of his cell. He rarely tried to find his way across the cell for fear of tripping or stumbling in the complete darkness. He looked up hearing the familiar sound of Joseph's voice and saw a faint light through the portal. John pushed himself up and tried to make his way to the door. He suddenly felt faint as he fell against a pillar. Even though he could now see the bodies strewn about the floor, it had become difficult for him to walk due to the weakness in his legs and trouble with balance. Finally reaching the door, John saw Joseph's wonderful face peering through the bars. Periodically, Joseph would shift his head in the portal, letting in new light and making John squint and shield his eyes with his hand.

As Joseph's face came into focus, John smiled, recognizing his friend. "Peace, Joseph. Back so soon?" They both laughed at his friendly greeting. Before Joseph could return it, John's smile sobered as he continued, "Although, sometimes I'm not sure what 'soon' is, because I lose track of time."

"It's been eight days, John—eight more days you shouldn't have been in here. I'm sorry you're having to go through this, John." Joseph paused as tears welled in his eyes. "If I hadn't introduced you to Pilate, none of this would have ever happened." The tears began to flow down his cheeks.

John shook his head. "No, it wasn't your fault, Joseph. I was the one who wanted to meet Pilate. Besides, that has nothing to do with it. It was my own foolishness that caused me to say things I shouldn't have."

Joseph brought a smile back to his face. "Well, no matter. I have some good news, or hope so, anyway. I told Pilate about what you said—"

John interrupted. "After you left, I thought long and hard about what I said, and I was wrong. I wish I had called you back when you were leaving." John paused, trying to catch his breath from what seemed to be difficult exertion. Something weighed on his lungs and his breath brought a slight pain, causing him to cough several times. Clearing his throat, John continued, "I wouldn't have said anything, Joseph. It wouldn't be right for me to bring you and Jesus down with me, no matter what I'm going through. I just don't feel I am thinking clearly." Getting out the words he had wanted to, John went back into a coughing spell, temporarily preventing Joseph's response.

After John had quieted down, Joseph said, "Think nothing of it, John. No one could imagine what you're going through. Besides, your ploy seems to have worked. It seems to have spurred Pilate to make an appeal to Antipas."

John smiled at the ray of hope, which carried over to Joseph. "Be of strong character, John. I've been praying for you, and I know God will answer my prayers. He's a just God, and surely he must see the injustice being done here." Lowering his voice, Joseph continued, "Antipas will pay for what he has done to you, John."

John and Joseph continued to talk for a while until the guards instructed Joseph it was time to leave. They said their good-byes, ending the conversation with renewed hope.

* * *

Two days later, while Joseph was still on his way back to Jerusalem, two guards opened the cell door calling for John. "Who is the one called 'John the Baptist'?"

All of the prisoners shielded their eyes from the sudden burst of light. John was surprised to hear his name. His immediate thought was of release. Feeling a jolt of life spring back into his body, John pushed himself to his feet. Having difficulty getting out the words and clearing his throat at the same time, John responded, "I am."

The guards motioned him to come to the door, seemingly repulsed from walking further into the filth of the cell. John felt a sense of elation, realizing he would soon be walking through the door. Just having it open was more freedom than he had had in months. And now it appeared he was actually going outside. John's pace quickened as he grew near the door, until finally the guards grabbed him, forcing him to move more rapidly. Out in the hallway, John could hear the cell door close behind him, but he could still see nothing due to the blinding light. John did all he could to catch a glimpse of the walls and floor as they walked through the corridor. Slowly, his eyes adjusted as they made their way down an endless maze of halls. For some reason, John began to sense they were going further into the depths of the prison rather than exiting, which slowly brought a sense of despair. The guards were emotionless and didn't speak as they proceeded. Finally, they came to a large room where another man was waiting. There were a few tables, a large block of wood in the center of the room, and a basket sitting beneath it. Sudden fear gripped his body as John realized where he was. The man waiting in the room walked over and picked up an ax hanging on the wall. John started backing away, but felt the grip of the guards tighten as they pulled him toward the large block of wood. John resisted with every ounce of his strength, but felt helpless as they tied his hands behind his back and forced him down onto the block. Tears came to his eyes as it became impossible for him to spit out words, pleading for his life. Finding it difficult to even catch his breath, John finally forced the words, "What have I done? There must be some mistake!"

His words fell upon deaf ears as the guards continued tying him down, lapping ropes across his back and looping them through eyelets on the wooden block. His breathing became even more difficult as the tightness of the ropes pressed his chest down. Somehow, John forced out the words, "Pontius... Pilate."

The guards paused slightly in their actions, but were not diverted from their morbid duty. John saw the shadow of the ax rise high against the wall, knowing that soon it would fall in his last witness. Seeing the shadow start to move, John wrenched his eyes closed and cried out with his last breath, "Father—"

25 ~ Food for Thought

John's head was brought back to Jerusalem and presented to Antipas on a platter. Joseph heard of the antics of the dinner party, Salome's dance, and the swift execution of the bizarre sentence. He was dumbfounded, grief-stricken, and infuriated. He could not believe John was dead. He could do little beyond wish a similar fate upon Antipas. He felt confused and frightened, wondering if the commotion he had stirred, the forced appeals to Antipas, and his frequent visits to Machaerus had somehow forced Antipas' hand.

Without thinking, Joseph went directly to the praetorium to confront Pilate, completely disregarding his usual care. Joseph's disbelief and overwhelming sadness were driving him far beyond the reach of his sanity. Walking up the steps, he began to feel this was not where he belonged. As Joseph approached the ruling chambers, an intense feeling of loneliness overshadowed his being. He hesitated, not knowing if he should proceed or turn around and let his anger settle. But he continued on, intent upon gaining an audience. Entering a large room outside of the ruling chambers, he saw Pilate standing outside the door talking to another member of the council. Eliakim turned towards Joseph as he approached. "Joseph, what brings you here?"

Pilate quickly interrupted, "This seems to be my day for working with the Jewish council. What have I done to deserve such an honor?" Pilate said with a token laugh.

Appearing a little annoyed, Eliakim responded, "Your honor, indeed. Perhaps undeserved."

Pilate lost his patronizing smile and returned to the subject of the interrupted conversation. "You must control the settlements outside the walls, or I will send soldiers to do your work. It's a breeding ground for your zealots. Attacks on Roman citizens have increased over the past several weeks, and I am certain it is a result of these hordes."

Eliakim shook his head in disgust and frustration. "The weather is turning colder, and they naturally come in from the wilderness to find shelter and food. This happens every year. If you can build roads, aqueducts, palaces, and monuments to Caesar, you can help provide food for these people."

Pilate responded with an obnoxious laugh. "I do not see taxes from these... people. Why do they deserve food from Rome? I don't even see taxes from residents inside these walls. Even the people we protect will not pay taxes. The barbarians outside the walls attack my soldiers and our families."

Eliakim turned towards Joseph and forced a smile. "Good day, Joseph. May God be with you and grant you the wisdom to deal with our Roman friends." He then walked away, ignoring any potential response from Pilate.

Pontius turned toward Joseph, but spoke loudly while Eliakim was still nearby. "And you, sir, have you come for a Roman handout?"

"No!" Joseph exclaimed, obviously in no mood for Pilate's antics. "John's been executed! Antipas' wife was behind this the whole time!" Joseph wrenched his fingers, wishing they could wrap around Herodias' throat. "I learned this today. I heard Antipas presented his head on a platter to his wretched wife!"

Pilate gave a convincing look of shock and horror as he shook his head, "A woman's scorn..."

Joseph continued, "You can have Antipas arrested and removed as tetrarch for executing a prisoner without authority from Rome! Perhaps you should even have *his* head!"

"Remove Antipas? I'm afraid it's not that simple, Joseph."

"What do you mean, 'not simple'! He murdered an innocent man! Antipas' own father was not allowed to execute his own son until granted authority from Rome, and that man was guilty of treason against his father! Now you're telling me Antipas can execute a man who has given much in his service to Rome—and nothing will come of it!"

Pilate motioned frantically with his hands, imploring Joseph to keep his voice down. "Rome would never take notice of someone like John, even though he was a soldier in service of her glory. Countless, nameless soldiers have fallen in battle, much like John. Being the son of Herod the Great is what made Rome take notice, treason or no treason." Pilate paused before his tone grew somber. "As for John, Rome would only laugh if I tried to depose Antipas for his sake." Pilate turned, looking away from Joseph. "John made an unfortunate mistake. He picked a battle with the wrong man and paid the price."

Joseph's fight and anger suddenly turned hopeless. His eyes drifted towards the floor. Support and confidence in the greatest power in the known world drifted away from his soul, shadowed by a deepening sorrow. Who could he trust anymore now that John was gone? Jesus did not have John's balance, wisdom, and fortitude. Joseph looked up to catch Pilate's gaze as he turned back around. The spark in Pilate's eyes seemed to dim to match his concern and despair.

* * *

The next day Pilate called Joseph back to Fortress Antonia to meet with Thaddaeus, who had traveled from Galilee.

After greeting Joseph, Thaddaeus smiled and said, "Jesus has heard of the death of John the Baptist and has withdrawn to the farmhouse on the southern shores of the Sea of Galilee. He wishes to meet with both of you."

Joseph shook his head, not receptive to the idea of traveling to Galilee to meet with Jesus. He noticed Pilate roll his eyes, obviously not receptive either. However, he thought how Jesus must feel having to carry forward the light of a man now gone.

Thaddaeus waited, eventually raising his hands for a response. Joseph finally spoke up. "What news do you bring from Galilee?"

Thaddaeus raised his eyebrows and took a deep breath. He looked at Pilate and replied, "It's mixed, at best, my lord."

Pilate's eyes widened. Joseph was also surprised at the melancholy nature of Thaddaeus' message. In his meetings with Jesus, he had only received good reports, which he in turn relayed to Pilate. Thaddaeus continued, "Jesus had a few confrontations with the local people of the area and exchanged some heated words." Thaddaeus went on to explain the recent encounters, and how Jesus had lost his temper, openly condemning all of the people of several cities.

Pontius slapped the table. "By the gods!" Looking over at Joseph, Pontius yelled, "What's wrong with you people? Can't you control what you say? He's supposed to be winning them over, not condemning them to hell!" Pontius paced around the room. "We told him to diminish the image of the religious order, not alienate himself from the people!" Pontius looked at Joseph as if expecting some kind of answer.

Thaddaeus interceded. "Things are really not as bad as they seem, my lord. There is still a great following, and Jesus has the support of his disciples. There are twelve of them now, counting Decius and myself."

Pilate calmed somewhat and replied, "Well, I can't go up to Galilee right now. There are just too many things going on here in Jerusalem for me to get away." Pilate turned a probing eye toward Joseph. "You will need to go up there, Joseph, with Glaucus." Pilate gave a sarcastic smirk and added, "Maybe you can convince the people camped outside the gates to go with you."

At first, Joseph took Pilate seriously with a look of surprise. Then he returned Pilate's sarcasm: "If I had that many people following me, Jesus would think he's losing his job."

Pontius laughed. "You?! A charismatic leader?" Pontius raised an eyebrow in levity. "Or perhaps he would think you have been promoted to Jewish centurion, leading the Jerusalem garrison against Galilee." Pontius and Thaddaeus burst into laughter as Joseph hesitated, not appreciating their humor.

Trying to sober the tone, Joseph replied, "I would not know the first thing about being a centurion, Noble Prefect, Jewish or Roman. It's a responsibility I would not care to embrace. I would not even know how to keep that many people alive in the wilderness, much less make them a threat."

Pontius calmed his laughter placing his hand on Joseph's shoulder. "Recognizing the demands of survival is half the battle, Joseph. There are some officers in our training who don't even know we must take water.

It's amazing how many men come to our schools thinking an army consists merely of men and weapons." Pontius paused; then, trying to make a point, he added, "You would make a fine general in the Roman army, Joseph, and I would be proud to have you serve under me. We were just joking, and I hope you didn't take offense."

A smile slowly returned to Joseph's face picturing himself in the uniform of a Roman centurion. Knowing Pilate's statement was purely hypothetical, Joseph played along. "I like my job just the way it is, Your Nobility." As he said this, Joseph thought about the journey he would take again, and quickly began to doubt the sincerity of his statement. He thought about all of the people outside the gates of Jerusalem, and Pilate's desire to get rid of them, which prompted an idea. His face lit up as he looked at Pilate. "How many people are camped outside the gates?"

"How many people?" Pontius repeated. "I don't know. It's hard to say exactly. My advisors have told me anywhere between ten and twenty thousand, counting women and children. Why?"

"I know how you can get the people to leave and win their hearts." Joseph noticed he had sparked Pilate's interest—and Thaddaeus' too. He walked over and picked up some bread. "Feed them. Promise them food somewhere else, and they'll go where the food is."

Pontius laughed. "Now you're starting to sound like Eliakim. We can't feed twenty thousand people." Pontius paused briefly as if correcting his thoughts. "Well, maybe we could. But if they knew it was from Rome, they would come to expect it from us. We can't do that. If you feed them once, they will expect more, and that would simply be impossible. Feeding twenty thousand people, even one time, would be difficult. That's four Roman legions!"

Joseph shook his head. "No, no. I'm not talking about feeding twenty thousand. Provide food for one of the large gatherings, probably no more than five to six hundred... and they will be drawn away from the city."

Pontius reacted favorably. "Five to six hundred people. You may have an idea, Joseph."

Joseph became more animated as he plotted. "That will be five to six hundred mouths to spread the news of a personal miracle. In the past, we've only had a handful of people to testify to miracles. Now hundreds will gain personal experience in one simple act."

Pontius fell into Joseph's excitement, but then voiced a concern. "On that scale, it may be difficult to conceal our involvement."

Joseph ran his fingers through his beard and twisted the hairs. "Jesus' disciples will serve the food. It will be a gift from God. That will win back their favor and more. The mobs will be more prone to listen to Jesus if they feel the satisfaction of food in their stomachs."

Thaddaeus interjected, "If we say the food is from their god, then why would the people not expect it every time they gather, instead of just occasionally? Don't you think it would follow that if their god showed compassion to feed them once, then he would be expected to show such compassion each time? How will that make sense?"

Joseph's smile softened realizing the wisdom of Thaddaeus' words. "For that matter, why would God let anyone starve to death? Maybe we would introduce theological questions that would eventually turn against us, as happened in Gadara."

Joseph started feeling uncomfortable again, sensing they were moving too quickly, stitching together a movement that needed better planning and design. "You're right, we obviously can't support every person, every time. There are times when you visit friends and receive gifts. That doesn't mean you expect gifts with every visit. You simply feel special and honored when it does happen. And so will be this gift of food... hopefully."

* * *

Joseph and Thaddaeus traveled to meet with Jesus to tell him of their plans. They took with them a wagon of bread and fish—enough to feed several hundred people. They planned the first gathering at a field, five miles west of Tiberias, hiding the food amongst the bushes and rocks. A single basket with only a few fish and bread was brought out to explain the aroma that filled the air, before the remaining disciples and other people began arriving. On that day four hundred people came to hear Jesus speak—less than they were expecting. Joseph and Jesus had worked carefully on a sermon based mainly on loving one's enemies and showing kindness, even to those who persecute. He openly ridiculed scribes, chief priests, Pharisees, Sadducees, and teachers of the Mosaic

Law, building upon a theme that had gained popularity with the masses.

Due to the early morning preparations, and late word of the gathering location, Jesus spoke into the late hours of the day. After the sermon was over, Jesus called his disciples together, most of whom were unaware of the hidden food, and said, "I have compassion on the crowd, for they have been with me the entire day and now have nothing to eat. I am unwilling to send them away hungry, lest they faint on the way."

Andrew questioned Jesus, "Where are we to get bread enough in the desert to feed these people?"

Jesus pointed to the basket of food and asked, "How many loaves have you?"

Andrew looked into the basket and counted. "Seven loaves and two fish."

Jesus broke the bread and fish into several pieces and gave them to ten of his disciples and said, "Go and serve the people, starting with those at the farthest reaches. As you go, tell them to sit in groups, and they will be fed."

With this the ten departed into the crowd as Jesus had instructed. While they were gone, Thaddaeus and Simon retrieved the hidden loaves and fish, which had already been broken. When the ten returned, they found the basket nearly full, which brought praise and glory to God for a wondrous miracle. Each was given more than before to distribute to the crowd. And with each return, there was still more. To each person they gave food, they spoke of the wondrous miracle they had just witnessed. The people were truly amazed, having had their fill, and still, great quantities of food remained.

Word quickly spread throughout the land. People came from great distances to witness the feast miracle. Some pulled their own wagons of traveling supplies and accompanying family, slowly dwindling the numbers outside Jerusalem, pleasantly fulfilling Pilate's expectations. As encampments began to spring up around Tiberias, Joseph and Jesus realized their next gathering would involve many more people. With what they'd learned from the first gathering, they devised better schemes for distributing the food and more elaborate tricks—some involving baskets with false bottoms, hidden compartments on wagons, and wagons pre-positioned amongst the crowd. The wagons, they surmised, would be perceived as belonging to those visiting. Pilate elicited the help of more undercover soldiers as the numbers grew larger. The fourth gathering included nearly five thousand men, women, and children. The numbers were so great that most could not hear Jesus' message, even though he strained to project his voice. Most of those gathered were not concerned about hearing a message, only witnessing a miracle—and the obvious draw of food to feed their families. Their plans, it seemed, had worked too well, and soon the area became overrun with too many people. Joseph and Jesus quickly realized it was necessary to leave the area, which became unmanageable. Jesus and his disciples traveled by boat to the other side of the Sea of Galilee, reaching land four miles south of Bethsaida. The multitudes, however, managed to follow, still numbering in the thousands.

26 ~ Word against Memory

The people related more closely to the firm reality of food, rather than the removed experience of staged healings. Joseph's idea provided a well-needed boost to Jesus' ministries. Jesus' popularity grew steadily, evidenced by the ever-growing crowds. Many were becoming accustomed to his new teachings and philosophies. However, pockets of discontent persisted.

Some of the disciples became drunk with popularity, even to the point of arguing amongst themselves as to who was the greatest. Jesus, too, became overwhelmed with the extremes of prominence, good and bad. It had been several months since he had thought of his family in Nazareth. Jesus was the oldest of five sons and two daughters. They all lived with their mother, Mary. His father, Joseph, had passed away several years before. Being the oldest, Jesus had been the head of the family. His new duties quickly changed all of that. He was no longer around to help with family matters, problems, and work, cultivating mounting tensions.

Joseph, Pilate, and Jesus knew that the best way to take advantage of their success was to travel around the country, getting the new message to as many people as possible. During their travels, Jesus avoided Nazareth. He kept the true nature of his teachings away from his family. He was in absolute agreement for the need of secrecy. But secrecy fed alienation, which at times spiraled into neglect, nurturing ill feelings that would otherwise lie dormant.

One day, Jesus was teaching to a large crowd at a synagogue in Magdala. His mother and three of his brothers had come to speak to him, but dared not go inside and interrupt while he was teaching. After waiting for some time, Mary elicited the help of a stranger to tell Jesus his family wanted to speak with him. Jesus replied to the man, "Who is my mother and who are my brothers?" Stretching out his hand toward his disciples, he proclaimed, "Here are my mother and my brothers! For whoever does the will of my Father in heaven is my brother, and sister, and mother."

The stranger shook his head in disbelief as several around him grumbled words of disapproval towards Jesus' apparent disrespect towards his family. The stranger turned and pushed his way through the crowd to deliver the disappointing message. Nearing the exit, another man pulled on the stranger's garment. "Did you come from up front?"

The stranger paused and nodded.

"I thought I heard Jesus refer to the Most High God as his Father. Did I hear him correctly?"

The stranger nodded again, and several people gasped, with one woman mumbling, "Blasphemy! King David is the Anointed One, begotten by God. It is stated in the Scriptures."

Another man in a different part of the audience stood up and yelled, "How is it that you refer to God as your father? What are you trying to say?"

Jesus pointed to everyone in the room. "Do you not know that we are *all* God's children? He loves us all. He created us in his own image." Looking at the man, whose expression had softened considerably, Jesus continued, "Have I not taught you to pray '*Our* Father, who art in heaven'? We should all refer to him as 'Father' since we are all his children."

Jesus felt cowardly: he had backed away from an opportunity to build upon the mystery of his image. However, he was weary of the pointed accusations of the past and enjoyed the more positive attention he received in the latest wave of gatherings. He realized there was a time for pushing the limit, and there was a time for consolidating your position. Consolidation was much less stressful. Jesus sensed favorable reaction from the crowd.

A man who had been a follower of John the Baptist raised his hand, pleading to ask a question. When Jesus recognized him, the man lowered his hand and slowly stood. He had a great sadness in his eyes and spoke with a tearful crackle in his voice: "Teacher, why is it that the one who came before you had to die at the hands of Antipas?"

The man's delivery brought the room to a somber silence. John was still greatly revered—a man never to be forgotten. With deep reverence filling his own soul, Jesus replied, "What did you go out into the wilderness to behold? A reed shaken by the wind? A man clothed in soft raiment? No! For those who wear soft raiment are pampered in the houses of kings." Jesus smiled as he looked directly at the man. "Why then did you go out? To see a prophet?" Jesus paused and looked around at every eye focused his way. Jesus took a deep breath. "Yes, I tell you, and more than a prophet."

With that, a gasp fell upon the entire crowd. The man's face turned to a blank stare as he slowly sat down. He leaned over to his wife and whispered, "I was there when John said he was not a prophet. He said it with such passion, I'll never forget it. Who should we believe?"

His wife placed her arm on his shoulder. "Maybe you remember wrong? We all know John was a wonderful and righteous man, who drew countless multitudes to the River Jordan. How could he not be a prophet? And you just heard Jesus."

The man shook his head and gritted his teeth. "No! I know what I heard and my memory does not fail me, woman!" Then softening his tone and looking into his wife's eyes, he continued, "I did not ask Jesus about the sanctity of the man. I was asking about the injustice of his death."

A scribe sitting next to the man and his wife asked, "You heard John speak?"

The man looked his way and nodded.

Before the scribe could continue, Jesus spoke again. "This is he of whom it is written, 'Behold, I send my messenger before thy face, who shall prepare the way before thee.'"

The scribe's expression grew puzzled and he leaned over closer to the man and his wife. "I know the verse. His words are from the book of Malachi. He does not know the meaning of the Scriptures."

The man and his wife looked attentively at the scribe, as several others around listened. "Everyone knows Malachi was referring to himself as a messenger of God. He was not prophesizing about John."

Those around nodded in agreement.

Continuing on, Jesus said, "Truly, I say to you, among those born of women there has risen no one greater than John the Baptist. If you are willing to accept it, he is Elijah who is to come."

Another gasp came from the crowd. The man jumped from his seat, shocked by the power of a crowd hypnotized in Jesus' words. He looked down at his wife and the scribe. "John must be turning in his grave. I heard John rebuke those referring to him so."

His wife eyed him in fear. "Sit down! You see how the crowd has reacted to his words. Everyone here loves John, as I know you do! If you attempt to refute his words, we will be driven out and stoned in the streets!"

The man shook his head, glancing towards the door. Looking back at Jesus, he suddenly called out, "You call those around you your family. But how can you neglect your real family waiting outside?"

Many in the crowd started jeering at the man, who now looked down at his wife and the scribe. "They were not there when John spoke. How can they be passing judgment on me?"

His wife pulled on his garment, forcing him to sit down.

In Jesus' defense, Peter stood and called out, "Look at our example. We have left our homes and followed you."

Having renewed confidence, Jesus bowed his head toward Peter in thankful acknowledgement. Turning back towards the crowd, Jesus continued, "Truly, I say to you, there is no man who has left house or wife or brothers or parents or children for the sake of the kingdom of God who will not be rewarded many times over now and in the eternal life to come. If anyone comes to me and does not hate his own father and mother and wife and children and brothers and sisters, yes, and even his own life, he cannot be my disciple."

The man leaned over to his wife and whispered, "I've heard enough. Come on, let's go." With that, his wife and several around them got up and left.

27 ~ Pushing the Limit

The masked slave dropped her tray of fruit on the stage as a heavyset nobleman pulled on her tunic. The nobleman's wife looked on with exaggerated disapproval. The audience burst into laughter, followed by applause as the wife took her plate and smashed it onto his round belly. Claudia brought her hand up to cover uncontrollable spurts of laughter as she eyed Pontius, wiping away tears streaming down his cheeks. The laughter and cheers of the audience seemed distant as she saw the man she loved, freed from the bonds of a foreign land and the demands of Rome.

Pontius took Claudia's hand as they walked back to Fortress Antonia in the cool air of the late afternoon. Entering their chambers, Pontius helped Claudia remove her hooded shawl. Claudia turned and placed her hand on Pontius' cheek. "Thank you, Pontius. What a wonderful day. It felt like we were back in Rome again."

Pontius turned his face in the contour of her hand until his lips touched her soft fingers. Gradually opening his eyes, Pontius whispered, "That's the necklace I gave you on our voyage here."

Claudia smiled as she brought her hand up to fondle the pendant. "I have worn it many times, Pontius. You have only just noticed?"

Pontius shrugged his shoulders. "Perhaps—I'm not sure."

Pontius reached up to touch the necklace and guided his hand down to the pendant. "I had forgotten how beautiful it was."

Claudia could feel tears welling in her eyes as Pontius looked up to meet hers. "But it pales to the glimmer in your eyes, the softness of your skin, and your enchanting face."

The tears fell down her cheeks as she caressed Pontius' hand against her chest. Pontius closed his eyes. "That day on the ship seems so long ago and far away. I wish I could go back and start again. Everything I've accomplished means nothing compared to my love for you."

Claudia put her arms around Pontius' waist and held him tight. "I love you, too. But don't belittle what you have done and your position. I'm proud of you, Pontius. I have grown to know the difficulties you must endure and the odd nature of these people. It would drive any ordinary man crazy, but you have grown stronger." Pulling back at arm's length, Claudia continued, "And you're still the same man I knew and loved back then—and always will."

Claudia felt Pontius return her hug with a compassionate embrace. He slowly released her and then walked over to the window. "Do you remember the Jewish man you mentioned several weeks ago?"

"Are you referring to the religious man Jesus?"

"Yes." Pontius turned and looked at Claudia. "He's not a religious man. He's not a man of their god. He is of Roman design."

Claudia's eyes widened. "He is of Roman design? What does that mean?"

"He is my emissary with the Jewish people—he and a few others."

Claudia's eyes widened as she brought her hand up to her mouth. "That's amazing, Pontius! Everyone speaks of him, Roman and Jew. How did you get a man like that to even talk to you, much less act as an emissary?"

"I created him. He did not attain his position through his own works. I chose him when he was but a common Jew, and built him to his position—with counsel from others, including Tacitus."

"Tacitus? Yes, I remember Tacitus. Marcellus speaks of him often, and I remember how much his death affected you. But that was over a year ago—maybe two."

"Yes, he was a good man. It was his idea to create an emissary with the Jewish people, starting with a seat on the Jewish council, and then John the Baptist."

"John the Baptist! Oh, by the mercy of the gods!" Claudia sat down in a chair, thoughts racing through her head. "Of course! Both Roman and

Jew speak favorably of Jesus—and John the Baptist. The Jewish people are perhaps more wary due to recent warnings from their priests, but they still think of him as a god..." Claudia looked up with amazement. "This was of your design? That's the most amazing thing I have ever heard!"

Pontius' demeanor seemed emboldened as he stood taller and smiled. "I should have told you long ago, but I saw the mob in Caesarea as a sign to protect you from the workings of government." Pontius shook his head, looking down at the floor. "Perhaps if I would have sought your counsel on the aquifer affair, Tacitus would still be alive."

Claudia rose and placed her hand on Pontius' shoulder. "That was not your fault. Tacitus was killed by zealots in the countryside. I know you have many difficult decisions in your position, and I shouldn't have been so hard on you."

Pontius turned and kissed Claudia, holding her tight. "You're right. This position would have driven me crazy, if it were not for you as my strength."

Claudia returned Pontius' kiss with love and confidence. Backing away, she grew elated with the thought: a world that seemed to be changing before her eyes. "So you have been the craftsmen behind the changes in this country. And I thought it was coincidence that these changes happened with our arrival." Claudia smiled as everything started making sense. "Of course—all of the talk about taxes and peaceful submission, bordering on welcoming our presence: the exact opposite of the character and culture I've seen in the marketplace. I have even heard of Jewish rebels laying down their arms upon hearing his words." Claudia paused for a moment. "What about all of the miracles and healings?"

Pontius smiled, but before he could respond, Claudia interrupted. "You were behind all of that, too?!" Claudia turned and paced around the room. "I knew when Esther first mentioned the man that it wasn't real. I was always skeptical that a man of their god could do such things! But the way she talked about him, and her witness of those healings, I was beginning to almost believe it myself! I found myself wanting to see him for my own witness!"

Pontius' smile grew concerned. "You could never go out into the wilderness. It would be far too dangerous. Even with escort, if they knew you were the prefect's wife, the zealots would stop at nothing."

"I would never venture outside the walls of this city without your knowledge." Claudia's eyes lit up with excitement. "Will he come to Jerusalem? I would like to meet him. The whole world is fascinated by him, and now I learn he is of your making!"

"No, I cannot bring him to Jerusalem. It would be too risky." Pontius paused. "John the Baptist came to Jerusalem, and people recognized him."

Claudia sighed with disappointment. "Risky?! The people love him here. This is where all of the people are, not in the wilderness."

* * *

Most considered Jesus a great teacher, offering new concepts and ideals beyond the traditional nature of the Mosaic Law and Jewish culture. Others considered him a prophet who had been given a special gift from God to speak of his divine will. Some spoke of him as the reincarnation of King David, the anointed son of God.

There were many, however, who stood fast to the teaching of the Scriptures. They heeded the warnings of prophets to steer clear of outside influences, and they considered Jesus' teachings to be blasphemous and took great despair in his growing popularity.

In early spring, Joseph and Jesus met Pilate in a farmhouse south of Aenon near Salim. Joseph felt uneasy as Pilate poured wine into three cups and offered him one. Joseph nervously sipped as Pilate approached Jesus and said, "I have been talking with Joseph about having you come to Jerusalem."

Joseph set his cup on a table and stood up from his chair. He had not agreed to Pilate's idea, and continued to voice opposition. "The Holy City is the sacred center of our faith. The Temple is in Jerusalem." Joseph paused, looking towards Jesus for support. "It is one thing to teach a variation of our faith in the countryside, but in Jerusalem... The people of Jerusalem are more traditional—closer to the watchful eye of the Jewish court. We can't be sure how they will react."

Pilate raised his voice. "You have been telling me the news of Jesus has grown favorable, even in Jerusalem!"

"I know! But news can be very different from personal witness!"

Joseph began shaking with anxiety. Lowering his voice, Joseph continued, "The people of Jerusalem are a different breed—more sophisticated, more educated in the Mosaic Law."

Pilate smiled. "I see your point, Joseph. But the time of your Passover is approaching, and many will come from all over Judea to celebrate the festival. Since they are 'unsophisticated,' this is the time for Jesus to make an appearance."

Joseph rubbed the back of his neck as he turned from Pilate's gaze. "With all due respect, Your Nobility, you do not understand the depth of conviction in the governing Jewish circles. There are great divisions and contrasting opinions among the people—not as unified as you might hope. There are many who are in awe of Jesus' miracles, but there are many who question the nature of his power and are intimidated by his popularity." Joseph paused drinking from his cup. Then he placed his hand on Jesus' shoulder. "We have had remarkable success. Even the simple act of helping Bartimius has changed people's hearts. I have noticed less anger and hatred when people speak of Rome. And having Matthew as one of Jesus' disciples—that was a stroke of genius. I have honestly noticed changing attitudes towards tax collectors."

Joseph could see he had Pilate's interest as he continued, "I have noticed growing suspicion and mistrust of the Saducees and Pharisees. Jesus' open challenge to their authority has worked well in the countryside, but I am not so sure about Jerusalem." Joseph paused, hoping Pontius would see the depth of his concern. "We must allow more time for these feelings and attitudes to become rooted, rather than force change too quickly."

Jesus nodded, but Pontius shook his head. "It has been over a year and a half—two and a half years, counting John. How much time do you think is necessary to push on?"

Joseph shook his head. "Maybe we don't need to push. Maybe we have attained enough. We have already done so much good. Maybe we should be pleased with what we have accomplished, sit back, and allow time for the people to adjust to this new order."

"No! We cannot sit back and let this stagnate! Stagnation breeds failure and lays the seeds of apathy. We must move forward while the interest is strong and developing. The time is right for Jesus to make his entrance into your Holy City, and I will not wait another year for your next Passover."

Joseph became combatant as he stood up. "Jerusalem is the seat of the Jewish council, the court of the high priest, and many of the priestly orders Jesus has been criticizing. They don't trust Jesus or the nature of his teachings, and openly profess so. It is not the masses I fear, but the condemnation from the Jewish court!"

Pontius calmed his voice and demeanor. "Hear me. It doesn't need to be very long. Jesus can make a brief appearance for a day or two and then return to Galilee. With time, his stay will grow longer as people become accustomed to his presence, where he can influence the politics of government and not just the hearts of the people."

Joseph took another drink of wine and sat back in his chair. Jesus smiled, giving Pilate a look of confidence. "I believe Pilate has a good idea. We are at the height of popularity, and I don't know if there would be a better opportunity to make an introduction to Jerusalem."

Joseph narrowed his eyes and turned to Jesus. "Remember what happened to John when he came to Jerusalem?"

Pontius' eyes twitched. Jesus glanced at Joseph with a look of disapproval. "John made the unfortunate mistake of personally attacking Antipas. I have made no such comments or had any interactions with Antipas." Jesus paused, taking a large drink from his cup. "Even when one would think that I, in my position, would have made appeals to Antipas for John's release, I did not do even that."

Joseph could see the wine bleeding between Jesus' lips. He knew Jesus had been forbidden to call out for John's release, but it still angered him. Joseph wondered where Jesus was going with this line of thought.

Jesus finally broke the awkward silence. "All of my teachings have dealt strictly with the people, and I have never felt any type of threat or concern from Antipas—or his wife."

Pontius nodded. "Jesus is right. We have nothing to worry about from Antipas."

Joseph sensed Pilate's confidence was reassuring Jesus, but he remained skeptical. He had heard the same reassurance for John. Something forced Joseph to hold his tongue, however, thinking he would overstep his bounds to question Pilate's word.

The next morning, Joseph gradually warmed towards Pilate's plan. Scanning through the book of Zechariah he found an interesting verse. "If I may, one of the last great prophets, Zechariah—the one John spoke of, common with his father's name—prophesized in the Scriptures, 'Shout aloud, O daughter of Jerusalem! Lo, your king comes to you triumphant and riding on the foal of an ass.' Granted, he was speaking of Zerubbabel, but it might be fitting to have Jesus enter in such a manner. It is subtle, but the people may take notice of the ancient scriptures as prophecy."

Pontius smiled. "Excellent idea, Joseph. It's simple and could be effective. Your knowledge of the scripture has been invaluable."

Joseph felt a strong sense of pride with Pilate's compliment. They were rare, but when they came, he knew he meant it. Pontius looked over at Jesus. "It is certainly within my wishes you become king of the Jews—a position Antipas will never attain. Perhaps you will be revered with divine reputation as was your King David."

Joseph's temporary delight turned dispirited with Pilate's persistent reference to King David. Returning to his line of planning, Joseph continued, "I know a man who has asses in a village just outside Jerusalem, near the Mount of Olives. I will make arrangements for a young foal to be tied up on the outskirts of the village on the day Jesus enters Jerusalem."

Pilate nodded his approval. "We still have a few weeks before Passover. I want you to give sermons building upon the mistrust of priests and scribes. It should be fresh in their minds as they enter Jerusalem."

* * *

As the time approached, Joseph arranged for Jesus and his disciples to stay in Jericho on their way to Jerusalem. Joseph knew the chief tax collector, Zacchaeus, and made plans for Jesus and the disciples to meet up with him and spend the evening at his home.

Great crowds gathered in Jericho upon hearing of Jesus' presence and his plans to go to Jerusalem. On the morning he was to leave, a large number of people gathered to accompany him. On the outskirts of Jericho, they came across Roman soldiers posing as blind beggars on the side of the road. Seeing that it was Jesus, one called out, "Have mercy on us, son of David!"

Before Jesus could get over to the men, most in the crowd became annoyed by the flagrant pleas of the filthy beggars. Some even rebuked them, telling them to be quiet and stop their obnoxious calls. This prompted the two soldiers to cry out even more, saying, "Lord, have mercy on us, son of David!"

Upon reaching them, Jesus asked in a loud voice, "What do you want me to do for you?"

One of the soldiers replied, "Master, my name is Bartimaeus, son of Timaeus. My friend and I have been blind since birth. Have mercy on us and let our eyes be opened."

Jesus assumed a look of compassion and touched their eyes with his hands, saying, "Stand up and go your way. Your faith has made you well!"

Immediately, the two stood, proclaiming their newly acquired sight. All who were there, including the disciples, proclaimed wonderment and praise to God.

From there, Jesus and his disciples proceeded to Bethany near Jerusalem. Jesus made arrangements for them to stay overnight with a friend of his, Lazarus, and his sisters, Martha and Mary. Jesus and Lazarus had worked together as carpenters in Nazareth since boyhood. Jesus had always liked Mary, but she had rarely returned his advances when they were younger.

That night at supper, while all of the men were seated around the dinner table, Lazarus said to Jesus, "There are rumors that the high priest, Joseph Caiaphas, is looking to have you arrested. He is wary of the works you have performed and thinks they are born of demonic forces."

"Caiaphas... wants to have me arrested!"

Mary, who was in the next room, began weeping. She walked over to a cabinet and pulled out a jar of fragrant ointment of pure nard. Everyone turned silent as Mary walked into the dining room with tears running down her cheeks. She walked over to Jesus and gently motioned for him to turn around in his chair. She then knelt down, anointed his feet, and wiped his feet with her hair. At first, Jesus felt apprehensive in front of the others, but gradually succumbed. He became entranced by the soft touch of her hands and the pleasant aroma of the ointment. The silence grew tense with the sound of the oil pressing through her fingers. Many of the disciples were noticeably embarrassed by Mary's forwardness. Judas leaned over to Andrew and whispered, "Why doesn't he rebuke her sinful brashness?" Then, breaking the silence, Judas called out, "Why was this ointment not sold for three hundred denarii and given to the poor?"

Jesus was immediately insulted by the unexpected interruption. Judas never backed down from confrontation, nor did he hesitate to start his own. His challenging demeanor created friction with many of the disciples, and this evening was no exception. It was difficult to keep secrets from Judas because he was always asking questions—too many questions. Jesus never liked Judas and feared him in some sense. Jesus was constantly on guard with him, more so than the other disciples, for fear of revealing the true nature of his ministries. But for reasons unknown to Jesus, Judas always remained.

Even though Judas' brazen approach was to be expected, Jesus felt cornered, being the sudden focus of everyone's attention in what had become an embarrassing situation. Feeling angered and personally attacked, Jesus yelled back, "Leave her alone! She means no harm by what she is doing! I'm sure the poor will not miss the three hundred denarii! The poor will be poor, with or without it! But you will not always have me, that I may receive her devotion, caring, and affection. And yes, the ointment and the touch of her hand please me."

A deathly silence fell upon the room, contrasting with the sweet fragrance. Mary immediately got up and went back to serving everyone at the table. Nothing more was said about the incident and even the simplest conversation became awkward.

* * *

The next morning, Jesus and his disciples stopped at the Mount of Olives to find the young ass before proceeding into Jerusalem.

A great crowd had gathered at the gates waiting to see Jesus. Toward late afternoon, Jesus entered the gates riding on the colt. Great cheers erupted from the crowd in their excitement. Many laid out their garments along the road in front of Jesus, while others laid out leafy branches they had cut from trees. Many were crying out his name and shouting, "Hosanna in the highest, blessed is he who comes in the name of the

Lord!"

Jesus was overwhelmed by the greetings and cheers. The adoration and admiration were beyond anything he had ever imagined, quelling any fear of the threat from the high priest. Jesus neared the temple, along with a great crowd that proceeded before and after him.

Pontius appeared on a balcony of Fortress Antonia and called back to Joseph, "It's Jesus! Do you hear them, Joseph? I have not heard such praises since I was in Rome! They are praising him as if he were their king!"

Joseph smiled and stood on a chair away from the window, trying to get a glimpse of the commotion below.

Reaching the temple, Jesus dismounted and said a few words to the crowd. After a short greeting, Jesus turned and walked into the temple to present his offering and say a few prayers. The showering of praise and adoration heightened his sense of self-importance, which in turn elevated his feeling of presence in the temple. The sudden tranquility eased his emotions as he knelt and bowed in prayer. He had never felt such peace before—a special connection with God. He *was* in his Father's house. The quiet air calmed his spirit from the day's intense theater. A few minutes turned into several. Jesus knew it was getting late and he would have to make his way back outside.

As Jesus was leaving through the square in front of the temple, he noticed several vendors presenting their goods and crafts, along with several other people searching through the goods for purchase. Their indifference to his presence angered him. With night quickly falling, Jesus went back to Lazarus' house in Bethany. The image of the vendors festered in his mind for the rest of the evening and through the night.

Lazarus' cupboards had become essentially bare after having prepared the large meal the night before. With all of the commotion, Lazarus had failed to replenish his store of food. Everyone went with very little food that evening. Fortunately, however, Jesus and his disciples were so exhausted from the day's activities that their weariness overwhelmed their hunger, and they had no problem falling asleep.

The next morning, Jesus and his disciples had to proceed to Jerusalem without a morning meal. Hunger tore at Jesus' stomach. Anger churned in his mind over what he had seen in the temple. As they neared Jerusalem, Jesus and his disciples saw a large, green fig tree in the distance. Forgetting that it was not the season for figs, Jesus ran up to the tree, only to find it didn't have any fruit. Jesus cursed the tree: "May no one ever eat fruit from you again!"

The disciples stood in disbelief as Jesus immediately turned and quickened a determined pace towards Jerusalem. One by one they followed, working to catch up.

Upon entering Jerusalem, Jesus went straight to the temple. The sore of hatred for the barterers in the courtyard had festered into an inflamed wound. Jesus noticed a whip on a vendor's table and was overcome with an urge to use it as a tool to punish the focus of his hatred. He cracked the whip, attempting to drive everyone out, yelling, "This is a house of prayer, not a den of thieves!" People started running as one man cried out from being hit. One woman dropped a jar of olive oil and bag of wheat, then picked up her children before running out of the square. Jesus overturned the tables with all of their goods and kicked at chairs, sending one crashing into the wall of the courtyard. He continued yelling, blindly cracking the whip at anything and anyone who stood nearby.

The screams subsided as Jesus found himself alone in the courtyard. He dropped the whip and kicked at pieces of broken pottery to clear a path to a pile of bread and a box of dried figs. He savored the bread that was still warm and the texture of the fruit, dried to perfection. A gulp of wine washed away the final grips of hunger as he eyed an axe propped up against a vendor's chair. Jesus laughed realizing his disciples had left, unable to share in his spoils. Jesus picked up the axe and nearly ran back to the fig tree on his return to Bethany. The trunk served as his final release of frustrations as he visualized each horrified face running from his whip with each swing of the axe, cutting deep into the outer rings.

The next day, when several of his disciples saw the tree was starting to wither, Peter proclaimed, "Master, look! The fig tree which you cursed has withered."

Jesus smiled, looking back at Peter. "Haven't I told you? Whatever you command and truly believe, will happen. In the same manner, whatever you ask in prayer, if you believe you will receive it, you will."

Shaking his head, Judas asked sarcastically, "Even if what you ask for is pointless and does harm to others? That tree could have borne fruit for others who pass along this way." Judas paused, and then added, "When it's the proper season for figs."

Some of the disciples laughed, but most held their silence, intimidated by the thought of a tree that had withered with his prophecy. Remembering a message John had told him long ago, Jesus looked sternly at Judas and said, "Even the fruit tree that does not bear good fruit will have the ax wielded against its root so that it will wither and die, and be cast into the fire!"

Judas backed off. Slowly, they all gathered and continued on their way to Jerusalem.

Going back to the temple, Jesus performed prearranged miracles and presented parables he and Joseph had prepared. At one point, a group of chief priests, scribes, and elders came up to him and asked, "By what authority are you doing these things?"

Over the past several months, Jesus had become skilled at maintaining the mystery, and using the power of rumors to get others to say for him what he dare not say himself. Knowing the great admiration the population still held for John, and knowing that almost everyone considered John to be a prophet, Jesus turned the question back on them. "Was the baptism of John from heaven or from men? Answer me, and I will answer you." Jesus knew if they responded "from men," which is the answer they presumed, then the crowd would quickly turn on them, supporting his efforts to discredit them in public. If they answered "from heaven," he could respond by saying, "I am John's servant, a disciple commissioned through his words and actions to carry on his good works."

The group argued amongst themselves and finally answered, "We do not know."

Smiling, Jesus said, "Neither will I tell you by what authority I do these things!" Then Jesus immediately went into the parable of a vineyard owner that he and Joseph had worked up a few weeks earlier.

A chief priest pointed to himself as he whispered to an elder standing beside him, "We are the subject of his attacks with these parables."

The elder nodded, but looked cautiously at the crowd gathered tightly around Jesus, some of them laughing as if in agreement.

The chief priest whispered, "He is smug in his hidden accusations. He must be arrested before this sedition spreads any further. His attacks on our authority are more dangerous, perhaps, than any attack from the outside. But we cannot arrest him in public with the popularity he is gaining, for fear of how they might react."

The elder nodded as they turned and pushed their way out of the crowd.

The chief priest approached Caiaphas in his court. "Here in Jerusalem, Jesus is brazen in his attacks against our authority. He even calls us hypocrites!"

Caiaphas nodded. "I have heard so."

The chief priest hesitated and then bowed humbly. "His words seem to be striking a chord with the public, Your Holiness."

Caiaphas rose from his chair and approached the chief priest. "Give the people of Israel a little credit, Rachamim. They will see through his false teachings and lies. We are the Chosen People of God who will not be swayed by the antics of one man."

Rachamim nodded and bowed further. "Yes, but we are an occupied nation in the midst of many changes. I have seen how the people react to his teachings, and we must not allow it to continue. He is sowing the seeds of mistrust for the Law of Moses and the teachings of the Scriptures—teachings that I would give my life to defend."

Caiaphas placed his hand on Rachamim's shoulder. "We would all give our life to defend our Holy Covenant with God." Caiaphas paused in thought. "Jesus has said some things that are not popular with the people. Rather than have him arrested and turn him into a martyr, we can turn sentiment against him."

Rachamim stood straight and smiled.

Caiaphas continued, "I have heard he has taken tax collectors as his disciples, and that he even stayed with the chief tax collector in Jericho before coming to Jerusalem. We can entrap Jesus in his own teachings. We will put the question directly to him. If he openly supports the payment of taxes, he will lose favor. If he publicly refutes the payment of taxes, he will be arrested and so charged by Rome."

Caiaphas sent a Pharisee and a courtier of Herod's palace to confront Jesus. The Pharisee and Herodian presented false airs to gain his favor and complimented Jesus. Then finally the Pharisee asked, "Is it lawful to pay taxes to Caesar, or not? Should we pay them, or should we not?"

With confidence Jesus remembered Joseph's words at the cabin long ago. "Why put me to the test? Bring me a coin."

The man dug around in his purse and gave a denarii to Jesus. Jesus looked at the coin briefly, and then handed it back to the man, asking, "Whose likeness and inscription is this?"

The man studied the coin closely and finally looked back up at Jesus. "Caesar's."

Jesus turned his attention to the crowd and said, "Render to Caesar the things that are Caesar's, and to God the things that are God's."

Many smiled and started nodding. The Pharisee put the coin back in his purse and glared at Jesus. "But this is the very coin I must tithe to God according to our law. It is also the coin that pays for the food to feed my family. Are you saying I should not tithe to God, but instead pay taxes to Rome?!"

Jesus smiled, looking back at the Pharisee with assurance. "Is tithing according to the old law really in God's service?"

The Pharisee shouted back, "You question tithing according to our law!" He reached for a dagger hidden in his cloak, as the Herodian grabbed his arm to pull him back.

"Not here, not now! We must report this to the court."

The Pharisee relaxed his arm, allowing the dagger to fall back into its sheath. As the Herodian pulled him away through the crowd, the Pharisee turned his head back and shouted, "You pervert our law, and in the same voice command us to pay taxes to Caesar! He is the god you serve, not Yahweh!"

Disfavor continued to build. Rumors were spreading over the seemingly random nature of Jesus' actions over the past week. The image of a godlike figure who had performed countless miracles was turning into a man, fraught with human frailties.

Still later that day, a scribe asked Jesus, "Which commandment is the first of all?"

Jesus thought through the commandments. The Scriptures did not state a preference or ranking, but Jesus quickly thought of one of his favorite verses. Quoting the book of Deuteronomy, Jesus said, "The first is, 'Hear, O Israel: The Lord our God is one Lord; and you shall love the Lord your God with all your heart, and with all your soul, and with all your might.'" And then quoting Leviticus, he added, "The second is this: 'You shall love your neighbor as yourself.' There is no other commandment greater than these."

The scribe then replied, "Neither of these are one of God's commandments." Then turning towards the crowd, the scribe continued, "The first was simply a statement from Moses. It was a powerful and wonderful statement of utmost merit, but not a commandment of God. This man does not understand the Law of Moses, and perverts it!"

The crowd was not receptive to the scribe's harsh accusation as they jeered, enforcing Jesus' confidence. "I do not pervert the Law, but shed new light into its meaning." Then, pointing at the scribe, Jesus continued, "These scribes have perverted their own understanding of the Law of Moses. They refer to King David as the first son of God." Jesus paused to see acknowledgement from the crowd. "David said in his Psalms, 'The Lord says to my lord: sit at my right hand, till I make your enemies your footstool.' If David referred to God as 'Lord,' then how can David be his son? Would he not refer to him as 'Father'?"

A low murmur spread through the crowd. Jesus could see the crowd stirring and the unrest that was developing. He suddenly realized he had overstepped his bounds. Attempting to refocus, Jesus waved his arms pleadingly. "Beware of the scribes, who like to go about in long robes, and to have salutations in the marketplaces and the best seats in the synagogues and the places of honor at feasts. They take money from poor widows and give long prayers that mean nothing. They will receive the greater condemnation."

Jesus successfully turned the focus of the taunting towards the priests and scribes, who suddenly left.

The gradual and carefully choreographed image that had been nurtured over the past year with carefully orchestrated appearances was beginning to unravel with the frequent, impromptu interactions. Word inevitably reached Joseph, who quickly relayed the information to Pilate. Deeply concerned over the developing events, Pontius called an emergency meeting to take place that evening at a supply office in Bethany.

28 ~ A Cornered Lion

Pilate could see Joseph's look of *I told you so*. Joseph turned his eyes to the ground. "As you both already know, Caiaphas is calling for Jesus' arrest. There are rumors he is even looking to have him killed."

"Killed!" Jesus exclaimed with a look of shock. "How is that possible? Even today, I was speaking freely to a large crowd in the temple, and among them were scribes and chief priests. Why didn't they arrest me then?"

"I suppose they fear the reaction of the masses. They know you have a strong following and they fear riots." Joseph nervously twiddled his fingers as he brought his hand up to massage his forehead. "I have even heard they seek to have you killed secretly, so as not to bear the burden of a public trial."

"Secretly! They couldn't do that! They are men of God! They are not murderers!"

Joseph nodded. "Men of God, yes, but they feel justified under Mosaic Law to have a man stoned to death for blasphemy." With a saddened look, Joseph added, "Your entry into Jerusalem has clearly been a mistake."

Jesus shook his head. "I haven't said anything blasphemous! I only hinted today that David might not be the son of God. I did not say that I was! I never have!"

Joseph raised his hands. "Yes, yes, I know. It's not what's been said. It's what's been done, and probably over the past year before coming to Jerusalem. I think your works on the Sabbath have pushed those of the religious order and possibly even some of the common people over the edge."

Pontius interceded, giving Joseph an apologetic glance. "Perhaps you were right, Joseph. Maybe we shouldn't have brought Jesus into Jerusalem. What's been done, has been done, and we must deal with it the best we can." Pontius turned toward Jesus. "The important thing is that we still have the support of the people and—"

Joseph interrupted, "I'm not so sure, sir. There are rumblings about Jesus' action in the temple a couple of days ago, and his statement about paying taxes to Caesar has not gone over well." Joseph shook his head in disappointment. "I've been hearing words of disfavor."

"Disfavor?" Jesus said with disgust and surprise in his voice.

Pontius, too, looked at Joseph with surprise. "That can't be. Only last week they were laying palm leaves to honor his entry into Jerusalem. I could hear the cheers from my office! Surely their admiration could not have turned so quickly!"

"I am not imagining this!" Joseph said emphatically. "Sentiment is changing, even as we speak, and I fear Caiaphas is growing bolder in his resolve."

Jesus wavered slightly and reached to steady himself on the back of a chair. "How quickly they turn on you!" Jesus began to tremble as he looked over at Pilate with pleading eyes. "At least I know I have the protection of Rome." Jesus' eyes shifted with a quiver in his voice. "We have been through a lot, and I have done all you have asked. I have done nothing wrong in the eyes of Rome. Surely this is not going to end in my death?"

Pontius perceived the fear in Jesus' eyes. It was a contagious emotion, reaching out and gripping every nerve in his body. "Of course not, Jesus. You are my friend; a man I can trust. We all have deep interests in ensuring the success of our goals. There has got to be a way out of this." Pontius paused briefly, rubbing the stubble on his chin. "Long ago, you mentioned you thought our plan would work—and it has been working. We have gained more in the submission and control of this land than I ever dreamed possible. If something caused these people to turn against you, maybe something can turn them back. There are many more outside of Jerusalem who still consider you their king."

Joseph agreed. "You're right. Jesus has a strong following outside of

Jerusalem. He should leave Jerusalem tonight, and let things cool down."

Pontius shook his head fervently. "No, that's not what I meant. Running away is not the answer. John wasn't in Jerusalem when he was arrested, and the countryside will not protect Jesus. If Jesus were to run now, his actions would be seen as weakness and cowardice. Whatever following he has outside of Jerusalem would soon disappear. The disfavor in Jerusalem, as you put it, would follow him."

Pontius noticed the concern growing on Joseph's face. Working on Joseph's uncertainty and changing the direction of the discussion, Pontius introduced another idea. "Perhaps we should call their bluff, force them to make an arrest. This could turn sentiment back in our favor." Seeing looks of shock and disagreement, Pontius quickly continued, "When word of your arrest gets out, people from all over the countryside will come to Jerusalem. You will not have to go to them." As their expressions softened, Pontius went on, "It is traditional at the time of Passover for the Roman prefect to release a prisoner. Usually the elders and priests make their appeal for a release, but this time I will use your own custom to work in our favor."

Pilate shifted his eyes from side to side, scheming as he went. "When I speak before the masses, I can have soldiers placed throughout the crowd crying out the name of Jesus. Surely the crowd will call for your release with the arrest fresh in their minds. Then the high priest will no longer have the power to bring charges against you."

It appeared Joseph was easing his resistance, but then suddenly he lashed out, "That's what we did with John! We allowed him to be arrested, and look where it got him!"

Not knowing the secret Pilate would take to his grave, Joseph had hit a nerve. Pilate slapped his hand on the table, surprising the three of them, including himself. Realizing the gravity of his display, he quickly took control of his senses. "Caiaphas is not Antipas! Caiaphas has very little power compared to Antipas. He cannot carry out any sentence without authorization from Rome." Pilate knew the same held true for Antipas, and he knew Joseph had brought that point up nearly a year before. However, the sternness in his voice and threatening look on his face were not met with rebuttal.

Joseph's confident opposition turned to forced submission as he frowned slightly and nodded. "An arrest by the high priest could bring strong opposition against him and almost certain sympathy toward Jesus." Joseph paused, then said with uncertainty, "Fine, maybe you're right."

Pilate smiled and gave a reassuring nod towards Jesus. Joseph sat down, seemingly exhausted. He leaned forward, placing his face in his hands, and spoke without looking up. "Caiaphas will never make a public arrest. The arrest will have to occur in private."

Pilate nodded. "You have a good point, Joseph."

Jesus helped himself to more wine. "If I am to be arrested in private, Caiaphas will need to know where I am in short order. Passover is only two days away. Someone will have to approach Caiaphas to affect my arrest." Jesus finished the cup before he continued. "It will have to be one of my disciples—Judas."

Joseph looked at Jesus with shock. "Judas? You are suggesting betrayal—from one of your disciples! That could look very bad having one of the twelve turn against you."

Jesus shook his head. "Well, who do you suggest? Who else would know where we spend our time away?"

"Maybe one of your other acquaintances, like Martha or Mary, or maybe the leper, Simon."

"No! They are my friends, very close friends. I would not even think of having one of them betray me. I know they would do almost anything I asked, but I will not ask them!" Jesus turned around and walked toward the window, looking out at the night sky. "But Judas. I feel that I can convince him to turn me in, as his duty. I will tell him it is necessary to have me arrested in order to force Caiaphas' hand. I will tell him just as we discussed it here—that it is a ploy to turn disfavor toward Caiaphas. I am certain I can convince him to do so."

Pontius agreed. "I like the idea. Besides, it's all we have on such short notice."

Before leaving, Jesus finished another cup of wine.

* * *

Jesus walked into a gathering of his disciples. They did not seem to notice him as they were huddled in devout prayer. The pious nature of their assembly seemed in stark contrast to the reality of his meeting with Joseph and Pilate. Half-drunk with wine, Jesus laughed at the irony, which turned all attention his way. Jesus walked over to Judas and pulled him aside.

Whispering when they were at a safe distance, Jesus stumbled on his words. "You are the greatest of my disciples. You're the one I can depend on in time of need. You have courage and strength above the others."

Jesus could see an expression of surprise in Judas' eyes, and uncertainty as he continued, "I will tell you of the true power behind the kingdom that none of the others know—"

Judas immediately interrupted, "The true nature is the One True God! I know this. We all know this."

Jesus shook his head as if in denial. "Yes, yes—but why here?—why now? I will tell you the answers to these questions, and more." Seeing he had sparked Judas' interest, Jesus continued, "But first I have something you must do. You will not understand now, but you will understand later when I tell you of the secrets of God's kingdom. But first, you must do what I ask."

Jesus went on to explain the orchestrated arrest, and the necessary timing while they were in Jerusalem. At first, Judas protested. But Jesus grew more emphatic and went on to explain the growing threat of being killed in secret compared to the protection of an arrest.

Finally, Judas reluctantly agreed. Jesus recognized the confusion and pain in his expression as Judas asked, "So when do you want me to do this?"

Jesus grabbed him by the shoulders in an affectionate grip. "Tomorrow night is the Passover feast. I wish to spend that time with all of you. I think it is important we share the Passover feast together. Then, after that, I want you to bring the guards of the high priest to have me arrested. I will go with the others to the Mount of Olives, in the Garden of Gethsemane, where we have gone many times to pray. I will stay there until you come with the guards."

Judas looked back at Jesus with saddened eyes. "Are you sure you want this, Master?"

Jesus looked squarely at Judas. "Have you no faith in my command?

Have you no faith that the people will call for my release? You have seen the depth and strength of their devotion to our teachings. They will call for my release, and the Roman prefect will be forced to release me, destroying any power Caiaphas will have over me. If I wait until after Passover, Caiaphas will still seek to have me arrested. Then where will I be?" Jesus could see his reassurance was having very little effect on Judas, but he did not have time to ease his discomfort. Still holding him by the shoulders and giving a more forceful look, Jesus added, "I want you to go to them today, to let them know ahead of time of your plans to turn me over. I must know whether they will carry through with my arrest, even in private. There isn't much time."

Jesus forced him on his way, and Judas immediately went to meet with the chief priests and elders. When they heard his offer, they were pleased and paid him thirty pieces of silver. At first, Judas took the money. But after leaving, having walked a short distance, he went back and returned the money.

Later that day, Jesus went to tell Joseph of his plans to spend Passover with his disciples before the arrest. Looking to Joseph for a favor, Jesus explained, "I would like to share the Passover feast with my disciples. Judas will go from there to affect my arrest at the Garden of Gethsemane. I had not thought of this, but it would be best if we had the Passover feast here in Jerusalem, rather than in Bethany." Jesus paused, hoping Joseph would see what he was alluding to. Since Joseph was not reacting, Jesus continued, "I do not have a place for us to stay here in Jerusalem. Could we use your home?"

Joseph looked away. Stuttering, Joseph replied, "We have to be careful here in Jerusalem. The council and the court have many spies throughout the city. They know I favor your teachings, having voiced support many times. But a direct connection is too risky—not just for me, but for my family. Are you sure you can't celebrate Passover with one of your friends in Bethany?"

"No, it will take most of the day to prepare the feast. The rest of the day will be spent at the temple. It will simply be too much if we keep going back and forth between here and Bethany. Besides, I doubt Caiaphas' soldiers will want to travel all the way to Bethany during the dark of night."

Joseph closed his eyes and let out a deep sigh. "We have a large upstairs room that would accommodate you and your disciples."

Jesus smiled. "Thank you, Joseph. That's very kind of you. That should be perfect." Jesus could still see the hesitancy in Joseph's demeanor as he placed his hands on his shoulder. "Hear my words. I will not tell my disciples whose home we are visiting." Seeing his reassurances had little effect, Jesus continued, "Andrew and James will come over first to prepare the meal."

"About what time will you send them?"

Jesus thought for a moment. "Oh, about midafternoon. That should give them enough time to prepare. I will give them careful instruction regarding the location of your house."

Joseph gave an anxious exhale. "It is not a good idea for them to go around the neighborhood knocking door-to-door, not knowing who to ask for. One door looks much like the next, and it would take time to find my home." Joseph paced back and forth, slapping his hand against the wall with each turn. "Tell your disciples to meet me outside of Nathaniel's Inn. I will be carrying a water jar. I will then lead them to my home from there."

Jesus gave a quick laugh. "Nathaniel's Inn? Why not outside your home?"

Joseph smiled. "I think it would draw too many questions if I were standing outside my own home all day long holding a jar."

Jesus returned Joseph's smile and nodded.

Noticeably more confident, Joseph added, "I will have plenty of food for them to prepare and will show them everything they need. After that, I think I will go with my wife to a friend's home. That way you and your disciples will have the place to yourselves."

The next day everything went nearly as planned. That evening, Jesus and all of the twelve were gathered in Joseph's home to celebrate the Passover feast.

As the night went on, Jesus served his disciples, showing them gratitude and compassion for all they had done for him and with him. He broke the bread his disciples had prepared, and distributed it among them. He also poured wine into each of their cups. Jesus began to feel apprehensive about the events to come realizing he would go through this without them.

Judas fidgeted in his chair, beads of sweat glistening on his forehead from the light of the oil lamps. Jesus sensed Judas' anxiety.

As the dinner ended and the evening grew late, Jesus became concerned that Judas might not follow through with his charge. Judas would not meet his stares, which only added to his anxiety. Jesus clinked his cup against one of the lamps, trying to get Judas' attention, motioning it was time for him to leave. But each time, Jesus was met with a blank stare. With time running short, his anxiety slowly turned to anger and an empty fear, resurfacing his dislike and mistrust for Judas. In a way, Jesus felt Judas' inaction as a betrayal in itself. Finally, Jesus knew he had to do something to get Judas to move. Drawing the attention of all of the disciples, Jesus said, "One of you, eating here with me, will betray me this very night."

The room became deathly quiet, followed by growing murmurs as each disciple quizzed those beside him. Unnoticed, Judas buried his face in his hands, then raked his hands through his hair. With tears beginning to show in his eyes, Judas interrupted the muddle of whispers. "Is it I, Master?"

Jesus looked back at Judas and nodded. "You have said so." With that Judas beat his breast, turned, and ran out of the room, half whimpering and half crying. The rest of the disciples were left speechless with the sound of Judas' footsteps plodding down the stairs. After the front door closed, Peter finally broke the silence. "How is it that Judas is to betray you?"

Looking back at Peter and feeling self-conscious about revealing too much, Jesus said, "He will turn me over to be arrested by the chief priests and scribes."

Peter showed shock and surprise. "Judas? How could he do such a thing, Master?"

"How is it that one can tell the true feelings of one that betrays? That is the meaning of betrayal. Having one who loved you, turn against you. Woe to the man by whom the Son of Man is betrayed! It would have been better for that man if he had not been born."

Having witnessed Judas' flight, most of the disciples expressed disgust as well as confusion. Peter's eyes burned with anger as he assured

Jesus, "We will never let anyone arrest you, Master!"

Frustrated by defiance that could ruin his plans, Jesus immediately responded, "Get behind me, Satan! You are a hindrance to me. This is the will of God, and who are we to interrupt the will of God? Who are we to judge the wisdom and purpose of his will?"

Peter's expression of anger quickly turned to baffled surprise. Peter blinked incredulously falling back into his chair. He looked back up at Jesus. "You have condemned Judas for the betrayal that is in his heart, and you have chastised me for wanting to protect you. What is it that a man must do to follow the will of God?"

Calming himself, Jesus looked back at his friend with compassion. "It is not necessarily what a man does, but what a man has in his heart that is driven by the will of God. Who can tell what truly lies in the hearts of the best of us?"

Peter appeared confused and unsettled by Jesus' words. "We can tell by his actions. Does it matter what a man thinks, if it does not manifest in his actions?" Peter then leaned over to the disciple next to him and whispered, "Is Jesus questioning what is in my heart?"

Jesus led the disciples in an uncomfortable hymn before ending dinner. He then stood and said, "It is time for us to leave. Servants will gather this up and clean later. For now, I want you to come with me to the Mount of Olives and pray in the Garden of Gethsemane." With the reality of the arrest drawing near, Jesus did not want to be alone.

Many of the disciples became noticeably upset about leaving the shelter of the home and finding their way through the dark. Grudgingly they gathered up their bedding and belongings, following Jesus out of the house and away from the city. When Jesus reached the spot he had prearranged with Judas, he instructed his disciples to sit and wait. The disciples fumbled to find flat areas on the ground on which to spread their bedding. Jesus went off a short distance, sat down on the ground, and looked up at the stars. The quarter moon was just beginning to drop below the horizon, and the stars stood out brighter than ever. If this had been any other night, the beautiful vision would have been enough to calm any soul, but Jesus was apprehensive of the events to unfold.

The night and the time wore on, only deepening Jesus' anxiety. After an hour had passed, he started feeling uneasy and got back up to check on the disciples. As he approached, he found them all asleep, which angered him to some degree. He realized they had no way of knowing the betrayal would happen that very evening. Jesus kicked lightly at Peter, trying to rouse him from his sleep. Slowly, Peter awoke, and his stirring brought others out of their sleep. Some started groaning and mumbling, asking what was going on, while others rubbed their heads and faces. As soon as he had their attention, Jesus said, "Do you not know that my hour is at hand? Could you not stay awake even for one hour to keep watch?"

Finally, James became aware enough to speak. "What do you mean, 'your hour has come'? Keep watch over what, Master?"

"Did I not tell you that Judas was to betray me? He could come at any moment with soldiers to arrest me!"

Peter rubbed his eyes and with a yawn said, "Judas doesn't know we are here. How could he lead an arresting party?" Peter leaned over to Andrew and whispered, "Why is Jesus so fearful of an arrest that is not going to happen? He is not acting rational. But I'm not going to say anything after the tongue lashing I received last night."

Through his own yawn, Andrew let out a quick laugh and shrugged his shoulders while leaning back against a nearby rock.

Thinking he had made his point, Jesus turned and went back to wait and pray. The disciples sat silently as Jesus' silhouette grew smaller against the stars. Time dragged on and Jesus became more and more frustrated, his anxiety continuing to mount. Even though his disciples were there, he still felt alone.

Finally, another hour passed, and doubt began to intrude on whether Judas would carry through with his mission. Getting up, he went back to his disciples, only to find them all asleep again. Selfishly, Jesus wondered how they could not feel the anxiety and fear gripping his own soul. He kicked at Peter again, who slowly awoke with only a few others stirring from the commotion. Impatient, Jesus said, "I asked you to stay awake with me! How can you fall back asleep with what is happening? Did I not ask you to stay awake and keep watch?"

Peter looked back at Jesus, aggressively moving his arm and pointing at him. "Master, earlier you yelled at me for wanting to protect you, and now you are yelling at us, telling us to keep watch! Sometimes I simply don't understand you! Why are you so worried about an arrest tonight?

We are alerting more to our presence by your fuss and racket. Perhaps if you just lie down and get some rest, it will be over by morning!"

Growing angrier still, Jesus called out, "Hear me! I told you my hour is at hand! I don't want this any more than you do! But if it be God's will, then so be it!"

Rolling his eyes, Peter replied, "Your hour is at hand? That's what you said half the night ago. If your hour stretches until morning, we will never get any sleep!"

As the rest continued to stir, Jesus added, "All that I am asking is for you to stay awake with me at the time of my betrayal."

Intimidated, Peter looked around at the other disciples and said, "Yes, Master. I will stay awake and stir the rest. I'm not sure if I can keep them all awake, but I will not fall back asleep."

Again, Jesus turned and went back to his solitary place, grumbling under his breath, "I'm sure you will."

Still another twenty minutes passed, then forty, and finally Jesus was starting to get so tired he could barely keep his own eyes open. Realizing his arrest might not happen that evening, Jesus began resigning himself to sleep as a welcome release from the weariness and apprehension. Then, in the distance, he saw several torch lights dancing against the darkness, away from the blanket of stars. The vision sparked a heightened anxiety as Jesus quickly recovered from his own muddled state, jumping to his feet.

As the arresting party approached, Judas leaned over to the chief priest. "I will walk up and touch the one who is called Jesus. They will let me walk amongst them as I approach."

Holding his torch up to Judas, the chief priest retorted, "I know what he looks like. We will have no trouble finding Jesus, if he is really here."

Judas looked away and shrugged his shoulders. Gaining his composure, he turned back and replied defiantly, "He's up there all right. All I ask is that you lead him away safely, and not let this mob get their hands on him."

The chief priest looked back at Judas with unconvincing reassurance.

Meanwhile, Jesus frantically felt his way along the moonless ground. Again, he found them all asleep, including Peter. Kicking at him, Jesus pleaded, "Peter! Peter! Quickly, get up!"

Peter stirred, unconsciously fending off the prodding. "I'm sorry, Master. I don't even remember falling asleep."

Feeling strong disgust, Jesus looked around at the rest of the disciples and started nudging all of them. "I told you my hour is at hand and see, now it happens!" Jesus pointed at the torchlights that were now much closer than before. "How can you be sleeping when the time is at hand for the Son of Man to be betrayed by sinners?"

Many of the disciples turned their gaze in the direction Jesus was pointing. Shocked, Peter jumped to his feet, followed by the others. A single torchlight broke off from the rest, coming amongst them. It was Judas, who immediately singled out and approached Jesus. Bringing his mouth up to Jesus' ear, Judas whispered with deepening sadness, "I am so sorry, Master. I do not understand. I have done as you asked."

Before Judas could move back, several in the approaching mob seized Jesus. The flickering light from the torches revealed the swords and clubs they were carrying, which heightened the sense of violence that hung in the air. Peter immediately drew his own sword and struck one of those seizing Jesus, cutting off his right ear. The slave of the high priest cried out in pain as he reached up to cover the wound. Jesus threw up his hands, yelling, "Stop! Put away your sword, Peter!" With the planned events finally taking place, Jesus regained his confidence. He would soon be in the protection of Rome. Looking boldly at all who were gathered, Jesus continued, "Do you think that I cannot appeal to my Father, and he will at once send more than twelve legions of angels?"

One of the slaves of the high priest leaned over to another and sneered, "Twelve legions?! Who does he think he is? A Roman centurion?"

Several nearby jeered, but were interrupted as Jesus continued, "Do not stoop to the level of this mob having come with clubs and swords as if they were coming after a robber!"

Peter dropped his sword as he reached up and pulled his hair. "We have been waiting here all night, preparing for this very moment, and now you tell us to do nothing!"

The flickering light from the torches and the constant screaming from the injured slave created an air of confusion. Peter rubbed his head as if to physically force some sense into his mind. Several soldiers from the mob approached Peter, but he turned and ran into the darkness. The rest of the disciples followed, fleeing into the night, leaving Jesus alone with his captors.

* * *

After fleeing a short distance, Peter turned and could see the mob moving back toward Jerusalem. All he had felt this day was conflict, and this was no exception. He wanted to keep running, but something urged him to stop and follow the mob back to Jerusalem. Making his way towards the dancing torches, when he was close enough, Peter noticed that Jesus offered no resistance, nor did he attempt any escape into the surrounding darkness. Peter felt helpless. His heart was telling him to do something, but he knew Jesus would stop him. Still, Peter followed along into the city until they reached the court of the high priest.

He went as far as the courtyard. He stood by a fire that guards had built to fight the chill of the night. After about thirty minutes, one of the maids of the high priest came up to the fire. After a couple of glances, she looked at Peter and said, "I remember seeing you with the Nazarene, Jesus, a couple of days ago at the temple. Aren't you one of his disciples?"

Startled by her inquiry, Peter quickly turned toward the woman, looking back into her peering eyes. He noticed her question had also brought the unwelcome attention of others around the fire. Peter tried to hide the fear that raced through his heart, stuttering out the words, "I-I don't know what you're talking about."

Even though some of the guards looked away, satisfied with his answer, the woman persisted. Her stare made Peter very uncomfortable as he shifted his feet, rubbing his hands faster and faster, betraying the anxiety building inside. He tried to avoid her stare, but periodically could not help but catch a glimpse.

Finally, Peter could not take it anymore. He shuffled his feet, then stepped back from the fire and proceeded out through the gateway. The maid followed. There were others gathered at the gate as the maid pointed an accusing finger. "This man is one of the disciples of the Nazarene, who was taken inside to be charged."

Peter lost his temper and turned back to her. "I told you, I don't know what you are talking about! I know nothing of this Nazarene!"

Another bystander spoke up. "You speak with a Galilean accent! Did you not come with the Nazarene?"

"No! How many times do I have to tell you that I don't know this man!" Frustrated and feeling the cowardice of his denial, Peter turned and ran into the street, hoping to lose himself in the night. Not looking back, Peter continued running until he was certain no one was following. The soft light of the morning sun was beginning to appear below the horizon.

Eventually, he turned a corner and leaned up against a wall to catch his breath. Realizing what he had done, Peter slowly slid down the wall until he was crumpled at its base, weeping. The night had been very long and tiring. The festive atmosphere of the dinner the night before seemed a world away. Everything had happened so quickly. So many things had occurred that he didn't understand, nor was he certain he wanted to. Peter had not believed himself capable of denying his master, and the very thought of it made him sob even more. He was exhausted and had little strength to hold back his emotions.

Peter then remembered what Jesus had told him the night before about what was in a man's heart. He was certain those words were meant for him. *Had his denials been acts of cowardice, or a reflection of waning loyalty from the week's events?* As the blinding brilliance of the first rays sliced the soft pre-dawn hours, his cries of despair broke the morning silence. Suddenly he heard a cock crow in the distance, and then another, followed by the sounds of an awakening world.

* * *

The chief priests, elders, and scribes were assembled to confront Jesus with the charges against him. They had gathered several witnesses to testify against the many miracles Jesus had performed. However, they had not found the actual subjects of his miracles, never realizing that most of them were Roman.

One of several people who had witnessed Jesus' miracles was asked to stand near the front of the courtroom. An elder approached him and asked, "Did you witness a case where Jesus supposedly healed a blind man, giving him sight?"

The witness nodded. "Yes."

A gasp filled the court as the elder waved his hands to quiet the room. "Did you know the man who was given sight?"

"No."

"Then how do you know he was blind before the healing?"

The witness looked down at the floor and thought back on the events. "He was being led by others and could not see his way."

The elder walked over to the witness and offered his arm. "Take my arm and follow me over to these benches." The witness placed his hand as instructed, and slowly followed with uncertain footsteps. As they reached the bench, the elder looked at the witness and asked, "Are you blind?"

The witness dropped his arm in surprise. "No!"

"But I led you over here with you grasping my arm. Does that make you blind?"

Chuckles arose from different corners of the court as the witness smiled. "I see your point, sir. I cannot be sure the man was blind."

The elder clapped his hands as he turned to the court. "But he was healed after Jesus touched his eyes! Healed from what?"

"I don't know, sir. I did not know this man—or those who escorted him."

"And where is this man now? Why is he not here presenting witness in defense of his master?"

The man shook his head in apparent confusion. "I don't know, sir. I told you, I didn't know him." After a short pause, the man looked up and added, "Jesus told him not to tell anyone. I thought this was the reason I did not hear of him afterwards."

The elder's eyes lit up. "Jesus told the man to tell no one?!"

"Yes. I will never forget his words, because they didn't make sense to me. He said it very sternly, as if by command. I have heard that Jesus commanded this on other occasions also."

"Jesus welcomes the spectacle of a public healing. Not once, but many times. But then commands of the subject—people we cannot seem to find—to tell no one!"

Many in the court started nodding. A low murmur stirred into open cries of accusation towards Jesus. The elder clapped his hands to regain order, and then walked over pointing at Jesus. "By what authority did he perform these works?!"

Shaking, the witness replied, "He called upon Almighty God, and no other, sir!"

The court erupted in cries of anger and blasphemy, as the witness cowered back to his bench.

Caiaphas stood and began hitting a club against a table, calling for calm. "Jesus has performed these acts in the name of Almighty God! There is no crime against that!"

The court erupted again in cries of objection. Caiaphas waved his arms in the air and walked over towards Jesus. "Unless we can call a witness to claim his power from none other than the Almighty God, we have no case against this man! God is all powerful, and can perform works beyond our understanding! How can we judge the nature of his works if he calls upon God?!"

The court became quiet as Caiaphas walked back to his chair. As he sat down, he said, "Call the next witness."

As the day dragged on, many of the testimonies were similar to the first. In the short time they had to prepare, a few of the chief priests gathered false witnesses. But the inconsistencies and absurdities of their hastily prepared testimony made it clear they were lying, creating a mockery of the case.

Throughout the whole affair, Jesus stood silently in the middle of the room with his hands bound behind him. The proceedings seemed to lose sight of the original purpose of the trial. Finally, Caiaphas rose and ended the spectacle by hitting his club against the table. "Enough witnesses! Enough testimony!" He approached Jesus, asking, "Have you no answer to make? What is it that these men testify against you?"

Jesus remained silent, barely even acknowledging the man standing next to him. His own exhaustion was starting to take its toll, and he had little interest in the proceedings of the trial since he knew he would soon be in Pilate's custody. Caiaphas began to shake with anger as he circled behind Jesus, waiting for an answer. Jesus did not move or blink an eye as Caiaphas came up on his other side, close enough to feel his breath. Suddenly Caiaphas backed away, asking another question, but seeming to address everyone in the court. "I was told by one of my guards that you called upon your 'Father' to command forth a legion of angels. I assume you were referring to the almighty God as your Father, were you not?" Then, looking back at Jesus, he asked, "Are you the Christ, the Son of the Blessed?!"

Jesus felt defiant at the charade going on around him and the parade of witnesses he knew were lying. He wanted this to end so that he could be placed in Roman custody. He had not expected the assault of false witnesses, which only strengthened his disgust for Jewish authority and swelled his pride in the foundation of his work: Rome. Caiaphas appeared surprised as Jesus finally turned his gaze his way and said, "I am."

A hush fell upon the court as Jesus said his first words. Feeling confident in the power of Rome, Jesus continued, "You will see the Son of Man sitting at the right hand of power."

Hearing these words, Caiaphas tore at his own clothing and let out a scream that cut through the deafening silence. Caiaphas looked back at the court, asking, "Why do we still need witnesses? You have heard his blasphemy. What is your decision?"

All of the chief priests, scribes, and elders emphatically echoed Caiaphas' charge. They all condemned Jesus to death. Some began to spit on him, covering his face with saliva and mucus, which Jesus could not wipe away. Still others struck him and slapped his face, sending blood and saliva flying across the room. One of the scribes yelled out in mockery, "Prophesy to us, you Christ! Who is it that struck you?"

Jesus fell to his knees from the blows. He would have fallen all the way if the guards hadn't grabbed him and continued with their own blows to his body. The severity and hatred of their reaction surprised Jesus far beyond his expectations. He could feel the depth of their hate and anger, not only from the pain of their blows and the shame from their spit, but from the look in their eyes. For the first time, Jesus felt vulnerable to the reality facing him, and intense fear filled his soul.

Jesus wasn't sure if he had passed out from the force of their blows or from sheer exhaustion. The next thing he knew he was being dragged through the street, out into the morning sky. A fair amount of time had passed for the sun was fairly high. Slowly regaining consciousness, Jesus could tell he was being taken to the praetorium to be brought before

Pontius Pilate. As they grew closer, the image of the familiar building became a welcome sight. The guards and the crowd that brought Jesus stopped short of entering the praetorium, not wanting to defile themselves during Passover. They threw Jesus to the ground and called to a Roman guard, requesting Pilate's presence. Even before the guard could turn around to make his way, Pilate appeared.

Looking up, Jesus saw the shock on Pilate's face. Pilate quickly changed his expression as he turned to the crowd. "What is this man accused of? Why do you bring him before me?"

One of the chief priests spoke up. "We found this man perverting our nation, forbidding us to give tribute to Caesar, and saying that he himself is Christ, a king."

Pilate let out a quick laugh. Jesus rolled his eyes and shook his head as he let out a deep sigh of relief. Jesus tried to get to his feet as Roman soldiers helped him and led him into the praetorium.

29 ~ Vengeance from Within

After running into the darkness, Andrew and James made their way back into Jerusalem to search for Judas. Jesus' arrest sparked haunting memories of John's arrest and the subsequent execution—now nearly two years ago. The sun was just beginning to light the morning sky, allowing them to study each face as they passed. First, they went to the court of the high priest. They waited across the street for some time. Andrew wondered if they should be risking their lives searching for Judas. While they were discussing and trying to decide the best way to find Judas, commotion at the front entrance caught Andrew's attention. Stricken with sadness and horror, he saw his master, nearly unconscious, being dragged by two guards, followed by Caiaphas. Jesus was trying to use his feet, but could not meet the pace. Several scribes and chief priests accompanied the procession. As the group drew near, Andrew could see marks and streams of blood covering Jesus' face and bruises on his stripped body. Both had difficulty holding back their tears. Andrew wanted to run up and tell Jesus they were there, but fear held him back. As Jesus passed by, the fear slowly turned to anger toward the man who'd caused this. The anger rekindled a flicker of courage as they walked back toward the courtyard. Finally, they came across a couple of guards who said they had seen Judas walk off to the east, toward the gates of the city.

Andrew and James looked for hours, but to no avail. In fact, there was little sign of any of the disciples. Eventually, they came across Thaddaeus and Simon. Andrew called out, "Simon, Thaddaeus! Over here!" Running up to them, Andrew was elated to lay eyes upon familiar faces.

Thaddaeus was the first to respond, acting surprised. "Peace to you, Andrew, James. What are you doing walking about Jerusalem?"

Andrew looked back, puzzled. "I was about to ask the same of you."

Thaddaeus stumbled slightly in his words. "We've been trying to find something to eat. I haven't eaten since last night, and my stomach is getting the best of me."

Andrew nodded, feeling his own stomach. His thoughts turned to what they had seen earlier in the day. "We saw Jesus being led off from the court this morning. He was beaten severely."

"Yes, we heard. He is being taken to Pontius Pilate. The high priest is seeking the death penalty, and Pilate is the only one who can carry out the sentence."

"The death penalty!" James exclaimed. "On what grounds?"

"Caiaphas considered his teachings blasphemy against God and condemned him."

James turned and walked away, shifting his eyes from side to side. "Merciful God! The death penalty?" He slapped his fist into his hand and turned back towards the others. "Have you seen Judas?"

Andrew did not feel comfortable telling Thaddaeus and Simon the reason for their inquiry. Even though Judas was least liked among the disciples, Thaddaeus and Simon always seemed more distant, and never was it more apparent than now.

"Judas? Yes, we saw him earlier in a field about a quarter mile outside the main gate, to the north, off the main road. We saw him as we were coming down from the Mount of Olives. He saw us, but didn't say anything. Of course, we were in no mood to go over and talk to him." Pausing as if in thought, Simon continued, "Nor was he, for that matter. Anyway, he was leaning against a tree and looked like he was trying to rest."

Excusing themselves, James called back, "Rest! I think I could use a little of that myself. Well, we will let you continue your search for food, and I'm going to find a place to lay my head." Andrew and James hurried away, almost before Thaddaeus and Simon could say good-bye.

Leaving the gates of the city, Andrew and James ran part of the way, carefully looking off to either side, hoping to catch a glimpse of Judas. After what seemed more than a quarter mile, Andrew was beginning to fear they had missed him or he was no longer there. Continuing on, he noticed a figure lying on the ground under a tree. As they got closer, he recognized the clothes and knew it to be Judas.

Judas was still asleep, for he did not move as they approached. Andrew came in close to get a better look at his face. Turning back to James, Andrew nodded. James searched for a good-sized rock, but instead found a sturdy piece of wood. Andrew pulled out his knife as he knelt down beside Judas. He concentrated on his hand, wondering if he could force his arm to move, sinking the blade into a body that had once been a friend. While he was wrestling with his thoughts, he noticed Judas' body jump as James made contact with Judas' head. Startled, Andrew jumped back as Judas nearly rolled over on top of him. Thinking it had been a fatal blow, Andrew was startled to see Judas begin to move. Judas was making an effort to climb to his knees, bringing one foot underneath as if to stand. As he did so, he looked up. Blood was streaming down his face from a caved indentation above his forehead. His saddened look and the streaming blood reminded Andrew of Jesus earlier in the day. In a way, it made him feel sorry for Judas, as Judas' eyes seemed to cry out, "Why?"

A fearful realization flooded his thoughts knowing they had to finish what now seemed all too real. The image of Jesus' bloody face impelled Andrew's body and hand into motion pushing the knife into Judas' stomach. Judas grabbed Andrew's arm which only served as a guide as Andrew pulled the knife out and thrust it in again and again, until Judas fell limp back onto the ground. Blood covered Andrew's hands as he threw the knife. Judas' chest moved in sporadic spasms, taking in short interrupted breaths. His eyes were closed in pain as he lifted his hand to feel his head with blood-soaked fingers. James started to cry as he walked over and stood above Judas. "Why? Why did you do it, Judas?"

Judas opened his eyes. In between random, short breaths that he could not seem to control, Judas finally got out a word: "Je—sus—" He then rolled over in pain and started coughing up blood that streamed to the ground.

James dropped his club and fell to his knees, sobbing uncontrollably. "What have we done?"

Andrew, too, began feeling a deepening horror as Judas jerked in strange, unnatural movements—the only indications he was still alive. With horror turning to a strong sense of pity, Andrew picked up the club and stood directly over Judas. With all of his strength, he brought the club down squarely on Judas' head, hoping to exact a final blow. The instant the club made contact, life flew from the body and motion ceased. Gone were the pain and the strange, gurgling, choking noises—and the man called Judas.

The pity turned to shame over the finality of their actions. They schemed to cover up the murder by claiming Judas had committed suicide. At first, James claimed Judas hanged himself. However, several days later, when the disciples learned of the severe head wounds and butchered abdomen, rumors surfaced that Judas had thrown himself over a cliff, hitting his head on a rock, causing his stomach to burst open with his bowels falling out onto the ground. Some even wondered if the man that had been found was really Judas. Before they could examine the body, the scribes and chief priests had him buried in the same field. From that day on, it was known as the Field of Blood.

30 ~ A Matter of Choice

A crowd gathered outside the praetorium. Pontius met with Jesus inside, voicing shock over his condition. "What did they do to you?"

Jesus lifted his hand to feel the blood, dirt, and grime on his face. "What does it look like they did to me? They spat in my face and beat me!" Jesus looked at his reflection in a mirror and carefully wiped at smudges on his face. His hand jerked as his fingers met cuts and bruises. Turning back toward Pilate, Jesus sarcastically added, "Well, I guess you could say this is going as planned!"

"Things are happening a little faster, but not to worry. Stay here. I'm going back outside to see if the crowd is still gathered."

Jesus shook his head. "Oh, they're still out there, all right. They'll stay as long as it takes to see me dead."

"Dead? Who said anything about execution?" Pontius asked with an honest sense of surprise. "Why would they want such a thing when you have done nothing wrong?"

"Nothing wrong! Sometimes I think you truly do not understand the thoughts and ways of my people! In their eyes I have blasphemed, and that is the worst sin in their eyes, worthy of death. Their hearts have hardened. Once they take the view that I have mocked the prophecies or falsely called upon the power of God, the fire will consume their thoughts. And there is no quenching it... until I'm dead."

Pontius shook his head and immediately left the room to see what was happening outside. Approaching the entrance, Pontius glimpsed the large crowd. Stepping back from the door before being detected, Pontius thought this might be the best time to call for the release of a prisoner. The turn of events was happening so quickly, and for a moment he wished Joseph was there. Calling Joseph to the praetorium would be far too risky, however, and he wasn't sure there was enough time.

Walking up to the sergeant of the guard, Pilate thought, *the same idea had worked so many years before, and surely it would work today. Only this time the men would be armed with words and the power of suggestion, not clubs.*

Trying to buy time, Pontius stepped back outside and addressed the crowd. "I have spoken with this man and find no fault in him! I find no crime with which to charge him!"

One of the chief priests stepped forward. "He has broken our law! He has blasphemed against God! A charge punishable by death! According to your law, Rome must carry out the execution. Jesus must be crucified."

Scattered cries erupted from the crowd: "Crucify him! Crucify the false prophet! Crucify the blasphemer!" It was not long before all of the cries became one, chanting "Crucify him!" over and over again. Events were quickly spiraling out of control. Pontius stepped back inside, thinking he should have waited until his soldiers were in place before addressing the crowd. With the deafening cries echoing down the halls, Pontius knew Jesus was hearing this. He rushed back to the room.

Pilate threw his hands in the air with a look of disgust and confusion. "What's wrong with these people? Just last week they were cheering you, laying down their own clothing in your path, and now look at them! They're calling for your death as if you were some sort of criminal!"

Jesus stood up and swung his arms angrily. "That's what we've been trying to tell you!"

On the verge of losing his temper, Pontius continued, "My understanding serves little to counsel their anger!" Pontius paced up and down, the incessant chanting echoing from outside. Finally, stopping in his tracks, Pontius looked at Jesus. "Soldiers are dressing to mix with the crowd. They should be in place shortly. We will wait a little longer, until the crowd has had time to settle. Then I will call for your release. My soldiers know what to do."

Jesus shook his head. "Do you hear what's going on out there? It'll never work!"

Almost striking Jesus for the tone he was using, Pontius yelled back, "What do you suggest I do? Take you outside and have you crucified?"

Jesus leaned back from the force of Pilate's anger. Treading more carefully, he replied, "Maybe we should wait for Joseph, and see what he has to say."

"There's no time. My men are already gathering, and I don't think there will be another time to call for your release. Passover ends tomorrow, and we must do it now." Trying to justify his decision, Pontius continued, "Besides, it's too risky to bring him here."

With anger rearing its weary head, Jesus cried out, "Too risky! What about me? I'm the one about to be crucified, hung on a cross to die like an animal!"

Pontius saw the desperation in Jesus' eyes and calmed himself. "Yes. Fine." Wondering if he was really making the right decision, Pontius added, "I'll call for Joseph." Stepping outside, Pontius walked down the hall, meeting the sergeant of the guard again. Pontius ordered him to send for Joseph and have him brought in through the back.

Outside the disorder was starting to calm, even though the crowd hadn't thinned. With or without Joseph, Pontius knew he had to address them, fearing they might grow suspicious. As Pilate stepped back outside, the crowd came to a complete hush. Seeing his men were in position, Pontius began to speak. "Each year, it is customary for Rome to release a prisoner in honor of your Passover season. Think well and carefully about whom you would have me release."

Immediately, Pontius heard Jesus' name ring out from several places in the crowd. The calls were quickly met with rebuttal and uproar. Calls of "No!" and "Boo!" quickly overpowered the outnumbered Roman soldiers. Pontius raised his hands, trying to calm the crowd so he could address them further, but to no avail. The soldiers persisted in calling the name of Jesus as the crowd turned on them. Eventually one of the chief priests precariously walked up the steps leading to Pilate's platform. Speaking to the crowd over the calls of the soldiers, the chief priest shouted, "The council of the chief priests and elders has come up with a name for release!" The crowd began to quiet as he continued. "We have chosen Barabbas!"

Immediately the crowd gave a thunderous cheer. Pontius' heart sank as the crowd began chanting, "Barabbas"—completely drowning out the efforts of the soldiers. Pontius began waving his arms frantically, trying to calm the crowd and gain their attention. Finally, after what seemed an embarrassingly long time, the crowd began to quiet, heeding the appeal from Pilate. "So who should I release, Barabbas or Jesus, who is called Christ, the King of the Jews. It's your choice: a murderer or your king?"

Immediately, the chanting resumed as strong as ever, calling the name of Barabbas. Upon hearing Pilate's plea, the chief priest who had been addressing the people went silent, giving a suspicious gaze towards Pilate. Pontius noticed the man's deep, quiet, burning stare.

The priest leaned over to his aide and whispered, "We have brought prisoners many times before Pilate, and he has never offered resistance to carry through with a crucifixion." The priest looked down and shuddered. "Most times I detest this burden of bringing a prisoner before the Roman prefect. I have seen a perverted pleasure in his eyes—granting the death of another Jew, criminal or otherwise."

The aide put his mouth to the priest's ear. "I have always detested his perverse satisfaction, too, Rabbi. No matter how much I have hated the prisoner, it sends chills down my spine to offer him up for Roman execution." The aide shook his head with a confused look. "Why does he persist in defense of this man?"

Pontius realized he was hopelessly up against overwhelming chants to release Barabbas as he called out, "Then what shall I do with the man whom you call 'the King of the Jews'?!"

The chief priest's face grew red as he gritted his teeth. Raising his voice so that all could hear, he said, "No one among us calls him this! He is not our king! These are Pilate's words—*not* ours!"

The crowd began screaming, "He is not our king!" and "Crucify him!"

Pontius' fear turned to anger as he started yelling over the crowd, "Why? What evil has he done? I told you I have found he is not guilty of the charges you have brought against him! I will, therefore, release him!"

The crowd persisted even more, "Crucify him!"

When Pilate saw he was gaining nothing, but rather that a riot was forming, he walked over to a water basin and washed his hands. "I am innocent of this man's blood." Appalled at the idea of crucifying a loyal subject of Rome, but questioning whether it was worth a riot that might turn into rebellion, Pilate cried out, "See to it yourselves!"

Pontius wondered what choice he had. How could he ignore their cries? His immediate thought was that if Jesus was going to be killed, then he would not be part of it. Thoughts of John's beheading haunted him as he finished vigorously washing his hands. Pilate pulled his hands from the water and slung them through the air. "Let his blood be on you and your children!"

The crowd came to a near silence. Fearing he had already said too much, and feeling defeated, Pontius turned and walked back into the praetorium.

Entering the room where Jesus was waiting, Pontius sat in a chair and buried his face in his hands. For the first time, he felt a real, deepening sense of failure and betrayal. He let out disbelieving sighs as Jesus stood in front of him shaking.

Joseph walked into the room and approached Jesus, who quickly explained the day's course of events. Joseph looked at Pilate, demanding, "You're not going to let them take Jesus and stone him, are you?"

Pontius lifted his face out of his hands. Still staring at the floor, he replied, "No, I won't let them stone Jesus."

"Well, that's what they will do if you release him to them."

Pontius shook his head. "I'm not going to release him to that mob. I can't anyway, by our own law. I was just reacting out of disgust."

Joseph continued, "If you hand him over, he's as good as dead. At least with us, he has a chance to survive."

With this statement, Pontius slowly but steadily turned his eyes toward Joseph. They began to light up with a spark of life. Standing to his feet, Pontius walked over to Joseph with a broadening grin. "Just because we hang someone on a cross, doesn't mean he has to die!" With intense pride he could hardly contain, Pontius turned back toward Jesus, saying, "Don't you see? We can pull you down long before you reach the point of death!"

Pilate's smile and uplifting spirit were contagious. A half-broken, uncertain smile appeared on Jesus' face as Pilate continued, "My soldiers will be guarding you, and my soldiers will pronounce your death. It's as simple as that!"

But then Jesus asked. "Won't everyone be able to see I am not dead or dying?"

Pontius looked back at Jesus. "You can play dead, can't you? Besides, I can have the guards keep everyone at a distance."

Joseph's brief smile turned to a look of concern. "Won't it be unusual to have guards at the crucifixion site? I have seen prisoners hang for days with no one around."

Pontius shook his head. "Not if we're concerned that someone will try to steal the prisoner."

Uncertain, Jesus added, "How can you justify keeping everyone at a distance?"

Pontius turned away, running his hands through his disheveled hair. "I can agree to crucify you, but I don't have to make a spectacle of it. I think the people will be pleased enough that I am offering the crucifixion." Pontius walked over to the window and looked down on the courtyard, his soldiers lying in wait. "Besides, I do not have to explain everything. I will just do it. It is problem enough when people come to gawk at the body."

Jesus took a deep breath and slowly let it out. "How long will I have to hang on the cross?"

Pontius scrunched his face in a matter-of-fact expression. "Oh, not more than a day. Usually, it takes several days for a body to hang until death, depending upon the health and condition of the prisoner. You're in good health, so I don't think a day would be much of a problem."

Joseph's tone grew skeptical. "How will a mere day be enough to convince everyone that Jesus is dead?"

"We'll have to make it appear that you were hung on the cross in very poor condition. You were brought in here, having been beaten. Tomorrow, we can make you appear even worse. It would be simple to assume you never recovered from the first beating. I can claim I had you beaten again by my soldiers."

Jesus shook his head. "After you publicly argued I had done nothing wrong? And you then threatened to release me, despite their cries for crucifixion? No one will believe you."

Joseph looked at Pilate with pleasant surprise. "You argued a case for Jesus in front of the crowd? Even when they were calling for his crucifixion?"

Pontius shrugged.

Jesus smiled, his expression reassuring. "I appreciated your defense, I assure you, even though it didn't work."

Joseph reiterated, "That contradicts a justification for having you beaten."

Pontius became annoyed at Joseph's probing. "It's funny you use the word 'justification.' I *am* the highest level of justice, and I do not have to explain all of my actions. Besides, would you rather Jesus hang on the cross for three to four days, until he is really near death?"

The room went quiet for a while. Finally, Jesus broke the silence with a quivering voice: "What happens afterward? How will I show my face without people knowing I didn't die?"

Joseph rolled his eyes. Pontius thought for a while and then let out a sigh of disappointment. "This may mean you will have to leave Judea and Galilee. I can send you to Perea, or perhaps down south to Idumaea."

Jesus raised quivering fingers to massage his forehead. "So it just ends here. After all of the work I've... we've done to win the hearts of so many people."

Joseph looked back and forth between Jesus and Pilate. "It doesn't have to end here. It could be the beginning. You've planted the seed that will continue to influence the hearts of our people. Sometimes it is a man's death, and not just his life, that makes him a legend... or a martyr."

Pontius was not convinced of Joseph's optimistic outlook. "I'm not so sure, Joseph. I think there's a good possibility that with Jesus' absence, people will slowly forget about him and go back to the way things were. Maybe we should name a successor as with John."

Joseph shrugged. "There isn't enough time. Jesus is technically incarcerated until his crucifixion, which may even be tomorrow. John had more time to prepare for a successor. I'm not sure it would be a good idea to repeat it again, anyway."

Jesus cleared his throat to gain their attention. "Aren't we getting off subject here? I think the important thing is that I will have my life! What happens to the movement as a result of my death, real or imaginary, is of no consequence—unfortunate, but of no concern. There is very little we can do now."

Joseph turned toward Jesus. "Do you think your disciples will carry on with your work?"

Jesus thought for a second, then shook his head. "I don't know. They've always worked under my direction. Without it, I'm afraid they will disperse. I should have prepared them better for this."

Joseph turned back toward Pilate. "What about Thaddaeus and Simon? Since they are Roman, we already have our connection."

While Pontius was nodding, Jesus interrupted. "No. They're rough around the edges, and I doubt the other disciples would follow them. They have always been perceived as different and never quite fit in." Jesus paused in thought. "Peter would be my choice. He's the leader among them, although at times he can be hotheaded. Sometimes, that's what it takes, I suppose. He knows nothing of the Roman connection. I think he would feel betrayed if he were informed."

Joseph interceded. "Perhaps Thaddaeus and Simon could serve as intermediaries. Peter would never have to know."

Pontius nodded. "Joseph has a good point. You've already laid the basis with your teachings. All we need is for someone to carry on with your work. We have grown to require very little interaction. My most recent interference resulted in exactly the opposite effect of what we were trying to achieve." Pontius shook his head, wishing he had never suggested that Jesus come to Jerusalem.

Jesus clasped his trembling hand and let out a sigh. "How will we get word to Peter? For something this important, he'll be very skeptical and hesitant, hearing it from Thaddaeus. If nothing else, he'll be suspicious, wondering how Thaddaeus came across this instruction." Pausing, Jesus added, "It's too bad I don't have time to talk to the disciples myself. Could you delay the crucifixion?"

Pontius looked at Jesus with surprise. "What good would that do? Do you think I can just let you walk out of here? That'll probably raise a few eyebrows on the Jewish court!"

Joseph's eyes started shifting back and forth as he took a deep breath and, with growing excitement, looked up at Pilate and Jesus. Touching his hand to his forehead, Joseph said, "Perhaps there is a way we can have plenty of time for you to interact with your disciples!"

Motionless, Jesus and Pontius stared at Joseph. Joseph's eyes widened. "You could go to them *after* the crucifixion."

Jesus blinked, then gave a blank stare. "Then they'll know I'm not dead—"

"Exactly! You have performed countless miracles, displaying power over physical infirmities of all kinds. Why not death?"

Pilate raised his eyebrows and let out a quick laugh. Joseph had come up with amazing and sometimes outlandish ideas in the past, but this one seemed beyond reason.

Pontius paced around the room, keeping his gaze on Joseph. Slowly he started feeling Joseph's excitement but voiced hesitation. "I don't know. I'm the one responsible for crucifying Jesus. If he appears alive afterward, people will become suspicious and think I spared his life. Then our connection will become all too obvious."

Joseph shook his head. "Don't you see? It's the only way. We could have Jesus appear for a short while, just long enough to get his message across to the disciples." He looked directly at Pilate, adding, "I agree. If he stayed around indefinitely, people would become suspicious. But if he shows up in short, controlled instances, then there will be mystery surrounding his appearances."

Joseph turned toward Jesus, who was also showing skepticism. "Don't you see the power in this? If we really want what we've done to maintain a permanent hold in the hearts of the people, then this will do it. If you are seen to have died on the cross, then everything will die with it. Not even your disciples will carry on with your teachings, no matter how much we kid ourselves. But if they see you have conquered death, see that you have been resurrected, then the fire will live on, and maybe even grow."

Pontius nodded and could sense Jesus was warming to the idea. Pontius turned his attention back towards Joseph, waiting for his next words. Joseph smiled, placing his hand on Jesus' shoulder. "Right now, the disciples are scattered to the four winds, and probably will be more so once you are crucified. Later, we could have Thaddaeus gather the disciples together where you will make an appearance. The vision of you amongst them, after they *know* you've been crucified, will truly amaze them. They've seen you perform miracles. How could they expect anything less?"

Pontius argued the point in his head. If someone did make the connection with Rome, that person would have a difficult time convincing a population that seemed bent on miraculous, supernatural explanations for everything and anything. The Jews seemed to burn with hunger for such revelations. But, offering a counterpoint, Pontius asked, "Then how would we explain his disappearance after that?"

Joseph's eyes lit up. "Think of the prophet Elijah! He was taken up, body and soul, into heaven. We could claim the same for Jesus. It is a well-accepted concept in the Scriptures. Quite frankly, the people would be amazed and feel incredibly privileged to have a prophet, like Elijah, in their own lifetime! I'm telling you, this could do more to change the attitudes of Jews than all of our previous work!"

Pontius liked Joseph's enthusiasm. He looked over at Jesus, who was nodding. Pontius closed his eyes and took a deep breath. "We'll do it."

With a sense of urgency, Joseph turned to leave. "I will instruct Thaddaeus and Simon to spread rumors of your impending resurrection to lay the seeds of prophecy."

31 ~ The Crucifixion

The next morning, the turning of the population weighed heavy on Pilate's mind with his decision to bring Jesus to Jerusalem. At the time he'd first met Joseph three years ago, Pontius never dreamed it would get this far. He felt he had done more to influence the culture and attitudes of the Jews than countless armies from Rome ever could. Jesus had been incredibly loyal and devoted to him, even in the face of great adversity. Having been sentenced to death, Jesus was facing the ultimate humiliation from his own people. Placing his hands on Jesus' shoulders as a sign of confidence, Pontius said, "Well, today's the day, Jesus. I assure you, I will not let you die on the cross. I have had a special cross made with a slight ledge for your feet. With it, you will be able to stand periodically on your heels to relieve the pressure from the ropes. You probably should alternate using your feet and hanging by your arms, so you can maintain your strength. By this time tomorrow, I will have you down from the cross, and Joseph will take you to the tomb."

"Joseph!" Jesus reacted. Then, closing his eyes, he added, "I understand. Of course."

"Yes. We have no other option on such short notice. It might seem odd—not being a member of your family, but what can we do?" Pontius nervously wrung his hands. "Joseph is known to be sympathetic to your movement, so it won't be too out of place. I'll have some food and water there for you. I will place guards at the tomb to keep people away, so you won't need to worry about anything."

Jesus took a deep breath. "Guards at the cross, guards at the tomb?

Don't you think that will raise suspicion?"

Pontius shook his head. "No. I'll just say the chief priests asked me to place soldiers, claiming they were worried your disciples might try to steal your body."

"What if they want to place their own guards at the tomb? It seems they would rather do that, don't you think?"

"No, when they see Roman guards there, I doubt they will want to share the duty." Pontius took his hands off Jesus' shoulders and walked over to the window to look down on the courtyard. Carefully considering the sequence of events for the next few days, Pontius continued, "None of this goes without risk. If guards from the high priest show up, then we'll just wait until they leave. They won't stay there forever. I'll just make sure you have enough food and water."

* * *

Pontius gathered the entire battalion of the elite guard into the praetorium. In his mind, Jesus *was* the king of the Jews and not a common criminal to be hung on the cross. Pontius presented Jesus with a royal cloak to wear at the ceremony. The robe was beautiful, made of the finest cloth that glistened in the light, showing off deep purples and gold trim.

As the entire battalion stood at attention in perfect rows and columns, Pilate brought Jesus before the power and glory of Rome. Jesus walked out on the elevated stage to stand next to Pilate. Pilate's chest swelled as he slowly looked around the sea of soldiers with confident eyes. Pilate raised his hands. "Behold a man who was condemned by his own people to be crucified this very day!"

One soldier leaned over to his friend and whispered, "By his own people?! We are standing before a Jew?!" The soldier exhaled a sarcastic sigh of disgust. Uneasiness filled the ranks as soldiers began to make slight movements, evidenced by the rattling of gear and equipment.

Oblivious to their thoughts, Pontius continued to bestow his own honor upon Jesus. "Behold a man who has done nothing wrong in the eyes of Rome. His only crime is that he *is* the king of the Jews! We have been forced to crucify this man by the ignorant and insane accusations of the Jewish court! A sentence he does not deserve. A sentence that should be bestowed on the accuser and not the accused. Standing before you is a man who should be honored, not condemned!"

The Roman soldier quickly smirked and whispered, "Honor a Jew?! I would rather run a sword through his chest than honor him."

His friend let out a short laugh, which he swallowed before it filled the room. More loudly, he replied, "Behold, a king the gods have forsaken!"

Several soldiers laughed, which caught Pilate's attention. Returning to attention, the first soldier whispered out of the corner of his mouth, "Where is his laurel wreath? Hail Judeas Caesar!"

Several soldiers burst into laughter. Raising a stiff hand, Pilate looked angrily in their direction, which quickly silenced the dissidence.

After dismissing the battalion, Pontius gathered a few of his best soldiers and a centurion to escort Jesus. He told the centurion of his plans to spare Jesus' death on the cross, telling him he had special interest to Rome, despite the judgment of the Jewish court. Without questioning Pilate's order, the centurion agreed he would pronounce Jesus dead when told to do so.

Pontius and Jesus went back into the praetorium. There wasn't much time until Jesus would be taken outside to face a crowd thirsting for his blood. Jesus changed back into his old, torn clothes, stained from the filth, sweat, blood, and spit from the days before. His appearance was embellished to imply further punishment. Pontius made small cuts on his arm, producing blood to smear on Jesus' face and clothes.

A company of Roman soldiers brought Jesus out to the waiting crowd. Everyone went silent when Jesus appeared. The soldier who had joked about the laurel wreath had plaited a crown of thorns. He held it up to Jesus' face. "Here is your crown, most noble king of the Jews. Here is your wreath from the very weeds of your beloved kingdom!" The soldier placed it on Jesus' head and spat in his face.

The centurion grabbed the soldier and pulled him back, tripping him to the ground. Before the soldier could get up, the centurion pulled out his sword and pushed the point against his chest, forcing him to back away.

Near the top of the cross, Pontius placed an inscription: *Jesus of Nazareth, the King of the Jews.*

Many in the crowd were noticeably offended by the inscription. Before the procession started, a chief priest approached Pilate and said, "Do not write 'The King of the Jews,' but, 'This man claims to be the King of the Jews.'"

Pontius turned toward the priest and looked at him with searing eyes. "What I have written, I have written." Turning away, Pontius then instructed a man from the crowd, Simon of Cyrene, to carry Jesus' cross to the place of Golgotha. He wanted to spare Jesus the indignity of carrying his own instrument of crucifixion. He also wanted to save Jesus' strength for the time he would spend on the cross.

Two thieves, carrying their own crosses, were taken with Jesus to be crucified. As they neared the site, the soldiers kept the people back as Pilate had instructed. The soldiers directed Simon to lay Jesus' cross on the ground, as did the two thieves. The soldiers tied the prisoners to the crosses, and then the crosses were raised using ropes, finally dropping into holes dug in the ground. It was the third hour after sunrise.

There was a strange mixture and milling about in the crowd. Most had cried out for Jesus' crucifixion, but seeing the morbid fruition of their demands, they were silent. Followers and accusers rubbed shoulders, almost as if they were unaware, or uncaring, of each other's presence.

As the day wore on, Pontius heard Jesus was thirsty and asking for water. Pontius instructed the centurion to have a bowl of water taken to the site. Using a sponge on the end of a long pole, they placed the sponge up to his lips so he could drink. To avoid suspicion, Pontius ordered the centurion to have his soldiers openly mock Jesus, claiming the drink to be vinegar.

It was Friday, the day before Passover Sabbath. It was about the sixth hour after sunrise when elders and priests of the Jewish court approached Pilate. The chief priest pleaded, "Tomorrow is our Passover celebration. The prisoners must not hang on the cross during Passover."

Flabbergasted, Pontius responded, "Yesterday you approached me, demanding that your king be crucified. Today you approach me, demanding he be taken down because of your Passover! You should have thought of that before we went through all of the trouble to carry out your sentence! I am not going to pull him down and then re-crucify him on Sunday!"

With a look of surprise, the chief priest gathered his composure. "The man, Jesus, is not our king, and we are not asking that he be re-crucified on Sunday. We are simply asking that the time of their death be hastened so they will not hang through tomorrow."

A sudden streak of fear ran through Pontius as he realized what they were asking. Caught off guard, he turned away in order to shield any signs written on his face. "Hasten their death?"

Pontius knew of the practice of breaking the legs of prisoners once they were on the cross to hasten death. This was rarely done, since doing so would rob the punishment of a slow, agonizing death and the example it served. Pontius turned back toward the chief priest. "The method of their death has been chosen—crucifixion—and their bodies will hang until they are dead. Their punishment is meant to extend through a slow death, and not be quickened through mercy."

"I understand your need to make an example of the criminals. But I am telling you, if their bodies are left hanging over the Passover Sabbath, it will create disgust and anger throughout all of our people. So much so, I have no doubt it will cause unrest and a riot that neither one of us will be able to stop or control. They will tear the bodies from the crosses and stone them, rather than let them hang in defilement."

Pontius had seen the fury and determination of a Jewish mob. He found himself wishing the plot had been even one day earlier. He could not believe the timing could lay ruin to all they had achieved. Pontius superficially agreed to the chief priest's request, realizing he would need to accelerate the timetable of their plans.

Pontius sent word to his soldiers to have the legs of the two robbers broken, but to leave Jesus alone. He would claim that Jesus was already dead. About two hours later, several of the chief priests returned asking why Jesus' legs had not been broken. Hoping his story was convincing, Pontius explained, "I did as you asked with the prisoners. When my soldiers prodded the prisoner called Jesus with their spears, they saw no signs of life. The centurion pronounced him dead."

With strong skepticism the chief priest asked, "Are you sure he is dead? He has only been on the cross for about five hours. Is your centurion skilled at making such a determination?"

"Yes! He has overseen many crucifixions, and I have no doubt in his judgment." Continuing in an effort to make his explanation more believable, Pilate voiced an image building in his mind: "Besides, in their prodding, one of the soldiers pierced his side, and water and blood gushed forth out of his bowels."

Seeing most were convinced by his account, Pontius continued, "Joseph of Arimathea, a member of your council, will take Jesus from the cross and lay him in a tomb."

One of the chief priests, Annas, shook his head. "I know the man you speak of. He is sympathetic to the Nazarenes. There are rumors among his followers that Jesus will rise from the dead. How do we know Joseph will not steal his body in order to claim false prophecy?"

Pilate smiled. "I assure you none of his followers will steal his body. I will place my own soldiers to guard the tomb."

Annas bowed in humble gratitude. "I am pleased you understand my position, for it is crucial that Jesus' disciples not obtain possession of his body. Perhaps a few of our own men could help your soldiers in keeping guard."

Annas quickly grimaced, realizing the error of his request. But before Annas could rescind, Pilate reacted violently. "Do you think my soldiers are incapable of their duties? Are you going to continue to stand there and insult me, or should I have you hung on a cross?"

Annas backed away turning to leave. The others quickly followed. An elder walked alongside Annas and whispered, "Pilate is possessed! It is difficult to understand his mind."

Annas nodded, quickening his pace.

The elder's face took on a concerned, questioning look. "Blood does not gush forth from the wound of a dead man! The blood would pool in his legs." The elder paused in thought. "Pilate was lying."

Annas stopped and stared intently at the elder. He looked back towards the praetorium and then back at the elder. "I'm not going back in there to accuse Pontius Pilate of lying."

32 ~ From the Lair

It was the twelfth hour as Joseph approached Golgotha. It was starting to turn dark, but Joseph could see and hear the crowd before him. Winding his way through the mass of people, he heard them talking about Jesus and how he was already dead. He could also hear people sobbing. Pushing his way to the front of the crowd, Joseph approached a Roman soldier who was maintaining control. Joseph announced his name and produced papers from Pontius Pilate. The Roman soldier held a torch to reveal the seal of the Roman prefect, immediately letting Joseph through.

As Joseph walked on, he could see the outlines of the bodies on the dusky horizon. The image sent shivers down his spine. It was one thing to lose a loved one in death, and another to watch them slowly and mercilessly wither away like a diseased fruit. Sometimes the bodies would start to rot, even before death, and it was hard to tell when the moment of mercy would finally arrive. This time, Joseph knew Jesus would defeat the cross. Knowing Jesus was alive was the only thing that kept him walking toward the horrid vision. As he got closer still, Joseph could hear sickening moans, and he wondered if it was Jesus.

Walking past the first cross he knew to be one of the robbers', Joseph tried not to look. His eyes were somehow lured, however, catching a glimpse of something that no longer looked human. The legs and feet were swollen beyond recognition. One leg was stretched, noticeably longer than the other. The sight produced a nauseating feeling in his chest realizing the man's legs had been broken and were dangling lifelessly. His arms were also stretched, appearing as if they had been pulled out of their sockets from supporting the full weight of his body. Once he was immediately abreast, Joseph could just make out the words of the man's moans, pleading for someone to end his life. A cowering feeling swept through his body as he ignored the man's pleas, quickening his pace towards Jesus.

Upon reaching Jesus, Joseph could tell he was still conscious and in a fair amount of pain. Standing at the base of the cross, Joseph called out softly, "Jesus! Jesus! It's me, Joseph. I've come to take you down."

Jesus opened his eyes and raised himself on his heels, relieving the strain on his arms. Jesus smiled and said in a weak voice, "Joseph, thank God you're here!"

Joseph motioned to Jesus to keep his voice down, fearing someone would hear, even though he knew the main crowd was too far away. Feeling intensely vulnerable, surrounded by instruments of death, Joseph reacted to Jesus' slight body movements: "Don't move so much. You're supposed to be dead!"

Jesus nodded slightly and then stopped. He cleared his throat. "Yes, sorry. It's hard to think clearly up here." Making slight movements, Jesus shifted his weight. "I am so glad we didn't wait until tomorrow. I don't think I could have lasted that long."

Joseph shook his head. "You should see the condition of the poor rogues crucified with you."

Jesus closed his eyes in painful thought. "Yes. I remember the sounds of the soldiers cracking their bones—and their screams." He shook his head as if trying to rid himself of the memory. "It seems like it was days ago. I can't keep track of time anymore."

Joseph pleaded with Jesus, "Stop that! I told you to stop moving!" Joseph looked back over his shoulder and saw one of the Roman guards approaching. "We'd better get you down right away!"

Looking back up at the crowd in the distance, Jesus shook his head ever so slightly. "They don't know what they do when they condemn a man to this fate." Tears welled in his eyes as they spilled over onto his cheeks, falling to his lips. "It is from the cruelest depths of mankind to sentence a man to spend his final moments in long, drawn-out, seemingly eternal suffering."

Joseph could tell Jesus was becoming delirious. By this time, the centurion had reached them, saying, "So you must be Joseph. I was told you would take the prisoner." Remaining cautious, the centurion studied Joseph carefully and added, "I was also told you would have orders, personally signed by Pontius Pilate."

Joseph quickly pulled out the orders, nearly dropping them to the ground. Unfolding the paper, Joseph handed it to the soldier. "Yes, I am Joseph. These are the orders."

The centurion looked the paper over carefully and then seemed satisfied, recognizing the Roman seal. Joseph pointed up toward Jesus, saying, "I will need help pulling this man down off the cross and carrying him to a resting place."

The centurion turned his head over his shoulder and barked out a deafening order that cracked through the eerie, near-silent moans of the other two prisoners. The sudden command caused both Joseph and Jesus to flinch, not expecting the indifferent attitude in the midst of such pain and suffering. Immediately, two soldiers came over to assist in whatever the centurion directed.

After helping Jesus down from the cross, Joseph wrapped him in a burial cloth. He was concerned they might run into people along the way, or be followed by curiosity seekers from the waning crowd.

Finally reaching the tomb Joseph stooped down, shoving his torch before him—almost as if he was expecting to find someone or something inside. Walking to the back of the tomb, he lit an oil lamp he had placed there earlier. He then directed the soldiers to lay Jesus on several layers of cloth, laid out on a rock ledge near the right side of the room. After laying Jesus on the ledge and assisting him into a sitting position, the two soldiers immediately exited to stand guard outside.

Joseph slowly removed Jesus' wrappings and helped him with clean garments. Jesus was barely conscious and extremely exhausted. Joseph pointed out where the food, water, and additional lamps were, even though he realized Jesus probably wasn't comprehending anything he said. Jesus fought to keep his eyes open, and his body swayed as if ready to fall. Joseph poured a cup of water and placed it to Jesus' lips. Jesus quickly reacted, revealing a thirst that had been overshadowed by his physical exhaustion. His face wrenched in pain as he tried to bring his arms up to grasp the cup, only to have them fall limp by his side. Joseph held the cup to his lips until he saw Jesus drift off into unconsciousness. Joseph slowly eased Jesus back onto the stone bed and covered him with blankets. He left the lamp burning, so Jesus would have some sense of whereabouts when he woke. Walking back outside the tomb, Joseph and the two soldiers rolled a large, rounded stone in front of the entrance.

* * *

Later the next day, on the Sabbath, Jesus opened his eyes to reveal the vague image of a rock ceiling and walls. Looking over to one side, he saw a lamp's motionless, steady flame as if it were frozen in time. For a moment he wondered if he was alive or dead, remembering his time on the cross. Trying to sit up, Jesus felt the pain in his arms. Slowly, he propped himself up. Looking about, he noticed faint hints of daylight outlining the imperfect seal of the stone on the entrance. On the floor next to the lamp, there were jars and loaves of bread, obviously meant for him. There were no windows and no way in or out besides the entrance. Jesus felt confused, but remembered talking to Joseph while he was still on the cross, and being helped down by the Roman soldiers. After that, he could not remember anything. Soon, Jesus realized he must be in the tomb that Joseph had prepared. He massaged the hunger pains in his stomach. *If I were dead, surely I wouldn't feel hunger.* The bits of daylight around the edge of the door did not offer a clue as to the time of day.

Feeling he could not stand, Jesus eased himself down onto the floor and crawled over to the food. The bread was still fresh, so he knew it hadn't been there long. Whether it was fresh or stale, he was thankful. He poured water from a jar into a small cup and washed down the bread still dry in his mouth. Scooting back up against the wall, Jesus took his time, savoring each bite as he rested his head against the rock. Slowly, he could feel his strength returning. He knew he needed to rest before trying to walk.

In what otherwise would have seemed a place of anxiety, Jesus felt comfort. The feeling of being alone, sealed off from the world, brought a sense of tranquility he had not known for some time. For the past two years, he had been constantly surrounded and followed by people.

Everywhere he went, people knew who he was, and they either adored him, or they hated him. Even when he would go off secretly to meet with Joseph or Pilate, he was still never alone, and those meetings were usually as nerve-racking and worrisome as facing a crowd of a thousand people. Now he was away from those constant duties, and it was a feeling he knew he would grow to like.

* * *

Trying not to be seen on the Passover Sabbath, Joseph went to visit Pilate. It was not an easy task because there were very few people on the streets of Jerusalem. Those walking about were eyed with contempt and suspicion. Finally, after carefully making his way, Joseph entered Fortress Antonia, asking to see Pontius Pilate.

Pilate was staring out of the window as Joseph entered. Joseph cleared his throat to get Pilate's attention. "I don't think Jesus will be able to reappear today or anytime soon. We really didn't discuss when he would make his appearance to the disciples, but I think he needs some time. Last night, he was much worse than I thought he would be. He's in pretty bad shape."

Joseph sensed Pilate was sincerely concerned about Jesus. Continuing, Joseph added, "I honestly think he needs to be seen by a doctor and receive medical attention. Otherwise, I don't know how long it will take him to recover."

"He was up there only a few hours. And my soldiers gave him water."

"He's been through a lot the past few days. I don't think it was simply the time on the cross. He was beaten severely in Caiaphas' court. And the whole trip to Jerusalem has worn on his soul."

Joseph ran his hands through his hair, painfully remembering the image from the night before. "And the stress he has been through, dealing with the horror of crucifixion, real or not. I'll never forget the image of the two crucified with him. I doubt I'll ever get it out of my mind."

"Calm yourself, Joseph. The worst is over now. I suppose you're right. I can send my doctor over to him tonight." Pontius paused in thought. "It must be far into the night. We must move him to a place where he can recover."

* * *

Mary Magdalene and Mary, the mother of James, John, and Salome, had planned to visit the body of Jesus in order to anoint his body with burial spices. They could not do so on the day of the Passover Sabbath, since it was forbidden according to Mosaic Law. Not wanting to wait much longer due to the decay of the body, they went to the tomb the very next morning, while it was still dark. Inching their way through the darkness and nearing the tomb, Mary Magdalene noticed a faint light moving in the area up ahead, which frightened her. Mary slowed her pace as she realized the light was coming from the area of Jesus' tomb.

Coming upon the tomb, she saw a man go inside where the stone had been rolled away. A short time later, another man came out carrying something in his arms, placing it in a small wagon. The scene frightened Mary as she screamed, turned, and ran. Her companion quickly followed close behind.

By the time Mary reached the place where Simon Peter and John were staying, a hint of light pierced the morning sky. She burst into their room, startling them from their sleep. Mary fell to the floor and started crying uncontrollably as Peter sat up, rubbing his eyes. John, too, sat up in bed. Getting out of bed, Peter went over to Mary and placed his arm around her shoulders. "Mary! Mary! What's wrong? Please stop crying."

Mary lifted her face with tears streaming down. "They have taken the Lord out of the tomb, and we do not know where they have laid him."

Peter looked at Mary with surprise and asked, "Do you mean Jesus? They have taken him from his tomb?"

As Mary nodded, Peter asked in confusion, "Who are *they*?"

Mary looked up at Peter and shook her head. "I don't know who *they* are. I just saw some men at Jesus' tomb, and the stone was rolled back."

Peter stood back and repeated her words in disbelief: "You saw some men at the tomb? What were they... what were *you* doing at the tomb?!"

Mary calmed herself. "Mary and I were going to the tomb to anoint Jesus' body with spices. We wanted to do it yesterday, but it was the Sabbath. Anyway, when we approached the tomb this morning, we saw a light. Some men were going in and out of his tomb." Mary started crying again as she recalled the scene.

Peter tried to comfort her. "You are in no harm, Mary. You are with us. Please stop crying."

John stood up and asked, "You said Mary. Are you talking about my mother?" As Mary nodded, John asked again, "Where is she? What happened to her?"

Mary looked up at John with a blank stare. "I don't know. I don't know what happened to her. I just ran." Mary immediately burst into tears again.

John frantically jumped up and immediately ran outside. Peter got up and quickly followed. Seeing she was alone, Mary rose and followed them.

John ran towards the tomb calling out his mother's name. When he neared the tomb, he stooped to look inside. It was empty. The burial cloths lay scattered on a rock ledge and on the floor. Peter came running up, nearly out of breath. Pointing inside the tomb, John said, "Peter! There's no one inside! It's empty!"

Peter stooped to look in and then crept inside. Another burial cloth was rolled up neatly away from the other linens. John followed Peter into the tomb and grabbed him by the arm. "Who could have taken him?"

Peter shook his head in disbelief. "I don't know. Who would do such a thing?"

"I don't understand. What could anyone gain by taking his body?" Pausing, John turned and headed back to the entrance, calling out his mother's name. Hearing no response, he immediately ran back toward her house.

Standing alone inside the tomb, Peter kept turning in circles.

Mary finally reached the tomb and called out, "John! Peter! Is that you in there? Who's in there?"

"Mary! It's me, Peter!"

Mary stooped down and stuck her head inside. "Do you see? He's not here! Someone has taken him!" She immediately started crying again.

"Mary, please stop." Peter crawled out of the tomb and held her with a comforting embrace. "So you don't know who they were? How many were there?"

Mary swallowed and wiped a tear. "There were two, I think. I couldn't make out who they were."

Holding her at arm's length, Peter asked, "Where were they taking his body?"

"I don't know. I wasn't here long enough. I remember a small wagon." Turning around, Mary pointed towards a path. "Over there. That's where it was."

Peter walked over to where Mary was pointing. There were several wagon tracks. Peter shook his head. "There's no way of knowing how old these are."

Peter kneeled down and picked up a small piece of bread. "This is odd. It couldn't have been here long without being scavenged by some bird or animal." Peter put the morsel to his nose and sniffed before tossing it back to the ground.

* * *

After a couple of days, Jesus fully recovered under the care of Pilate's doctor. He truly enjoyed the rest and relaxation of the convalescence, not remembering the last time he had laid his head in the same place for two nights in a row. The food was wonderful and plentiful, prepared for him at every meal. In a sense, Jesus didn't want the wardship to end, but realized there was still much to do. With the comfort and security of the respite, Jesus felt disheartened knowing he would have to go back out and face the world of Judea. The thought was softened, however, by knowing it would only be for a few brief encounters, and, hopefully, only to meet with his disciples. How surprised they would be, he thought, when they first saw his face.

Pontius and Joseph met with Jesus on the fourth day. With a strong embrace, Joseph said to Jesus, "It's good to see you doing so well! Last week, I have to admit, I was really worried about you."

Jesus smiled. "I know. I was worried about me, too."

Jesus' lighthearted demeanor brought a smile to Pontius' face. "I am glad you are doing well." Pontius walked over and embraced Jesus.

Seeing and feeling his embrace, Jesus was a little shocked at Pilate's reaction. Pulling away, Pontius added, "I hope they have treated you well."

Jesus quickly nodded. "Oh yes, can't complain." Smiling again, he added, "I've been treated like a king."

Pontius burst into laughter. "And so you are, Jesus! So you are!"

They all started laughing and slapping each other on the shoulders. After exchanging a few additional cordialities, they slowly settled down to business.

"Do you feel well enough to meet with your disciples?"

Jesus looked back at Pilate. He was fully capable of proceeding with the meeting, but regretted the answer he knew he had to give. "Yes, I think it's time."

The three made plans to have Jesus meet with his disciples in two days. Joseph got word to Thaddaeus and Simon to have the eleven gather in a farmhouse just outside of Jerusalem. As enticement for the gathering, Joseph instructed Thaddaeus and Simon to tell everyone that they had already seen Jesus and that they wanted to discuss what they had witnessed.

Getting word to the remaining nine disciples was not an easy task, for some were in hiding, cowering for their lives. With the help of those they found, Thaddaeus and Simon finally got the message to everyone.

When the time came for the gathering, Thaddaeus and Simon brought another soldier, Cleopas, to assist in offering witness to the story. They told the other nine that they had seen Jesus and talked to him while walking on the road to Emmaus—a place about seven miles from Jerusalem.

Few of the disciples believed their testimony. They were skeptical of the two they considered as least of the disciples. If it had been Peter or John, then more of them would have believed. It was also a matter of principle of who Jesus would appear to first. As Thaddaeus described the encounter and the disciples were arguing among themselves, Jesus came in from a side room and stood amongst them.

First Matthew saw Jesus, and then James. They became silent. Matthew's eyes widen as he froze and could barely get out the words: "The ghost of Jesus."

All of the remaining disciples fixed their eyes on Jesus, and the entire room grew deathly silent. Jesus wore a brilliant white garment, pure in its weave and texture. It covered the full length of his body.

Seeing the fear in their eyes, Jesus said to them, "Why are you troubled, and why do questions fill your hearts?" He held out his hand from beneath his garment, showing his flesh to reassure them he was not a ghost. "See my hands and my feet—that is myself." Walking amongst them, he directed them to feel his shoulders and his arms, adding, "Handle me, and see; for a spirit has not flesh and bones as you see that I have."

Gradually, some of the disciples reached out to feel Jesus as he had directed. The rest backed away in fear. Still trying to prove that he was flesh and blood, Jesus asked, "Have you anything here to eat?"

They gave him a piece of broiled fish, and he took it and ate before them.

Then he said to them, "These are my words, which I spoke to you while I was still with you, that everything written about me in the Law of Moses and the prophets and the Psalms must be fulfilled." Then Jesus opened the Scriptures and read to them from the book of Hosea: "Come, let us return to the Lord; for he has torn, that he may heal us; he has stricken and he will bind us up. After two days he will revive us; on the third day he will raise us up, that we may live before him." Rolling the scroll closed, Jesus then continued, "Thus it is written that the Christ should suffer and on the third day rise from the dead, and that repentance and forgiveness of sins should be preached in his name to all of the people of Israel, beginning from Jerusalem."

Soon, all of the disciples started gathering closer to Jesus. Thomas, one of the twelve, said, "But Master, it has been nearly a week and a half since your crucifixion. Why do you speak of the third day?"

Jesus looked at Thomas and said, "Because it was on the third day that I left the tomb, and shortly thereafter first appeared to Thaddaeus, Simon, and Cleopas."

Thomas nodded with a confused look. "But Master, that passage deals with healing several people from an affliction rather than raising one person from the dead." Thomas shook his head as if trying to remember. "That was Ephraim who had a sickness, and Judah who had a wound. They were not dead."

Jesus lost his smile and gave Thomas a heavy look. The mistrust he had felt towards Judas seemed to resurrect with Thomas. Taking short, quick breaths, Jesus slowly turned his growing anger into a forced smile. Slapping Thomas on the back with more force than usual, Jesus replied,

"Well, I'm here with you now, aren't I?"

Jesus met with the disciples a few more times, challenging them to continue with his mission and spread his new version of the Jewish faith. He challenged them to continue working with the people of Israel in the hopes that their work would finally take a permanent hold.

In his last meeting, feeling a sense of abandoning them, Jesus said, "I will return again in the glory of my Father with the holy angels. Truly, I say to you, there are some standing here who will not taste death before they see the kingdom of God come with power." Jesus knew this was not in the plans, but he felt a need to leave them with a sense of impending hope.

* * *

Claudia ran her fingers through Pontius' hair. "I am so glad I finally get to meet the man all of Jerusalem is talking about. It's as if the ground is alive with new growth from the gardens of Rome." Cheerful tears welled in her eyes. "I am so proud of you, Pontius. With everything you have done, Tiberius will grant you a position on the senate."

Pontius smiled placing his arms around Claudia's waist. "That will have to wait a few years, my love. My term here as gardener has only begun."

Claudia let out a short laugh as she kissed Pontius. "The flowers of Rome will make this place almost bearable."

Pontius offered a comforting smile. "You make this country bearable, not the flowers of Rome or the work of my hands."

Pontius took a deep breath. "Jesus will be here soon. You must speak of this to no one—at least while we are still in Judea, or else this Roman garden will wither and die."

They were interrupted by a loud knock on the door. Pilate opened the door and Jesus entered. The Roman escort remained outside. Jesus staggered forward, bracing himself with one hand against the wall. He bowed slowly. As he looked up, his bloodshot eyes grew wide with a confident smile. Jesus couldn't keep his eyes off of Claudia as Pilate made the introductions.

Bowing again unsteadily, his words were slurred and wavering. "I didn't know Roman women were so beautiful."

Pilate's lips tightened and his mouth twitched. Claudia noticed Jesus' glance drop to the pendant on her chest. She raised her hand to cover the pendant as her eyes narrowed in a stern look of enchanting beauty and power. "Are all of your people so bold and inappropriate?"

Jesus lost his smile as Claudia continued, "You know you're supposed to be dead."

Author's Note

Rome's influence on the birth of Christianity is unmistakable, more so than many might realize. Rome's influence is clearly illustrated in two categories: the commonality with Roman culture and cults as it existed prior to Christianity, and the evidence that can be seen in realistic and historical interpretation of the early Christian writings. The discussion that follows proposes a new theory on the origins of Christianity. Was Christianity born of human conflict—the conflict between the imperialism of the Roman Empire and the self-perceived entitlement of the ancient Jewish culture, resulting in Roman attempts at manipulation of religious forces in Judea?

Preexisting Roman Culture and Cults

In Volume II of the *Theological Dictionary of the New Testament*,[1] on page 724 in a discussion of the Greek term *evangelion*, the editors make the following statement regarding the ruler of the Roman Empire:

> The ruler is divine by nature.[2] His power extends to men, to animals, to the earth and to the sea. Nature belongs to him; wind and waves are subject to him.[3] He works miracles and heals men.[4] He is the saviour of the world who also redeems individuals from their difficulties. He has appeared on earth as a deity in human form.[5]

This is a powerful and far-reaching statement that encompasses a great deal of classical literature—far more than references 2 through 5 above. For a thorough discussion and listing of appropriate classical references, see a book by Lily Ross Taylor entitled *The Divinity of the Roman Emperor*.[6]

The mythology of divinity began with the founding of Rome (attributed to the date 753 BCE). The Roman historian Livy (59 BCE – 17 CE) acknowledges in *The Early History of Rome, I.3*[7] the myth concerning the founders of Rome, the brothers Romulus and Remus, being born of a Vestal Virgin, Sylvia, with the god Mars as their father. Livy refers to "Romulus, the son of a god and himself divine."[8] The Greek historian Plutarch wrote:

> For it is said that their [Romulus' and Remus'] mother [Sylvia] conceived by a God. It is reported concerning the begetting of Romulus, that the sun was eclipsed at the time as the immortal God Mars was with the mortal Sylvia. The same is said to have happened about the time of his death.... the sun was under an eclipse.[9]

This sets precedence to Christianity in terms of human divinity, virgin birth, and divine conception. These concepts were by no means unique or original to Roman culture (Egypt and Greece come to mind), but Rome was in control of Judea during the birth of Christianity, granting it preference. With regard to the solar eclipse (a relatively rare natural event), the *New Testament* also speaks of an eclipse of the sun upon Christ's death.[10] Livy acknowledges other possible explanations for Sylvia's placement in history, but clearly the mythology existed prior to Christianity concerning the divinity of the founders of Rome, their virgin birth, and a god as their father. Plutarch writes of another virgin birth:

> Queen Tanaquil ... dressed up the virgin in all her bridal ornaments and attire, and then shut her up in a room together with this apparition. Some attribute this amour to Lar the household God, and others to Vulcan; but which-soever it was,

Ocresia was with child, and gave birth to Sevius [the sixth Roman king, 579 – 535 BCE].[11]

After the time of Romulus, Romans strongly resisted the concept of deity for Roman rulers for hundreds of years until the time of the Caesars in the middle of the first century BCE. Romans accepted Romulus as a god due to his distance in ancient history and an attributed myth that he never actually died, but was swept up into heaven by a whirlwind. Livy states, "… and at last every man present hailed him as a god and a son of god, and prayed to him."[12] But after the era of the Roman kings (753 – 510 BCE) the Roman people shunned the title of *rex*, or king, and the idea of god incarnate, until the time of Julius Caesar.

It was during the reign of Julius Caesar (60 – 44 BCE) and Augustus Caesar (44 BCE – 14 CE) that the concept of god incarnate gained prominence. The idea of the ruler's divinity was especially promoted in the eastern provinces. An inscription in Ephesus honored Julius Caesar as "a revealed god, offspring of Mars and Venus, and universal saviour of the human race."[13] In 45 BCE in Rome in the temple of Quirinus, a statue of Caesar was erected with the inscription, "To the unconquered god."[14] The Roman senate decreed Julius Caesar to be a god and commanded the erection of a temple to him and his *Clementia*.[15] In 45 BCE Caesar's portrait appears for the first time on coins from the Roman mint, which had usually contained images of the gods, and had never before shown a representation of a living man.[16]

Julius Caesar's adopted son and heir, Octavian, continued the practice of having his portrait on minted coins when he became Emperor Augustus Caesar. Inscriptions on the coins included *divi filius*, son of a god. Augustus Caesar was considered by popular mythology to be the son of the god Apollo. Augustus' mother, Atia, spent the night in the temple of Apollo and was impregnated by the god in the form of a serpent (the Roman representation of fertility).[17] In Book 6 of *Aeneid* written by the Roman poet Virgil around 19 BCE, Virgil refers to Augustus as "descended from God." Contemporary rivals to Augustus Caesar, Mark Antony and Sextus Pompey, also claimed rights to divinity. Mark Antony masqueraded as Dionysus, and Sextus claimed to be the son of Neptune,

Neptune dux, as the Roman author Horace referred to him.[18] Sextus claimed dominion over the seas and the favor of Neptune when his opponent's fleet was destroyed by storm.[19] Julius Caesar was also said to have dominion over the waves. In reference to a boat-pilot fearful of putting to sea due to violent waves, Plutarch quotes Caesar as saying, "Put on, brave fellow, and fear nothing, but commit the sails to [the goddess] Fortune, and expose all boldly to the winds; for thou carriest Caesar and Caesar's fortune."[20] Plutarch goes on to write that the goddess Fortune favored Caesar and "it was her province to give calmness to the sea." Compare this to Matthew 8:26–27:

> And he [Jesus] said to them, "Why are you afraid, O men of little faith?" Then he rose and rebuked the winds and the sea; and there was a great calm. And the men marveled, saying, "What sort of man is this, that even the winds and the sea obey him?"

The concept of god incarnate and being the son of a god was not unique to the Roman and Greek culture. In Judaism, King David was considered to be the firstborn son of God.[21] In the *New Testament* Jesus disputes this,[22] presumably in promoting his own rights to this claim.

In the *New Testament* Jesus had twelve disciples.[23] In *The Early History of Rome, I.7*, in reference to the first king of Rome, Livy writes, "… of which the most important was the creation of the twelve lictors to attend his person. Some have fancied that he made the lictors twelve in number because the vultures, in the augury, had been twelve." In *The Divine Augustus*, section 70, in reference to a gala Augustus Caesar would throw, Suetonius writes, "A private entertainment which he gave, commonly called the *Supper of the Twelve Gods*, and at which the guests were dressed in the habit of gods and goddesses…." Does Livy's emphasis of the number twelve somehow carry over to the number of disciples in Christian literature? However, the number twelve also has strong importance in Jewish culture with the twelve tribes of Israel coming from the twelve sons of Jacob.[24]

Religious scholars are not certain of the origins of Christian baptism (from the Greek word *baptismos*, which means the act of bathing or washing). Many note that the Jewish rite of initiation for gentiles called *proselyte ablution* also originated around this time. But a precedent also existed in Roman culture. In *The Early History of Rome, I.45*, Livy writes:

> Surely you do not mean to sacrifice to Diana without first performing the act of purification? You must bathe yourself, before the ceremony, in a living stream. Down there in the valley the Tiber [River] flows.

Roman culture placed a strong emphasis on bathing for cleanliness, and according to the above passage, in preparation for religious ceremony. If the original purpose of baptism in river waters relates to a type of cleansing or bathing (i.e., the meaning of *baptismos*), then the ritual has strong similarity to the practice described by Livy. There were also Jewish sects of the time that practiced ritualistic cleansing, but not necessarily in a river.

In the first century BCE, the Greek historian Nicolaus of Damascus (teacher to Herod the Great and ambassador to Augustus Caesar) writes in the *Life of Augustus*:

> Octavius, at the age of about nine years [twelve[25]], was an object of no little admiration to the Romans, exhibiting as he did great excellence of nature, young though he was; for he gave an oration before a large crowd and received much applause from grown men.

Compare this to Luke 2:42–47:

> And when he [Jesus] was twelve years old ... they found him in the temple, sitting among the teachers, listening to them and asking them questions; and all who heard him were amazed at his understanding and his answers.

Both passages refer to child prodigies prior to their entrances as profound leaders in adulthood.

After the death of Julius Caesar, Suetonius writes in *The Divine Augustus, Section 96*, that a Thessalian claimed the "Divine Julius Caesar" appeared to him while he was traveling on a byroad. This story has similarities to the appearance of Jesus to Simon while traveling on the road in Luke 24.

The term *gospel* is an old-English form of "good news," which stems from the Greek word *evangelion*. Prior to the Middle Ages and the English translations, the term *gospel* didn't exist. The Greek term *evangelion* is of importance here (root term for the modern-day "evangelical"). Prior to Christianity, the term *evangelion* had as much or more meaning and emotion in Roman culture as *gospel* has in Christianity today. Reference 1 explains in detail the use of this term in Greek and Roman culture along with associated references. In brief, the Greeks first used the term to mean "reward for good news." The Greeks eventually modified the term to mean "news of victory in battle" brought by a messenger. The Romans also adapted this term to announce a new Caesar or the birth of a divine heir to the throne.[26] The following decree in the Roman province of Asia in 9 BCE marks the birthday of Augustus (September 23) as the beginning of the civil year:[27]

> Providence ... has ordained the most perfect consummation for human life by giving to it Augustus, by filling him with virtue for doing the work of a benefactor among men, and by sending in him, as it were, a saviour for us and those who come after us, to make war to cease, to create order everywhere ... and whereas the birthday of the God [Augustus] was the beginning for the world of the *Evangel* that have come to men through him ... the reckoning of time for the course of human life should begin with his birth.

The earliest Christian writings (the first three Gospels in their original translations) used the term in nearly identical fashion to the Roman use. *Evangelion* appears fifteen times in Matthew, Mark, and Luke. Mark 1:1 states, "The beginning of the *evangel* of Jesus Christ, the Son of God." In Luke 1:19 an angel proclaims *evangel* announcing the birth of John the

Baptist to his father. In Luke 2:10 an angel proclaims *evangel* announcing the birth of Jesus to shepherds.

Later, as Christianity developed, the apostle Paul enthusiastically adapted this term in his letters of the *New Testament*—using it over 60 times. It is interesting to note that *evangelion* appears almost 80 times in *New Testament* writings, but never appears in the prior Jewish religious writings of the *Old Testament*.

Some may think the commonalties mentioned above are coincidence. But all of these were *preexisting* human concepts associated with a society in control of Judea—concepts which gained fervor in Rome in the few decades preceding Christianity. The commonalties mentioned in this paper are not exhaustive.

Historical Perspective of Early Christian Writings

Several independent sources suggest that Christianity began in the first century CE in the Roman province of Judea during the reign of Pontius Pilate as governor. The Roman historian Publius Cornelius Tacitus (56 – 117 CE) wrote in *The Annals of Imperial Rome, XV.42*:

> To suppress this rumor [suspicions on the burning of Rome in 64 CE], Nero fabricated scapegoats—and punished with every refinement the notoriously depraved Christians (as they were popularly called). Their originator, Christ, had been executed in Tiberius' reign by the governor of Judea, Pontius Pilatus. But in spite of this temporary setback the deadly superstition had broken out afresh, not only in Judea (where the mischief had started) but even in Rome.

This is an historical, independent reference to the origins of Christianity. The *New Testament* writings are not considered in the classical sense "historical." There is disagreement even on which century they were written. Since the writings are filled with stories of miracles and fantastical events, many consider these folklore, which takes time to develop in human culture. However, some scholars believe the first three

Gospels (Matthew, Mark, and Luke) were written much earlier, soon after the time of Jesus. If the Gospels were written by people of that time and period, then they can be used to hypothesize real human events and attitudes representative of the movement.

Two dominant forces present in Judea during the birth of Christianity included Roman authority and the established Jewish religious order. Both of these forces were very strong and influential, and oftentimes in conflict. Even though the established Jewish religious order was not as organized and well-defined as Roman authority, it formed the basis for very bitter, fervent, and sometimes violent resistance to Roman occupation. The province of Judea presented numerous problems to the Roman Empire in terms of collecting taxes, enlisting men to serve in their fielded armies, and enforcing control and order in a disobedient population.

It was not unheard of for Roman authority to meddle in the religious affairs of the Jews. The Roman governor prior to Pontius Pilate, Valerius Gratus, appointed and fired a succession of five high priests to the Jewish court. In many of Rome's provinces (and especially the eastern provinces), the cult of the Roman Emperor was promoted as an effective means of government.[28] Showing great flexibility in their governing model, Rome also permitted the practice of local religious customs in order to pacify the masses. However, the intensity of Jewish religious beliefs was the primary source of their resistance to Roman authority. The mere presence of the Roman occupation was a defilement to the Holy Land of the Jews and their covenant with God. Did Christianity begin as a result of Roman manipulation to soften the resistance of Jews to Roman rule?

According to written documentation from that time period, Jesus offered teachings very different from Judaism. He was consistently critical of the Jewish religious order, while offering startling public praise of a Roman centurion. He encouraged submissive behavior towards oppression and obedience to taxes. Jesus' criticism of the Jewish religious order (the keepers of the Mosaic Law,[29] the scribes,[30] the chief priests,[31] the Pharisees,[32] Saducees,[33] etc.) would have been consistent with Roman goals of breaking down competition to their authority. The Jewish religious order was strongly resistant to any outside influence to the Jewish faith. Disruption of this core precept by Rome would have assisted in instilling obedience and servitude in the common people. In contrast, Jesus publicly referred to a Roman centurion as having the greatest faith in all of Israel.[34] In turn Roman centurions referred to Jesus as "Lord,"[35] and in another case as "[a or the] Son of God."[36] It is interesting that the only documented spoken reference to Jesus as the Son of God comes from a Roman—from the very culture where this concept had prominence in the preceding decades.

Positive and obedient references towards paying taxes are repeated many times in the *New Testament* writings.[37] Jesus was referred to as a "friend of tax collectors."[38] When Jesus was asked if it was lawful to pay taxes to Rome, Jesus responded, "Render to Caesar the things that are Caesar's."[39] In another written story regarding the payment of the half-shekel tax,[40] Jesus instructs Peter to pay for both of them, taking special care not to offend the collector. One of the twelve disciples was highlighted as being a tax collector (Matthew/Levi).[41] While staying the night in Jericho, Jesus stayed with the chief tax collector, Zacchaeus.[42] Jews detested paying taxes to Rome, many even considering the profession of tax collector as sinful. Jesus' teachings and actions were well in line with Roman goals to change this attitude.

Another dominant theme of Jesus' teachings promoted submissive behavior towards oppression. "But if any one strikes you on the right cheek, turn to him the other also."[43] "Love your enemies and pray for those who persecute you."[44] "Blessed are the meek, the poor, the peacemakers."[45] This is in direct contrast to the proud, priestly nature of the Jews. Jews felt they were the chosen people of God, bound by a Holy Covenant that, by definition, would last forever.[46] The Hebrew God of the *Old Testament* demanded merciless treatment of enemies with no room for forgiveness.[47] In 1 Samuel 15:25–30, the Jewish King Saul repented and asked for forgiveness, twice, for not having killed every living thing of the enemy (men, women, children, babies, and animals), but was rejected by God—fatally. In obvious contrast, the passive, submissive tendencies of Jesus' teachings offer clear advantages to Roman control.

There were two primary ways people in a conquered province could be productive subjects to the Roman Empire: (1) pay taxes to Rome, and (2) serve in the fielded Roman armies. Rome employed a unique and highly successful policy of enlisting men from the conquered provinces to serve in their fielded armies. However, this was very expensive, as were many other aspects of maintaining the Empire. In the early stages of the Christian movement, John the Baptist is documented as having baptized men from only two professions: tax collectors and soldiers. These were public exhibitions, which may have provided an acceptant light towards the named professions. John professes that the proper behavior for a tax collector is to collect no more than the appointed amount.[48] This implies that the appointed amount is legitimate and proper. As for soldiers, John professes, "Rob no one by violence or by false accusation, and be content with your wages."[49] Having soldiers be content with their wages has obvious advantages to Rome. In these public baptisms, when a tax collector and a soldier asked what was needed for righteousness, John did not tell them to stop practicing their professions, which is probably what the people wanted to hear. Instead, he instructed them in ways conducive to Roman rule.

Public miracles were a noted aspect of Jesus' ministries. The Jewish historian Flavius Josephus writes in *The Antiquities of the Jews*, "... he performed admirable and amazing works." Assuming for the moment that this reference and the numerous references in the *New Testament* have some basis in human events, it is fair to say that only a handful of consortiums in the region had the means and ability to orchestrate the documented miracles. And there was probably only one that had the means and ability to feed four and five thousand people in remote areas.[50] Rome was well versed at feeding legions in the field. It is, quite frankly, the most logical conclusion that Rome was behind such exhibitions. It is even documented in written accounts that a centurion initiated and was directly involved in the performance of a miracle.[51]

Ironically, a point of contention that many may have towards this theory actually turns out to be a very strong point of support. The crucifixion of Jesus was carried out by the Romans, albeit through the demands of the Jews. But if one studies closely what is written about this event—versus what has been passed down by word of mouth in Christian tradition—a very different story emerges. None of the Gospel accounts of the crucifixion mention Jesus having been nailed to the cross. Why would such an unusual and exceedingly cruel aspect of crucifixion be missing from written accounts? The most obvious and simplest answer to this question is that Jesus wasn't nailed to the cross. He was probably supported in the more common fashion with ropes. This is not the only answer to the posed question, but it is a viable and reasonable answer.

Written accounts suggest Jesus spent relatively little time on the cross—approximately six hours, and that he appeared alive after the crucifixion. There are three primary arguments suggesting his post-appearance may have been a real event:

(1) The event is documented in two independent sources: the *New Testament* and *Antiquities* by Josephus. Josephus wrote, "And when Pilate, at the suggestion of the principal men among us [the Jewish elders and chief priests], had condemned him to the cross, those that loved him at first did not forsake him, for he appeared to them alive again the third day."

(2) The event is very likely the primary reason why Christianity persisted. If Jesus had died upon crucifixion, the movement probably would have died with him.

(3) The documented story of Jesus' post-appearance after the crucifixion in Luke 24:36–43 is realistic, granting it credibility:

> As they were saying this, Jesus himself stood among them. But they were startled and frightened, and supposed that they saw a spirit. And he said to them, "Why are you troubled, and why do questionings rise in your hearts? See my hands and my feet, that it is I myself; handle me, and see; for a spirit has not flesh and bones as you see that I have." And while they still disbelieved for joy, and wondered, he said to them, "Have you anything here to eat?" They gave him a piece of broiled fish, and he took it and ate before them.

If one reads this account without the common preconception that Jesus was nailed to the cross, the story takes on a different meaning. Why is there no mention of nail wounds in this written account? Jesus asks his disciples to "see" exposed parts of his body (i.e., parts not covered by clothing, like his hands and feet) and to physically handle other parts of his body to prove he is flesh and blood, and not spirit. Jesus is doing this to calm their fears by proving he is not a ghost.

As shocking as this next statement may appear, it is a relatively simple statement with complete viability. It is a statement well in line with the motivation of Roman authority to protect its interest in light of violent demands from a Jewish mob. The next statement is not only simple, but also exceedingly logical if one throws off the intense cultural emotion placed upon it. If Jesus appeared alive after the crucifixion (as suggested by the arguments above), then this necessarily means he did not die on the cross. This strongly hints that Rome was involved in allowing Jesus to live. Rome carried out the crucifixion and a Roman centurion pronounced his supposed death.[52]

The strong possibility that nails were not used in Jesus' crucifixion and his relatively short time on the cross fits well with a Roman design to protect Jesus from a death demanded by a Jewish mob. And Jesus' documented post-appearance to his followers suggests a continuation, if not enhancement, of this design in a viable sequence of human events in no need of supernatural explanation.

It is easy to conceptualize how the religious fervor of early Christians may have sensationalized the crucifixion with the introduction of nails. Or rumors may have been introduced by the Romans to explain Jesus' supposed quick death on the cross. The first written account suggesting this method may have been used does not appear until many decades later when the Gospel of John is written in a modified version of the post-appearance story called the "doubting Thomas."[53] Most biblical scholars agree that the Gospel of John was written long after the other three. If one carefully maps out the chronology of major events in the Gospels, the first three have fair agreement. The Gospel of John, however, varies significantly from the other three. The Gospel of John re-tells the post-appearance story in a slightly modified version from Luke, first introducing the concept of nail wounds in Jesus' hands.

There are several other *very* important differences in the Gospel of John compared to the other three Gospels that I will mention briefly:

(1) John is the only Gospel that mentions any type of physical violation to Jesus while he was on the cross (i.e., the stabbing of Jesus in the side with a spear *after* he was supposedly dead).[54] The stabbing results from Jewish demands that the legs of the prisoners be broken, and Rome's reaction of breaking those of the other two, but not Jesus'. The medically improbable account regarding fluid expulsion from a corpse (from the testimony of a Roman, Pontius Pilate, after probing from Jewish elders) suggests fabricated witness.

(2) In the first three Gospels, the Romans direct Simon of Cyrene to carry Jesus' cross. John is the only Gospel that states Jesus carried his own cross.

(3) John is the only Gospel to mention that women and his acquaintances were near the cross,[55] which contradicts all of the other three, which state they watched from a distance.[56]

(4) The Gospel of John never uses the Greek term *evangelion*. Many theologians surmise that the author of John was sensitive to the use of this term and that it may have come from Jesus' lips. I contend the author's sensitivity was associated with the timing of the writing of that Gospel and the spread of Christianity to Rome (discussed in more detail later).

(5) The first three Gospels quote Jesus as promising his disciples his glorious "Second-Coming" would occur within their lifetimes.[57] This quote is completely missing from the Gospel of John, probably since it became all too apparent in later years this was not going to happen.

Before the crucifixion, when a Jewish crowd[58] brought Jesus before Roman authority, Pontius Pilate argued profusely *against* crucifying Jesus.[59] Pilate carried Jesus' defense to the point that a riot was forming.[60] Why would a Roman prefect defend a Jewish peasant, whom he supposedly had never known, in front of a Jewish crowd vehemently calling for his execution? In addition, there are several points regarding the crucifixion which suggest Rome was involved in concealing a staged execution. Roman soldiers (including a centurion) stood guard over the crucifixion site.[61] A heretofore unexplained person in the *New Testament*, Joseph of Arimathea, took possession of Jesus' body (not a member of his family, which was the traditional practice).[62] And according to scholarly opinion (historians/theologians Albert Roper, Mgr. E. Le Camus, A. T. Robertson, Professor T. J. Thorburn, A. B. Bruce, Arndt, Gingrich, Professor Harold Smith, Lewis, and Short noted in *Evidence* by Josh McDowell) and my own conclusion from the *New Testament* writings,[63] Roman soldiers stood guard over Jesus' tomb. In any case, written accounts state that Pontius Pilate was directly involved in directing the guards for Jesus' tomb. Why did the Romans take such a strong interest in what was otherwise the corpse of a Jewish peasant? It is absurd to think of Roman soldiers expending man-hours to guard the gravesite of an executed Jewish criminal. It is reasonable to consider that the Jewish Court would have been highly motivated to dispatch Jewish guards to the gravesite without involving, or needing, Pilate's approval. But this is not what's documented in written accounts.

The only documented conflict to Roman support of the Jesus movement is written accounts that Jesus was mocked, spat upon, and struck with a reed while under Roman custody.[64] The incident occurred in the Roman praetorium and, as such, probably was based strictly on Roman witness—the very ones who would have been involved in deceit. John 18:28 records that Jews did not enter the praetorium on that day. The reference of being struck in the head with a reed is hardly the beating commonly portrayed in Christian folklore. And such a beating conflicts significantly with Pilate's *public* defense of Jesus in front of the Jewish mob. Luke makes no reference to these interactions with Roman soldiers, but instead records a similar incident in Antipas' court without anyone striking Jesus.[65] A much more violent and angry encounter occurs in the court of the Jewish high priest and is recorded in all four Gospels.[66]

The *traditional* word-of-mouth version of the "crown of thorns" in Christian folklore describes long, menacing thorns tearing into Jesus' scalp causing great pain with blood streaming down his face. These *are* strictly word-of-mouth images since written documentation says nothing about thorns piercing his skin, the blood they may have caused, or the pain they may have inflicted. The Gospels refer to Roman soldiers "plaiting a crown of thorns."[67] The word *plait* means to braid, as in hair or straw, which suggests a softer weave of some flexible stalk. Given that there are no written accounts of long thorns, piercing skin, and blood, then where did these accounts come from? One could investigate Christian art history to get a feel for when the word-of-mouth versions originated.

Despite common perceptions held by modern-day Christians, Jesus is never documented as supporting the overthrow of Roman authority. And Roman authority is never documented as pursuing Christ's crucifixion. Modern-day theologians and religious historians may conjecture how they think it should have been, hypothesizing that Pilate had no qualms crucifying Jesus, or even sought Jesus' crucifixion in order to keep the peace. But such conjecture is pointless when it goes against the only written knowledge we have of these events. Any number of human events is possible for any number of underlying reasons.

There is one other point of contention that many people might have towards this theory that is actually a strong point of support. Early Christians in Rome were persecuted by the ruling authority. But a very important question is: Why did Christianity spread so quickly to Rome—within a few decades? Without modern-day communications it is easy to see how the true nature of Christianity's beginning may have been lost, particularly if the beginning was concealed in local secrecy in Judea. This would not be the first example in history where something is started for one reason, but develops into something else entirely—with unforeseen consequences. What were the forces behind the seemingly paradoxical shift of an offshoot of Judaism from Judea to Rome? From the land of the "chosen people of God" to the land of their oppressors—oppressors who continued world domination under the eventual banner of Christianity itself. Could it be that Christianity gravitated towards Rome due to the Western leanings of its teachings and philosophies? The Christian philosophy was embraced wholeheartedly by the common people of Rome, but was shunned in Judea. As with anything new, the early Christian movement in Rome was looked upon with caution and disdain by the ruling authority. But they, too, gradually embraced Christianity, making it the official religion of the Roman Empire under Emperor Constantine over two hundred years later.

Lesser-Known Disciples

In order for Rome's manipulation of religious forces in Judea to succeed, very few of Jesus' immediate followers or disciples would have been aware of the Roman connection. There are numerous references in the *New Testament* of Jesus going off by himself, away from the disciples for days at a time or overnight.[68] If the Gospel writers went to the trouble of noting these occurrences, then these sojourns were probably prevalent or frequent events.

A few of the less-important disciples may have been involved in the Roman connection—"less important" for two main reasons. First, they would have maintained a low profile in order to conceal their involvement. Second, the very reason the more prominent or famous disciples *are* famous (Peter, James, John, etc.) is because they would have been the ones who were so completely duped and unaware of the Roman connection. They were the ones who carried on the movement, especially after having witnessed the "miraculous" appearance of Jesus after his crucifixion. Joseph of Arimathea would have been instrumental in the Roman connection since he was the person who is documented as having taken Jesus' body from the cross.

At what point did Christianity take on a life of its own and possibly lose the true nature of its beginnings (whatever form that may have been)? Pontius Pilate reigned as governor for only a few years after the time of Jesus. Documentation suggests that Pilate either died in 36 CE during his trip back to Rome, or he continued a life in exile in Gaul. There are some sects of Christianity that even speculate that Pilate and his wife, Claudia Procula, converted to Christianity. Is there a connection between a sketchy perception of conversion to Christianity and Pilate's involvement in its formation? There are historical references that suggest Joseph of Arimathea ended up in Gaul, just as Pontius Pilate might have. And one of the "lesser" disciples (Simon Zelotes) came to Gaul per Joseph's request. Eventually he went on to Britain where he was executed by a

Roman commander in 61 CE. The puzzle gets very complicated and it is difficult to decipher Christian folklore—the true knowledge of its beginnings and perceived plots in related or unrelated power struggles.

Did the true nature of Christianity's beginning disappear after Pilate's departure from Judea? One intriguing event suggests otherwise. Herod Agrippa, a Jewish king appointed by Rome after Pilate's departure, ruled Judea during the period of 37 to 44 CE. Early on, Agrippa was looked upon with disdain and mistrust by Jews, complicating his efforts in gaining their approval. However, towards the end of his rule, Agrippa gained great popularity amongst the populace by taking on a policy of persecuting the early Christians in Judea. He carried it to the point of having one of the original disciples, James, executed, and Peter jailed. Many historians suspect that Herod Agrippa was poisoned soon after this by the Romans. But historians are perplexed as to why Rome would have done such a thing in light of Agrippa's increasing popularity. Christian folklore suggests God caused Agrippa's death due to his persecution of the Christians. A combination of the historical and Christian-folklore versions may be the true circumstances, with Rome playing the role of God. If *local* Roman authority still had an interest in nurturing what was still a *local* Christian subversion of Judaism, therein lies a possible motive for Rome to eliminate Agrippa. And perhaps it was Rome's involvement that subsequently freed Peter from a Jewish prison, which could have easily been staged to appear as a miracle. Is it possible that Peter had positive interactions from Roman encounters, compared to the rejections and persecution he received from Jews? Could this be the reason Peter eventually carried his ministries to Rome, not realizing that in doing so, he would lose the protection of the *local* Roman authority back in Judea? Or could it be that by the time Peter was executed in Rome (64 CE), the true nature of Christianity's beginnings had been lost?

The Birth Story

The birth of Jesus is discussed in only two of the four Gospels, Matthew and Luke. Of the two Gospels, Luke provides the most standard sequence of events when Mary and Joseph are living in Nazareth (of

Galilee) and Mary is conceived with Jesus. When Mary is nearly full term, she and Joseph are forced to travel to Bethlehem (of Judea) for a Roman census. Since Joseph is of the lineage of David, he has to travel to the city of David, Bethlehem. The birthplace occurs in a manger since there was no room at the inn. The birthplace is visited by shepherds, not kings or wise men, and there is no mention of a star. There is also no mention of Herod having all of the male children killed. After Bethlehem, Mary, Joseph, and Jesus go directly to Jerusalem for purification according to the Law of Moses. They then return to their home in Nazareth.

The story in Matthew is different. There is no mention of Mary and Joseph having first lived in Nazareth, or the census. The story in Matthew implies that they start out living in Bethlehem, and as such, Jesus is born in Bethlehem. They end up moving to Nazareth (where Jesus is known to have grown up, being a Nazarene) under different circumstances. Reading Matthew, one gets the impression that Bethlehem is the original home of Mary and Joseph. Matthew 2:11 refers to the wise men (or astrologers or Magi in some versions of the Bible, or three kings according to Holy Tradition from the Catholic Church) going into a "house" where Mary and Jesus are, rather than a stable. Matthew refers to a star that guides the wise men. After Bethlehem, Mary, Joseph, and Jesus go to Egypt in order to avoid Herod's wrath in having all of the male children killed.

In contrast to trying to avoid Herod's wrath, Luke states that after Jesus' birth they go to Jerusalem, which is precisely where Herod is. In Matthew, after having spent some unknown time in Egypt awaiting Herod's death, Joseph desires to return to his "home" in Judea (presumably Bethlehem in Matthew, in contrast to Nazareth in Luke) but is afraid because of Herod's successor, Herod's son Archelaus. Instead, Matthew 2:22–23 implies that they withdraw to a new location, Nazareth of Galilee (which, in contrast, is their original home in Luke). However, this version of how they ended up in Nazareth does not make complete sense, since another of Herod's sons, Antipas, was tetrarch over Galilee (they would have had the same fear to return to either location).

Both of these stories coincide with the apparent fact that Jesus grew up in Nazareth until his late twenties or early thirties, which was probably all too obvious to people who lived in Nazareth in 26 CE. What is different between these two Gospels are the details of Jesus' earlier childhood and how he came to be born in Bethlehem. Both stories attempt to place Jesus' birth in Bethlehem, despite having grown up in Nazareth. This was an important issue for Jews at the time. They knew from the Scriptures regarding the prophecies of a messiah (the anticipated deliverer and king of the Jews) that he would come from Bethlehem (Micah 5:2). The fact that Jesus was known to be from Nazareth disturbed them considerably. This was the concern behind the Pharisees directing a question toward Jesus about where he was really from in John 8:19 and accusing Jesus of bearing false witness in John 8:13. It was also an expressed concern in John 7:41–42:

> ... But some said, "Is this the Christ to come from Galilee? Has not the scripture said that the Christ is descended from David, and comes from Bethlehem, the village where David was?"

And in John 7:52:

> ... Search and you will see that no prophet is to rise from Galilee.

And in John 1:46, when Nathanael asks:

> "Can anything good come out of Nazareth?"

If Jesus really was born in the place of his childhood, Nazareth, the two different stories in Matthew and Luke appear to be differing attempts toward meeting the need of the prophecy.

The killing of all male children two years of age and younger in all of Bethlehem and all the region would seem to be a very significant event. This particular story is only mentioned in a single sentence in Matthew 2:16. Other related events are well documented in several sources that Herod the Great suffered from mental illness toward the end of his reign and eventual death in 4 BCE. Herod had ten different wives, one of whom he loved very much (Mariame, a Hasmonean princess). Due to his paranoia and mental instability, he murdered her one day in a violent, jealous rage. Herod also had her two sons, her brother, her grandfather, and her mother killed. Amongst many other problems toward the end of his life, Herod suffered from arteriosclerosis, experiencing great pain that exacerbated his mental instability. He altered his will three times, and finally disinherited and killed his own firstborn, Antipater. Herod even made an unsuccessful attempt at suicide before he died. There is, however, no other documentation stating he had all the male children in Bethlehem killed. It is an event that is not even mentioned in Luke in his story of Jesus' birth. One cannot help but think that the story of having the firstborn killed was fabricated to equate Jesus' birth to the story of the birth of Moses in the *Old Testament* in which the Pharaoh ordered all of the males born of Hebrew women killed (Exodus 1:22).

There is also some discrepancy regarding dates between the year Jesus was born and the death of Herod the Great in 4 BCE. The birth story in Matthew would place the year of Jesus' birth prior to 4 BCE (possibly 5 or 6 BCE). In contrast, a summation of the accounts in other parts of the *New Testament* would place the year of his birth at the transition from BCE to CE. As a point-in-time reference, the reign of Pontius Pilate as governor of Judea started in 26 CE. Luke 3:1 states that John the Baptist (who preceded Jesus' ministry) started his ministry in the fifteenth year of the reign of Tiberius Caesar (29 CE). Luke, chapter 3, goes on to say that Jesus followed John the Baptist, beginning his ministry when he was about thirty years of age. Simple math of these accounts places Jesus' birth three to five years after the death of Herod the Great. Of course, the statement "about thirty years of age" places ambiguity in the timeline. In order to have preceded Herod's death, Jesus would have been a minimum of thirty-five years old for the tightest sequencing of events, and more realistically, thirty-six or thirty-seven, allowing for more reasonable timing.

Another interesting point regarding Jesus' birth pertains to Matthew 1:1 through 1:17 in which the genealogy from Abraham to David to Joseph to Jesus is spelled out in forty-one generations (again making the important tie to fulfill the prophecy that the Messiah would be a descendent of David). But this succession appears to be irrelevant since Joseph, as the story goes, was not the real father of Jesus. In stark contrast, an entirely different genealogy is presented in Luke 3:23 showing fifty-seven generations from Abraham to Jesus. They differ even in naming Joseph's father (Jacob in Matthew and Heli in Luke). From King David backward, both genealogies are nearly identical, aside from Luke having one more generation with a man named Arni. But from King David forward, the genealogies widely differ. The genealogy in Matthew goes through many of the great kings of Judah/Israel (Solomon, Ahaz, Hezekiah, Manasseh, Josiah, and Zerubbabel), whereas in Luke, only one of these (Zerubbabel) is mentioned. Zerubbabel was one of the last great kings of Judah who was prophesized by Haggai and Zechariah in 520 BCE as a messianic hopeful. However, this never came to be. Immediately following King David, Matthew lists Solomon, while Luke lists Nathan. The two books then list sixteen and twenty-two generations down through Zerubbabel, with another eleven and twenty generations down through Jesus. One could attempt to explain the differences (but not all of the differences) by claiming one of the lineages was through Jesus' mother, Mary, rather than Joseph. But both passages specifically refer to Joseph's father for the lineage, and not a reference to his "father-in-law," or Mary's father. Why do the two accounts go to all of the trouble of listing forty to fifty generations, when neither is in agreement? And why do they even bother since, theoretically, Joseph wasn't Jesus' biological father? One can't help but think that one or both lists were fabricated to establish an ancestry relationship to King David.

Conclusion

Below are six follow-on points to gleam from this Author's Note. The first three are most assuredly fact. Statement (1) warrants volumes of obvious arguments that will not be addressed here. Statement (2) follows naturally from the first. Statement (3) is obvious, even with a cursory examination of Christianity and Judaism, which should be of concern in Christian theology inheriting a God that supposedly doesn't change.[69] Questions (4) through (6) are speculative and assume there was a man in history filling the role of Jesus. This speculation is supported by independent references from Tacitus and Josephus mentioned earlier in this Author's Note.

(1) The supernatural explanation of Christianity's birth is myth.
(2) Christianity started as a result of human endeavors.
(3) Christian culture and its theological basis differ significantly from Judaism.
(4) If Christianity's birth was highlighted by numerous marvelous works/miracles (as documented by Flavius Josephus and the *New Testament*), these exhibitions would have been orchestrated. Did a single Judean peasant have the means or even the motivation to pull off such feats?
(5) Would a single Judean peasant promote and pursue drastic changes to Jewish culture knowing how sensitive (i.e., life-threatening) his actions would have been to the general population?
(6) Could a single Judean peasant do all of this and somehow survive a Roman execution to ensure the continuation of his movement?

The answers to questions (4) through (6) are most assuredly no. It is more likely such an individual had the organized backing of a capable organization—and evidence points squarely to Rome.

Bibliography

ABC: Appian of Alexandria, *Bellum Civile (The Civil Wars)*

ABD: David Noel Freedman editor-in-chief, *Anchor Bible Dictionary, Vol. 5 O–Sh*, Doubleday, New York, 1992

AOJ: Flavius Josephus, *Antiquities of the Jews*. Flavius Josephus was a Jewish historian who wrote the *Antiquities* in 93–94 CE at about the same time the gospels were written, 60–100 CE.

CAA: Marcus Tullius Cicero, *Ad Atticum*

CDR: Cassius Dio, *Roman History*

DRE: Lily Ross Taylor, *The Divinity of the Roman Emperor*, Scholars Press, the American Philological Association, Middletown, Connecticut, 1931

EHR: Livy, *The Early History of Rome, Rome Under the Kings*, probably written around 20 BCE

HEP: Horace, *Epodes*

JTB: Carl H. Kraeling, *John the Baptist*, Scribner, New York, 1951

NDA: Nicolaus of Damascus, *Life of Augustus*

NEB: *The New Encyclopedia Britannica, Vol. 22, Macropedic, Knowledge in Depth, 15th Edition*, 1997

NID: Collin Brown, *The New International Dictionary of New Testament Theology, Volume 2*, Zondervan Publishing House, Grand Rapids, Michigan, c. 1975–1978

ONT: *The Old and the New Testaments of The Holy Bible*, Revised Standard Version, Thomas Nelson Inc., Camden, New Jersey, 1962

OWG: Otto Weinreich, *Antikes Gottmenschentum*, N. Jbch. Wiss. U. Jugendbilding, 2, 1926, pp. 633–651

OWH: Otto Weinreich, *Antike Heilungswunder*, RVV, 8, 1909, pp. 65–75

PCA: Plutarch, *Caesar*

PCF: Plutarch's essay entitled *Concerning the Fortune of the Romans*, written around 75 CE, from *Plutarch's Essays and Miscellanies*, otherwise known as *Moralia*, The Colonial Company, Limited, New York and Pittsburg, 1905

PGA: Philo, *Gaium*

PGI: *Papyrus Giessen* I, 3, 3, n. 31

TDA: Gaius Suetonius Tranquillus, *The Divine Augustus*, referencing theological works of Asclepiades the Mendesian

TDN: Gerhard Kittel, *Theological Dictionary of the New Testament, Volume II*, Wm. B. Eerdmans Publishing Company, Grand Rapids, Michigan, 1964

WCP: Chaim Potok, *Wanderings, Chaim Potok's History of the Jews*, Alfred Knopf, New York, 1978

WDO: Wilhelm Dittenberger, *Orientis graeci inscriptions selectae*, Leipzig, S. Hirzel, 1903–05

WDS: Wilhelm Dittenberger, *Sylloge Inscriptionum Graecarum, 3rd Edition*, Leipzig, S. Hirzel, 1915

Notes and References

Reference acronyms are found in the Bibliography.

1) TDN

2) OWG

3) PCF 6

4) OWH

5) WDO, PGI

6) DRE

7) EHR 1.3

8) EHR 1.40

9) PCF 8

10) Matthew 27:45, Mark 15:33, Luke 23:44–45

11) PCF 10

12) EHR 1.16

13) WDS 760

14) DRE pg. 65, CDR 43.45.3, CAA 12.45.3

15) CDR 44.6.4, ABC 2.106, PCA 57

16) DRE pg. 66, CDR 44.4.4

17) TDA 94, CDR 45.1.2

18) DRE pg. 120, HEP 9.7

19) ABC 5.100, CDR 48.48

20) PCF 6

21) NEB pg. 383, Psalms 2:17, 2 Samuel 7:14

22) Matthew 22:43–45, Mark 12:36–37, Luke 20:42–44

23) Matthew 10:1–2, Mark 6:7, etc.

24) Genesis 49:1–28

25) This oration took place in 51 BCE at his grandmother Julia's funeral (sister of Julius Caesar) when Octavian would have been closer to twelve years old. TDA Section 8 refers to Augustus being in his twelfth year for the funeral oration.

26) WCP pg. 280

27) NID pg. 108

28) DRE pg. 208

29) Luke 11:45–47 11:52

30) Matthew 15:1–7 23:2–3 23:13–29, Mark 12:38–40, Luke 20:46

31) Matthew 21:23 21:31

32) Matthew 15:1–7 16:6 16:11–12 23:2–3 23:13–29, Mark 8:15, Luke 11:42–44 12:1

33) Matthew 16:6 16:11–12 22:23–29

34) Matthew 8:10–13, Luke 7:9

35) Matthew 8:8, Luke 7:6

36) Matthew 27:54, Mark 15:39

37) Matthew 9:9–10 11:19 17:24–27 21:31 22:17–21, Mark 2:14–15 12:14–17, Luke 3:13 5:27–29 7:29 7:34 15:1 18:10–13 19:1–10 20:22–25

38) Matthew 11:19, Luke 7:34

39) Matthew 22:21, Mark 12:17, Luke 20:25

40) Matthew 17:24–27

41) Matthew 9:9–10

42) Luke 19:1–7

43) Matthew 5:39

44) Matthew 5:44

45) Matthew 5:3–10

46) Deuteronomy 7:6–24, Exodus 3:7, 2 Samuel 7:8–16 23–24, Isaiah 49:6–7

47) See the story of King Saul in 1 Samuel 15, as one example.

48) Luke 3:13

49) Luke 3:14

50) Matthew 14:19–21 15:35–38, Mark 6:39–44 8:6–9, Luke 9:14–17

51) Matthew 8:5–10, Luke 7:2–10

52) Mark 15:45

53) John 20:19–29

54) John 19:31–34

55) John 19:25–26

56) Matthew 27:55, Mark 15:40–41, Luke 23:49

57) Matthew 16:27–28 24:34, Mark 8:38–9:1 13:30, Luke 21:32

58) Mark 15:8, Luke 23:1, "multitudes" in Luke 23:4

59) Matthew 27:21–24, Mark 15:14, Luke 23:4 23:13–22, John 18:38 19:4 19:12 19:15

60) Matthew 27:24

61) Matthew 27:36 27:54, Mark 15:39, Luke 23:47

62) Matthew 27:57–60, Mark 15:43–46, Luke 23:50–53, John 19:38

63) Matthew 27:64–66 28:11–15

64) Matthew 27:27–31, Mark 15:16–20, John 19:1–3

65) Luke 23:8–11

66) Matthew 26:57–68, Mark 14:53–65, Luke 22:54–65, John 18:19–24

67) Matthew 27:29, Mark 15:17, John 19:2

68) Matthew 4:1 14:13 14:23 21:17–18, Mark 1:35 3:13 6:32 6:46 9:2, Luke 4:1–2 4:42 5:16 6:12 6:15, John 10:40 11:54 12:36

69) Malachi 3:16

Made in the USA
San Bernardino, CA
13 May 2018